COLLECTED WORKS OF
ROBERT W. SERVICE

Copyright © 2007 BiblioBazaar
All rights reserved
ISBN: 978-1-4346-4815-0

COLLECTED WORKS OF ROBERT W. SERVICE

The Trail of '98
and
Ballads of a Bohemian

BIBLIOBAZAAR

COLLECTED WORKS OF
ROBERT W. SERVICE

CONTENTS

THE TRAIL OF '98

BOOK I
 The Road to Anywhere 21
BOOK II
 The Trail 55
BOOK III
 The Camp 141
BOOK IV
 The Vortex 251

ILLUSTRATIONS

We were in a caldron of fire. The roar of doom
 was in our ears 13
"No," she said firmly, "you can't see the girl" 103
Then, as I hung half in, half out of the window, he clutched
 me by the throat 246
"Garry," I said, "this is—this is Berna" 358

BALLADS OF A BOHEMIAN

Prelude 387

BOOK ONE
SPRING

I

My Garret 389
Julot the *Apache* 391

II

L'Escargot D'Or 395
It Is Later Than You Think 397
Noctambule 399

III

Insomnia 402
Moon Song 404
The Sewing-Girl 405

IV

Lucille 408
On the Boulevard 412
Facility 415

V

Golden Days 417
The Joy of Little Things 418
The Absinthe Drinkers 419

BOOK TWO
EARLY SUMMER

I

The Release 423
The Wee Shop 424
The Philistine and the Bohemian 427

II

The Bohemian Dreams 430
A Domestic Tragedy 432
The Pencil Seller 433

III

Fi-Fi in Bed 438
Gods in the Gutter 439
The Death of Marie Toro 440

IV

The Bohemian 443
The Auction Sale 444
The Joy of Being Poor 447

V

My Neighbors 449
   Room 4: The Painter Chap 449
   Room 6: The Little Workgirl 452
   Room 5: The Concert Singer 453
   Room 7: The Coco-Fiend 455

BOOK THREE
LATE SUMMER

I

The Philanderer	462
The *Petit Vieux*	463
My Masterpiece	463
My Book	464
My Hour	466

II

A Song of Sixty-Five	469
Teddy Bear	471
The Outlaw	472
The Walkers	474

III

Poor Peter	477
The Wistful One	478
If You Had a Friend	479
The Contented Man	480
The Spirit of the Unborn Babe	481

IV

Finistere	483
Old David Smail	485
The Wonderer	487
Oh, It Is Good	489

V

I Have Some Friends	490
The Quest	492

The Comforter 493
The Other One 494
Catastrophe 495

BOOK FOUR
WINTER

I

Priscilla 499
A Casualty 502
The Blood-Red *Fourragere* 504
Jim 506

II

Kelly of the Legion 508
The Three Tommies 511
The Twa Jocks 514

III

His Boys 517
The Booby-Trap 519
Bonehead Bill 521

IV

A Lapse of Time and a Word of Explanation 524
Michael 525
The Wife 526
Victory Stuff 528
Was It You? 529

Les Grands Mutilés 531
The Sightless Man 531
The Legless Man 534
The Faceless Man 537

L'Envoi 541

We were in a caldron of fire. The roar of doom was in our ears

THE TRAIL OF '98

A Northland Romance

With illustrations by
MAYNARD DIXON

PRELUDE

The north wind is keening overhead. It minds me of the howl of a wolf-dog under the Arctic stars. Sitting alone by the glow of the great peat fire I can hear it high up in the braeside firs. It is the voice, inexorably scornful, of the Great White Land.

Oh, I hate it, I hate it! Why cannot a man be allowed to forget? It is near ten years since I joined the Eager Army. I have travelled: I have been a pilgrim to the shrines of beauty; I have pursued the phantom of happiness even to the ends of the earth. Still it is always the same—I cannot forget.

Why should a man be ever shadowed by the vampire wing of his past? Have I not a right to be happy? Money, estate, name, are mine, all that means an open sesame to the magic door. Others go in, but I beat against its flinty portals with hands that bleed. No! I have no right to be happy. The ways of the world are open; the banquet of life is spread; the wonder-workers plan their pageants of beauty and joy, and yet there is no praise in my heart. I have seen, I have tasted, I have tried. Ashes and dust and bitterness are all my gain. I will try no more. It is the shadow of the vampire wing.

So I sit in the glow of the great peat fire, tired and sad beyond belief. Thank God! at least I am home. Everything is so little changed. The fire lights the oak-panelled hall; the crossed claymores gleam; the eyes in the mounted deer-heads shine glassily; rugs of fur cover the polished floor; all is comfort, home and the haunting atmosphere of my boyhood. Sometimes I fancy it has been a dream, the Great White Silence, the lure of the gold-spell, the delirium of the struggle; a dream, and I will awake to hear Garry calling me to shoot over the moor, to see dear little Mother with her meek, sensitive mouth, and her cheeks as delicately tinted as the leaves of a briar rose. But no! The hall is silent. Mother has gone to her long rest. Garry sleeps under the snow. Silence everywhere; I am alone, alone.

So I sit in the big, oak-carved chair of my forefathers, before the great peat fire, a peak-faced drooping figure of a man with hair untimely grey. My crutch lies on the floor by my side. My old nurse comes up quietly to look at the fire. Her rosy, wrinkled face smiles cheerfully, but I can see the anxiety in her blue eyes. She is afraid for me. Maybe the doctor has told her—*something*.

No doubt my days are numbered, so I am minded to tell of it all: of the Big Stampede, of the Treasure Trail, of the Gold-born City; of those who followed the gold-lure into the Great White Land, of the evil that befell them, of Garry and of Berna. Perhaps it will comfort me to tell of these things. To-morrow I will begin; to-night, leave me to my memories.

Berna! I spoke of her last. She rises before me now with her spirit-pale face and her great troubled grey eyes, a little tragic figure, ineffably pitiful. Where are you now, little one? I have searched the world for you. I have scanned a million faces. Day and night have I sought, always hoping, always baffled, for, God help me, dear, I love you. Among that mad, lusting horde you were so weak, so helpless, yet so hungry for love.

With the aid of my crutch I unlatch one of the long windows, and step out onto the terrace. From the cavernous dark the snowflakes sting my face. Yet as I stand there, once more I have a sense of another land, of imperious vastitudes, of a silent empire, unfathomably lonely.

Ghosts! They are all around me. The darkness teems with them, Garry, my brother, among them. Then they all fade and give way to one face . . .

Berna, I love you always. Out of the night I cry to you, Berna, the cry of a broken heart. Is it your little, pitiful ghost that comes down to me? Oh, I am waiting, waiting! Here will I wait, Berna, till we meet once more. For meet we will, beyond the mists, beyond the dreaming, at last, dear love, at last.

* * * * *

This is the law of the Yukon, and ever she makes it plain:
"Send not your foolish and feeble; send me your strong and your sane.
Strong for the red rage of battle; sane, for I harry them sore;
Send me men girt for the combat, men who are grit to the core;
Swift as the panther in triumph, fierce as the bear in defeat,
Sired of a bulldog parent, steeled in the furnace heat.
Send me the best of your breeding, lend me your chosen ones;
Them will I take to my bosom, them will I call my sons;
Them will I gild with my treasure, them will I glut with my meat;
But the others—the misfits, the failures—I trample under my feet."

—"Songs of a Sourdough."

* * * * *

BOOK I

THE ROAD TO ANYWHERE

Can you recall, dear comrade, when we tramped God's land together,
> And we sang the old, old Earth-Song, for our youth was very sweet;

When we drank and fought and lusted, as we mocked at tie and tether,
> Along the road to Anywhere, the wide world at our feet.

Along the road to Anywhere, when each day had its story;
> When time was yet our vassal, and life's jest was still unstale;

When peace unfathomed filled our hearts as, bathed in amber glory,
> Along the road to Anywhere we watched the sunsets pale.

Alas! the road to Anywhere is pitfalled with disaster;
> There's hunger, want, and weariness, yet O we loved it so!

As on we tramped exultantly, and no man was our master,
> And no man guessed what dreams were ours, as swinging heel and toe,

We tramped the road to Anywhere, the magic road to Anywhere,
> The tragic road to Anywhere such dear, dim years ago.

>   —"Songs of a Sourdough."

CHAPTER I

As far back as I can remember I have faithfully followed the banner of Romance. It has given colour to my life, made me a dreamer of dreams, a player of parts. As a boy, roaming alone the wild heather hills, I have heard the glad shouts of the football players on the green, yet never ettled to join them. Mine was the richer, rarer joy. Still can I see myself in those days, a little shy-mannered lad in kilts, bareheaded to the hill breezes, with health-bright cheeks, and a soul happed up in dreams.

And, indeed, I lived in an enchanted land, a land of griffins and kelpies, of princesses and gleaming knights. From each black tarn I looked to see a scaly reptile rise, from every fearsome cave a corby emerge. There were green spaces among the heather where the fairies danced, and every scaur and linn had its own familiar spirit. I peopled the good green wood with the wild creatures of my thought, nymph and faun, naiad and dryad, and would have been in nowise surprised to meet in the leafy coolness the great god Pan himself.

It was at night, however, that my dreams were most compelling. I strove against the tyranny of sleep. Lying in my small bed, I revelled in delectable imaginings. Night after night I fought battles, devised pageants, partitioned empires. I gloried in details. My rugged war-lords were very real to me, and my adventures sounded many periods of history. I was a solitary caveman with an axe of stone; I was a Roman soldier of fortune; I was a Highland outlaw of the Rebellion. Always I fought for a lost cause, and always my sympathies were with the rebel. I feasted with Robin Hood on the King's venison; I fared forth with Dick Turpin on the gibbet-haunted heath; I followed Morgan, the Buccaneer, into strange and exotic lands of trial and treasure. It was a wonderful gift of visioning that was mine in those days. It was the bird-like flight of the pure child-mind to whom the unreal is yet the real.

Then, suddenly, I arrived at a second phase of my mental growth in which fancy usurped the place of imagination. The modern equivalents of Romance attracted me, and, with my increasing grasp of reality, my gift of vision faded. As I had hitherto dreamed of knight-errants, of corsairs and of outlaws, I now dreamed of cowboys, of gold-seekers, of beach-combers. Fancy painted scenes in which I, too, should play a rousing part. I read avidly all I could find dealing with the Far West, and ever my wistful gaze roved over the grey sea. The spirit of Romance beaconed to me. I, too, would adventure in the stranger lands, and face their perils and brave their dangers. The joy of the thought exulted in my veins, and scarce could I bide the day when the roads of chance and change would be open to my feet.

It is strange that in all these years I confided in no one. Garry, who was my brother and my dearest friend, would have laughed at me in that affectionate way of his. You would never have taken us for brothers. We were so different in temperament and appearance that we were almost the reverse of each other. He was the handsomest boy I have ever seen, frank, fair-skinned and winning, while I was dark, dour and none too well favoured. He was the best runner and swimmer in the parish, and the idol of the village lads. I cared nothing for games, and would be found somewhere among the heather hills, always by my lone self, and nearly always with a story book in my pocket. He was clever, practical and ambitious, excelling in all his studies; whereas, except in those which appealed to my imagination, I was a dullard and a dreamer.

Yet we loved each others as few brothers do. Oh, how I admired him! He was my ideal, and too often the hero of my romances. Garry would have laughed at my hero-worship; he was so matter-of-fact, effective and practical. Yet he understood me, my Celtic ideality, and that shy reserve which is the armour of a sensitive soul. Garry in his fine clever way knew me and shielded me and cheered me. He was so buoyant and charming he heartened you like Spring sunshine, and braced you like a morning wind on the mountain top. Yes, not excepting Mother, Garry knew me better than any one has ever done, and I loved him for it. It seems overfond to say this, but he did not have a fault: tenderness, humour, enthusiasm, sympathy and the beauty of a young god—all that was manfully endearing was expressed in this brother of mine.

So we grew to manhood there in that West Highland country, and surely our lives were pure and simple and sweet. I had never been further from home than the little market town where we sold our sheep. Mother managed the estate till Garry was old enough, when he took hold with a vigour and grasp that delighted every one. I think our little Mother stood rather in awe of my keen, capable, energetic brother. There was in her a certain dreamy, wistful idealism that made her beautiful in my eyes, and to look on she was as fair as any picture. Specially do I remember the delicate colouring of her face and her eyes, blue like deep corn-flowers. She was not overstrong, and took much comfort from religion. Her lips, which were fine and sensitive, had a particularly sweet expression, and I wish to record of her that never once did I see her cross, always sweet, gentle, smiling.

Thus our home was an ideal one; Garry, tall, fair and winsome; myself, dark, dreamy, reticent; and between us, linking all three in a perfect bond of love and sympathy, our gentle, delicate Mother.

* * * * *

CHAPTER II

So in serenity and sunshine the days of my youth went past. I still maintained my character as a drone and a dreamer. I used my time tramping the moorland with a gun, whipping the foamy pools of the burn for trout, or reading voraciously in the library. Mostly I read books of travel, and especially did I relish the literature of Vagabondia. I had come under the spell of Stevenson. His name spelled Romance to me, and my fancy etched him in his lonely exile. Forthright I determined I too would seek these ultimate islands, and from that moment I was a changed being. I nursed the thought with joyous enthusiasm. I would be a frontiersman, a trail-breaker, a treasure-seeker. The virgin prairies called to me; the susurrus of the giant pines echoed in my heart; but most of all, I felt the spell of those gentle islands where care is a stranger, and all is sunshine, song and the glowing bloom of eternal summer.

About this time Mother must have worried a good deal over my future. Garry was now the young Laird, and I was but an idler, a burden on the estate. At last I told her I wanted to go abroad, and then it seemed as if a great difficulty was solved. We remembered of a cousin who was sheep-ranching in the Saskatchewan valley and had done well. It was arranged that I should join him as a pupil, then, when I had learned enough, buy a place of my own. It may be imagined that while I apparently acquiesced in this arrangement, I had already determined that as soon as I reached the new land I would take my destiny into my own hands.

I will never forget the damp journey to Glasgow and the misty landscape viewed through the streaming window pane of a railway carriage. I was in a wondrous state of elation. When we reached the great smoky city I was lost in amazement not unmixed with fear. Never had I imagined such crowds, such houses, such hurry. The three of us, Mother, Garry and I, wandered and wondered for three days. Folks gazed at us curiously, sometimes admiringly, for our cheeks were bright with Highland health, and our eyes candid as the June skies. Garry in particular, tall, fair and handsome, seemed to call forth glances of interest wherever he went. Then as the hour of my departure drew near a shadow fell on us.

I will not dwell on our leave-taking. If I broke down in unmanly grief, it must be remembered I had never before been from home. I was but a lad, and these two were all in all to me. Mother gave up trying to be brave, and mingled her tears with mine. Garry alone contrived to make some show of cheerfulness. Alas! all my elation had gone. In its place was a sense of guilt, of desertion, of unconquerable gloom. I had an inkling then of the tragedy of motherhood, the tender love that would hold yet cannot, the world-call and the ruthless, estranging years, all the memories of clinging love given only to be taken away.

"Don't cry, sweetheart Mother," I said; "I'll be back again in three years."

"Mind you do, my boy, mind you do."

She looked at me woefully sad, and I had a queer, heartrending prevision I would never see her more. Garry was supporting her, and she seemed to have suddenly grown very frail. He was pale and quiet, but I could see he was vastly moved.

"Athol," said he, "if ever you need me just send for me. I'll come, no matter how long or how hard the way."

I can see them to this day standing there in the drenching rain, Garry fine and manly, Mother small and drooping. I can see her with her delicate rose colour, her eyes like wood violets drowned in tears, her tender, sensitive lips quivering with emotion.

"Good-bye, laddie, good-bye."

I forced myself away, and stumbled on board. When I looked back again they were gone, but through the grey shadows there seemed to come back to me a cry of heartache and irremediable loss.

"Good-bye, good-bye."

* * * * *

CHAPTER III

It was on a day of early Autumn when I stood knee-deep in the heather of Glengyle, and looked wistfully over the grey sea. 'Twas but a month later when, homeless and friendless, I stood on the beach by the Cliff House of San Francisco, and gazed over the fretful waters of another ocean. Such is the romance of destiny.

Consigned, so to speak, to my cousin the sheep-raiser of the Saskatchewan, I found myself setting foot on the strange land with but little heart for my new vocation. My mind, cramful of book notions, craved for the larger life. I was valiantly mad for adventure; to fare forth haphazardly; to come upon naked danger; to feel the bludgeonings of mischance; to tramp, to starve, to sleep under the stars. It was the callow boy-idea perpetuated in the man, and it was to lead me a sorry dance. But I could not overbear it. Strong in me was the spirit of the gypsy. The joy of youth and health was brawling in my veins. A few thistledown years, said I, would not matter. And there was Stevenson and his glamorous islands winning me on.

So it came about I stood solitary on the beach by the seal rocks, with a thousand memories confusing in my head. There was the long train ride with its strange pictures: the crude farms, the glooming forests, the gleaming lakes that would drown my whole country, the aching plains, the mountains that rip-sawed the sky, the fear-made-eternal of the desert. Lastly, a sudden, sunlit paradise, California.

I had lived through a week of wizardry such as I had never dreamed of, and here was I at the very throne of Western empire. And what a place it was, and what a people—with the imperious mood of the West softened by the spell of the Orient and mellowed by the glamour of Old Spain. San Francisco! A score of tongues clamoured in her streets and in her byways a score of races lurked austerely. She suckled at her breast the children of the old grey nations and gave them of her spirit, that swift purposeful spirit so proud of past achievement and so convinced of glorious destiny.

I marvelled at the rush of affairs and the zest of amusement. Every one seemed to be making money easily and spending it eagerly. Every one was happy, sanguine, strenuous. At night Market Street was a dazzling alley of light, where stalwart men and handsome women jostled in and out of the glittering restaurants. Yet amid this eager, passionate life I felt a dreary sense of outsideness. At times my heart fairly ached with loneliness, and I wandered the pathways of the park, or sat forlornly in Portsmouth Square as remote from it all as a gazer on his mountain top beneath the stars.

I became a dreamer of the water front, for the notion of the South Seas was ever in my head. I loafed in the sunshine, sitting on the pier-edge, with eyes fixed on the lazy shipping. These were care-free, irresponsible days, and not, I am now convinced, entirely misspent. I came to know the worthies of the wharfside, and plunged into an under-world of fascinating repellency. Crimpdom eyed and tempted me, but it was always with whales or seals, and never with pearls or copra. I rubbed shoulders with eager necessity, scrambled for free lunches in frowsy bar-rooms, and amid the scum and débris of the waterside found much food for sober thought. Yet at times I blamed myself for thus misusing my days, and memories of Glengyle and Mother and Garry loomed up with reproachful vividness.

I was, too, a seeker of curious experience, and this was to prove my undoing. The night-side of the city was unveiled to me. With the assurance of innocence I wandered everywhere. I penetrated the warrens of underground Chinatown, wondering why white women lived there, and why they hid at sight of me. Alone I poked my way into the opium joints and the gambling dens. Vice, amazingly unabashed, flaunted itself in my face. I wondered what my grim, Covenanting ancestors would have made of it all. I never thought to have seen the like, and in my inexperience it was like a shock to me.

My nocturnal explorations came to a sudden end. One foggy midnight, coming up Pacific Street with its glut of saloons, I was clouted shrewdly from behind and dropped most neatly in the gutter. When I came to, very sick and dizzy in a side alley, I found

I had been robbed of my pocketbook with nearly all my money therein. Fortunately I had left my watch in the hotel safe, and by selling it was not entirely destitute; but the situation forced me from my citadel of pleasant dreams, and confronted me with the grimmer realities of life.

I became a habitué of the ten-cent restaurant. I was amazed to find how excellent a meal I could have for ten cents. Oh for the uncaptious appetite of these haphazard days! With some thirty-odd dollars standing between me and starvation, it was obvious I must become a hewer of wood and a drawer of water, and to this end I haunted the employment offices. They were bare, sordid rooms, crowded by men who chewed, swapped stories, yawned and studied the blackboards where the day's wants were set forth. Only driven to labour by dire necessity, their lives, I found, held three phases— looking for work, working, spending the proceeds. They were the Great Unskilled, face to face with the necessary evil of toil.

One morning, on seeking my favourite labour bureau, I found an unusual flutter among the bench-warmers. A big contractor wanted fifty men immediately. No experience was required, and the wages were to be two dollars a day. With a number of others I pressed forward, was interviewed and accepted. The same day we were marched in a body to the railway depot and herded into a fourth-class car.

Where we were going I knew not; of what we were going to do I had no inkling. I only knew we were southbound, and at long last I might fairly consider myself to be the shuttlecock of fortune.

* * * * *

CHAPTER IV

I left San Francisco blanketed in grey fog and besomed by a roaring wind; when I opened my eyes I was in a land of spacious sky and broad, clean sunshine. Orange groves rushed to welcome us; orchards of almond and olive twinkled joyfully in the limpid air; tall, gaunt and ragged, the scaly eucalyptus fluttered at us a morning greeting, while snowy houses, wallowing in greenery, flashed a smile as we rumbled past. It seemed like a land of promise, of song and sunshine, and silent and apart I sat to admire and to enjoy.

"Looks pretty swell, don't it?"

I will call him the Prodigal. He was about my own age, thin, but sun-browned and healthy. His hair was darkly red and silky, his teeth white and even as young corn. His eyes twinkled with a humorsome light, but his face was shrewd, alert and aggressive.

"Yes," I said soberly, for I have always been backward with strangers.

"Pretty good line. The banana belt. Old Sol working overtime. Blossom and fruit cavorting on the same tree. Eternal summer. Land of the *mañana*, the festive frijole, the never-chilly chili. Ever been here before?"

"No."

"Neither have I. Glad I came, even if it's to do the horny-handed son of toil stunt. Got the makings?"

"No, I'm sorry; I don't smoke."

"All right, guess I got enough."

He pulled forth a limp sack of powdery tobacco, and spilled some grains into a brown cigarette paper, twisting it deftly and bending over the ends. Then he smoked with such enjoyment that I envied him.

"Where are we going, have you any idea?" I asked.

"Search me," he said, inhaling deeply; "the guy in charge isn't exactly a free information bureau. When it comes to peddling the bull con he's there, but when you try to pry off a few slabs of cold hard fact it's his Sunday off."

"But," I persisted, "have you no idea?"

"Well, one thing you can bank on, they'll work the Judas out of us. The gentle grafter nestles in our midst. This here's a cinch game and we are the fall guys. The contractors are a bum outfit. They'll squeeze us at every turn. There was two plunks to the employment man; they got half. Twenty for railway fare; they come in on that. Stop at certain hotels: a rake-off there. Stage fare: more graft. Five dollars a week for board: costs them two-fifty, and they will be stomach robbers at that. Then they'll ring in twice as many men as they need, and lay us off half the time, so that we just about even up on our board bill. Oh, I'm onto their curves all right."

"Then," I said, "if you know so much why did you come with us?"

"Well, if I know so much you just bet I know some more. I'll go one better. You watch my smoke."

He talked on with a wonderful vivid manner and an outpouring knowledge of life, so that I was hugely interested. Yet ever and anon an allusion of taste would betray him, and at no time did I fail to see that his roughness was only a veneer. As it turned out he was better educated by far than I, a Yale boy taking a post-graduate course in the University of Hard Luck.

My reserve once thawed, I told him much of my simple life. He listened, intently sympathetic.

"Say," said he earnestly when I had finished, "I'm rough-and-ready in my ways. Life to me's a game, sort of masquerade, and I'm the worst masquerader in the bunch. But I know how to handle myself, and I can jolly my way along pretty well. Now, you're green, if you'll excuse me saying it, and maybe I can help you some. Likewise you're the only one in all the gang of hoboes that's my kind. Come on, let's be partners."

I felt greatly drawn to him and agreed gladly.

"Now," said he, "I must go and jolly along the other boys. Aren't they a fierce bunch? Coloured gentlemen, Slavonians, Polaks, Dagoes, Swedes—well, I'll go prospecting, and see what I can strike."

He went among them with a jabber of strange terms, a bright smile and ready banter, and I could see that he was to be a quick favourite. I envied him for his ease of manner, a thing I could never compass. Presently he returned to me.

"Say, partner, got any money?"

There was something frank and compelling in his manner, so that I produced the few dollars I had left, and spread them before him.

"That's all my wealth," I said smilingly.

He divided it into two equal portions and returned one to me. He took a note of the other, saying:

"All right, I'll settle up with you later on."

He went off with my money. He seemed to take it for granted I would not object, and on my part I cared little, being only too eager to show I trusted him. A few minutes later behold him seated at a card-table with three rough-necked, hard-bitten-looking men. They were playing poker, and, thinks I: "Here's good-bye to my money." It minded me of wolves and a lamb. I felt sorry for my new friend, and I was only glad he had so little to lose.

We were drawing in to Los Angeles when he rejoined me. To my surprise he emptied his pockets of wrinkled notes and winking silver to the tune of twenty dollars, and dividing it equally, handed half to me.

"Here," says he, "plant that in your dip."

"No," I said, "just give me back what you borrowed; that's all I want."

"Oh, forget it! You staked me, and it's well won. These guinneys took me for a jay. Thought I was easy, but I've forgotten more than they ever knew, and I haven't forgotten so much either."

"No, you keep it, please. I don't want it."

"Oh, come! put your Scotch scruples in your pocket. Take the money."

"No," I said obstinately.

"Look here, this partnership of ours is based on financial equality. If you don't like my gate, you don't need to swing on it."

"All right," said I tartly, "I don't want to."

Then I turned on my heel.

* * * * *

CHAPTER V

On either side of us were swift hills mottled with green and gold, ahead a curdle of snow-capped mountains, above a sky of robin's-egg blue. The morning was lyric and set our hearts piping as we climbed the canyon. We breathed deeply of the heady air, exclaimed at sight of a big bee ranch, shouted as a mule team with jingling bells came swinging down the trail. With cries of delight we forded the little crystal stream wherever the trail plunged knee-deep through it. Higher and higher we climbed, mile after mile, our packs on our shoulders, our hearts very merry. I was as happy as a holiday schoolboy, willing this should go on for ever, dreading to think of the grim-visaged toil that awaited us.

About midday we reached the end. Gangs of men were everywhere, ripping and tearing at the mountain side. There was a roar of blasting, and rocks hurtled down on us. Bunkhouses of raw lumber sweated in the sun. Everywhere was the feverish activity of a construction camp.

We were assigned to a particular bunkhouse, and there was a great rush for places. It was floorless, doorless and in part roofless. Above the medley of voices I heard that of the Prodigal:

"Say, fellows, let's find the softest side of this board! Strikes me the Company's mighty considerate. All kinds of ventilation. Good chance to study astronomy. Wonder if I couldn't borrow a mattress somewhere? Ha! Good eye! Watch me, fellows!"

We saw him make for a tent nearby where horses were stabled. He reconnoitred carefully, then darted inside to come out in a twinkling, staggering under a bale of hay.

"How's that for rustling? I guess I'm slow—hey, what? Guess this is poor!"

He was wadding his bunk with the hay, while the others looked on rather enviously. Then, as a bell rang, he left off.

"Hash is ready, boys; last call to the dining-car. Come on and see the pigs get their heads in the trough."

We hurried to the cookhouse, where a tin plate, a tin cup, a tin spoon and a cast-iron knife was laid for each of us at a table of unplaned boards. A great mess of hash was ready, and excepting myself every one ate voraciously. I found something more to my taste, a can of honey and some soda crackers, on which I supped gratefully.

When I returned to the bunkhouse I found my bunk had been stuffed with nice soft hay, and my blankets spread on top. I looked over to the Prodigal. He was reading, a limp cigarette between his yellow-stained fingers. I went up to him.

"It's very good of you to do this," I said.

"Oh no! Not at all. Don't mention it," he answered with much politeness, never raising his eyes from the book.

"Well," I said, "I've just got to thank you. And look here, let's make it up. Don't let the business of that wretched money come between us. Can't we be friends anyway?"

He sprang up and gripped my hand.

"Sure! nothing I want more. I'm sorry. Another time I'll make allowance for that shorter-catechism conscience of yours. Now let's go over to that big fire they've made and chew the rag."

So we sat by the crackling blaze of mesquite, sagebrush and live-oak limbs, while over us twinkled the friendly stars, and he told me many a strange story of his roving life.

"You know, the old man's all broke up at me playing the fool like this. He's got a glue factory back in Massachusetts. Guess he stacks up about a million or so. Wanted me to go into the glue factory, begin at the bottom, stay with it. 'Stick to glue, my boy,' he says; 'become the Glue King,' and so on. But not with little Willie. Life's too interesting a proposition to be turned down like that. I'm not repentant. I know the fatted calf's waiting for me, getting fatter every day. One of these days I'll go back and sample it."

It was he I first heard talk of the Great White Land, and it stirred me strangely.

"Every one's crazy about it. They're rushing now in thousands, to get there before the winter begins. Next spring there will be the biggest stampede the world has ever seen. Say, Scotty, I've the greatest notion to try it. Let's go, you and I. I had a partner once, who'd been up there. It's a big, dark, grim land, but there's the gold, shining, shining, and it's calling us to go. Somehow it haunts me, that soft, gleamy, virgin gold there in the solitary rivers with not a soul to pick it up. I don't care one rip for the value of it. I can make all I want out of glue. But the adventure, the excitement, it's that that makes me fit for the foolish house."

He was silent a long time while my imagination conjured up terrible, fascinating pictures of the vast, unawakened land, and a longing came over me to dare its shadows.

As we said good-night, his last words were:

"Remember, Scotty, we're both going to join the Big Stampede, you and I."

* * * * *

CHAPTER VI

I slept but fitfully, for the night air was nipping, and the bunkhouse nigh as open as a cage. A bonny morning it was, and the sun warmed me nicely, so that over breakfast I was in a cheerful humour. Afterwards I watched the gang labouring, and showed such an injudicious interest that that afternoon I too was put to work.

It was very simple. Running into the mountain there was a tunnel, which they were lining with concrete, and it was the task of I and another to push cars of the stuff from the outlet to the scene of operations. My partner was a Swede who had toiled from boyhood, while I had never done a day's work in my life. It was as much as I could do to lift the loaded boxes into the car. Then we left the sunshine behind us, and for a quarter of a mile of darkness we strained in an uphill effort.

From the roof, which we stooped to avoid, sheets of water descended. Every now and then the heavy cars would run off the rails, which were of scantling, worn and frayed by friction. Then my Swede would storm in Berserker rage, and we would lift till the veins throbbed in my head. Never had time seemed so long. A convict working in the salt mines of Siberia did not revolt more against his task than I. The sweat blinded me; a bright steel pain throbbed in my head; my heart seemed to hammer. Never so thankful was I as when we had made our last trip, and sick and dizzy I put on my coat to go home.

It was dark. There was a cable line running from the tunnel to the camp, and down this we shot in buckets two at a clip. The descent gave me a creepy sensation, but it saved a ten minutes' climb down the mountain side, and I was grateful.

Tired, wet and dirty, how I envied the Prodigal lying warm and cosy on his fragrant hay. He was reading a novel. But the thought that I had earned a dollar comforted me. After supper he, with Ginger and Dutchy, played solo till near midnight, while I tossed on my bunk too weary and sore to sleep.

Next day was a repetition of the first, only worse. I ached as if I had been beaten. Stiff and sore I dragged myself to the tunnel again. I lifted, strained, tugged and shoved with a set and tragic face. Five hours of hell passed. It was noon. I nursed my strength for the after effort. Angrily I talked to myself, and once more I pulled through. Weary and slimy with wet mud, I shot down the cable line. Snugly settled in his bunk, the Prodigal had read another two hundred pages of "Les Misérables." Yet—I reflected somewhat sadly—I had made two dollars.

On the third day sheer obstinacy forced me to the tunnel. My self-respect goaded me on. I would not give in. I must hold this job down, I *must*, I MUST. Then at the noon hour I fainted.

No one saw me, so I gritted my teeth and once more threw my weight against the cars. Once more night found me waiting to descend in the bucket. Then as I stood there was a crash and shouts from below. The cable had snapped. My Swede and another lay among the rocks with sorely broken bones. Poor beggars! how they must have suffered jolting down that boulder-strewn trail to the hospital.

Somehow that destroyed my nerve. I blamed myself indeed. I flogged myself with reproaches, but it was of no avail. I would sooner beg my bread than face that tunnel once again. The world seemed to be divided into two parts, the rest of it and that tunnel. Thank God, I didn't *have* to go into it again. I was exultantly happy that I didn't. The Prodigal had finished his book, and was starting another. That night he borrowed some of my money to play solo with.

Next day I saw the foreman. I said:

"I want to go. The work up there's too hard for me."

He looked at me kindly.

"All right, sonny," says he, "don't quit. I'll put you in the gravel pit."

So next day I found a more congenial task. There were four of us. We threw the gravel against a screen where the finer stuff that sifted through was used in making concrete.

The work was heart-breaking in its monotony. In the biting cold of the morning we made a start, long before the sun peeped above the wall of mountain.

We watched it crawl, snail-like, over the virgin sky. We panted in its heat. We saw it drop again behind the mountain wall, leaving the sky gorgeously barred with colour from a tawny orange glow to an ice-pale green—a regular *pousse café* of a sunset. Then when the cold and the dark surged back, by the light of the evening star we straightened our weary spines, and throwing aside pick and shovel hurried to supper.

Heigh-ho! what a life it was. Resting, eating, sleeping; negative pleasures became positive ones. Life's great principle of compensation worked on our behalf, and to lie at ease, reading an old paper, seemed an exquisite enjoyment.

I was much troubled about the Prodigal. He complained of muscular rheumatism, and except to crawl to meals was unable to leave his bunk. Every day came the foreman to inquire anxiously if he was fit to go to work, but steadily he grew worse. Yet he bore his suffering with great spirit, and, among that nondescript crew, he was a thing of joy and brightness, a link with that other world which was mine own. They nicknamed him "Happy," his cheerfulness was so invincible. He played cards on every chance, and he must have been unlucky, for he borrowed the last of my small hoard.

One morning I woke about six, and found, pinned to my blanket, a note from my friend.

"Dear Scotty:

"I grieve to leave you thus, but the cruel foreman insists on me working off my ten days' board. Racked with pain as I am, there appears to be no alternative but flight. Accordingly I fade away once more into the unknown. Will write you general delivery, Los Angeles. Good luck and good-bye. Yours to a cinder,

"Happy."

There was a hue and cry after him, but he was gone, and a sudden disgust for the place came over me. For two more days I worked, crushed by a gloom that momently intensified. Clamant and imperative in me was the voice of change. I could not become toil-broken, so I saw the foreman.

"Why do you want to go?" he asked reproachfully.

"Well, sir, the work's too monotonous."

"Monotonous! Well, that's the rummest reason I ever heard a man give for quitting. But every man knows his own business best. I'll give you a time-cheque."

While he was making it out I wondered if, indeed, I did know my own business best; but if it had been the greatest folly in the world, I was bound to get out of that canyon.

Treasuring the slip of paper representing my labour, I sought one of the bosses, a sour, stiff man of dyspeptic tendencies. With a smile of malicious sweetness he returned it to me.

"All right, take it to our Oakland office, and you'll get the cash."

Expectantly I had been standing there, thinking to receive my money, the first I had ever earned (and to me so distressfully earned, at that). Now I gazed at him very sick at heart: for was not Oakland several hundred miles away, and I was penniless.

"Couldn't you cash it here?" I faltered at last.

"No!" (very sourly).

"Couldn't you discount it, then?"

"No!" (still more tartly).

I turned away, crestfallen and smarting. When I told the other boys they were indignant, and a good deal alarmed on their own account. I made my case against the Company as damning as I could, then, slinging my blankets on my back, set off once more down the canyon.

* * * * *

CHAPTER VII

I was gaining in experience, and as I hurried down the canyon and the morning burgeoned like a rose, my spirits mounted invincibly. It was the joy of the open road and the care-free heart. Like some hideous nightmare was the memory of the tunnel and the gravel pit. The bright blood in me rejoiced; my muscles tensed with pride in their toughness; I gazed insolently at the world.

So, as I made speed to get the sooner to the orange groves, I almost set heel on a large blue envelope which lay face up on the trail. I examined it and, finding it contained plans and specifications of the work we had been at, I put it in my pocket.

Presently came a rider, who reined up by me.

"Say, young man, you haven't seen a blue envelope, have you?"

Something in the man's manner aroused in me instant resentment. I was the toiler in mud-stiffened overalls, he arrogant and supercilious in broadcloth and linen.

"No," I said sourly, and, going on my way, heard him clattering up the canyon.

It was about evening when I came onto a fine large plain. Behind me was the canyon, gloomy like the lair of some evil beast, while before me the sun was setting, and made the valley like a sea of golden glaze. I stood, knight-errant-wise, on the verge of one of those enchanted lands of precious memory, seeking the princess of my dreams; but all I saw was a man coming up the trail. He was reeling homeward, with under one arm a live turkey, and swinging from the other a demijohn of claret.

He would have me drink. He represented the Christmas spirit, and his accent was Scotch, so I up-tilted his demijohn gladly enough. Then, for he was very merry, he would have it that we sing "Auld Lang Syne." So there, on the heath, in the golden dance of the light, we linked our hands and lifted our voices like two daft folk. Yet, for that it was Christmas Eve, it seemed not to be so mad after all.

There was my first orange grove. I ran to it eagerly, and pulled four of the largest fruit I could see. They were green-like of rind and bitter sour, but I heeded not, eating the last before I was satisfied. Then I went on my way.

As I entered the town my spirits fell. I remembered I was quite without money and had not yet learned to be gracefully penniless. However, I bethought me of the time-cheque, and entering a saloon asked the proprietor if he would cash it. He was a German of jovial face that seemed to say: "Welcome, my friend," and cold, beady eyes that queried: "How much can I get of your wad?" It was his eyes I noticed.

"No, I don'd touch dot. I haf before been schvindled. Himmel, no! You take him avay."

I sank into a chair. Catching a glimpse of my face in a bar mirror, I wondered if that hollow-cheeked, weary-looking lad was I. The place was crowded with revellers of the Christmastide, and geese were being diced for. There were three that pattered over the floor, while in the corner the stage-driver and a red-haired man were playing freeze-out for one of them.

I drowsed quietly. Wafts of bar-front conversation came to me. "Envelope . . . lost plans . . . great delay." Suddenly I sat up, remembering the package I had found.

"Were you looking for some lost plans?" I asked.

"Yes," said one man eagerly, "did you find them?"

"I didn't say I did, but if I could get them for you, would you cash this time-cheque for me?"

"Sure," he says, "one good turn deserves another. Deliver the goods and I'll cash your time-cheque."

His face was frank and jovial. I drew out the envelope and handed it over. He hurriedly ran through the contents and saw that all were there.

"Ha! That saves a trip to 'Frisco," he said, gay with relief.

He turned to the bar and ordered a round of drinks. They all had a drink on him, while he seemed to forget about me. I waited a little, then pressed forward with my time-cheque.

"Oh that," said he, "I won't cash that. I was only joshing."

A feeling of bitter anger welled up within me. I trembled like a leaf.

"You won't go back on your word?" I said.

He became flustered.

"Well, I can't do it anyway. I've got no loose cash."

What I would have said or done I know not, for I was nigh desperate; but at this moment the stage-driver, flushed with his victory at freeze-out, snatched the paper from my hand.

"Here, I'll discount that for you. I'll only give you five dollars for it, though."

It called for fourteen, but by this time I was so discouraged I gladly accepted the five-dollar goldpiece he held out to tempt me.

Thus were my fortunes restored. It was near midnight and I asked the German for a room. He replied that he was full up, but as I had my blankets there was a nice dry shed at the back. Alas! it was also used by his chickens. They roosted just over my head, and I lay on the filthy floor at the mercy of innumerable fleas. To complete my misery the green oranges I had eaten gave me agonizing cramps. Glad, indeed, was I when day dawned, and once more I got afoot, with my face turned towards Los Angeles.

* * * * *

CHAPTER VIII

Los Angeles will always be written in golden letters in the archives of my memory. Crawling, sore and sullen, from the clutch of toil, I revelled in a lotus life of ease and idleness. There was infinite sunshine, and the quiet of a public library through whose open windows came the fragrance of magnolias. Living was incredibly cheap. For seventy-five cents a week I had a little sunlit attic, and for ten cents I could dine abundantly. There was soup, fish, meat, vegetables, salad, pudding and a bottle of wine. So reading, dreaming and roaming the streets, I spent my days in a state of beatitude.

But even five dollars will not last for ever, and the time came when once more the grim face of toil confronted me. I must own that I had now little stomach for hard labour, yet I made several efforts to obtain it. However, I had a bad manner, being both proud and shy, and one rebuff in a day always was enough. I lacked that self-confidence that readily finds employment, and again I found myself mixing with the spineless residuum of the employment bureau.

At last the morning came when twenty-five cents was all that remained to me in the world. I had just been seeking a position as a dish-washer, and had been rather sourly rejected. Sitting solitary on the bench in that dreary place, I soliloquized:

"And so it has come to this, that I, Athol Meldrum, of gentle birth and Highland breeding, must sue in vain to understudy a scullion in a third-rate hash joint. I am, indeed, fallen. What mad folly is this that sets me lower than a menial? Here I might be snug in the Northwest raising my own fat sheep. A letter home would bring me instant help. Yet what would it mean? To own defeat; to lose my self-esteem; to call myself a failure. No, I won't. Come what may, I will play the game."

At that moment the clerk wrote:—

"Man Wanted to Carry Banner."

"How much do you want for that job?" I asked.

"Oh, two bits will hold you," he said carelessly.

"Any experience required?" I asked again.

"No, I guess even you'll do for that," he answered cuttingly.

So I parted with my last quarter and was sent to a Sheeny store in Broadway. Here I was given a vociferous banner announcing:

"Great retiring sale," and so forth.

With this hoisted I sallied forth, at first very conscious and not a little ashamed. Yet by and by this feeling wore off, and I wandered up and down with no sense of my employment, which, after all, was one adapted to philosophic thought. I might have gone through the day in this blissful coma of indifference had not a casual glance at my banner thrilled me with horror. There it was in hideous, naked letters of red:

"Retireing Sale."

I reeled under the shock. I did not mind packing a banner, but a misspelt one . . .

I hurried back to the store, resolved to throw up my position. Luckily the day was well advanced, and as I had served my purpose I was given a silver dollar.

On this dollar I lived for a month. Not every one has done that, yet it is easy to do. This is how I managed.

In the first place I told the old lady who rented me my room that I could not pay her until I got work, and I gave her my blankets as security. There remained only the problem of food. This I solved by buying every day or so five cents' worth of stale bread, which I ate in my room, washing it down with pure spring water. A little imagination and lo! my bread was beef, my water wine. Thus breakfast and dinner. For supper there was the Pacific Gospel Hall, where we gathered nightly one hundred strong, bawled hymns, listened to sundry good people and presently were given mugs of coffee and chunks of bread. How good the fragrant coffee tasted and how sweet the fresh bread!

At the end of the third week I got work as an orange-picker. It was a matter of swinging long ladders into fruit-flaunting trees, of sunshiny days and fluttering leaves, of golden branches plundered, and boxes filled from sagging sacks. There is no more ideal occupation. I revelled in it. The others were Mexicans; I was "El Gringo." But on an average I only made fifty cents a day. On one day, when the fruit was unusually large, I made seventy cents.

Possibly I would have gone on, contentedly enough, perched on a ladder, high up in the sunlit sway of treetops, had not the work come to an end. I had been something of a financier on a picayune scale, and when I counted my savings and found that I had four hundred and ninety-five cents, such a feeling of affluence came over me that I resolved to gratify my taste for travel. Accordingly I purchased a ticket for San Diego, and once more found myself southward bound.

* * * * *

CHAPTER IX

A few days in San Diego reduced my small capital to the vanishing point, yet it was with a light heart I turned north again and took the All-Tie route for Los Angeles. If one of the alluring conditions of a walking tour is not to be overburdened with cash surely I fulfilled it, for I was absolutely penniless. The Lord looks after his children, said I, and when I became too inexorably hungry I asked for bread, emphasising my willingness to do a stunt on the woodpile. Perhaps it was because I was young and notably a novice in vagrancy, but people were very good to me.

The railway track skirts the ocean side for many a sonorous league. The mile-long waves roll in majestically, as straight as if drawn with a ruler, and crash in thunder on the sandy beach. There were glorious sunsets and weird storms, with underhanded lightning stabs at the sky. I built little huts of discarded railway ties, and lit camp-fires, for I was fearful of the crawling things I saw by day. The coyote called from the hills. Uneasy rustlings came from the sagebrush. My teeth, a-chatter with cold, kept me awake, till I cinched a handkerchief around my chin. Yet, drenched with night-dews, half-starved and travel-worn, I seemed to grow every day stronger and more fit. Between bondage and vagabondage I did not hesitate to choose.

Leaving the sea, I came to a country of grass and she-oaks very pretty to see, like an English park. I passed horrible tulé swamps, and reached a cattle land with corrals and solitary cowboys. There was a quaint old Spanish Mission that lingers in my memory, then once again I came into the land of the orange-groves and the irrigating ditch. Here I fell in with two of the hobo fraternity, and we walked many miles together. One night we slept in a refrigerator car, where I felt as if icicles were forming on my spine. But walking was not much in their line, so next morning they jumped a train and we separated. I was very thankful, as they did not look over-clean, and I had a wholesome horror of "seam-squirrels."

On arriving in Los Angeles I went to the Post Office. There was a letter from the Prodigal dated New York, and inclosing fourteen dollars, the amount he owed me. He said:

> "I returned to the paternal roof, weary of my rôle. The fatted calf awaited me. Nevertheless, I am sick again for the unhallowed swine-husks. Meet me in 'Frisco about the end of February, and I will a glorious proposition unfold. Don't fail. I must have a partner and I want you. Look for a letter in the General Delivery."

There was no time to lose, as February was nearly over. I took a steerage passage to San Francisco, resolving that I would mend my fortunes. It is so easy to drift. I was already in the social slough, a hobo and an outcast. I saw that as long as I remained friendless and unknown nothing but degraded toil was open to me. Surely I could climb up, but was it worth while? A snug farm in the Northwest awaited me. I would work my way back there, and arrive decently clad. Then none would know of my humiliation. I had been wayward and foolish, but I had learned something.

The men who toiled, endured and suffered were kind and helpful, their masters mean and rapacious. Everywhere was the same sordid grasping for the dollar. With my ideals and training nothing but discouragement and defeat would be my portion. Oh, it is so easy to drift!

I was sick of the whole business.

* * * * *

CHAPTER X

What with steamer fare and a few small debts to settle, I found when I landed in San Francisco that once more I was flatly broke. I was arrestively seedy, literally on my uppers, for owing to my long tramp my boots were barely holding together. There was no letter for me, and perhaps it was on account of my disappointment, perhaps on account of my extreme shabbiness, but I found I had quite lost heart. Looking as I did, I would not ask any one for work. So I tightened my belt and sat in Portsmouth Square, cursing myself for the many nickels I had squandered in riotous living.

Two days later I was still drawing in my belt. All I had eaten was one meal, which I had earned by peeling half a sack of potatoes for a restaurant. I slept beneath the floor of an empty house out the Presidio way.

On this day I was drowsing on my bench when some one addressed me.

"Say, young fellow, you look pretty well used up."

I saw an elderly, grey-haired man.

"Oh no!" I said, "I'm not. That's just my acting. I'm a millionaire in disguise, studying sociology."

He came and sat by me.

"Come, buck up, kid, you're pretty near down and out. I've been studyin' you them two days."

"Two days," I echoed drearily. "It seems like two years." Then, with sudden fierceness:

"Sir, I am a stranger to you. Never in my life before have I tried to borrow money. It is asking a great deal of you to trust me, but it will be a most Christian act. I am starving. If you have ten cents that isn't working lend it to me for the love of God. I'll pay you back if it takes me ten years."

"All right, son," he said cheerfully; "let's go and feed."

He took me to a restaurant where he ordered a dinner that made my head swim. I felt near to fainting, but after I had had some brandy, I was able to go on with the business of eating. By the time I got to the coffee I was as much excited by the food as if I had been drinking wine. I now took an opportunity to regard my benefactor.

He was rather under medium height, but so square and solid you felt he was a man to be reckoned with. His skin was as brown as an Indian's, his eyes light-blue and brightly cheerful, as from some inner light. His mouth was firm and his chin resolute. Altogether his face was a curious blend of benevolence and ruthless determination.

Now he was regarding me in a manner entirely benevolent.

"Feel better, son? Well, go ahead an' tell me as much of your story as you want to."

I gave an account of all that had happened to me since I had set foot on the new land.

"Huh!" he ejaculated when I had finished. "That's the worst of your old-country boys. You haven't got the get-up an' nerve to rustle a job. You go to a boss an' tell him: 'You've no experience, but you'll do your best.' An American boy says: 'I can do anything. Give me the job an' I'll just show you.' Who's goin' to be hired? Well, I think I can get you a job helpin' a gardener out Alameda way."

I expressed my gratitude.

"That's all right," he said; "I'm glad by the grace of God I've been the means of givin' you a hand-up. Better come to my room an' stop with me till somethin' turns up. I'm goin' North in three days."

I asked if he was going to the Yukon.

"Yes, I'm goin' to join this crazy rush to the Klondike. I've been minin' for twenty years, Arizona, Colorado, all over, an' now I am a-goin' to see if the North hasn't got a stake for me."

Up in his room he told me of his life.

"I'm saved by the grace of God, but I've been a Bad Man. I've been everything from a city marshal to boss gambler. I have gone heeled for two years, thinking to get my pass to Hell at any moment."

"Ever killed any one?" I queried.

He was beginning to pace up and down the room.

"Glory to God, I haven't, but I've shot . . . There was a time when I could draw a gun an' drive a nail in the wall. I was quick, but there was lots that could give me cards and spades. Quiet men, too, you would never think it of 'em. The quiet ones was the worst. Meek, friendly, decent men, to see them drinkin' at a bar, but they didn't know Fear, an' every one of 'em had a dozen notches on his gun. I know lots of them, chummed with them, an' princes they were, the finest in the land, would give the shirts off their backs for a friend. You'd like them—but Lord be praised, I'm a saved man."

I was deeply interested.

"I know I'm talking as I shouldn't. It's all over now, an' I've seen the evil of my ways, but I've got to talk once in a while. I'm Jim Hubbard, known as 'Salvation Jim,' an' I know minin' from Genesis to Revelation. Once I used to gamble an' drink the limit. One morning I got up from the card-table after sitting there thirty-six hours. I'd lost five thousand dollars. I knew they'd handed me out 'cold turkey,' but I took my medicine.

"Right then I said I'd be a crook too. I learned to play with marked cards. I could tell every card in the deck. I ran a stud-poker game, with a Jap an' a Chinaman for partners. They were quicker than white men, an' less likely to lose their nerve. It was easy money, like taking candy from a kid. Often I would play on the square. No man can bluff strong without showing it. Maybe it's just a quiver of the eyelash, maybe a shuffle of the foot. I've studied a man for a month till I found the sign that gave him away. Then I've raised an' raised him till the sweat pricked through his brow. He was my meat. I went after the men that robbed me, an' I went one better. Here, shuffle this deck."

He produced a pack of cards from a drawer.

"I'll never go back to the old trade. I'm saved. I trust in God, but just for diversion I keep my hand in."

Talking to me, he shuffled the pack a few times.

"Here, I'm dealing; what do you want? Three kings?"

I nodded.

He dealt four hands. In mine there were three kings.

Taking up another he showed me three aces.

"I'm out of practice," he said apologetically. "My hands are calloused. I used to keep them as soft as velvet."

He showed me some false shuffles, dealing from under the deck, and other tricks.

"Yes, I got even with the ones that got my money. It was eat or be eaten. I went after the suckers. There was never a man did me dirt but I paid him with interest. Of course, it's different now. The Good Book says: 'Do good unto them that harm you.' I guess I would, but I wouldn't recommend no one to try and harm me. I might forget."

The heavy, aggressive jaw shot forward; the eyes gleamed with a fearless ferocity, and for a moment the man took on an air that was almost tigerish. I could scarce believe my sight; yet the next instant it was the same cheerful, benevolent face, and I thought my eyes must have played me some trick.

Perhaps it was that sedate Puritan strain in me that appealed to him, but we became great friends. We talked of many things, and most of all I loved to get him to tell of his early life. It was just like a story: thrown on the world while yet a child; a shoeblack in New York, fighting for his stand; a lumber-jack in the woods of Michigan; lastly a miner in Arizona. He told me of long months on the desert with only his pipe for company, talking to himself over the fire at night, and trying not to go crazy. He told me of the girl he married and worshipped, and of the man who broke up his home. Once more I saw that flitting tiger-look appear on his face and vanish immediately. He told me of his wild days.

"I was always a fighter, an' I never knew what fear meant. I never saw the man that could beat me in a rough-an'-tumble scrap. I was uncommon husky an' as quick as a cat, but it was my fierceness that won out for me. Get a man down an' give him the leather. I've kicked a man's face to a jelly. It was kick, bite an' gouge in them days—anything went.

"Yes, I never knew fear. I've gone up unarmed to a man I knew was heeled to shoot me on sight, an' I've dared him to do it. Just by the power of the eye I've made him take water. He thought I had a gun an' could draw quicker'n him. Then, as the drink got hold of me, I got worse and worse. Time was when I would have robbed a bank an' shot the man that tried to stop me. Glory to God! I've seen the evil of my ways."

"Are you sure you'll never backslide?" I asked.

"Never! I'm born again. I don't smoke, drink or gamble, an' I'm as happy as the day's long. There was the drink. I would go on the water-wagon for three months at a stretch, but day and night, wherever I went, the glass of whisky was there right between my eyes. Sooner or later it got the better of me. Then one night I went half-sober into a Gospel Hall. The glass was there, an' I was in agony tryin' to resist it. The speaker was callin' sinners to come forward. I thought I'd try the thing anyway, so I went to the penitents' bench. When I got up the glass was gone. Of course it came back, but I got rid of it again in the same way. Well, I had many a struggle an' many a defeat, but in the end I won. It's a divine miracle."

I wish I could paint or act the man for you. Words cannot express his curious character. I came to have a great fondness for him, and certainly owed him a huge debt of gratitude.

One day I was paying my usual visit to the Post Office, when some one gripped me by the arm.

"Hullo, Scotty! By all that's wonderful. I was just going to mail you a letter."

It was the Prodigal, very well dressed and spruce-looking.

"Say, I'm so tickled I got you; we're going to start in two days."

"Start! Where?" I asked.

"Why, for the Golden North, for the land of the Midnight Sun, for the treasure-troves of the Klondike Valley."

"You maybe," I said soberly; "but I can't."

"Yes you can, and you are, old sport. I fixed all that. Come on, I want to talk to you. I went home and did the returned prodigal stunt. The old man was mighty decent when I told him it was no good, I couldn't go into the glue factory yet awhile. Told him I had the gold-bug awful bad and nothing but a trip up there would cure me. He was rather tickled with the idea. Staked me handsomely, and gave me a year to make good. So here I am, and you're in with me. I'm going to grubstake you. Mind, it's a business proposition. I've got to have some one, and when you make the big strike you've got to divvy up."

I said something about having secured employment as an under-gardener.

"Pshaw! you'll soon be digging gold-nuggets instead of potatoes. Why, man, it's the chance of a lifetime, and anybody else would jump at it. Of course, if you're afraid of the hardships and so on—"

"No," I said quickly, "I'll go."

"Ha!" he laughed, "you're too much of a coward to be afraid. Well, we're going to be blighted Argonauts, but we've got to get busy over our outfits. We haven't got any too much time."

So we hustled around. It seemed as if half of San Francisco was Klondike-crazy. On every hand was there speculation and excitement. All the merchants had their outfitting departments, and wild and vague were their notions as to what was required. We did not do so badly, though like every one else we bought much that was worthless and foolish. Suddenly I bethought me of Salvation Jim, and I told the Prodigal of my new friend.

"He's an awfully good sort," I said; "white all through; all kinds of experience, and he's going alone."

"Why," said the Prodigal, "that's just the man we want. We'll ask him to join us."

I brought the two together, and it was arranged. So it came about that we three left San Francisco on the fourth day of March to seek our fortunes in the Frozen North.

* * * * *

BOOK II

THE TRAIL

Gold! We leaped from our benches. Gold! We sprang from our stools.
Gold! We wheeled in the furrow, fired with the faith of fools.
Fearless, unfound, unfitted, far from the night and the cold,
Heard we the clarion summons, followed the master-lure—
Gold!

CHAPTER I

"Say! you're looking mighty blue. Cheer up, darn you! What's the matter?" said the Prodigal affectionately.

And indeed there was matter enough, for had I not just received letters from home, one from Garry and one from Mother? Garry's was gravely censorious, almost remonstrant. Mother, he said, was poorly, and greatly put out over my escapade. He pointed out that I was in a fair way of being a rolling stone, and hoped that I would at once give up my mad notion of the South Seas and soberly proceed to the Northwest.

Mother's letter was reproachful, in parts almost distressful. She was failing, she said, and she begged me to be a good son, give up my wanderings and join my cousin at once. Also she enclosed post-office orders for forty pounds. Her letter, written in a fine faltering hand and so full of gentle affection, brought the tears to my eyes; so that it was very bleakly I leaned against the ship's rail and watched the bustle of departure. Poor Mother! Dear old Garry! With what tender longing I thought of those two in far-away Glengyle, the Scotch mist silvering the heather and the wind blowing caller from the sea. Oh, for the clean, keen breath of it! Yet alas, every day was the memory fading, and every day was I fitting more snugly into the new life.

"I've just heard from the folks," I said, "and I feel like going back on you."

"Oh, beat it," he cried; "you can't renig now. You've got to see the thing through. Mothers are all like that when you cut loose from their apron-strings. Ma's scared stiff about me, thinks the devil's got an option on my future sure. They get wised up pretty soon. What you want to do is to get busy and make yourself acquainted. Here I've been snooping round for the last two hours, and got a line on nearly every one on board. Say! Of all the locoed outfits this here aggregation has got everything else skinned to a hard-boiled finish. Most of them are indoor men, ink-slingers and calico snippers; haven't done a day's hard work in their lives, and don't know a pick from a mattock. They've got a notion they've just got to get up there and pick big nuggets out of the water like cherries out of a cocktail. It's the limit."

"Tell me about them," I said.

"Well, see that young fellow standing near us?"

I looked. He was slim, with gentle, refined features and an unnaturally fresh complexion.

"That fellow was a pen-pusher in a mazuma emporium—I mean a bank clerk. Pinklove's his name. He wanted to get hitched to some girl, but the directors wouldn't stand for it. Now he's chucked his job and staked his savings on this trip. There's his girl in the crowd."

Bedded in that mosaic of human faces I saw one that was all sweetness, yet shamelessly tear-stained.

"Lucky beggar," I said, "to have some one who cares so much about his going."

"Unlucky, you mean, lad. You don't want to have any strings on you when you play this game."

He pointed to a long-haired young man in a flowing-end tie.

"See that pale-faced, artistic-looking guy alongside him. That's his partner. Ineffectual, moony sort of a mut. He's a wood-carver; they call him Globstock; told me his knowledge of wood-carving would come in handy when we came to make boats at Lake Bennett. Then there's a third. See that little fellow shooting off his face?"

I saw a weazened, narrow-chested mannikin, with an aggressive certainty of feature.

"He's a professor, plumb-full of book dope on the Yukon. He's Mister Wise Mike. He knows it all. Hear his monologue on 'How It Should Be Done.' He's going to live on deck to inure himself to the rigours of the Arctic climate. Works with a pair of spring dumb-bells to get up his muscle so's he can shovel out the nuggets."

Our eyes roved round from group to group, picking out characteristic figures.

"See that big bleached-blond Englishman? Came over with me on the Pullman from New York. 'Awfully bored, don't you know.'

When we got to 'Frisco, he says to me: 'Thank God, old chappie, the worst part of the journey's over.' Then there's Romulus and Remus, the twins, strapping young fellows. Only way I know them apart is one laces his boots tight, the other slack. They think the world of each other."

He swung around to where Salvation Jim was talking to two men.

"There's a pair of winners. I put my money on them. Nothing on earth can stop those fellows, native-born Americans, all grit and get-up. See that tall one smoking a cigar and looking at the women? He's an athlete. Name's Mervin; all whipcord and whalebone; springy as a bent bow. He's a type of the Swift. He's bound to get there. See the other. Hewson's his name; solid as a tower; muscled like a bear; built from the ground up. He represents the Strong. Look at the grim, determined face of him. You can't down a man like that."

He indicated another group.

"Now there's three birds of prey. Bullhammer, Marks and Mosher. The big, pig-eyed heavy-jowled one is Bullhammer. He's in the saloon business. The middle-sized one in the plug hat is Marks. See his oily, yellow face dotted with pimples. He's a phoney piece of work; calls himself a mining broker. The third's Jake Mosher. He's an out-and-out gambler, a sure-thing man, once was a parson."

I looked again. Mosher had just taken off his hat. His high-domed head was of monumental baldness, his eyes close-set and crafty, his nose negligible. The rest of his face was mostly beard. It grew black as the Pit to near the bulge of his stomach, and seemed to have drained his scalp in its rank luxuriance. Across the deck came the rich, oily tones of his voice.

"A bad-looking bunch," I said.

"Yes, there's heaps like them on board. There's a crowd of dance-hall girls going up, and the usual following of parasites. Look at that Halfbreed. There's a man for the country now, part Scotch, part Indian; the quietest man on the boat; light, but tough as wire nails."

I saw a lean, bright-eyed brown man with flat features, smoking a cigarette.

"Say! Just get next to those two Jews, Mike and Rebecca Winklestein. They're going to open up a sporty restaurant."

The man was a small bandy-legged creature, with eyes that squinted, a complexion like ham fat and waxed moustaches. But it was the woman who seized my attention. Never did I see such a strapping Amazon, six foot if an inch, and massive in proportion. She was handsome too, in a swarthy way, though near at hand her face was sensuous and bold. Yet she had a suave, flattering manner and a coarse wit that captured the crowd. Dangerous, unscrupulous and cruel, I thought; a man-woman, a shrew, a termagant!

But I was growing weary of the crowd and longed to go below. I was no longer interested, yet the voice of the Prodigal droned in my ear.

"There's an old man and his granddaughter, relatives of the Winklesteins, I believe. I think the old fellow's got a screw loose. Handsome old boy, though; looks like a Hebrew prophet out of a job. Comes from Poland. Speaks Yiddish or some such jargon; Only English he knows is 'Klondike, Klondike.' The girl looks heartbroken, poor little beggar."

"Poor little beggar!" I heard the words indeed, but my mind was far away. To the devil with Polish Jews and their granddaughters. I wished the Prodigal would leave me to my own thoughts, thoughts of my Highland home and my dear ones. But no! he persisted:

"You're not listening to what I'm saying. Look, why don't you!"

So, to please him, I turned full round and looked. An old man, patriarchal in aspect, crouched on the deck. Erect by his side, with her hand on his shoulder, stood a slim figure in black, the figure of a girl. Indifferently my eyes travelled from her feet to her face. There they rested. I drew a deep breath. I forgot everything else. Then for the first time I saw—Berna.

I will not try to depict the girl. Pen descriptions are so futile. I will only say that her face was very pale, and that she had large pathetic grey eyes. For the rest, her cheeks were woefully pinched and her lips drooped wistfully. 'Twas the face, I thought, of a virgin martyr with a fear-haunted look hard to forget. All this I saw, but most of all I saw those great, grey eyes gazing unseeingly over the crowd, ever so sadly fixed on that far-away East of her dreams and memories.

"Poor little beggar!"

Then I cursed myself for a sentimental impressionist and I went below. Stateroom forty-seven was mine. We three had been separated in the shuffle, and I knew not who was to be my roommate. Feeling very downhearted, I stretched myself on the upper berth, and yielded to a mood of penitential sadness. I heard the last gang-plank thrown off, the great crowd cheer, the measured throb of the engines, yet still I sounded the depths of reverie. There was a bustle outside and growing darkness. Then, as I lay, there came voices to my door, guttural tones blended with liquid ones; lastly a timid knock. Quickly I answered it.

"Is this room number forty-seven?" a soft voice asked.

Even ere she spoke I divined it was the Jewish girl of the grey eyes, and now I saw her hair was like a fair cloud, and her face fragile as a flower.

"Yes," I answered her.

She led forward the old man.

"This is my grandfather. The Steward told us this was his room."

"Oh, all right; he'd better take the lower berth."

"Thank you, indeed; he's an old man and not very strong."

Her voice was clear and sweet, and there was an infinite tenderness in the tone.

"You must come in," I said. "I'll leave you with him for a while so that you can make him comfortable."

"Thank you again," she responded gratefully.

So I withdrew, and when I returned she was gone; but the old man slept peacefully.

It was late before I turned in. I went on deck for a time. We were cleaving through blue-black night, and on our right I could dimly discern the coast festooned by twinkling lights. Every one had gone below, I thought, and the loneliness pleased me. I was very quiet, thinking how good it all was, the balmy wind, the velvet vault of the night frescoed with wistful stars, the freedom-song of the sea; how restful, how sane, how loving!

Suddenly I heard a sound of sobbing, the merciless sobbing of a woman's breast. Distinct above the hollow breathing of the sea it assailed me, poignant and insistent. Wonderingly I looked around. Then, in a shadow of the upper deck, I made out a slight girl-figure, crouching all alone. It was Grey Eyes, crying fit to break her heart.

"Poor little beggar!" I muttered.

* * * * *

CHAPTER II

"Gr-r-r—you little brat! If you open your face to him I'll kill you, kill you, see!"

The voice was Madam Winklestein's, and the words, hissed in a whisper of incredible malignity, arrested me as if I had been struck by a live wire. I listened. Behind the stateroom door there followed a silence, grimly intense; then a dull pounding; then the same savage undertone.

"See here, Berna, we're next to you two—we're onto your curves. We know the old man's got the stuff in his gold-belt, two thousand in bills. Now, my dear, my sweet little angel what thinks she's too good to mix with the likes o' us, we need the mon, see!" (Knock, knock.) "And we're goin' to have it, see!" (Knock, knock.) "That's where you come in, honey, you're goin' to get it for us. Ain't you now, darlin'!" (Knock, knock, knock.)

Faintly, very faintly, I heard a voice:

"No."

If it be possible to scream in a whisper, the woman did it.

"You will! you will! Oh! oh! oh! There's the cursed mule spirit of your mother in you. She'd never tell us the name of the man that was the ruin of 'er, blast 'er."

"Don't speak of my mother, you vile woman!"

The voice of the virago contracted to an intensity of venom I have never heard the equal of.

"Vile woman! Vile woman! You, you to call *me* a vile woman, me that's been three times jined in holy wedlock . . . Oh, you bastard brat! You whelp of sin! You misbegotten scum! Oh, I'll fix you for that, if I've got to swing for it."

Her scalding words were capped with an oath too foul to repeat, and once more came the horrible pounding, like a head striking the woodwork. Unable to bear it any longer, I rapped sharply on the door.

Silence, a long, panting silence; then the sound of a falling body; then the door opened a little and the twitching face of Madam appeared.

"Is there somebody sick?" I asked. "I'm sorry to trouble you, but I was thinking I heard groans and—I might be able to do something."

Piercingly she looked at me. Her eyes narrowed to slits and stabbed me with their spite. Her dark face grew turgid with impotent anger. As I stood there she was like to have killed me. Then like a flash her expression changed. With a dirty bejewelled hand she smoothed her tousled hair. Her coarse white teeth gleamed in a gold-capped smile. There was honey in her tone.

"Why, no! my niece in here's got a toothache, but I guess we can fix it between us. We don't need no help, thanks, young feller."

"Oh, that's all right," I said. "If you should, you know, I'll be nearby."

Then I moved away, conscious that her eyes followed me malevolently.

The business worried me sorely. The poor girl was being woefully abused, that was plain. I felt indignant, angry and, last of all, anxious. Mingled with my feelings was a sense of irritation that I should have been elected to overhear the affair. I had no desire just then to champion distressed damsels, least of all to get mixed up in the family brawls of unknown Jewesses. Confound her, anyway! I almost hated her. Yet I felt constrained to watch and wait, and even at the cost of my own ease and comfort to prevent further violence.

For that matter there were all kinds of strange doings on board, drinking, gambling, nightly orgies and hourly brawls. It seemed as if we had shipped all the human dregs of the San Francisco deadline. Never, I believe, in those times when almost daily the Argonaut-laden boats were sailing for the Golden North, was there one in which the sporting element was so dominant. The social hall reeked with patchouli and stale whiskey. From the staterooms came shrill outbursts of popular melody, punctuated with the popping of champagne corks. Dance-hall girls, babbling incoherently, reeled in the passageways, danced on the cabin table, and were only held back from licentiousness by the restraint of their bullies. The day was one long round of revelry, and the night was pregnant with sinister sound.

Already among the better element a moral secession was apparent. Convention they had left behind with their boiled shirts and their store clothes, and crazed with the idea of speedy fortune, they were even now straining at the leash of decency. It was a howling mob, elately riotous, and already infected by the virus of the goldophobia.

Oh, it was good to get on deck of a night, away from this saturnalia, to watch the beacon stars strewn vastly in the skyey uplift, to listen to the ancient threnody of the outcast sea. Blue and silver the nights were, and crystal clear, with a keen wind that painted the cheek and kindled the eye. And as I sat in silent thought there came to me Salvation Jim. His face was grim, his eyes brooding. From the brilliantly lit social hall came a blare of music-hall melody.

"I don't like the way of things a bit," he said; "I don't like it. Look here now, lad, I've lived round mining camps for twenty years, I've followed the roughest callings on earth, I've tramped the States all over, yet never have I seen the beat of this. Mind you, I ain't prejudiced, though I've seen the error of my ways, glory to God! I can make allowance once in a while for the boys gettin' on a jamboree, but by Christmas! Say! There's enough evil on this boat to stake a sub-section in Hell. There's men should be at home with their dinky little mothers an' their lovin' wives an' children, down there right now in that cabin buyin' wine for them painted Jezebels.

"There's doctors an' lawyers an' deacons in the church back in old Ohio, that never made a bad break in their lives, an' now they're rowin' like barroom bullies for the kisses of a baggage. In the bay-window of their souls the devil lolls an' grins an' God is freezin' in the attic. You mark my words, boy; there's a curse on this northern gold. The Yukon's a-goin' to take its toll. You mark my words."

"Oh, Jim," I said, "you're superstitious."

"No, I ain't. I've just got a hunch. Here we are a bit of floatin' iniquity glidin' through the mystery of them strange seas, an' the very officers on dooty sashed to the neck an' reekin' from the arms of the scented hussies below. It'll be God's mercy if we don't crash on a rock, an' go down good an' all to the bitter bottom. But it don't matter. Sooner or later there's goin' to be a reckonin'. There's many a one shoutin' an' singin' to-night'll leave his bones to bleach up in that bleak wild land."

"No, Jim," I protested, "they will be all right once they get ashore."

"Right nothin'! They're a pack of fools. They think they've got a bulge on fortune. Hear them a-howlin' now. They're all millionaires in their minds. There's no doubt with them. It's a cinch. They're spendin' it right now. You mark my words, young feller, for I'll never live to see them fulfilled—there's ninety in a hundred of all them fellers that's goin' to this here Klondike will never make good, an' of the other ten, nine won't *do* no good."

"One per cent. that will keep their stakes—that's absurd, Jim."

"Well, you'll see. An' as for me, I feel as sure as God's above us guidin' us through the mazes of the night, I'll never live to make the trip back. I've got a hunch. Old Jim's on his last stampede."

He sighed, then said sharply:

"Did you see that feller that passed us?"

It was Mosher, the gambler and ex-preacher.

"That man's a skunk, a renegade sky-pilot. I'm keepin' tabs on that man. Maybe him an' me's got a score to settle one of them days. Maybe."

He went off abruptly, leaving me to ponder long over his gloomy words.

We were now three days out. The weather was fine, and nearly every one was on deck in the sunshine. Even Bullhammer, Marks and Mosher had deserted the card-room for a time. The Bank clerk and the Wood-carver talked earnestly, planned and dreamed. The Professor was busy expounding a theory of the gold origin to a party of young men from Minnesota. Silent and watchful the athletic Mervin smoked his big cigar, while, patient and imperturbable, the iron Hewson chewed stolidly. The twins were playing checkers. The Winklesteins were making themselves solid with the music-hall clique. In and out among the different groups darted the Prodigal, as volatile as a society reporter at a church bazaar. And besides these, always alone, austerely aloof as if framed in a picture by themselves, a picture of dignity and sweetness, were the Jewish maid and her aged grandfather.

Although he was my room-mate I had seen but little of him. He was abed before I retired and I was up and out ere he awoke. For the rest I avoided the two because of their obvious connection with the Winklesteins. Surely, thought I, she cannot be mixed up with those two and be everything that's all right. Yet there was something in the girl's clear eyes, and in the old man's fine face, that reproached me for my doubt.

It was while I was thus debating, and covertly studying the pair, that something occurred.

Bullhammer and Marks were standing by me, and across the deck came the acridly nasal tones of the dance-hall girls. I saw the libertine eyes of Bullhammer rove incontinently from one unlovely demirep to another, till at last they rested on the slender girl standing by the side of her white-haired grandfather. Appreciatively he licked his lips.

"Say, Monkey, who's the kid with old Whiskers there?"

"Search me, Pete," said Marks; "want a knockdown?"

"Betcher! Seems kind-a standoffish, though, don't she?"

"Standoffish be darned! Never yet saw the little bit of all right that could stand off Sam Marks. I'm a winner, I am, an' don' you forget it. Just watch my splash."

I must say the man was expensively dressed in a flashy way. His oily, pimple-garnished face wreathed itself in a smirk of patronising familiarity, and with the bow of a dancing master he advanced. I saw her give a quick start, bite her lip and shrink back. "Good for you, little girl," I thought. But the man was in no way put out.

"Say, Sis, it's all right. Just want to interdooce you to a gentleman fren' o' mine."

The girl gazed at him, and her dilated eyes were eloquent of fear and distrust. It minded me of the panic of a fawn run down by the hunter, so that I found myself trembling in sympathy. A startled moment she gazed; then swiftly she turned her back.

This was too much for Marks. He flushed angrily.

"Say! what's the matter with you? Come off the perch there. Ain't we good enough to associate with you? Who the devil are you, anyhow?"

His face was growing red and aggressive. He closed in on her. He laid a rough hand on her shoulder. Thinking the thing had gone far enough I stepped forward to interfere, when the unexpected happened.

Suddenly the old man had risen to his feet, and it was a surprise to me how tall he was. Into his face there had come the ghost of ancient power and command. His eyes blazed with wrath, and his clenched fist was raised high in anathema. Then it came swiftly down on the head of Marks, crushing his stiff hat tightly over his eyes.

The climax was ludicrous in a way. There was a roar of laughter, and hearing it Marks spluttered as he freed himself. With a curse of rage he would have rushed the old man, but a great hand seized him by the shoulder. It was the grim, taciturn Hewson, and judging by the way his captive squirmed, his grip must have been peculiarly vise-like. The old man was pale as death, the girl crying, the passengers crowding round. Every one was gabbling and curious, so feeling I could do no good, I went below.

What was there about this slip of a girl that interested me so? Ever and anon I found myself thinking of her. Was it the conversation I had overheard? Was it the mystery that seemed to surround her? Was it the irrepressible instinct of my heart for the romance of life? With the old man, despite our stateroom propinquity, I had made no advances. With the girl I had passed no further words.

But the Gods of destiny act in whimsical ways. Doubtless the voyage would have finished without the betterment of our acquaintance; doubtless our paths would have parted, nevermore to cross; doubtless our lives would have been lived out to their fulness and this story never have been told—had it not been for the luckless fatality of the Box of Grapes.

* * * * *

CHAPTER III

Puget Sound was behind us and we had entered on that great sea that stretched northward to the Arctic barrens. Misty and wet was the wind, and cold with the kiss of many icebergs. Under a grey sky, glooming to purple, the gelid water writhed nakedly. Spectral islands elbowed each other, to peer at us as we flitted past. Still more wraithlike the mainland, fringed to the sea foam with saturnine pine, faded away into fastnesses of impregnable desolation. There was a sense of deathlike passivity in the land, of overwhelming vastitude, of unconquerable loneliness. It was as if I had felt for the first time the Spirit of the Wild; the Wild where God broods amid His silence; the Wild, His infinite solace and His sanctuary.

As we forged through the vague sea lanes, we were like a glittering trinket on the bosom of the night. Our mad merriment scarce ever abated. We were a blare of revelry and a blaze of light. Excitement mounted to fever heat. In the midst of it the women with the enamelled cheeks reaped a bountiful harvest. I marvel now that, with all the besotted recklessness of those that were our pilots, we met with no serious mishap.

"Don't mind you much of a Sunday-school picnic, does it?" commented the Prodigal. "It's fierce the way the girls are prying some of these crazy jays loose from their wads. They're all plumb batty. I'm tired trying to wise them up. 'Go and chase yourself,' they say; 'we're all right. Don't matter if we do loosen up a bit now, there's all kinds of easy money waiting for us up there.' Then they talk of what they're going to do when they've got the dough. One gazebo wants to buy a castle in the old country; another wants a racing stable; another a steam yacht. Oh, they're a hot bunch of sports. They're all planning to have a purple time in the sweet by-and-bye. I don't hear any of them speak of endowing a home for decrepit wash-ladies or pensioning off their aged grandmothers. They make me sick. There's a cold juicy awakening coming."

He was right. In their visionary leaps to affluence they soared to giddy heights. They strutted and bragged as if the millions were already theirs. To hear them, you would think they had an exclusive option on the treasure-troves of the Klondike. Yet, before and behind us, were dozens of similar vessels, bearing just as eager a mob of fortune-hunters, all drawn irresistibly northward by the Golden Magnet.

Nevertheless, it was hard not to be affected by the prevailing spirit of optimism. For myself the gold had but little attraction, but the adventure was very dear to my heart. Once more the clarion call of Romance rang in my ears, and I leapt to its summons. And indeed, I reflected, it was a wonderful kaleidoscope of a world, wherein I, but a half-year back cooling my heels in a highland burn, should be now part and parcel of this great Argonaut army. Already my native uncouthness was a thing of the past, and the quaint mannerisms of my Scots tongue were yielding to the racy slang of the frontier. More to the purpose, too, I was growing in strength and wiry endurance. As I looked around me I realised that there were many less fitted for the trail than I, and there was none with such a store of glowing health. You may picture me at this time, a tallish young man, with a fine colour in my cheeks, black hair that curled crisply, and dark eyes that were either alight with eagerness or agloom with dreams.

I have said that we were all more or less in a ferment of excitement, but to this I must make a reservation. One there was who, amid all our unrest, remained cold, distant and alien—the Jewish girl, Berna. Even in the old man the gold fever betrayed itself in a visionary eye and a tremor of the lips; but the girl was a statue of patient resignation, a living reproof to our febrile and purblind imaginings.

The more I studied her, the more out of place she seemed in my picture, and, almost unconsciously, I found myself weaving about her a fabric of romance. I endowed her with a mystery that piqued and fascinated me, yet without it I have no doubt I would have been attracted to her. I longed to know her uncommon well, to win her regard, to do something for her that should make her eyes rest very kindly on me. In short, as is the way of young men,

I was beginning to grope blindly for that affection and sympathy which are the forerunners of passion and love.

The land was wintry and the wind shrilled so that the attendant gulls flapped their wings hard in the face of it. The wolf-pack of the sea were snarling whitely as they ran. The decks were deserted, and so many of the brawlers were sick and lay like dead folk that it almost seemed as if a Sabbath quiet lay on the ship. That day I had missed the old man, and on going below, found him lying as one sore stricken. A withered hand lay on his brow, and from his lips, which were almost purple, thin moans issued.

"Poor old beggar," I thought; "I wonder if I cannot do anything for him." And while I was thus debating, a timid knock came to the door. I opened it, and there was the girl, Berna.

There was a nervous anxiety in her manner, and a mute interrogation in her grey eyes.

"I'm afraid he's a little sick to-day," I said gently; "but come in, won't you, and see him?"

"Thank you." Pity, tenderness and love seemed to struggle in her face as she softly brushed past me. With some words of endearment, she fell on her knees beside him, and her small white hand sought his thin gnarled one. As if galvanised into life, the old man turned gratefully to her.

"Maybe he would care for some coffee," I said. "I think I could rustle him some."

She gave me a queer, sad look of thanks.

"If you could," she answered.

When I returned she had the old man propped up with pillows. She took the coffee from me, and held the cup to his lips; but after a few sips he turned away wearily.

"I'm afraid he doesn't care for that," I said.

"No, I'm afraid he won't take it."

She was like an anxious nurse hovering over a patient. She thought a while.

"Oh, if I only had some fruit!"

Then it was I bethought me of the box of grapes. I had bought them just before leaving, thinking they would be a grateful surprise to my companions. Obviously I had been inspired, and now I produced them in triumph, big, plump, glossy fellows, buried in the fragrant cedar dust. I shook clear a large bunch, and once more we tried the old man. It seemed as if we had hit on the one thing needful, for he ate eagerly. She watched him for a while with a growing sense of relief, and when he had finished and was resting quietly, she turned to me.

"I don't know how I can thank you, sir, for your kindness."

"Very easily," I said quickly; "if you will yourself accept some of the fruit, I shall be more than repaid."

She gave me a dubious look; then such a bright, merry light flashed into her eyes that she was radiant in my sight. It was as if half a dozen years had fallen from her, revealing a heart capable of infinite joy and happiness.

"If you will share them with me," she said simply.

So, for the lack of chairs, we squatted on the narrow stateroom floor, under the old man's kindly eye. The fruit minded us of sunlit vines, and the careless rapture of the South. To me the situation was one of rare charm. She ate daintily, and as we talked, I studied her face as if I would etch it on my memory forever.

In particular I noticed the wistful contour of her cheek, her sensitive mouth, and the fine modelling of her chin. She had clear, candid eyes and sweeping lashes, too. Her ears were shell-like, and her hair soft, wavy and warm. These things I marked minutely, thinking she was more than beautiful—she was even pretty. I was in a state of extraordinary elation, like a man that has found a jewel in the mire.

It must be remembered, lest I appear to be taking a too eager interest in the girl, that up till now the world of woman had been *terra incognita* to me; that I had lived a singularly cloistered life, and that first and last I was an idealist. This girl had distinction, mystery and charm, and it is not to be wondered at that I found a joy in her presence. I proved myself a perfect artesian well of conversation, talking freely of the ship, of our fellow-passengers and of the chances of the venture. I found her wonderfully quick in the uptake. Her mind seemed nimbly to outrun mine, and she divined my words ere I had them uttered. Yet she never spoke of herself, and when I left them together I was full of uneasy questioning.

Next day the old man was still abed, and again the girl came to visit him. This time I noticed that much of her timid manner was gone, and in its stead was a shy friendliness. Once more the box of grapes proved a mediator between us, and once more I found in her a reticent but sympathetic audience—so much so that I was frank in telling her of myself, my home and my kinsfolk. I thought that maybe my talk would weary her, but she listened with a bright-eyed regard, nodding her head eagerly at times. Yet she spoke no word of her own affairs, so that when again I left them together I was as much in the dark as ever.

It was on the third day I found the old man up and dressed, and Berna with him. She looked brighter and happier than I had yet seen her, and she greeted me with a smiling face. Then, after a little, she said:

"My grandfather plays the violin. Would you mind if he played over some of our old-country songs? It would comfort him."

"No, go ahead," I said; "I wish he would."

So she got an ancient violin, and the old man cuddled it lovingly and played soft, weird melodies, songs of the Czech race, that made me think of Romance, of love and hate, and passion and despair. Piece after piece he played, as if pouring out the sadness and heart-hunger of a burdened people, until my own heart ached in sympathy.

The wild music throbbed with passionate sweetness and despair. Unobserved, the pale twilight stole into the little cabin. The ruggedly fine face of the old man was like one inspired, and with clasped hands, the girl sat, very white-faced and motionless. Then I saw a gleam on her cheek, the soft falling of tears. Somehow, at that moment, I felt drawn very near to those two, the music, the tears, the fervent sadness of their faces. I felt as if I had been allowed to share with them a few moments consecrated to their sorrow, and that they knew I understood.

That day as I was leaving, I said to her:

"Berna, this is our last night on board."

"Yes."

"To-morrow our trails divide, maybe never again to cross. Will you come up on deck for a little while to-night? I want to talk to you."

"Talk to me?"

She looked startled, incredulous. She hesitated.

"Please, Berna, it's the last time."

"All right," she answered in a low tone.

Then she looked at me curiously.

* * * * *

CHAPTER IV

She came to meet me, lily-white and sweet. She was but thinly wrapped, and shivered so that I put my coat around her. We ventured forward, climbing over a huge anchor to the very bow of the boat, and crouching down in its peak, were sheltered from the cold breeze.

We were cutting through smooth water, and crowding in on us were haggard mountains, with now and then the greenish horror of a glacier. Overhead, in the desolate sky, the new moon nursed the old moon in her arms.

"Berna!"

"Yes."

"You're not happy, Berna. You're in sore trouble, little girl. I don't know why you come up to this God-forsaken country or why you are with those people. I don't want to know; but if there's anything I can do for you, any way I can prove myself a true friend, tell me, won't you?"

My voice betrayed emotion. I could feel her slim form, very close to me, all a-tremble. In the filtered silver of the crescent moon, I could see her face, wan and faintly sweet. Gently I prisoned one of her hands in mine.

She did not speak at once. Indeed, she was quiet for a long time, so that it seemed as if she must be stricken dumb, or as if some feelings were conflicting within her. Then at last, very gently, very quietly, very sweetly, as if weighing her words, she spoke.

"No, there's nothing you can do. You've been too kind all along. You're the only one on the boat that's been kind. Most of the others have looked at me—well, you know how men look at a poor, unprotected girl. But you, you're different; you're good, you're honourable, you're sincere. I could see it in your face, in your eyes. I knew I could trust you. You've been kindness itself to grandfather and I, and I never can thank you enough."

"Nonsense! Don't talk of thanks, Berna. You don't know what a happiness it's been to help you. I'm sorry I've done so little. Oh, I'm going to be sincere and frank with you. The few hours I've had with you have made me long for others. I'm a lonely beggar. I never had a sister, never a girl friend. You're the first, and it's been like sudden sunshine to me. Now, can't I be really and truly your friend, Berna; your friend that would do much for you? Let me do something, anything, to show how earnestly I mean it?"

"Yes, I know. Well, then, you are my dear, true friend—there, now."

"Yes,—but, Berna! To-morrow you'll go and we'll likely never see each other again. What's the good of it all?"

"Well, what do you want? We will both have a memory, a very sweet, nice memory, won't we? Believe me, it's better so. You don't want to have anything to do with a girl like me. You don't know anything about me, and you see the kind of people I'm going with. Perhaps I am just as bad as they."

"Don't say that, Berna," I interposed sternly; "you're all that's good and pure and sweet."

"No, I'm not, either. We're all of us pretty mixed. But I'm not so bad, and it's nice of you to think those things . . . Oh! if I had never come on this terrible trip! I don't even know where we are going, and I'm afraid, afraid."

"No, little girl."

"Yes, I can't tell you how afraid I am. The country's so savage and lonely; the men are so like brute beasts; the women—well, they're worse. And here are we in the midst of it. I don't know what's going to become of us."

"Well, Berna, if it's like that, why don't you and your grandfather turn back? Why go on?"

"He will never turn back. He'll go on till he dies. He only knows one word of English and that's Klondike, Klondike. He mutters it a thousand times a day. He has visions of gold, glittering heaps of it, and he'll stagger and struggle on till he finds it."

"But can't you reason with him?"

"Oh, it's all no use. He's had a dream. He's like a man that's crazy. He thinks he has been chosen, and that to him will a great treasure be revealed. You might as well reason with a stone. All I can do is to follow him, is to take care of him."

"What about the Winklesteins, Berna?"

"Oh, they're at the bottom of it all. It is they who have inflamed his mind. He has a little money, the savings of a lifetime, about two thousand dollars; and ever since he came to this country, they've been trying to get it. They ran a little restaurant in New York. They tried to get him to put his little store in that. Now they are using the gold as a bait, and luring him up here. They'll rob and kill him in the end, and the cruel part is—he's not greedy, he doesn't want it for himself—but for me. That's what breaks my heart."

"Surely you're mistaken, Berna; they can't be so bad as that."

"Bad! I tell you they're *vile*. The man's a worm, and the woman, she's a devil incarnate. She's so strong and so violent in her tempers that when she gets drinking—well, it's just awful. I should know it, I lived with them for three years."

"Where?"

"In New York. I came from the old country to them. They worked me in the restaurant at first. Then, after a bit, I got employment in a shirt-waist factory. I was quick and handy, and I worked early and late. I attended a night school. I read till my eyes ached. They said I was clever. The teacher wanted me to train and be a teacher too. But what was the good of thinking of it? I had my living to get, so I stayed at the factory and worked and worked. Then when I had saved a few dollars, I sent for grandfather, and he came and we lived in the tenement and were very happy for a while. But the Winklesteins never gave us any peace. They knew he had a little money laid away, and they itched to get their hands on it. The man was always telling us of get-rich-quick schemes, and she threatened me in horrible ways. But I wasn't afraid in New York. Up here it's different. It's all so shadowy and sinister."

I could feel her shudder.

"Oh, Berna," I said, "can't I help you?"

She shook her head sadly.

"No, you can't; you have enough trouble of your own. Besides it doesn't matter about me. I didn't mean to tell you all this, but now, if you want to be a true friend, just go away and forget me. You don't want to have anything to do with me. Wait! I'll tell you something more. I'm called Berna Wilovich. That's my grandfather's name. My mother ran away from home. Two years later she came back—with me. Soon after she died of consumption. She would never tell my father's name, but said he was a Christian, and of good family. My grandfather tried to find out. He would have killed the man. So, you see, I am nameless, a child of shame and sorrow. And you are a gentleman, and proud of your family. Now, see the kind of friend you've made. You don't want to make friends with such as I."

"I want to make friends with such as need my friendship. What is going to happen to you, Berna?"

"Happen! God knows! It doesn't matter. Oh, I've always been in trouble. I'm used to it. I never had a really happy day in my life. I never expect to. I'll just go on to the end, enduring patiently, and getting what comfort I can out of things. It's what I was made for, I suppose."

She shrugged her shoulders and shivered a little.

"Let me go now, my friend. It's cold up here; I'm chilled. Don't look so terribly downcast. I expect I'll come out all right. Something may happen. Cheer up! Maybe you'll see me a Klondike queen yet."

I could see that her sudden brightness but hid a black abyss of bitterness and apprehension. What she had told me had somehow stricken me dumb. There seemed a stark sordidness in the situation that repelled me. She had arisen and was about to step over the fluke of the great anchor, when I aroused myself.

"Berna," I said, "what you have told me wrings my heart. I can't tell you how terribly sorry I feel. Is there nothing I can do for you, nothing to show I am not a mere friend of words and phrases? Oh, I hate to let you go like this."

The moon had gone behind a cloud. We were in a great shadow. She halted, so that, as we stood, we were touching each other. Her voice was full of pathetic resignation.

"What can you do? If we were going in together it might be different. When I met you at first I hoped, oh, I hoped—well, it doesn't matter what I hoped. But, believe me, I'll be all right. You won't forget me, will you?"

"Forget you! No, Berna, I'll never forget you. It cuts me to the heart I can do nothing now, but we'll meet up there. We can't be divided for long. And you'll be all right, believe me too, little girl. Be good and sweet and true and every one will love and help you. Ah, you must go. Well, well—God bless you, Berna."

"And I wish you happiness and success, dear friend of mine."

Her voice trembled. Something seemed to choke her. She stood a moment as if reluctant to go.

Suddenly a great impulse of tenderness and pity came over me, and before I knew it, my arms were around her. She struggled faintly, but her face was uplifted, her eyes starlike. Then, for a moment of bewildering ecstasy, her lips lay on mine, and I felt them faintly answer.

Poor yielding lips! They were cold as ice.

* * * * *

CHAPTER V

Never shall I forget the last I saw of her, a forlorn, pathetic figure in black, waving a farewell to me as I stood on the wharf. She wore, I remember, a low collar, and well do I mind the way it showed off the slim whiteness of her throat; well do I mind the high poise of her head, and the silken gloss of her hair. The grey eyes were clear and steady as she bade good-bye to me, and from where we stood apart, her face had all the pathetic sweetness of a Madonna.

Well, she was going, and sad enough her going seemed to me. They were all for Dyea, and the grim old Chilcoot, with its blizzard-beaten steeps, while we had chosen the less precipitous, but more drawn-out, Skagway trail. Among them I saw the inseparable twins; the grim Hewson, the silent Mervin, each quiet and watchful, as if storing up power for a tremendous effort. There was the large unwholesomeness of Madam Winklestein, all jewellery, smiles and coarse badinage, and near her, her perfumed husband, squinting and smirking abominably. There was the old man, with his face of a Hebrew Seer, his visionary eye now aglow with fanatical enthusiasm, his lips ever muttering: "Klondike, Klondike"; and lastly, by his side, with a little wry smile on her lips, there was the white-faced girl.

How my heart ached for her! But the time for sentiment was at an end. The clarion call to action rang out. Inflexibly the trail was mustering us. The hour was come for every one to give of the best that was in him, even as he had never given it before. The reign of peace was over; the fight was on.

On all sides were indescribable bustle, confusion and excitement; men shouting, swearing, rushing hither, thither; wrangling, anxious-eyed and distracted over their outfits. A mood of unsparing energy dominated them. Their only thought was to get away on the gold-trail. A frantic eagerness impelled them; insistent, imperative; the trail called to them, and the light of the gold-lust smouldered and flamed in their uneasy eyes. Already the spirit of the gold-trail was awakening.

Hundreds of scattered tents; a few frame buildings, mostly saloons, dance-halls and gambling joints; an eager, excited mob crowding on the loose sidewalks, floundering knee-deep in the mire of the streets, struggling and squabbling and cursing over their outfits—that is all I remember of Skagway. The mountains, stark and bare to the bluff, seemed to overwhelm the flimsy town, and between them, like a giant funnel, a great wind was roaring.

Lawlessness was rampant, but it did not touch us. The thugs lay in wait for the men with pokes from the "inside." To the great Cheechako army, they gave little heed. They were captained by one Smith, known as "Soapy," whom I had the fortune to meet. He was a pleasant-appearing, sociable man, and no one would have taken him for a desperado, a killer of men.

One picture of Skagway is still vivid in my memory. The scene is a saloon, and along with the Prodigal, I am having a glass of beer. In a corner sits a befuddled old man, half asleep. He is long and lank, with a leathery face and a rusty goatee beard—as ragged, disreputable an old sinner as ever bellied up to a bar. Suddenly there is a sound of shooting. We rush out and there are two toughs blazing away at each other from the sheltering corners of an opposite building.

"Hey, Dad! There's some shootin' goin' on," says the barkeeper.

The old man rouses and cocks up a bleary, benevolent eye.

"Shooting', did ye say? Pshaw! Them fellers don't know how to shoot. Old Dad'll show 'em how to shoot."

He comes to the door, and lugging out a big rusty revolver, blazes away at one of the combatants. The man, with a howl of surprise and pain, limps away. The old man turns to the other fellow. Bang! We see splinters fly, and a man running for dear life.

"Told you I'd show 'em how to shoot," remarks old Dad to us. "Thanks, I'll have a gin-fizz for mine."

The Prodigal developed a wonderful executive ability about this time; he was a marvel of activity, seemed to think of everything and to glory in his responsibility as a leader. Always cheerful, always thoughtful, he was the brains of our party. He never abated in his efforts a moment, and was an example and a stimulus to us all. I say "all," for we had added the "Jam-wagon"[1] to our number. It was the Prodigal who discovered him. He was a tall, dissolute Englishman, gaunt, ragged and verminous, but with the earmarks of a gentleman. He seemed indifferent to everything but whiskey and only anxious to hide himself from his friends. I discovered he had once been an officer in a Hussar regiment, but he was obviously reluctant to speak of his past. A lost soul in every sense of the word, the North was to him a refuge and an unrestricted stamping-ground. So, partly in pity, partly in hope of winning back his manhood, we allowed him to join the party.

Pack animals were in vast demand, for it was considered a pound of grub was the equal of a pound of gold. Old horses, fit but for the knacker's yard, and burdened till they could barely stand, were being goaded forward through the mud. Any kind of a dog was a prize, quickly stolen if left unwatched. Sheep being taken in for the butcher were driven forward with packs on their backs. Even was there an effort to make pack animals out of pigs, but they grunted, squealed and rolled their precious burdens in the mire. What crazy excitement, what urging and shouting, what desperate device to make a start!

We were lucky in buying a yoke of oxen from a packer for four hundred dollars. On the first day we hauled half of our outfit to Canyon City, and on the second we transferred the balance. This was our plan all through, though in bad places we had to make many relays. It was simple enough, yet, oh, the travail of it! Here is an extract from my diary of these days.

> "Turn out at 4 A.M. Breakfasted on flapjacks and coffee. Find one of our oxen dying. Dies at seven o'clock. Harness remaining ox and start to remove goods up Canyon. Find trail in awful condition, yet thousands are struggling to get through. Horses often fall in pools of water ten to fifteen feet deep, trying to haul loads over the boulders that render trail almost impassable. Drive with sleigh over places that at other times one would be afraid

---

1   A Jam-wagon was the general name given to an Englishman on the trail.

to walk over without any load. Two feet of snow fell during the night, but it is now raining. Rains and snows alternately. At night bitterly cold. Hauled five loads up Canyon to-day. Finished last trip near midnight and turned in, cold, wet and played out."

The above is a fairly representative day and of such days we were to have many ere we reached the water. Slowly, with infinite effort, with stress and strain to every step of the way, we moved our bulky outfit forward from camp to camp. All days were hard, all exasperating, all crammed with discomfort; yet, bit by bit, we forged ahead. The army before us and the army behind never faltered. Like a stream of black ants they were, between mountains that reared up swiftly to storm-smitten palisades of ice. In the darkness of night the army rested uneasily, yet at the first streak of dawn it was in motion. It was an endless procession, in which every man was for himself. I can see them now, bent under their burdens, straining at their hand-sleighs, flogging their horses and oxen, their faces crimped and puckered with fatigue, the air acrid with their curses and heavy with their moans. Now a horse stumbles and slips into one of the sump-holes by the trail side. No one can pass, the army is arrested. Frenzied fingers unhitch the poor frozen brute and drag it from the water. Men, frantic with rage, beat savagely at their beasts of burden to make up the precious time lost. There is no mercy, no humanity, no fellowship. All is blasphemy, fury and ruthless determination. It is the spirit of the gold-trail.

At the canyon head was a large camp, and there, very much in evidence, the gambling fraternity. Dozens of them with their little green tables were doing a roaring business. On one side of the canyon they had established a camp. It was evening and we three, the Prodigal, Salvation Jim and myself, strolled over to where a three-shell man was holding forth.

"Hullo!" says the Prodigal. "It's our old friend Jake. Jake skinned me out of a hundred on the boat. Wonder how he's making out?"

It was Mosher, with his bald head, his crafty little eyes, his flat nose, his black beard. I saw Jim's face harden. He had always shown a bitter hatred of this man, and often I wondered why.

We stood a little way off. The crowd thinned and filtered away until but one remained, one of the tall young men from Minnesota. We heard Mosher's rich voice.

"Say, pard, bet ten dollars you can't place the bean. See! I put the little joker under here, right before your eyes. Now, where is it?"

"Here," said the man, touching one of the shells.

"Right you are, my hearty! Well, here's your ten."

The man from Minnesota took the money and was going away.

"Hold on," said Mosher; "how do I know you had the money to cover that bet?"

The man laughed and took from his pocket a wad of bills an inch thick.

"Guess that's enough, ain't it?"

Quick as lightning Mosher had snatched the bills from him, and the man from Minnesota found himself gazing into the barrel of a six-shooter.

"This here's my money," said Mosher; "now you *git*."

A moment only—a shot rang out. I saw the gun fall from Mosher's hand, and the roll of bills drop to the ground. Quickly the man from Minnesota recovered them and rushed off to tell his party. Then the men from Minnesota got their Winchesters, and the shooting began.

From their camp the gamblers took refuge behind the boulders that strewed the sides of the canyon, and blazed away at their opponents. A regular battle followed, which lasted till the fall of night. As far as I heard, only one casualty resulted. A Swede, about half a mile down the trail, received a spent bullet in the cheek. He complained to the Deputy Marshal. That worthy, sitting on his horse, looked at him a moment. Then he spat comprehensively.

"Can't do anything, Ole. But I'll tell you what. Next time there's bullets flying round this section of the country, don't go sticking your darned whiskers in the way. See!"

That night I said to Jim:

"How did you do it?"

He laughed and showed me a hole in his coat pocket which a bullet had burned.

"You see, having been in the game myself, I knew what was comin' and acted accordin'."

"Good job you didn't hit him worse."

"Wait a while, sonny, wait a while. There's something mighty familiar about Jake Mosher. He's mighty like a certain Sam Mosely I'm interested in. I've just written a letter outside to see, an' if it's him—well, I'm saved; I'm a good Christian, but—God help him!"

"And who was Sam Mosely, Jim?"

"Sam Mosely? Sam Mosely was the skunk that busted up my home an' stole my wife, blast him!"

* * * * *

CHAPTER VI

Day after day, each man of us poured out on the trail the last heel-tap of his strength, and the coming of night found us utterly played out. Salvation Jim was full of device and resource, the Prodigal, a dynamo of eager energy; but it was the Jam-wagon who proved his mettle in a magnificent and relentless way. Whether it was from a sense of gratitude, or to offset the cravings that assailed him, I know not, but he crammed the days with merciless exertion.

A curious man was the Jam-wagon, Brian Wanless his name, a world tramp, a derelict of the Seven Seas. His story, if ever written, would be a human document of moving and poignant interest. He must once have been a magnificent fellow, and even now, with strength and will-power impaired, he was a man among men, full of quick courage and of a haughty temper. It was ever a word and a blow with him, and a fight to the desperate finish. He was insular, imperious and aggressive, and he was always looking for trouble.

Though taciturn and morose with men, the Jam-wagon showed a tireless affection for animals. From the first he took charge of our ox; but it was for horses his fondness was most expressed, so that on the trail, where there was so much cruelty, he was constantly on the verge of combat.

"That's a great man," said the Prodigal to me, "a fighter from heel to head. There's one he can't fight, though, and that's old man Booze."

But on the trail every man was a fighter. It was fight or fall, for the trail would brook no weaklings. Good or bad, a man must be a man in the primal sense, dominant, savage and enduring. The trail was implacable. From the start it cried for strong men; it weeded out its weaklings. I had seen these fellows on the ship feed their vanity with foolish fancies; kindled to ardours of hope, I had seen debauch regnant among them; now I was to see them crushed, cowed, overwhelmed, realising each, according to his kind, the menace and antagonism of the way. I was to see the weak falter and fall by the trail side; I was to see the fainthearted quail and turn back; but I was to see the strong, the brave, grow grim, grow elemental in their desperate strength, and tightening up their belts, go forward unflinchingly to the bitter end. Thus it was the trail chose her own. Thus it was, from passion, despair and defeat, the spirit of the trail was born.

The spirit of the Gold Trail, how shall I describe it? It was based on that primal instinct of self-preservation that underlies our thin veneer of humanity. It was rebellion, anarchy; it was ruthless, aggressive, primitive; it was the man of the stone age in modern garb waging his fierce, incessant warfare with the forces of nature. Spurred on by the fever of the gold-lust, goaded by the fear of losing in the race; maddened by the difficulties and obstacles of the way, men became demons of cruelty and aggression, ruthlessly thrusting aside and trampling down the weaker ones who thwarted their progress. Of pity, humanity, love, there was none, only the gold-lust, triumphant and repellent. It was the survival of the fittest, the most tenacious, the most brutal. Yet there was something grandly terrible about it all. It was a barbaric invasion, an army, each man fighting for his own hand under the banner of gold. It was conquest. Every day, as I watched that human torrent, I realised how vast, how irresistible it was. It was Epic, it was Historical.

Many pitiful things I saw—men with haggard, hopeless faces, throwing their outfits into the snow and turning back broken-hearted; men staggering blindly on, exhausted to despair, then dropping wearily by the trail side in the bitter cold and sinister gloom; weaklings, every one. Many terrible things I saw—men cursing each other, cursing the trail, cursing their God, and in the echo of their curses, grinding their teeth and stumbling on. Then they would vent their fury and spite on the poor dumb animals. Oh, what cruelty there was! The life of the brute was as nothing; it was the tribute of the trail; it was a sacrifice on the altar of human greed.

Long before dawn the trail awakened and the air was full of breakfast smells, chiefly that of burnt porridge: for pots were seldom scraped, neither were dishes washed. Soon the long-drawn-out army was on the march, jaded animals straining at their loads, their drivers reviling and beating them. All the men were bearded, and many of them wore parkas. As many of the women had discarded petticoats, it was often difficult at a short distance to tell the sex of a person. There were tents built on sleighs, with faces of women and children peering out from behind. It was a wonderful procession, all classes, all nationalities, greybeards and striplings, parsons and prostitutes, rich and poor, filing past in their thousands, drawn desperately on by the golden magnet.

One day we were making a trip with a load of our stuff when, just ahead, there was a check in the march, so I and the Jam-wagon went forward to investigate. It was our old friend Bullhammer in difficulties. He had rather a fine horse, and in passing a sump-hole, his sled had skidded and slipped downhill into the water. Now he was belabouring the animal unmercifully, acting like a crazy man, shouting in a frenzy of rage.

The horse was making the most gallant efforts I ever saw, but, with every fresh attempt, its strength weakened. Time and again it came down on its knees, which were raw and bleeding. It was shining with sweat so that there was not a dry hair on its body, and if ever a dumb brute's eyes spoke of agony and fear, that horse's did. But Bullhammer grew every moment more infuriated, wrenching its mouth and beating it over the head with a club. It was a sickening sight and, used as I was to the inhumanity of the trail, I would have interfered had not the Jam-wagon jumped in. He was deadly pale and his eyes burned.

"You infernal brute! If you strike that horse another blow, I'll break your club over your shoulders."

Bullhammer turned on him. Surprise paralysed the man, rage choked him. They were both big husky fellows, and they drew up face to face. Then Bullhammer spoke.

"Curse you, anyway. Don't interfere with me. I'll beat bloody hell out of the horse if I like, an' you won't say one word, see?"

With that he struck the horse another vicious blow on the head. There was a quick scuffle. The club was wrenched from Bullhammer's hand. I saw it come down twice. The man sprawled on his back, while over him stood the Jam-wagon, looking very grim. The horse slipped quietly back into the water.

"You ugly blackguard! I've a good mind to beat you within an ace of your life. But you're not worth it. Ah, you cur!"

He gave Bullhammer a kick. The man got on his feet. He was a coward, but his pig eyes squinted in impotent rage. He looked at his horse lying shivering in the icy water.

"Get the horse out yourself, then, curse you. Do what you please with him. But, mark you—I'll get even with you for this—I'll—get—even."

He shook his fist and, with an ugly oath, went away. The block in the traffic was relieved. The trail was again in motion. When we got abreast of the submerged horse, we hitched on the ox and hastily pulled it out, and (the Jam-wagon proving to have no little veterinary skill) in a few days it was fit to work again.

* * * * *

Another week had gone and we were still on the trail, between the head of the canyon and the summit of the Pass. Day after day was the same round of unflinching effort, under conditions that would daunt any but the stoutest hearts. The trail was in a terrible condition, sometimes well-nigh impassable, and many a time, but for the invincible spirit of the Prodigal, would I have turned back. He had a way of laughing at misfortune and heartening one when things seemed to have passed the limit of all endurance.

Here is another day selected from my diary:

> "Rose at 4:30 A.M. and started for summit with load. Trail all filled in with snow, and had dreadful time shovelling it out. Load upsets number of times. Got to summit at three o'clock. Ox almost played out. Snowing and blowing fearfully on summit. Ox tired; tries to lie down every few yards. Bitterly cold and have hard time trying to keep hands and feet from freezing. Keep on going to make Balsam City. Arrived there about ten o'clock at night. Clothing frozen stiff. Snow from seven to one hundred feet deep. No wood within a quarter mile and then only soft balsam. Had to go for wood. Almost impossible to start fire. Was near midnight when I had fire going well and supper cooked. Eighteen hours on the trail without a square meal. The way of the Klondike is hard, hard."

And yet I believe, compared with others, we were getting along finely. Every day, as the difficulties of the trail increased, I saw more and more instances of suffering and privation, and to many the name of the White Pass was the death-knell of hope. I could see their faces blanch as they gazed upward at that white immensity; I could see them tighten their pack-straps, clench their teeth and begin the ascent; could see them straining every muscle as they climbed, the grim lines harden round their mouths, their eyes full of hopeless misery and despair; I could see them panting at every step, ghastly with fatigue, lurching and stumbling on under their heavy packs. These were the weaker ones, who, sooner or later, gave up the struggle.

Then there were the strong, ruthless ones, who had left humanity at home, who flogged their staggering skin-and-bone pack animals till they dropped, then, with a curse, left them to die.

Far, far above us the monster mountains nuzzled among the clouds till cloud and mountain were hard to tell apart. These were giant heights heaved up to the stars, where blizzards were cradled and the storm-winds born, stupendous horrific familiars of the tempest and the thunder. I was conscious of their absolute sublimity. It was like height piled on height as one would pile up sacks of flour. As Jim remarked: "Say, wouldn't it give you crick in the neck just gazin' at them there mountains?"

How ant-like seemed the black army crawling up the icy pass, clinging to its slippery face in the blinding buffet of snow and rain! Men dropped from its ranks uncared for and unpitied. Heedless of those that fell, the gap closed up, the march went on. The great army crawled up and over the summit. Far behind could we see them, hundreds, thousands, a countless host, all with "Klondike" on their lips and the lust of the gold-lure in their hearts. It was the Great Stampede.

"Klondike or bust," was the slogan. It was ever on the lips of those bearded men. "Klondike or bust"—the strong man, with infinite patience, righted his overturned sleigh, and in the face of the blinding blizzard, pushed on through the clogging snow. "Klondike or bust"—the weary, trail-worn one raised himself from the hole where he had fallen, and stiff, cold, racked with pain, gritted his teeth doggedly and staggered on a few feet more. "Klondike or bust"—the fanatic of the trail, crazed with the gold-lust, performed mad feats of endurance, till nature rebelled, and raving and howling, he was carried away to die.

"'Member Joe?" some one would say, as a pack-horse came down the trail with, strapped on it, a dead, rigid shape. "Joe used to be plumb-full of fun; always joshin' or takin' some guy off; well—that's Joe."

Two weary, woe-begone men were pulling a hand-sleigh down from the summit. On it was lashed a man. He was in a high fever, raving, delirious. Half-crazed with suffering themselves, his partners plodded on unheedingly. I recognised in them the Bank clerk and the Professor, and I hailed them. From black hollows their eyes stared at me unrememberingly, and I saw how emaciated were their faces.

"Spinal meningitis," they said laconically, and they were taking him down to the hospital. I took a look and saw in that mask of terror and agony the familiar face of the Wood-carver.

He gazed at me eagerly, wildly: "I'm rich," he cried, "rich. I've found it—the gold—in millions, millions. Now I'm going outside to spend it. No more cold and suffering and poverty. I'm going down there to *live*, thank God, to live."

Poor Globstock! He died down there. He was buried in a nameless grave. To this day I fancy his old mother waits for his return. He was her sole support, the one thing she lived for, a good, gentle son, a man of sweet simplicity and loving kindness. Yet he lies under the shadow of those hard-visaged mountains in a nameless grave.

The trail must have its tribute.

* * * * *

CHAPTER VII

It was at Balsam City, and things were going badly. Marks and Bullhammer had formed a partnership with the Halfbreed, the Professor and the Bank clerk, and the arrangement was proving a regrettable one for the latter two. It was all due to Marks. At the best of times, he was a cross-grained, domineering bully, and on the trail, which would have worn to a wire edge the temper of an angel, his yellow streak became an eyesore. He developed a chronic grouch, and it was not long before he had the two weaker men toeing the mark. He had a way of speaking of those who had gone up against him in the past and were "running yet," of shooting scrapes and deadly knife-work in which he had displayed a spirit of cold-blooded ferocity. Both the Professor and the Bank clerk were men of peace and very impressionable. Consequently, they conceived for Marks a shuddering respect, not unmixed with fear, and were ready to stand on their heads at his bidding.

On the Halfbreed, however, his intimidation did not work. While the other two trembled at his frown, and waited on him hand and foot, the man of Indian blood ignored him, and his face was expressionless. Whereby he incurred the intense dislike of Marks.

Things were going from bad to worse. The man's aggressions were daily becoming more unbearable. He treated the others like Dagoes and on every occasion he tried to pick a quarrel with the Halfbreed, but the latter, entrenching himself behind his Indian phlegm, regarded him stolidly. Marks mistook this for cowardice and took to calling the Halfbreed nasty names, particularly reflecting on the good character of his mother. Still the Halfbreed took no notice, yet there was a contempt in his manner that stung more than words. This was the state of affairs when one evening the Prodigal and I paid them a visit.

Marks had been drinking all day, and had made life a little hell for the others. When we arrived he was rotten-ripe for a quarrel. Then the Prodigal suggested a game of poker, so four of them, himself, Marks, Bullhammer and the Halfbreed, sat in.

At first they made a ten-cent limit, which soon they raised to twenty-five; then, at last, there was no limit but the roof. A bottle passed from mouth to mouth and several big jack-pots were made. Bullhammer and the Prodigal were about breaking even, Marks was losing heavily, while steadily the Halfbreed was adding to his pile of chips.

Through one of those freaks of chance the two men seemed to buck one another continually. Time after time they would raise and raise each other, till at last Marks would call, and always his opponent had the cards. It was exasperating, maddening, especially as several times Marks himself was called on a bluff. The very fiend of ill-luck seemed to have gotten into him, and as the game proceeded, Marks grew more flushed and excited. He cursed audibly. He always had good cards, but always somehow the other just managed to beat him. He became explosively angry and abusive. The Halfbreed offered to retire from the game, but Marks would not hear of it.

"Come on, you nigger!" he shouted. "Don't sneak away. Give me a chance to get my money back."

So they sat down once more, and a hand was dealt. The Halfbreed called for cards, but Marks did not draw. Then the betting began. After the second round the others dropped out, and Marks and the Halfbreed were left. The Halfbreed was inimitably cool, his face was a perfect mask. Marks, too, had suddenly grown very calm. They started to boost each other.

Both seemed to have plenty of money and at first they raised in tens and twenties, then at last fifty dollars at a clip. It was getting exciting. You could hear a pin drop. Bullhammer and the Prodigal watched very quietly. Sweat stood on Marks's forehead, though the Halfbreed was utterly calm. The jack-pot held about three hundred dollars. Then Marks could stand it no longer.

"I'll bet a hundred," he cried, "and see you."

He triumphantly threw down a straight.

"There, now," he snarled, "beat that, you stinking Malamute."

There was a perceptible pause. I felt sorry for the Halfbreed. He could not afford to lose all that money, but his face showed no shade of emotion. He threw down his cards and there arose from us all a roar of incredulous surprise.

For the Halfbreed had thrown down a royal flush in diamonds. Marks rose. He was now livid with passion.

"You cheating swine," he cried; "you crooked devil!"

Quickly he struck the other on the face, a blow that drew blood. I thought for a moment the Halfbreed would return the blow. Into his eyes there came a look of cold and deadly fury. But, no! quickly bending down, he scooped up the money and left the tent.

We stared at each other.

"Marvellous luck!" said the Prodigal.

"Marvellous hell!" shouted Marks. "Don't tell me it's luck. He's a sharper, a dirty thief. But I'll get even. He's got to fight now. He'll fight with guns and I'll kill the son of a dog."

He was drinking from the bottle in big gulps, fanning himself into an ungovernable fury with fiery objurgations. At last he went out, and again swearing he would kill the Halfbreed, he made for another tent, from which a sound of revelry was coming.

Vaguely fearing trouble, the Prodigal and I did not go to bed, but sat talking. Suddenly I saw him listen intently.

"Hist! Did you hear that?"

I seemed to hear a sound like the fierce yelling of a wild animal.

We hurried out. It was Marks running towards us. He was crazy with liquor, and in one hand he flourished a gun. There was foam on his lips and he screamed as he ran. Then we saw him stop before the tent occupied by the Halfbreed, and throw open the flap.

"Come out, you dirty tin-horn, you crook, you Indian bastard; come out and fight."

He rushed in and came out again, dragging the Halfbreed at arm's length. They were tussling together, and we flung ourselves on them and separated them.

I was holding Marks, when suddenly he hurled me off, and flourishing a revolver, fired one chamber, crying:

"Stand back, all of you; stand back! Let me shoot at him. He's my meat."

We stepped back pretty briskly, for Marks had cut loose. In fact, we ducked for shelter, all but the Halfbreed, who stood straight and still.

Marks took aim at the man waiting there so coolly. He fired, and a tide of red stained the other man's shirt, near the shoulder. Then something happened. The Halfbreed's arm rose quickly. A six-shooter spat twice.

He turned to us. "I didn't want to do it, boys, but you see he druv' me to it. I'm sorry. He druv' me to it."

Marks lay in a huddled, quivering heap. He was shot through the heart and quite dead.

* * * * *

CHAPTER VIII

We were camping in Paradise Valley. Before us and behind us the great Cheechako army laboured along with infinite travail. We had suffered, but the trail of the land was near its end. And what an end! With every mile the misery and difficulty of the way seemed to increase. Then we came to the trail of Rotting Horses.

Dead animals we had seen all along the trail in great numbers, but the sight as we came on this particular place beggared description. There were thousands of them. One night we dragged away six of them before we could find room to put up the tent. There they lay, sprawling horribly, their ribs protruding through their hides, their eyes putrid in the sunshine. It was like a battlefield, hauntingly hideous.

And every day was adding to their numbers. The trail ran over great boulders covered with icy slush, through which the weary brutes sank to their bellies. Struggling desperately, down they would come between two boulders. Then their legs would snap like pipe-stems, and there usually they were left to die.

One would see, jammed in the cleft of a rock, the stump of a hoof, or sticking up sharply, the jagged splinter of a leg; while far down the bluff lay the animal to which it belonged. One would see the poor dead brutes lying head and tail for an hundred yards at a stretch. One would see them deserted and desperate, wandering round foraging for food. They would come to the camp at night whinnying pitifully, and with a look of terrible entreaty on their starved faces. Then one would take pity on them—and shoot them.

I remember stumbling across a big, heavy horse one night in the gloom. It was swaying from side to side, and as I drew near I saw its throat was hideously cut. It looked at me with such agony in its eyes that I put my handkerchief over its face, and, with the blow of an axe, ended its misery. The most spirited of the horses were the first to fall. They broke their hearts in gallant effort. Goaded to desperation, sometimes they would destroy themselves, throw themselves frantically over the bluff. Oh, it was horrible! horrible!

Our own horse proved a ready victim. To tell the truth, no one but the Jam-wagon was particularly sorry. If there was a sump-hole in sight, that horse was sure to flounder into it. Sometimes twice in one day we had to unhitch the ox and pull him out. There was a place dug out of the snow alongside the trail, which was being used as a knacker's yard, and here we took him with a broken leg and put a bullet in his brain. While we waited there were six others brought in to be shot.

It was a Sunday and we were in the tent, indescribably glad of a day's rest. The Jam-wagon was mending a bit of harness; the Prodigal was playing solitaire. Salvation Jim had just returned from a trip to Skagway, where he had hoped to find a letter from the outside regarding one Jake Mosher. His usually hale and kindly face was drawn and troubled. Wearily he removed his snow-sodden clothes.

"I always did say there was God's curse on this Klondike gold," he said; "now I'm sure of it. There's a hoodoo on it. What it's a-goin' to cost, what hearts it's goin' to break, what homes it's goin' to wreck no man'll ever know. God only knows what it's cost already. But this last is the worst yet."

"What's the matter, Jim?" I said; "what last?"

"Why, haven't you heard? Well, there's just been a snow-slide on the Chilcoot an' several hundred people buried."

I stared aghast. Living as we did in daily danger of snow-slides, this disaster struck us with terror.

"You don't say!" said the Prodigal. "Where?"

"Oh, somewhere's near Lindeman. Hundreds of poor sinners cut off without a chance to repent."

He was going to improve on the occasion when the Prodigal cut in.

"Poor devils! I guess we must know some of them too." He turned to me. "I wonder if your little Polak friend's all right?"

Indeed my thoughts had just flown to Berna. Among the exigencies of the trail (when we had to fix our minds on the trouble of the moment and every moment had its trouble) there was little time for reflection. Nevertheless, I had found at all times visions of her flitting before me, thoughts of her coming to me when I least expected them. Pity, tenderness and a good deal of anxiety were in my mind. Often I wondered if ever I would see her again. A feeling of joy and a great longing would sweep over me in the hope. At these words then of the Prodigal, it seemed as if all my scattered sentiments crystallised into one, and a vast desire that was almost pain came over me. I suppose I was silent, grave, and it must have been some intuition of my thoughts that made the Prodigal say to me:

"Say, old man, if you would like to take a run over the Dyea trail, I guess I can spare you for a day or so."

"Yes, indeed, I'd like to see the trail."

"Oh, yes, we've observed your enthusiastic interest in trails. Why don't you marry the girl? Well, cut along, old chap. Don't be gone too long."

So next morning, travelling as lightly as possible, I started for Bennett. How good it seemed to get off unimpeded by an outfit, and I sped past the weary mob, struggling along on the last lap of their journey. I had been in some expectation of the trail bettering itself, but indeed it appeared at every step to grow more hopelessly terrible. It was knee-deep in snowy slush, and below that seemed to be literally paved with dead horses.

I only waited long enough at Bennett to have breakfast. A pie nailed to a tent-pole indicated a restaurant, and there, for a dollar, I had a good meal of beans and bacon, coffee and flapjacks. It was yet early morning when I started for Linderman.

The air was clear and cold, ideal mushing weather, and already parties were beginning to struggle into Bennett, looking very weary and jaded. On the trail a man did a day's work by nine in the morning, another by four in the afternoon, and a third by nightfall. You were lucky to get off at that.

I was jogging along past the advance guard of the oncoming army, when who should I see but Mervin and Hewson. They looked thoroughly seasoned, and had made record time with a large outfit. In contrast to the worn, weary-eyed men with faces pinched and puckered, they looked insolently fit and full of fight. They had heard of the snow-slide but could give me no particulars. I inquired for Berna and the old man. They were somewhere behind, between

Chilcoot and Lindeman. "Yes, they were probably buried under the slide. Good-bye."

I hurried forward, full of apprehension. A black stream of Cheechakos were surging across Lindeman; then I realised the greatness of the other advancing army, and the vastness of the impulse that was urging these indomitable atoms to the North. It was blowing quite hard and many had put up sails on their sleds with good effect. I saw a Jew driving an ox, to which he had four small sleds harnessed. On each of these he had hoisted a small sail. Suddenly the ox looked round and saw the sails. Here was something that did not come within the scope of his experience. With a bellow of fear, he stampeded, pursued by a yelling Hebrew, while from the chain of sleds articles scattered in all directions. When last I saw them in the far distance, Jew and ox were still going.

Why was I so anxious about Berna? I did not know, but with every mile my anxiety increased. A dim unreasoning fear possessed me. I imagined that if anything happened to her I would forever blame myself. I saw her lying white and cold as the snow itself, her face peaceful in death. Why had I not thought more of her? I had not appreciated her enough, her precious sweetness and her tenderness. If only she was spared, I would show her what a good friend I could be. I would protect her and be near her in case of need. But then how foolish to think anything could have happened to her. The chances were one in a hundred. Nevertheless, I hurried forward.

I met the Twins. They had just escaped the slide, they told me, and had not yet recovered from the shock. A little way back on the trail it was. I would see men digging out the bodies. They had dug out seventeen that morning. Some were crushed as flat as pancakes.

Again, with a pain at my heart, I asked after Berna and her grandfather. Twin number one said they were both buried under the slide. I gasped and was seized with sudden faintness. "No," said twin number two, "the old man is missing, but the girl has escaped and is nearly crazy with grief. Good-bye."

Once more I hurried on. Gangs of men were shovelling for the dead. Every now and then a shovel would strike a hand or a skull. Then a shout would be raised and the poor misshapen body turned out.

Again I put my inquiries. A busy digger paused in his work. He was a sottish-looking fellow, and there was something of the glare of a ghoul in his eyes.

"Yes, that must have been the old guy with the whiskers they dug out early on from the lower end of the slide. Relative, name of Winklestein, took charge of him. Took him to the tent yonder. Won't let any one go near."

He pointed to a tent on the hillside, and it was with a heavy heart I went forward. The poor old man, so gentle, so dignified, with his dream of a golden treasure that might bring happiness to others. It was cruel, cruel . . .

"Say, what d'ye want here? Get to hell outa this."

The words came with a snarl. I looked up in surprise.

There at the door of the tent, all a-bristle like a gutter-bred cur, was Winklestein.

* * * * *

CHAPTER IX

I stared at the man a moment, for little had I expected so gracious a reception.

"Mush on, there," he repeated truculently; "you're not wanted 'round here. Mush! Pretty darned smart."

I felt myself grow suddenly, savagely angry. I measured the man for a moment and determined I could handle him.

"I want," I said soberly, "to see the body of my old friend."

"You do, do you? Well, you darned well won't. Besides, there ain't no body here."

"You're a liar!" I observed. "But it's no use wasting words on you. I'm going on anyhow."

With that I gripped him suddenly and threw him sideways with some force. One of the tent ropes took away his feet violently, and there on the snow he sprawled, glowering at me with evil eyes.

"Now," said I, "I've got a gun, and if you try any monkey business, I'll fix you so quick you won't know what's happened."

The bluff worked. He gathered himself up and followed me into the tent, looking the picture of malevolent impotence. On the ground lay a longish object covered with a blanket. With a strange feeling of reluctant horror I lifted the covering. Beneath it lay the body of the old man.

He was lying on his back, and had not been squeezed out of all human semblance like so many of the others. Nevertheless, he was ghastly enough, with his bluish face and wide bulging eyes. What had worn his fingers to the bone so? He must have made a desperate struggle with his bare hands to dig himself out. I will never forget those torn, nailless fingers. I felt around his waist. Ha! the money belt was gone!

"Winklestein," I said, turning suddenly on the little Jew, "this man had two thousand dollars on him. What have you done with it?"

He started violently. A look of fear came into his eyes. It died away, and his face was convulsed with rage.

"He did not," he screamed; "he didn't have a red cent. He's no more than an old pauper I was taking in to play the fiddle. He owes *me*, curse him! And who are you anyways, you blasted meddler, that accuses a decent man of being a body robber?"

"I was this dead man's friend. I'm still his granddaughter's friend. I'm going to see justice done. This man had two thousand dollars in a gold belt round his waist. It belongs to the girl now. You've got to give it up, Winklestein, or by—"

"Prove it, prove it!" he spluttered. "You're a liar; she's a liar; you're all a pack of liars, trying to blackmail a decent man. He had no money, I say! He had no money, and if ever he said so, he's a liar."

"Oh, you vile wretch!" I cried. "It's you that's lying. I've a mind to choke your dirty throat. But I'll hound you till I make you cough up that money. Where's Berna?"

Suddenly he had become quietly malicious.

"Find her," he jibed; "find her for yourself. And take yourself out of my sight as quickly as you please."

I saw he had me over a barrel, so, with a parting threat, I left him. A tent nearby was being run as a restaurant, and there I had a cup of coffee. Of the man who kept it, a fat, humorous cockney, I made enquiries regarding the girl. Yes, he knew her. She was living in yonder tent with Madam Winklestein.

"They sy she's tykin' on horful baht th' old man, pore kid!"

I thanked him, gulped down my coffee, and made for the tent. The flap was down, but I rapped on the canvas, and presently the dark face of Madam appeared. When she saw me, it grew darker.

"What d'you want?" she demanded.

"I want to see Berna," I said.

"Then you can't. Can't you hear her? Isn't that enough?"

Surely I could hear a very low, pitiful sound coming from the tent, something between a sob and a moan, like the wailing of an Indian woman over her dead, only infinitely subdued and anguished. I was shocked, awed, immeasurably grieved.

"Thank you," I said; "I'm sorry. I don't want to intrude on her in her hour of affliction. I'll come again."

"All right," she laughed tauntingly; "come again."

I had failed. I thought of turning back, then I thought I might as well see what I could of the far-famed Chikoot, so once more I struck out.

The faces of the hundreds I met were the same faces I had passed by the thousand, stamped with the seal of the trail, seamed with lines of suffering, wan with fatigue, blank with despair. There was the same desperate hurry, the same indifference to calamity, the same grim stoical endurance.

A snowstorm was raging on the summit of the Chikoot and the snow was drifting, covering the thousands of caches to the depth of ten and fifteen feet. I stood on the summit of that nearly perpendicular ascent they call the "Scales." Steps had been cut in the icy steep, and up these men were straining, each with a huge pack on his back. They could only go in single file. It was the famous "Human Chain." At regular distances, platforms had been cut beside the trail, where the exhausted ones might leave the ranks and rest; but if a worn-out climber reeled and crawled into one of the shelters, quickly the line closed up and none gave him a glance.

The men wore ice-creepers, so that their feet would clutch the slippery surface. Many of them had staffs, and all were bent nigh double under their burdens. They did not speak, their lips were grimly sealed, their eyes fixed and stern. They bowed their heads to thwart the buffetings of the storm-wind, but every way they turned it seemed to meet them. The snow lay thick on their shoulders and covered their breasts. On their beards the spiked icicles glistened. As they moved up step by step, it seemed as if their feet were made of lead, so heavily did they lift them. And the resting-places by the trail were never empty.

You saw them in the canyon at the trail top, staggering in the wind that seemed to blow every way at once. You saw them blindly groping for the caches they had made but yesterday and now fathoms deep under the snowdrift. You saw them descending swiftly, dizzily, leaning back on their staffs, for the down trail was like a slide. In a moment they were lost to sight, but to-morrow they would come again, and to-morrow and to-morrow, the men of the Chilcoot.

The Trail of Travail—surely it was all epitomised in the tribulations of that stark ascent. From my eyrie on its blizzard-beaten crest I could see the Human Chain drag upward link by link, and every link a man. And as he climbed that pitiless treadmill, on each man's face there could be deciphered the palimpsest of his soul.

Oh, what a drama it was, and what a stage! The Trail of '98—high courage, frenzied fear, despotic greed, unflinching sacrifice. But over all—its hunger and its hope, its passion and its pain—triumphed the dauntless spirit of the Pathfinder—the mighty Pioneer.

"No," she said firmly, "you can't see the girl"

Then I knew, I knew. These silent, patient, toiling ones were the Conquerors of the Great White Land; the Men of the High North, the Brotherhood of the Arctic Wild. No saga will ever glorify their deeds, no epic make them immortal. Their names will be written in the snows that melt and vanish at the smile of Spring; but in their works will they live, and their indomitable spirit will be as a beacon-light, shining down the dim corridors of Eternity.

* * * * *

I slept at a bunkhouse that night, and next morning I again made a call at the tent within which lay Berna. Again Madam, in a gaudy wrapper, answered my call, but this time, to my surprise, she was quite pleasant.

"No," she said firmly, "you can't see the girl. She's all prostrated. We've given her a sleeping powder and she's asleep now. But she's mighty sick. We've sent for a doctor."

There was indeed nothing to be done. With a heavy heart I thanked her, expressed my regrets and went away. What had got into me, I wondered, that I was so distressed about the girl. I thought of her continually, with tenderness and longing. I had seen so little of her, yet that little had meant so much. I took a sad pleasure in recalling her to mind in varying aspects; always she appeared different to me somehow. I could get no definite idea of her; ever was there something baffling, mysterious, half revealed.

To me there was in her, beauty, charm, every ideal quality. Yet must my eyes have been anointed, for others passed her by without a second glance. Oh, I was young and foolish, maybe; but I had never before known a girl that appealed to me, and it was very, very sweet.

So I went back to the restaurant and gave the fat cockney a note which he promised to deliver into her own hands. I wrote:

> "Dear Berna: I cannot tell you how deeply grieved I am over your grandfather's death, and how I sympathise with you in your sorrow. I came over from the other trail to see you, but you were too ill. Now I must go back at once. If I could only have said a word to comfort you! I feel terribly about it.
>
> "Oh, Berna, dear, go back, go back. This is no country for you. If I can help you, Berna, let me know. If you come on to Bennett, then I will see you.

"Believe me again, dear, my heart aches for you.
"Be brave.

"Always affectionately yours,
"Athol Meldrum."

Then once more I struck out for Bennett.

* * * * *

CHAPTER X

Our last load was safely landed in Bennett and the trail of the land was over. We had packed an outfit of four thousand pounds over a thirty-seven-mile trail and it had taken us nearly a month. For an average of fifteen hours a day we had worked for all that was in us; yet, looking back, it seems to have been more a matter of dogged persistence and patience than desperate endeavour and endurance.

There is no doubt that to the great majority, the trail spelt privation, misery and suffering; but they were of the poor, deluded multitude that never should have left their ploughs, their desks and their benches. Then there were others like ourselves to whom it meant hardship, more or less extreme, but who managed to struggle along fairly well. Lastly, there was a minority to whom it was little more than discomfort. They were the seasoned veterans of the trail to whom its trials were all in the day's work. It was as if the Great White Land was putting us to the test, was weeding out the fit from the unfit, was proving itself a land of the Strong, a land for men.

And indeed our party was well qualified to pass the test of the trail. The Prodigal was full of irrepressible enthusiasm, and always loaded to the muzzle with ideas. Salvation Jim was a mine of foresight and resource, while the Jam-wagon proved himself an insatiable glutton for work. Altogether we fared better than the average party.

We were camped on the narrow neck of water between Lindeman and Bennett, and as hay was two hundred and fifty dollars a ton, the first thing we did was to butcher the ox. The next was to see about building a boat. We thought of whipsawing our own boards, but the timber near us was poor or thinned out, so that in the end we bought lumber, paying for it twenty cents a foot. We were all very unexpert carpenters; however, by watching others, we managed to make a decent-looking boat.

These were the busy days. At Bennett the two great Cheechako armies converged, and there must have been thirty thousand people camped round the lake. The night was ablaze with countless camp-fires, the day a buzz of busy toil. Everywhere you heard the racket of hammer and saw, beheld men in feverish haste over their boat-building. There were many fine boats, but the crude makeshift effort of the amateur predominated. Some of them, indeed, had no more shape than a packing-case, and not a few resembled a coffin. Anything that would float and keep out the water was a "boat."

Oh, it was good to think that from thenceforward, the swift, clear current would bear us to our goal. No more icy slush to the knee, no more putrid horse-flesh under foot, no more blinding blizzards and heart-breaking drift of snows. But the blue sky would canopy us, the gentle breezes fan us, the warm sun lock us in her arms. No more bitter freezings and sinister dawns and weary travail of mind and body. The hills would busk themselves in emerald green, the wild crocus come to gladden our eyes, the long nights glow with sunsets of theatric splendour. No wonder, in the glory of reaction, we exulted and laboured on our boat with brimming hearts. And always before us gleamed the Golden Magnet, making us chafe and rage against the stubborn ice that stayed our progress.

The days were full of breezy sunshine and at all times the Eager Army watched the rotting ice with anxious eyes. In places it was fairly honeycombed now, in others corroded and splintered into silver spears. Here and there it heaved up and cracked across in gaping chasms; again it sagged down suddenly. There were sheets of surface water and stretches of greenish slush that froze faintly overnight. In large, flaming letters of red, the lake was dangerous, near to a break-up, a death trap; yet every day the reckless ones were going over it to be that much nearer the golden goal.

In this game of taking desperate chances, many a wild player lost, many a foolhardy one never reached the shore. No one will ever know the number of victims claimed by these black unfathomable waters.

It was the Professor who opened our eyes to the danger of crossing the lake. He and the Bank clerk quarrelled over the wisdom of delay. The Professor was positive it was quite safe. The ice was four feet thick. Go fast over the weak spots and you would be all right. He argued, fumed and ranted. They were losing precious time, time which might mean all the difference between failure and success. It was expedient to get ahead of the rabble. He, for one, was no craven; he had staked his all on this trip. He had studied the records of Arctic explorers. He thought he was no man's fool. If others were cowardly enough to hold back, he would go alone.

The upshot of it was that one grey morning he took his share of the outfit and started off by himself.

Said the Bank clerk, half crying:

"Poor old Pondersby! In spite of the words we had, we parted the best of friends. We shook hands and I wished him all godspeed. I saw him twisting and wriggling among the patches of black and white ice. For a long time I watched him with a heavy heart. Yet he seemed to be getting along nicely, and I was beginning to think he was right and to call myself a fool. He was getting quite small in the distance, when suddenly he seemed to disappear. I got the glasses. There was a big hole in the ice, no sleigh, no Pondersby. Poor old fellow!"

There were many such cases of separation on the shores of Lake Bennett. Parties who had started out on that trail as devoted chums, finished it as lifelong enemies. Tempers were ground to a razor-edge; words dropped crudely; anger flamed to meet anger. You could scarcely blame them. They did not realise that the trail demanded all that was in a man of gentleness, patience and forbearance. Poor human nature was strained and tested inexorably, and the most loving friends became the most deadly foes forevermore.

One instance of this was the twins.

"Say," said the Prodigal, "you ought to see Romulus and Remus. They're scrapping like cat and dog. Seems they've had a bunch of trouble right along the line—you know how the trail brings out the yellow streak in a man. Well, they're both fiery as Hades, so after a particularly warm evening they swore that as soon as they got to Bennett, they'd divvy up the stuff and each go off by his lonesome. Somehow, they patched it up when they reached here and got busy on their boat. Now it seems they've quarrelled worse than ever. Romulus is telling Remus his real name and *vice-versa*. They're raking up old grievances of their childhood days, and the end of it is they've once more decided to halve tip the outfit. They're mad enough to kill each other. They've even decided to cut their boat in two."

It was truly so. We went and watched them. Each had a bitter determination on his face. They were sawing the boat through the middle. Afterwards, I believe, they patched up their ends and made a successful trip to Dawson.

The ice was going fast. Strangers were still coming in over the trail with awful tales of its horrors. Bennett was all excitement and seething life. Thousands of ungainly boats, rafts and scows were waiting to be launched. Already craft were beginning to come through from Lindeman, rushing down the fierce torrent between the two lakes. From where we were camped we saw them pass. There were ugly rapids and a fang-like rock, against which many a luckless craft was piled up.

It was the most fascinating thing in the world to watch these daring Argonauts rush the rapids, to speculate whether or not they would get through. The stroke of an oar, a few feet to right or left, meant unspeakable calamity. Poor souls! Their faces of utter despair as they landed dripping from the water and saw their precious goods disappearing in the angry foam would have moved a heart of stone. As one man said, in the bitterness of his heart:

"Oh, boys, what a funny God we've got!"

There was a man who came sailing through the passage with a fine boat and a rich outfit. He had lugged it over the trail at the cost of infinite toil and weariness. Now his heart was full of hope. Suddenly he was in the whirl of the current, then all at once loomed up the cruel rock. His face blanched with horror. Frantically he tried to avoid it. No use. Crash! and his frail boat splintered like matchwood.

But this man was a fighter. He set his jaw. Once more he went back over that deadly trail. He bought, at great expense, a new outfit and had packers hustle it over the trail. He procured a new boat. Once more he sailed through the narrow canyon. His face was set and grim.

Suddenly, like some iron Nemesis, once more loomed up the fatal rock. He struggled gallantly, but again the current seemed to grip him and throw him on that deadly fang. With another sickening crash he saw his goods sink in the seething waters.

Did he give up? No! A third time he struggled, weary, heartbroken, over that trail. He had little left now, and with that little he bought his third outfit, a poor, pathetic shadow of the former ones, but enough for a desperate man.

Once more he packed it over the trail, now a perfect Avernus of horror. He reached the river, and in a third poor little boat, again he sailed down the passage. There was the swift-leaping current, the ugly tusk of rock staked with wreckage. A moment, a few feet, a turn of the oar-blade, and he would have been past. But, no! The rock seemed to fascinate him as the eyes of a snake fascinate a bird. He stared at it fearfully, a look of terror and despair. Then for the third time, with a hideous crash, his frail boat was piled up in a pitiful ruin.

He was beaten now.

He climbed on the bank, and there, with a last look at the ugly snarl of waters, and the jagged up-thrust of that evil rock, he put a bullet smashing through his brain.

* * * * *

The ice was loose and broken. We were all ready to start in a few days. The mighty camp was in a ferment of excitement. Every one seemed elated beyond words. On, once more, to Eldorado!

It was near midnight, but the sky, where the sun had dipped below the mountain rim, was a sea of translucent green, weirdly and wildly harmonious with the desolation of the land. On the bleak lake one could hear the lap of waves, while the high, rocky shore to the left was a black wall of shadow. I stood by the beach near our boat, all alone in the wan light, and tried to think calmly of the strange things that had happened to me.

Surely there was something of Romance left in this old world yet if one would only go to seek it. Here I was, sun-browned, strong, healthy, having come through many trials and still on the edge of adventure, when I might, but for my own headstrong perversity, have yet been vegetating on the hills of Glengyle. A great exultation welled up in me, the voice of youth and ambition, the lust to conquer. I would succeed, I would wrest from the vast, lonely, mysterious North some of its treasure. I would be a conqueror.

Silent and abstracted, I looked into the brooding disk of sheeny sky, my eyes dream-troubled.

Then I felt a ghostly hand touch my arm, and with a great start of surprise, I turned.

"Berna!"

* * * * *

CHAPTER XI

The girl was wearing a thin black shawl around her shoulders, but in the icy wind blowing from the lake, she trembled like a wand. Her face was pale, waxen, almost spiritual in its expression, and she looked at me with just the most pitiably sweet smile in the world.

"I'm sorry I startled you; but I wanted to thank you for your letter and for your sympathy."

It was the same clear voice, with the throb of tender feeling in it.

"You see, I'm all alone now." The voice faltered, but went on bravely. "I've got no one that cares about me any more, and I've been sick, so sick I wonder I lived. I knew you'd forgotten me, and I don't blame you. But I've never forgotten you, and I wanted to see you just once more."

She was speaking quite calmly and unemotionally.

"Berna!" I cried; "don't say that. Your reproach hurts me so. Indeed I did try to find you, but it's such a vast camp. There are so many thousands of people here. Time and again I inquired, but no one seemed to know. Then I thought you must surely have gone back, and it's been such a busy time, building our boat and getting ready. No, Berna, I didn't forget. Many's and many's a night I've lain awake thinking of you, wondering, longing to see you again—but haven't you forgotten a little?"

I saw the sensitive lips smile almost bitterly.

"No! not even a little."

"Oh! I'm sorry, Berna. I'm sorry I've looked after you so badly. I'll never forgive myself. You've been terribly sick, too. What a little white whisp you are! You look as if a breeze would blow you away. You shouldn't be out this night, girl. Put my coat around you, come now."

I wrapped her in it and saw with gladness her shivering cease. As I buttoned it at her throat I marvelled at the thinness of her, and at the delicacy of her face. In the opal light of the luminous sky her great grey eyes were lustrous.

"Berna," I said again, "why did you come in here, why? You should have gone back."

"Gone back," she repeated; "indeed I would have, oh, so gladly. But you don't understand—they wouldn't let me. After they had got all his money—and they *did* get it, though they swear he had nothing—they made me come on with them. They said I owed them for his burial, and for the care and attention they gave me when I was sick. They said I must come on with them and work for them. I protested, I struggled. But what's the use? I can't do anything against them any more. I'm weak, and I'm terribly afraid of her."

She shuddered, then a look of fear came into her eyes. I put my hand on her arm and drew her close to me.

"I just slipped away to-night. She thinks I'm asleep in the tent. She watches me like a cat, and will scarce let me speak to any one. She's so big and strong, and I'm so slight and weak. She would kill me in one of her rages. Then she tells every one I'm no good, an ingrate, everything that's bad. Once when I threatened to run away, she said she would accuse me of stealing and have me put in gaol. That's the kind of woman she is."

"This is terrible, Berna. What have you been doing all the time?"

"Oh, I've been working, working for them. They've been running a little restaurant and I've waited on table. I saw you several times, but you were always too busy or too far away in dreams to see me, and I couldn't get a chance to speak. But we're going down the lake to-morrow, so I thought I would just slip away and say good-bye."

"Not good-bye," I faltered; "not good-bye."

Her tone was measured, her eyes closed almost.

"Yes, I'm afraid I must say it. When we get down there, it's good-bye, good-bye. The less you have to do with me, the better."

"What do you mean?"

"Well, I mean this. These people are not decent. They're vile. I must go with them; I cannot get away. Already, though I'm as pure as your sister would be, already my being with them has smirched me in everybody's eyes. I can see it by the way the men look at me. No, go your way and leave me to whatever fate is in store for me."

"Never!" I said harshly. "What do you take me for, Berna?"

"My friend . . . you know, after his death, when I was so sick, I wanted to die. Then I got your letter, and I felt I must see you again for—I thought a lot of you. No man's ever been so kind to me as you have. They've all been—the other sort. I used to think of you a good deal, and I wanted to do some little thing to show you I was really grateful. On the boat I used to notice you because you were so quiet and abstracted. Then you were grandfather's room-mate and gentle and kind to him. You looked different from the others, too; your eyes were good—"

"Oh, come, Berna, never mind that."

"Yes, I mean it. I just wanted to tell you the things a poor girl thought of you. But now it's all nearly over. We've neither of us got to think of each other any more . . . and I just wanted to give you this—to remind you sometimes of Berna."

It was a poor little locket and it contained a lock of her silken hair.

"It's worth nothing, I know, but just keep it for me."

"Indeed I will, Berna, keep it always, and wear it for you. But I can't let you go like this. See here, girl, is there nothing I can do? Nothing? Surely there must be some way. Berna, Berna, look at me, listen to me! Is there? What can I do? Tell me, tell me, my girl."

She seemed to sway to me gently. Indeed I did not intend it, but somehow she was in my arms. She felt so slight and frail a thing, I feared to hurt her.

Then I felt her bosom heaving greatly, and I knew she was crying. For a little I let her cry, but presently I lifted up the white face that lay on my shoulder. It was wet with tears. Again and again I kissed her. She lay passively in my arms. Never did she try to escape nor hide her face, but seemed to give herself up to me. Her tears were salt upon my lips, yet her own lips were cold, and she did not answer to my kisses.

At last she spoke. Her voice was like a little sigh.

"Oh, if it could only be!"

"What, Berna? Tell me what?"

"If you could only take me away from them, protect me, care for me. Oh, if you could only *marry* me, make me your wife. I would be the best wife in the world to you; I would work my fingers to the bone for you; I would starve and suffer for you, and walk the world barefoot for your sake. Oh, my dear, my dear, pity me!"

It seemed as if a sudden light had flashed upon my brain, stunning me, bewildering me. I thought of the princess of my dreams. I thought of Garry and of Mother. Could I take her to them?

"Berna," I said sternly, "look at me."

She obeyed.

"Berna, tell me, by all you regard as pure and holy, do you love me?"

She was silent and averted her eyes.

"No, Berna," I said, "you don't; you're afraid. It's not the sort of love you've dreamed of. It's not your ideal. It would be gratitude and affection, love of a kind, but never that great dazzling light, that passion that would raise to heaven or drag to hell."

"How do I know? Perhaps that would come in time. I care a great deal for you. I think of you always. I would be a true, devoted wife—"

"Yes, I know, Berna; but you don't love me, love me; see, dear. It's so different. You might care and care till doomsday, but it wouldn't be the other thing; it wouldn't be love as I have conceived of it, dreamed of it. Listen, Berna! Here's where our difference in race comes in. You would rush blindly into this. You would not consider, test and prove yourself. It's the most serious matter in life to me, something to be looked at from every side, to be weighed and balanced."

As I said this, my conscience was whispering fiercely: "Oh, fool! Coward! Paltering, despicable coward! This girl throws herself on you, on your honour, chivalry, manhood, and you screen yourself behind a barrier of convention."

However, I went on.

"You might come to love me in time, but we must wait a while, little girl. Surely that is reasonable? I care for you a great, great deal, but I don't know if I love you in the great way people should love. Can't we wait a little, Berna? I'll look after you, dear; won't that do?"

She disengaged herself from me, sighing woefully.

"Yes, I suppose that'll do. Oh, I'll never forgive myself for saying that to you. I shouldn't, but I was so desperate. You don't know what it meant to me. Please forget it, won't you?"

"No, Berna, I'll never forget it, and I'll always bless you for having said it. Believe me, dear, it will all come right. Things aren't so bad. You're just scared, little one. I'll watch no one harms you, and love will come to both of us in good time, that love that means life and death, hate and adoration, rapture and pain, the greatest thing in the world. Oh, my dear, my dear, trust me! We have known each other such a brief space. Let us wait a little longer, just a little longer."

"Yes, that's right, a little longer."

Her voice was faint and toneless. She disengaged herself.

"Now, good-night; they may have missed me."

Almost before I could realise it she had disappeared amid the tents, leaving me there in the gloom with my heart full of doubt, self-reproach and pain.

Oh, despicable, paltering coward!

* * * * *

CHAPTER XII

Spring in the Yukon! Majestic mountains crowned with immemorial snow! The mad midnight melodies of birds! From the kindly stars to the leaves of grass that glimmer in the wind, a world pregnant with joy, a land jewel-bright and virgin-sweet!

After the obsession of the long, long night, Spring leaps into being with a sudden sun-thrilled joy, a radiant uplift. The shy emerald mantles the valleys and fledges the heights; the pussy-willows tremble by lake and stream; the wild crocus brims the hollows with a haze of violet; trailing his last ragged pennants of snow on the hills, winter makes his sullen retreat.

Perhaps I am over-sensitive, but I have ecstasied moments when to me it seems the grass is greener, the sky bluer than they are to most; I surrender my heart to wonder and joy; I am in tune with the triumphant cadence of Things; I am an atom of praise; I live, therefore I exult.

Only in hyperbole could I express that golden Spring, as we set sail on the sunlit waters of Lake Bennett. Never had I felt so glad. And indeed it was a vastly merry mob that sailed with us, straining their eyes once more to the Eldorado of their dreams. Bottled-up spirits effervesced wildly; hearts beat bravely; hopes were high. The bitter landtrail was forgotten. The clear, bright water leaped laughingly at the bow; the gallant breeze was blowing behind. The strong men bared their breasts and drank of it deeply.

Yes, they were the strong, the fit, suffered by the North to survive, stiffened and braced and seasoned, the Chosen of the Test, the Proven of the Trail. Songs of jubilation rang in the night air; men, eager-eyed and watchful, roared snatches of melody as they toiled at sweep and oar; banjos, mandolins, fiddles, flutes, mingled in maddest confusion. Once more the great invading army of the

Cheechakos moved forward tumultuously, but now with mirth and rejoicing.

The great calm night was never dark, the great deep lakes infinitely serene, the great mountains majestically solemn. In the lighted sky the pale ghost-moon seemed ever apologising for itself. The world was a grand harmonious symphony that even the advancing tide of the Argonauts could not mar.

Yet, under all the mirth and gaiety, you could feel, tense, ruthless and dominant, the spirit of the trail. In that invincible onrush of human effort, as the oars bent with their strokes of might, as the sail bellied before the breeze, as the eager wave leapt at the bow, you could feel the passion that quickened their hearts and steeled their arms. Klondike or bust! Once more the slogan rang on bearded lips; once more the gold-lust smouldered in their eyes. The old primal lust resurged: to win at any cost, to thrust down those in the way, to fight fiercely, brutally, even as wolf-dogs fight, this was the code, the terrible code of the Gold-trail. The basic passions upleapt, envy and hate and fear triumphed, and with ever increasing excitement the great fleet of the gold-hunters strained onward to the valley of the treasure.

Of all who had started out with us but a few had got this far. Of these Mervin and Hewson were far in front, victors of the trail, qualified to rank with the Men of the High North, the Sourdoughs of the Yukon Valley. Somewhere in the fleet were the Bank clerk, the Halfbreed and Bullhammer, while three days' start ahead were the Winklesteins.

"These Jews have the only system," commented the Prodigal; "they ran the 'Elight' Restaurant in Bennett and got action on their beans and flour and bacon. The Madam cooked, the old man did the chores and the girl waited on table. They've roped in a bunch of money, and now they've lit out for Dawson in a nice, tight little scow with their outfits turned into wads of the long green."

I kept a keen lookout for them and every day I hoped we would overtake their scow, for constantly I thought of Berna. Her little face, so wistfully tender, haunted me, and over and over in my mind I kept recalling our last meeting.

At times I blamed myself for letting her go so easily, and then again I was thankful that I had not allowed my heart to run away with my head. For I was beginning to wonder if I had not given her my heart, given it easily, willingly and without reserve. And in truth at the idea I felt a strange thrill of joy. The girl seemed to me all that was fair, lovable and sweet.

We were now skimming over Tagish Lake. With grey head bared to the breeze and a hymn stave on his lips, Salvation Jim steered in the strong sunlight. His face was full of cheer, his eyes alight with kindly hope. Leaning over the side, the Prodigal was dragging a spoon-bait to catch the monster trout that lived in those depths. The Jam-wagon, as if disgusted at our enforced idleness, slumbered at the bow. As he slept I noticed his fine nostrils, his thin, bitter lips, his bare brawny arms, tattooed with strange devices. How clean he kept his teeth and nails! There was the stamp of the thoroughbred all over him. In what strange parts of the world had he run amuck? What fair, gracious women mourned for him in far-away England?

Ah, those enchanted days, the sky spaces abrim with light, the gargantuan mountains, the eager army of adventurers, undismayed at the gloomy vastness!

We came to Windy Arm, rugged, desolate and despairful. Down it, with menace and terror on its wings, rushes the furious wind, driving boats and scows crashing on an iron shore. In the night we heard shouts; we saw wreckage piled up on the beach, but we pulled away. For twelve weary hours we pulled at the oars, and in the end our danger was past.

We came to Lake Tagish; a dead calm, a blazing sun, a seething mist of mosquitoes. We sweltered in the heat; we strained, with blistered hands, at the oars; we cursed and toiled like a thousand others of that grotesque fleet. There were boats of every shape, square, oblong, circular, three-cornered, flat, round—anything that would float. They were made mostly of boards, laboriously hand-sawn in the woods, and from a half-inch to four inches thick. Black pitch smeared the seams of the raw lumber. They travelled sideways as well as in any other fashion. And in such crazy craft were thousands of amateur boatmen, sailing serenely along, taking danger with sang-froid, and at night, over their camp-fires, hilariously telling of their hairbreadth escapes.

We entered the Fifty-mile River; we were in a giant valley; tier after tier of benchland rose to sentinel mountains of austerest grandeur. There at the bottom the little river twisted like a silver wire, and down it rowed the eager army. They shattered the silence into wildest echo, they roused the bears out of their frozen sleep; the forest flamed from their careless fires.

The river was our beast of burden now, a tireless, gentle beast. Serenely and smoothly it bore us onward, yet there was a note of menace in its song. They had told us of the canyon and of the rapids, and as we pulled at the oars and battled with the mosquitoes, we wondered when the danger was coming, how we would fare through it when it came.

Then one evening as we were sweeping down the placid river, the current suddenly quickened. The banks were sliding past at a strange speed. Swiftly we whirled around a bend, and there we were right on top of the dreadful canyon. Straight ahead was what seemed to be a solid wall of rock. The river looked to have no outlet; but as we drew nearer we saw that there was a narrow chasm in the stony face, and at this the water was rearing and charging with an angry roar.

The current was gripping us angrily now; there was no chance to draw back. At his post stood the Jam-wagon with the keen, alert look of the man who loves danger. A thrill of excitement ran through us all. With set faces we prepared for the fight.

I was in the bow. All at once I saw directly in front a scow struggling to make the shore. In her there were three people, two women and a man. I saw the man jump out with a rope and try to snub the scow to a tree. Three times he failed, running along the bank and shouting frantically. I saw one of the women jump for the shore. Then at the same instant the rope parted, and the scow, with the remaining woman, went swirling on into the canyon.

* * * * *

CHAPTER XIII

All this I saw, and so fascinated was I that I forgot our own peril. I heard a shrill scream of fear; I saw the solitary woman crouch down in the bottom of the scow, burying her face in her hands; I saw the scow rise, hover, and then plunge downward into the angry maw of the canyon.

The river hurried us on helplessly. We were in the canyon now. The air grew dark. On each side, so close it seemed we could almost touch them with our oars, were black, ancient walls, towering up dizzily. The river seemed to leap and buck, its middle arching four feet higher than its sides, a veritable hog-back of water. It bounded on in great billows, green, hillocky and terribly swift, like a liquid toboggan slide. We plunged forward, heaved aloft, and the black, moss-stained walls brindled past us.

About midway in the canyon is a huge basin, like the old crater of a volcano, sloping upwards to the pine-fringed skyline. Here was a giant eddy, and here, circling round and round, was the runaway scow. The forsaken woman was still crouching on it. The light was quite wan, and we were half blinded by the flying spray, but I clung to my place at the bow and watched intently.

"Keep clear of that scow," I heard some one shout. "Avoid the eddy."

It was almost too late. The ill-fated scow spun round and swooped down on us. In a moment we would have been struck and overturned, but I saw Jim and the Jam-wagon give a desperate strain at the oars. I saw the scow swirling past, just two feet from us. I looked again—then with a wild panic of horror I saw that the crouching figure was that of Berna.

I remember jumping—it must have been five feet—and I landed half in, half out of the water. I remember clinging a moment, then pulling myself aboard. I heard shouts from the others as the current swept them into the canyon. I remember looking round and cursing because both sweeps had been lost overboard, and lastly I remember bending over Berna and shouting in her ear:

"All right, I'm with you!"

If an angel had dropped from high heaven to her rescue I don't believe the girl could have been more impressed. For a moment she stared at me unbelievingly. I was kneeling by her and she put her hands on my shoulders as if to prove to herself that I was real. Then, with a half-sob, half-cry of joy, she clasped her arms tightly around me. Something in her look, something in the touch of her slender, clinging form made my heart exult. Once again I shouted in her ear.

"It's all right, don't be frightened. We'll pull through, all right."

Once more we had whirled off into the main current; once more we were in that roaring torrent, with its fearsome dips and rises, its columned walls corroded with age and filled with the gloom of eternal twilight. The water smashed and battered us, whirled us along relentlessly, lashed us in heavy sprays; yet with closed eyes and thudding hearts we waited. Then suddenly the light grew strong again. The primæval walls were gone. We were sweeping along smoothly, and on either side of us the valley sloped in green plateaus up to the smiling sky.

I unlocked my arms and peered down to where her face lay half hidden on my breast.

"Thank God, I was able to reach you!"

"Yes, thank God!" she answered faintly. "Oh, I thought it was all over. I nearly died with fear. It was terrible. Thank God for you!"

But she had scarce spoken when I realised, with a vast shock, that the danger was far from over. We were hurrying along helplessly in that fierce current, and already I heard the roar of the Squaw Rapids. Ahead, I could see them dancing, boiling, foaming, blood-red in the sunset glow.

"Be brave, Berna," I had to shout again; "we'll be all right. Trust me, dear!"

She, too, was staring ahead with dilated eyes of fear. Yet at my words she became wonderfully calm, and in her face there was a great, glad look that made my heart rejoice. She nestled to my side. Once more she waited.

We took the rapids broadside on, but the scow was light and very strong. Like a cork in a mill-stream we tossed and spun around. The vicious, mauling wolf-pack of the river heaved us into the air, and worried us as we fell. Drenched, deafened, stunned with fierce, nerve-shattering blows, every moment we thought to go under. We were in a caldron of fire. The roar of doom was in our ears. Giant hands with claws of foam were clutching, buffeting us. Shrieks of fury assailed us, as demon tossed us to demon. Was there no end to it? Thud, crash, roar, sickening us to our hearts; lurching, leaping, beaten, battered . . . then all at once came a calm; we must be past; we opened our eyes.

We were again sweeping round a bend in the river in the shadow of a high bluff. If we could only make the bank—but, no! The current hurled us along once more. I saw it sweep under a rocky face of the hillside, and then I knew that the worst was coming. For there, about two hundred yards away, were the dreaded Whitehorse Rapids.

"Close your eyes, Berna!" I cried. "Lie down on the bottom. Pray as you never prayed before."

We were on them now. The rocky banks close in till they nearly meet. They form a narrow gateway of rock, and through those close-set jaws the raging river has to pass. Leaping, crashing over its boulder-strewn bed, gaining in terrible impetus at every leap, it gathers speed for its last desperate burst for freedom. Then with a great roar it charges the gap.

But there, right in the way, is a giant boulder. Water meets rock in a crash of terrific onset. The river is beaten, broken, thrown back on itself, and with a baffled roar rises high in the air in a raging hell of spume and tempest. For a moment the chasm is a battleground of the elements, a fierce, titanic struggle. Then the river, wrenching free, falls into the basin below.

"Lie down, Berna, and hold on to me!"

We both dropped down in the bottom of the scow, and she clasped me so tightly I marvelled at the strength of her. I felt her wet cheek pressed to mine, her lips clinging to my lips.

"Now, dear, just a moment and it will all be over."

Once again the angry thunder of the waters. The scow took them nose on, riding gallantly. Again we were tossed like a feather in a whirlwind, pitchforked from wrath to wrath. Once more, swinging, swerving, straining, we pelted on. On pinnacles of terror our hearts poised nakedly. The waters danced a fiery saraband; each wave was a demon lashing at us as we passed; or again they were like fear-maddened horses with whipping manes of flame. We clutched each other convulsively. Would it never, never end . . . then . . . then . . .

It seemed the last had come. Up, up we went. We seemed to hover uncertainly, tilted, hair-poised over a yawning gulf. Were we going to upset? Mental agony screamed in me. But, no! We righted. Dizzily we dipped over; steeply we plunged down. Oh! it was terrible! We were in a hornets' nest of angry waters and they were stinging us to death; we were in a hollow cavern roofed over with slabs of seething foam; the fiery horses were trampling us under their myriad hoofs. I gave up all hope. I felt the girl faint in my arms. How long it seemed! I wished for the end. *The flying hammers of hell were pounding us, pounding us—Oh, God! Oh, God! . . .*

Then, swamped from bow to stern, half turned over, wrecked and broken, we swept into the peaceful basin of the river below.

* * * * *

CHAPTER XIV

On the flats around the Whitehorse Rapids was a great largess of wild flowers. The shooting stars gladdened the glade with gold; the bluebells brimmed the woodland hollow with amethyst; the fireweed splashed the hills with the pink of coral. Daintily swinging, like clustered pearls, were the petals of the orchid. In glorious profusion were begonias, violets, and Iceland poppies, and all was in a setting of the keenest emerald. But over the others dominated the wild rose, dancing everywhere and flinging its perfume to the joyful breeze.

Boats and scows were lined up for miles along the river shore. On the banks water-soaked outfits lay drying in the sun. We, too, had shipped much water in our passage, and a few days would be needed to dry out again. So it was that I found some hours of idleness and was able to see a good deal of Berna.

Madam Winklestein I found surprisingly gracious. She smiled on me, and in her teeth, like white quartz, the creviced gold gleamed. She had a smooth, flattering way with her that disarmed enmity. Winklestein, too, had conveniently forgotten our last interview, and extended to me the paw of spurious friendship. I was free to see Berna as much as I chose.

Thus it came about that we rambled among the woods and hills, picking wild flowers and glad almost with the joy of children. In these few days I noted a vast change in the girl. Her cheeks, pale as the petals of the wild orchid, seemed to steal the tints of the briar-rose, and her eyes beaconed with the radiance of sun-waked skies. It was as if in the poor child a long stifled capacity for joy was glowing into being.

One golden day, with her cheeks softly flushed, her eyes shining, she turned to me.

"Oh, I could be so happy if I only had a chance, if I only had the chance other girls have. It would take so little to make me the happiest girl in the world—just to have a home, a plain, simple home where all was sunshine and peace; just to have the commonest comforts, to be care-free, to love and be loved. That would be enough." She sighed and went on:

"Then if I might have books, a little music, flowers—oh, it seems like a dream of heaven; as well might I sigh for a palace."

"No palace could be too fair for you, Berna, no prince too noble. Some day, your prince will come, and you will give him that great love I told you of once."

Swiftly a shadow came into the bright eyes, the sweet mouth curved pathetically.

"Not even a beggar will seek me, a poor nameless girl travelling in the train of dishonour . . . and again, I will never love."

"Yes, you will indeed, girl—infinitely, supremely. I know you, Berna; you'll love as few women do. Your dearest will be all your world, his smile your heaven, his frown your death. Love was at the fashioning of you, dear, and kissed your lips and sent you forth, saying, 'There goeth my handmaiden.'"

I thought for a while ere I went on.

"You cared for your grandfather; you gave him your whole heart, a love full of self-sacrifice, of renunciation. Now he is gone, you will love again, but the next will be to the last as wine is to water. And the day will come when you will love grandly. Yours will be a great, consuming passion that knows no limit, no assuagement. It will be your glory and your shame. For him will your friends be foes, your light darkness. You will go through fire and water for your beloved's sake; your parched lips will call his name, your frail hands cling to him in the shadow of death. Oh, I know, I know. Love has set you apart. You will immolate yourself on his altars. You will dare, defy and die for him. I'm sorry for you, Berna."

Her face hung down, her lips quivered. As for me, I was surprised at my words and scarce knew what I was saying.

At last she spoke.

"If ever I loved like that, the man I loved must be a king among men, a hero, almost a god."

"Perhaps, Berna, perhaps; but not needfully. He may be a grim man with a face of power and passion, a virile, dominant brute, but—well, I think he will be more of a god. Let's change the subject."

I found she had all the sad sophistication of the lowly-born, yet with it an invincible sense of purity, a delicate horror of the physical phases of love. She was a finely motived creature with impossible ideals, but out of her stark knowledge of life she was naïvely outspoken.

Once I asked of her:

"Berna, if you had to choose between death and dishonour, which would you prefer?"

"Death, of course," she answered promptly.

"Death's a pretty hard proposition," I commented.

"No, it's easy; physical death, compared with the other, compared with moral death."

She was very emphatic and angry with me for my hazarded demur. In an atmosphere of disillusionment and moral miasma she clung undauntedly to her ideals. Never was such a brave spirit, so determined in goodness, so upright in purity, and I blessed her for her unfaltering words. "May such sentiments as yours," I prayed, "be ever mine. In doubt, despair, defeat, oh Life, take not away from me my faith in the pure heart of woman!"

Often I watched her thoughtfully, her slim, well-poised figure, her grey eyes that were fuller of soul than any eyes I have ever seen, her brown hair wherein the sunshine loved to pick out threads of gold, her delicate features with their fine patrician quality. We were dreamers twain, but while my outlook was gay with hope, hers was dark with despair. Since the episode of the scow I had never ventured to kiss her, but had treated her with a curious reserve, respect and courtesy.

Indeed, I was diagnosing my case, wondering if I loved her, affirming, doubting on a very see-saw of indetermination. When with her I felt for her an intense fondness and at times an almost irresponsible tenderness. My eyes rested longingly on her, noting with tremulous joy the curves and shading of her face, and finding in its very defects, beauties.

When I was away from her—oh, the easeless longing that was almost pain, the fanciful elaboration of our last talk, the hint of her graces in bird and flower and tree! I wanted her wildly, and the thought of a world empty of her was monstrous. I wondered how in the past we had both existed and how I had lived, carelessly, happy and serenely indifferent. I tried to think of a time when she should no longer have power to make my heart quicken with joy or contract with fear—and the thought of such a state was insufferable pain. Was I in love? Poor, fatuous fool! I wanted her more than everything else in all the world, yet I hesitated and asked myself the question.

Hundreds of boats and scows were running the rapids, and we watched them with an untiring fascination. That was the most exciting spectacle in the whole world. The issue was life or death, ruin or salvation, and from dawn till dark, and with every few minutes of the day, was the breathless climax repeated. The faces of the actors were sick with dread and anxiety. It was curious to study the various expressions of the human countenance unmasked and confronted with gibbering fear. Yes, it was a vivid drama, a drama of cheers and tears, always thrilling and often tragic. Every day were bodies dragged ashore. The rapids demanded their tribute. The men of the trail must pay the toll. Sullen and bloated the river disgorged its prey, and the dead, without prayer or pause, were thrown into nameless graves.

On our first day at the rapids we met the Halfbreed. He was on the point of starting downstream. Where was the Bank clerk? Oh, yes; they had upset coming through; when last he had seen little Pinklove he was struggling in the water. However, they expected to get the body every hour. He had paid two men to find and bury it. He had no time to wait.

We did not blame him. In those wild days of headstrong hurry and gold-delirium human life meant little. "Another floater," one would say, and carelessly turn away. A callousness to death that was almost mediæval was in the air, and the friends of the dead hurried on, the richer by a partner's outfit. It was all new, strange, sinister to me, this unveiling of life's naked selfishness and lust.

Next morning they found the body, a poor, shapeless, sodden thing with such a crumpled skull. My thoughts went back to the sweet-faced girl who had wept so bitterly at his going. Even then, maybe, she was thinking of him, fondly dreaming of his return, seeing the glow of triumph in his boyish eyes. She would wait and hope; then she would wait and despair; then there would be another white-faced woman saying, "He went to the Klondike, and never came back. We don't know what became of him."

Verily, the way of the gold-trail was cruel.

Berna was with me when they buried him.

"Poor boy, poor boy!" she repeated.

"Yes, poor little beggar! He was so quiet and gentle. He was no man for the trail. It's a funny world."

The coffin was a box of unplaned boards loosely nailed together, and the men were for putting him into a grave on top of another coffin. I protested, so sullenly they proceeded to dig a new grave. Berna looked very unhappy, and when she saw that crude, shapeless pine coffin she broke down and cried bitterly.

At last she dried her tears and with a happier look in her eyes bade me wait a little until she returned. Soon again she came back, carrying some folds of black sateen over her arm. As she ripped at this with a pair of scissors, I noticed there was a deep frilling to it. Also a bright blush came into her cheek at the curious glance I gave to the somewhat skimpy lines of her skirt. But the next instant she was busy stretching and tacking the black material over the coffin.

The men had completed the new grave. It was only three feet deep, but the water coming in had prevented them from digging further. As we laid the coffin in the hole it looked quite decent now in its black covering. It floated on the water, but after some clods had been thrown down, it sank with many gurglings. It was as if the dead man protested against his bitter burial. We watched the grave-diggers throw a few more shovelsful of earth over the place, then go off whistling. Poor little Berna! she cried steadily. At last she said:

"Let's get some flowers."

So out of briar-roses she fashioned a cross and a wreath, and we laid them reverently on the muddy heap that marked the Bank clerk's grave.

Oh, the pitiful mockery of it!

* * * * *

CHAPTER XV

Soon I knew that Berna and I must part, and but two nights later it came. It was near midnight, yet in no ways dark, and everywhere the camp was astir. We were sitting by the river, I remember, a little way from the boats. Where the sun had set, the sky was a luminous veil of ravishing green, and in the elusive light her face seemed wanly sweet and dreamlike.

A sad spirit rustled amid the shivering willows and a great sadness had come over the girl. All the happiness of the past few days seemed to have ebbed away from her and left her empty of hope. As she sat there, silent and with hands clasped, it was as if the shadows that for a little had lifted, now enshrouded her with a greater gloom.

"Tell me your trouble, Berna."

She shook her head, her eyes wide as if trying to read the future.

"Nothing."

Her voice was almost a whisper.

"Yes, there is, I know. Tell me, won't you?"

Again she shook her head.

"What's the matter, little chum?"

"It's nothing; it's only my foolishness. If I tell you, it wouldn't help me any. And then—it doesn't matter. You wouldn't care. Why should you care?"

She turned away from me and seemed absorbed in bitter thought.

"Care! why, yes, I would care; I do care. You know I would do anything in the world to help you. You know I would be unhappy if you were unhappy. You know—"

"Then it would only worry you."

She was regarding me anxiously.

"Now you must tell me, Berna. It will worry me indeed if you don't."

Once more she refused. I pleaded with her gently. I coaxed, I entreated. She was very reluctant, yet at last she yielded.

"Well, if I must," she said; "but it's all so sordid, so mean, I hate myself; I despise myself that I should have to tell it."

She kneaded a tiny handkerchief nervously in her fingers.

"You know how nice Madam Winklestein's been to me lately—bought me new clothes, given me trinkets. Well, there's a reason—she's got her eye on a man for me."

I gave an exclamation of surprise.

"Yes; you know she's let us go together—it's all to draw him on. Oh, couldn't you see it? Didn't you suspect something? You don't know how bitterly they hate you."

I bit my lip.

"Who's the man?"

"Jack Locasto."

I started.

"Have you heard of him?" she asked. "He's got a million-dollar claim on Bonanza."

Had I heard of him! Who had not heard of Black Jack, his spectacular poker plays, his meteoric rise, his theatric display?

"Of course he's married," she went on, "but that doesn't matter up here. There's such a thing as a Klondike marriage, and they say he behaves well to his discarded mis—"

"Berna!" angry and aghast, I had stopped her. "Never let me hear you utter that word. Even to say it seems pollution."

She laughed harshly, bitterly.

"What's this whole life but pollution? . . . Well, anyway, he wants me."

"But you wouldn't, surely you wouldn't?"

She turned on me fiercely.

"What do you take me for? Surely you know me better than that. Oh, you almost make me hate you."

Suddenly she pressed the little handkerchief to her eyes. She fell to sobbing convulsively. Vainly I tried to soothe her, whispering:

"Oh, my dear, tell me all about it. I'm sorry, girl, I'm sorry."

She ceased crying. She went on in her fierce, excited way.

"He came to the restaurant in Bennett. He used to watch me a lot. His eyes were always following me. I was afraid. I trembled when I served him. He liked to see me tremble, it gave him a feeling of power. Then he took to giving me presents, a diamond ring, a heart-shaped locket, costly gifts. I wanted to return them, but she wouldn't let me, took them from me, put them away. Then he and she had long talks. I know it was all about me. That was why I came to you that night and begged you to marry me—to save me from him. Now it's gone from bad to worse. The net's closing round me in spite of my flutterings."

"But he can't get you against your will," I cried.

"No! no! but he'll never give up. He'll try so long as I resist him. I'm nice to him just to humour him and gain time. I can't tell you how much I fear him. They say he always gets his way with women. He's masterly and relentless. There's a cold, sneering command in his smile. You hate him but you obey him."

"He's an immoral monster, Berna. He spares neither time nor money to gratify his whims where a woman is concerned. And he has no pity."

"I know, I know."

"He's intensely masculine, handsome in a vivid, gipsy sort of way; big, strong and compelling, but a callous libertine."

"Yes, he's all that. And can you wonder then my heart is full of fear, that I am distracted, that I asked you what I did? He is relentless and of all women he wants me. He would break me on the wheel of dishonour. Oh, God!"

Her face grew almost tragic in its despair.

"And everything's against me; they're all helping him. I haven't a single friend, not one to stand by me, to aid me. Once I thought of you, and you failed me. Can you wonder I'm nearly crazy with the terror of it? Can you wonder I was desperate enough to ask you to save me? I'm all alone, friendless, a poor, weak girl. No, I'm wrong. I've one friend—death; and I'll die, I'll die, I swear it, before I let him get me."

Her words came forth in a torrent, half choked by sobs. It was hard to get her calmed. Never had I thought her capable of such force, such passion. I was terribly distressed and at a loss how to comfort her.

"Hush, Berna," I pleaded, "please don't say such things. Remember you have a friend in me, one that would do anything in his power to help you."

She looked at me a moment.

"How can you help me?"

I held both of her hands firmly, looking into her eyes.

"By marrying you. Will you marry me, dear? Will you be my wife?"

"No!"

I started. "Berna!"

"No! I wouldn't marry you if you were the last man left in the world," she cried vehemently.

"Why?" I tried to be calm.

"Why! why, you don't love me; you don't care for me."

"Yes, I do, Berna. I do indeed, girl. Care for you! Well, I care so much that—I beg you to marry me."

"Yes, yes, but you don't love me right, not in your great, grand way. Not in the way you told me of. Oh, I know; it's part pity, part friendship. It would be different if I cared in the same way, if—if I didn't care so very much more."

"You do, Berna; you love me like that?"

"How do I know? How can I tell? How can any of us tell?"

"No, dear," I said, "love has no limits, no bounds, it is always holding something in reserve. There are yet heights beyond the heights, that mock our climbing, never perfection; no great love but might have been eclipsed by a greater. There's a master key to every heart, and we poor fools delude ourselves with the idea we are opening all the doors. We are on sufferance, we are only understudies in the love drama, but fortunately the star seldom appears on the scene. However, this I know—"

I rose to my feet.

"Since the moment I set eyes on you, I loved you. Long before I ever met you, I loved you. I was just waiting for you, waiting. At first I could not understand, I did not know what it meant, but now I do, beyond the peradventure of a doubt; there never was any but you, never will be any but you. Since the beginning of time it was all planned that I should love you. And you, how do you care?"

She stood up to hear my words. She would not let me touch her, but there was a great light in her eyes. Then she spoke and her voice was vibrant with passion, all indifference gone from it.

"Oh, you blind! you coward! Couldn't you see? Couldn't you feel? That day on the scow it came to me—Love. It was such as I had never dreamed of, rapture, ecstasy, anguish. Do you know what I wished as we went through the rapids? I wished that it might be the end, that in such a supreme moment we might go down clinging together, and that in death I might hold you in my arms. Oh, if you'd only been like that afterwards, met love open-armed with love. But, no! you slipped back to friendship. I feel as if there were a barrier of ice between us now. I will try never to care for you any more. Now leave me, leave me, for I never want to see you again."

"Yes, you will, you must, you must, Berna. I'd sell my immortal soul to win that love from you, my dearest, my dearest; I'd crawl around the world to kiss your shadow. If you called to me I would come from the ends of the earth, through storm and darkness, to your side. I love you so, I love you so."

I crushed her to me, I kissed her madly, yet she was cold.

"Have you nothing more to say than fine words?" she asked.

"Marry me, marry me," I repeated.

"Now?"

Now! I hesitated again. The suddenness of it was like a cold douche. God knows, I burned for the girl, yet somehow convention clamped me.

"Now if you wish," I faltered; "but better when we get to Dawson. Better when I've made good up there. Give me one year, Berna, one year and then—"

"One year!"

The sudden gleam of hope vanished from her eyes. For the third time I was failing her, yet my cursed prudence overrode me.

"Oh, it will pass swiftly, dear. You will be quite safe. I will be near you and watch over you."

I reassured her, anxiously explaining how much better it would be if we waited a little.

"One year!" she repeated, and it seemed to me her voice was toneless. Then she turned to me in a sudden spate of passion, her face pleading, furrowed, wretchedly sad.

"Oh, my dear, my dear, I love you better than the whole world, but I hoped you would care enough for me to marry me now. It would have been best, believe me. I thought you would rise to the occasion, but you've failed me. Well, be it so, we'll wait one year."

"Yes, believe me, trust me, dear; it will be all right. I'll work for you, slave for you, think only of you, and in twelve short months— I'll give my whole life to make you happy."

"Will you, dear? Well, it doesn't matter now . . . I've loved you."

* * * * *

All that night I wrestled with myself. I felt I ought to marry her at once to shield her from the dangers that encompassed her. She was like a lamb among a pack of wolves. I juggled with my conscience. I was young and marriage to me seemed such a terribly all-important step.

Yet in the end my better nature triumphed, and ere the camp was astir I arose. I was going to marry Berna that day. A feeling of relief came over me. How had it ever seemed possible to delay? I was elated beyond measure.

I hurried to tell her, I pictured her joy. I was almost breathless. Love words trembled on my tongue tip. It seemed to me I could not bear to wait a moment.

Then as I reached the place where they had rested I gazed unbelievingly. A sickening sense of loss and failure crushed me.

For the scow was gone.

* * * * *

CHAPTER XVI

It was three days before we made a start again, and to me each day was like a year. I chafed bitterly at the delay. Would those sacks of flour never dry? Longingly I gazed down the big, blue Yukon and cursed the current that was every moment carrying her farther from me. Why her sudden departure? I had no doubt it was enforced. I dreaded danger. Then in a while I grew calmer. I was foolish to worry. She was safe enough. We would meet in Dawson.

At last we were under way. Once more we sped down that devious river, now swirling under the shadow of a steep bank, now steering around a sandspit. The scenery was hideous to me, bluffs of clay with pines peeping over their rims, willow-fringed flats, swamps of niggerhead, ugly drab hills in endless monotony.

How full of kinks and hooks was the river! How vicious with snags! How treacherous with eddies! It was beginning to bulk in my thoughts almost like an obsession. Then one day Lake Labarge burst on my delighted eyes. The trail was nearing its end.

Once more with swelling sail we drove before the wind. Once more we were in a fleet of Argonaut boats, and now, with the goal in sight, each man redoubled his efforts. Perhaps the rich ground would all be gone ere we reached the valley. Maddening thought after what we had endured! We must get on.

There was not a man in all that fleet but imagined that fortune awaited him with open arms. They talked exultantly. Their eyes shone with the gold-lust. They strained at sweep and oar. To be beaten at the last! Oh, it was inconceivable! A tigerish eagerness filled them; a panic of fear and cupidity spurred them on.

Labarge was a dream lake, mirroring noble mountains in its depths (for soon after we made it, a dead calm fell). But we had no eyes for its beauty. The golden magnet was drawing us too strongly now. We cursed that exquisite serenity that made us sweat at the oars; we cursed the wind that never would arise; the currents that always were against us. In that breathless tranquillity myriads of mosquitoes assailed us, blinded us, covered our food as we ate, made our lives a perfect hell of misery. Yet the trail was nearing its finish.

What a relief it was when a sudden storm came up! Whitecaps tossed around us, and the wind drove us on a precipitous shore, so that we nearly came to a sorry end. But it was over at last, and we swept on into the Thirty-mile River.

A furious, hurling stream was this, that matched our mad, impatient mood; but it was staked with hidden dangers. We gripped our weary oars. Keenly alert we had to be, steering and watching for rocks that would have ripped us from bow to stern. There was a famously terrible one, on which scows smashed like egg-shells under a hammer, and we missed it by a bare hand's-breadth. I felt sick to think of our bitterness had we piled up on it. That was an evil, ugly river, full of capricious turns and eddies, and the bluffs were high and steep.

Hootalinqua, Big Salmon, Little Salmon, these are names to me now. All I can remember is long days of toil at the oar, fighting the growing obsession of mosquitoes, ever pressing on to the golden valley. The ceaseless strain was beginning to tell on us. We suffered from rheumatism, we barked with cold. Oh, we were weary, weary, yet the trail was nearing its end.

One sunlit Sabbath evening I remember well. We were drifting along and we came on a lovely glade where a creek joined the river. It was a green, velvety, sparkling place, and by the creek were two men whipsawing lumber. We hailed them jauntily and asked them if they had found prospects. Were they getting out lumber for sluice-boxes?

One of the men came forward. He was very tired, very quiet, very solemn. "No," he said, "we are sawing out a coffin for our dead."

Then we saw a limp shape in their boat and we hurried on, awed and abashed.

The river was mud colour now, swirling in great eddies or convulsed from below with sudden upheavals. Drifting on that oily current one seemed to be quite motionless, and only the gliding banks assured us of progress. The country seemed terrible to me, sinister, guilty, God-forsaken. At the horizon, jagged mountains stabbed viciously at the sky.

The river overwhelmed me. Sometimes it was a stream of blood, running into the eye of the setting sun, beautiful, yet weird and menacing. It broadened, deepened, and every day countless streams swelled its volume. Islands waded in it greenly. Always we heard it *singing*, a seething, hissing noise supposed to be the pebbles shuffling on the bottom.

The days were insufferably hot and mosquito-curst; the nights chilly, damp and mosquito-haunted. I suffered agonies from neuralgia. Never mind, it would soon be over. We were on our last lap. The trail was near its end.

Yes, it was indeed the homestretch. Suddenly sweeping round a bend we raised a shout of joy. There was that great livid scar on the mountain face—the "Slide," and clustered below it like shells on the seashore, an army of tents. It was the gold-born city.

Trembling with eagerness we pulled ashore. Our troubles were over. At last we had gained our Eldorado, thank God, thank God!

A number of loafers were coming to meet us. They were strangely calm.

"How about the gold?" said the Prodigal; "lots of ground left to stake?"

One of them looked at us contemptuously. He chewed a moment ere he spoke.

"You Cheechakers better git right home. There ain't a foot of ground to stake. Everything in sight was staked last Fall. The rest is all mud. There's nothing doin' an' there's ten men for every job! The whole thing's a fake. You Cheechakers better git right home."

Yes, after all our travail, all our torment, we had better go right home. Already many were preparing to do so. Yet what of that great oncoming horde of which we were but the vanguard? What of the eager army, the host of the Cheechakos? For hundreds of miles were lake and river white with their grotesque boats. Beyond them again were thousands and thousands of others struggling on through mosquito-curst morasses, bent under their inexorable burdens. Reckless, indomitable, hope-inspired, they climbed the passes and shot the rapids; they drowned in the rivers, they rotted in the swamps. Nothing could stay them. The golden magnet was drawing them on; the spell of the gold-lust was in their hearts.

And this was the end. For this they had mortgaged homes and broken hearts. For this they had faced danger and borne suffering: to be told to return.

The land was choosing its own. All along it had weeded out the weaklings. Now let the fainthearted go back. This land was only for the Strong.

Yet it was sad, so much weariness, and at the end disenchantment and failure.

Verily the ways of the gold-trail were cruel.

* * * * *

BOOK III

THE CAMP

For once you've panned the speckled sand and seen the bonny dust,
    Its peerless brightness blinds you like a spell;
It's little else you care about; you go because you must,
    And you feel that you could follow it to hell.
You'd follow it in hunger, and you'd follow it in cold;
    You'd follow it in solitude and pain;
And when you're stiff and battened down let some one whisper "Gold,"
    You're lief to rise and follow it again.

—"The Prospector."

CHAPTER I

I will always remember my first day in the gold-camp. We were well in front of the Argonaut army, but already thousands were in advance of us. The flat at the mouth of Bonanza was a congestion of cabins; shacks and tents clustered the hillside, scattered on the heights and massed again on the slope sweeping down to the Klondike. An intense vitality charged the air. The camp was alive, ahum, vibrant with fierce, dynamic energy.

In effect the town was but one street stretching alongside the water front. It was amazingly packed with men from side to side, from end to end. They lounged in the doorways of oddly assorted buildings, and jostled each other on the dislocated sidewalks. Stores of all kinds, saloons, gambling joints flourished without number, and in one block alone there were half a dozen dance-halls. Yet all seemed plethorically prosperous.

Many of the business houses were installed in tents. That huge canvas erection was a mining exchange; that great log barn a dance-hall. Dwarfish log cabins impudently nestled up to pretentious three-story hotels. The effect was oddly staccato. All was grotesque, makeshift, haphazard. Back of the main street lay the red-light quarter, and behind it again a swamp of niggerheads, the breeding-place of fever and mosquito.

The crowd that vitalised the street was strikingly cosmopolitan. Mostly big, bearded fellows they were, with here the full-blooded face of the saloon man, and there the quick, pallid mask of the gambler. Women too I saw in plenty, bold, free, predacious creatures, a rustle of silk and a reek of perfume. Till midnight I wandered up and down the long street; but there was no darkness, no lull in its clamorous life.

I was looking for Berna. My heart hungered for her; my eyes ached for her; my mind was so full of her there seemed no room for another single thought. But it was like looking for a needle in a strawstack to find her in that seething multitude. I knew no one, and it seemed futile to inquire regarding her. These keen-eyed men with eager talk of claims and pay-dirt could not help me. There seemed to be nothing for it but to wait. So with spirits steadily sinking zerowards I waited.

We found, indeed, that there was little ground left to stake. The mining laws were in some confusion, and were often changing. Several creeks were closed to location, but always new strikes were being made and stampedes started. So, after a session of debate, we decided to reserve our rights to stake till a good chance offered. It was a bitter awakening. Like all the rest we had expected to get ground that was gold from the grass-roots down. But there was work to be had, and we would not let ourselves be disheartened.

The Jam-wagon had already deserted us. He was off up on Eldorado somewhere, shovelling dirt into a sluice-box for ten dollars a day. I made up my mind I would follow him. Jim also would get to work, while the Prodigal, we agreed, would look after all our interests, and stake or buy a good claim.

Thus we planned, sitting in our little tent near the beach. We were in a congeries of tents. The beach was fast whitening with them. If one was in a hurry it was hard to avoid tripping over ropes and pegs. As each succeeding party arrived they had to go further afield to find camping-ground. And they were arriving in thousands daily. The shore for a mile was lined five deep with boats. Scows had been hauled high and dry on the gravel, and there the owners were living. A thousand stoves were eloquent of beans and bacon. I met a man taking home a prize, a porterhouse steak. He was carrying it over his arm like a towel, paper was so scarce. The camp was a hive of energy, a hum of occupation.

But how many, after they had paraded that mile-long street with its mud, its seething foam of life, its blare of gramophones and its blaze of dance-halls, ached for their southland homes again! You could read the disappointment in their sun-tanned faces. Yet they were the eager navigators of the lakes, the reckless amateurs of the rivers. This was a something different from the trail. It was as if, after all their efforts, they had butted up against a stone wall. There was "nothing doing," no ground left, and only hard work, the hardest on earth.

Moreover, the country was at the mercy of a gang of corrupt officials who were using the public offices for their own enrichment. Franchises were being given to the favourites of those in power, concessions sold, liquor permits granted, and abuses of every kind practised on the free miner. All was venality, injustice and exaction.

"Go home," said the Man in the Street; "the mining laws are rotten. All kinds of ground is tied up. Even if you get hold of something good, them dam-robber government sharks will flim-flam you out of it. There's no square deal here. They tax you to mine; they tax you to cut a tree; they tax you to sell a fish; pretty soon they'll be taxing you to breathe. Go home!"

And many went, many of the trail's most indomitable. They could face hardship and danger, the blizzards, the rapids, nature savage and ravening; but when it came to craft, graft and the duplicity of their fellow men they were discouraged, discomfited.

"Say, boys, I guess I've done a slick piece of work," said the Prodigal with some satisfaction, as he entered the tent. "I've bought three whole outfits on the beach. Got them for twenty-five per cent. less than the cost price in Seattle. I'll pull out a hundred per cent. on the deal. Now's the time to get in and buy from the quitters. They so soured at the whole frame-up they're ready to pull their freights at any moment. All they want's to get away. They want to put a few thousand miles between them and this garbage dump of creation. They never want to hear the name of Yukon again except as a cuss-word. I'm going to keep on buying outfits. You boys see if I don't clean up a bunch of money."

"It's too bad to take advantage of them," I suggested.

"Too bad nothing! That's business; your necessity, my opportunity. Oh, you'd never make a money-getter, my boy, this side of the millennium—and you Scotch too."

"That's nothing," said Jim; "wait till I tell you of the deal I made to-day. You recollect I packed a flat-iron among my stuff, an' you boys joshed me about it, said I was bughouse. But I figured out: there's camp-meetin's an' socials up there, an' a nice, dinky, white shirt once in a way goes pretty good. Anyway, thinks I, if there ain't no one else to dress for in that wilderness, I'll dress for the Almighty. So I sticks to my old flat-iron."

He looked at us with a twinkle in his eye and then went on.

"Well, it seems there's only three more flat-irons in camp, an' all the hot sports wantin' boiled shirts done up, an' all the painted Jezebels hollerin' to have their lingery fixed, an' the wash-ladies just goin' round crazy for flat-irons. Well, I didn't want to sell mine, but the old coloured lady that runs the Bong Tong Laundry (an' a sister in the Lord) came to me with tears in her eyes, an' at last I was prevailed on to separate from it."

"How much, Jim?"

"Well, I didn't want to be too hard on the old girl, so I let her down easy."

"How much?"

"Well, you see there's only three or four of them flat-irons in camp, so I asked a hundred an' fifty dollars, an' quick's a flash, she took me into a store an' paid me in gold-dust."

He flourished a little poke of dust in our laughing faces.

"That's pretty good," I said; "everything seems topsy-turvy up here. Why, to-day I saw a man come in with a box of apples which the crowd begged him to open. He was selling those apples at a dollar apiece, and the folks were just fighting to get them."

It was so with everything. Extraordinary prices ruled. Eggs and candles had been sold for a dollar each, and potatoes for a dollar a pound; while on the trail in '97 horse-shoe nails were selling at *a dollar a nail*.

Once more I roamed the long street with that awful restless agony in my heart. Where was she, my girl, so precious now it seemed I had lost her? Why does love mean so much to some, so little to others? Perhaps I am the victim of an intensity of temperament, but I craved for her; I visioned evils befalling her; I pierced my heart with dagger-thrusts of fear for her. Oh, if I only knew she was safe and well! Every slim woman I saw in the distance looked to be her, and made my heart leap with emotion. Yet always I chewed on the rind of disappointment. There was never a sign of Berna.

In the agitation and unrest of my mind I climbed the hill that overshadows the gold-born city. The Dome they call it, and the face of it is vastly scarred, blanched as by a cosmic blow. There on its topmost height by a cairn of stone I stood at gaze, greatly awestruck.

The view was a spacious one, and of an overwhelming grandeur. Below me lay the mighty Yukon, here like a silken ribbon, there broadening out to a pool of quicksilver. It seemed motionless, dead, like a piece of tinfoil lying on a sable shroud.

The great valley was preternaturally still, and pall-like as if steeped in the colours of the long, long night. The land so vast, so silent, so lifeless, was round in its contours, full of fat creases and bold curves. The mountains were like sleeping giants; here was the swell of a woman's breast, there the sweep of a man's thigh. And beyond that huddle of sprawling Titans, far, far beyond, as if it were an enclosing stockade, was the jagged outline of the Rockies.

Quite suddenly they seemed to stand up against the blazing sky, monstrous, horrific, smiting the senses like a blow. Their primordial faces were hacked and hewed fantastically, and there they posed in their immemorial isolation, virgin peaks, inviolate valleys, impregnably desolate and savagely sublime.

And beyond their stormy crests, surely a world was consuming in the kilns of chaos. Was ever anything so insufferably bright as the incandescent glow that brimmed those jagged clefts? That fierce crimson, was it not the hue of a cooling crucible, that deep vermillion the rich glory of a rose's heart? Did not that tawny orange mind you of ripe wheat-fields and the exquisite intrusion of poppies? That pure, clear gold, was it not a bank of primroses new washed in April rain? What was that luminous opal but a lagoon, a pearly lagoon, with floating in it islands of amber, their beaches crisped with ruby foam? And, over all the riot of colour, that shimmering chrysoprase so tenderly luminous—might it not fitly veil the splendours of paradise?

I looked to where gulped the mouth of Bonanza, cavernously wide and filled with the purple smoke of many fires. There was the golden valley, silent for centuries, now strident with human cries, vehement with human strife. There was the timbered basin of the Klondike bleakly rising to mountains eloquent of death. It was dominating, appalling, this vastness without end, this unappeasable loneliness. Glad was I to turn again to where, like white pebbles on a beach, gleamed the tents of the gold-born city.

Somewhere amid that confusion of canvas, that muddle of cabins, was Berna, maybe lying in some wide-eyed vigil of fear, maybe staining with hopeless tears her restless pillow. Somewhere down there—Oh, I must find her!

I returned to the town. I was tramping its long street once more, that street with its hundreds of canvas signs. It was a city of signs. Every place of business seemed to have its fluttering banner, and beneath these banners moved the ever restless throng. There were men from the mines in their flannel shirts and corduroys, their Stetsons and high boots. There were men from the trail in sweaters and mackinaws, German socks and caps with ear-flaps. But all were bronzed and bearded, fleshless and clean-limbed. I marvelled at the seriousness of their faces, till I remembered that here was no problem of a languorous sunland, but one of grim emergency. It was a man's game up here in the North, a man's game in a man's land, where the sunlight of the long, long day is ever haunted by the shadow of the long, long night.

Oh, if I could only find her! The land was a great symphony; she the haunting theme of it.

I bought a copy of the "Nugget" and went into the Sourdough Restaurant to read it. As I lingered there sipping my coffee and perusing the paper indifferently, a paragraph caught my eye and made my heart glow with sudden hope.

* * * * *

CHAPTER II

Here was the item:

Jack Locasto loses $19,000.
"One of the largest gambling plays that ever occurred in Dawson came off last night in the Malamute Saloon. Jack Locasto of Eldorado, well known as one of the Klondike's wealthiest claim-owners, Claude Terry and Charlie Haw were the chief actors in the game, which cost the first-named the sum of $19,000.

"Locasto came to Dawson from his claim yesterday. It is said that before leaving the Forks he lost a sum ranging in the neighbourhood of $5,000. Last night he began playing in the Malamute with Haw and Terry in an effort, it is supposed, to recoup his losses at the Forks. The play continued nearly all night, and at the wind-up, Locasto, as stated above, was loser to the amount of $19,000. This is probably the largest individual loss ever sustained at one sitting in the history of Klondike poker playing."

Jack Locasto! Why had I not thought of him before? Surely if any one knew of the girl's whereabouts, it would be he. I determined I would ask him at once.

So I hastily finished my coffee and inquired of the emasculated-looking waiter where I might find the Klondike King.

"Oh, Black Jack," he said: "well, at the Green Bay Tree, or the Tivoli, or the Monte Carlo. But there's a big poker game on and he's liable to be in it."

Once more I paraded the seething street. It was long after midnight, but the wondrous glow, still burning in the Northern sky, filled the land with strange enchantment. In spite of the hour the town seemed to be more alive than ever. Parties with pack-laden mules were starting off for the creeks, travelling at night to avoid the heat and mosquitoes. Men with lean brown faces trudged sturdily along carrying extraordinary loads on their stalwart shoulders. A stove, blankets, cooking utensils, axe and shovel usually formed but a part of their varied accoutrement.

Constables of the Mounted Police were patrolling the streets. In the drab confusion their scarlet tunics were a piercing note of colour. They walked very stiffly, with grim mouths and eyes sternly vigilant under the brims of their Stetsons. Women were everywhere, smoking cigarettes, laughing, chaffing, strolling in and out of the wide-open saloons. Their cheeks were rouged, their eye-lashes painted, their eyes bright with wine. They gazed at the men like sleek animals, with looks that were wanton and alluring. A libertine spirit was in the air, a madcap freedom, an effluence of disdainful sin.

I found myself by the stockade that surrounded the Police reservation. On every hand I saw traces of a recent overflow of the river that had transformed the street into a navigable canal. Now in places there were mudholes in which horses would flounder to their bellies. One of the Police constables, a tall, slim Englishman with a refined manner, proved to me a friend in need.

"Yes," he said, in answer to my query, "I think I can find your man. He's downtown somewhere with some of the big sporting guns. Come on, we'll run him to earth."

As we walked along we compared notes, and he talked of himself in a frank, friendly way.

"You're not long out from the old country? Thought not. Left there myself about four years ago—I joined the Force in Regina. It's altogether different 'outside,' patrol work, a free life on the open prairie. Here they keep one choring round barracks most of the time. I've been for six months now on the town station. I'm not sorry, though. It's all devilish interesting. Wouldn't have missed it for a farm. When I write the people at home about it they think I'm yarning—stringing them, as they say here. The governor's a clergyman. Sent me to Harrow, and wanted to make a Bishop out of me. But I'm restless; never could study; don't seem to fit in, don't you know."

I recognised his type, the clean, frank, breezy Englishman that has helped to make an Empire. He went on:

"Yes, how the old dad would stare if I could only have him in Dawson for a day. He'd never be able to get things just in focus any more. He would be knocked clean off the pivot on which he's revolved these thirty years. Seems to me every one's travelling on a pivot in the old country. It's no use trying to hammer it into their heads there are more points of view than one. If you don't just see things as they see them, you're troubled with astigmatism. Come, let's go in here."

He pushed his way through a crowded doorway and I followed. It was the ordinary type of combined saloon and gambling-joint. In one corner was a very ornate bar, and all around the capacious room were gambling devices of every kind. There were crap-tables, wheel of fortune, the Klondike game, Keno, stud poker, roulette and faro outfits. The place was chock-a-block with rough-looking men, either looking on or playing the games. The men who were running the tables wore shades of green over their eyes, and their strident cries of "Come on, boys," pierced the smoky air.

In a corner, presiding over a stud-poker game, I was surprised to see our old friend Mosher. He was dealing with one hand, holding the pack delicately and sending the cards with a dexterous flip to each player. Miners were buying chips from a man at the bar, who with a pair of gold scales was weighing out dust in payment.

My companion pointed to an inner room with a closed door.

"The Klondike Kings are in there, hard at it. They've been playing now for twenty-four hours, and goodness knows when they'll let up."

At that moment a peremptory bell rang from the room and a waiter hurried up.

"There they are," said my friend, as the door opened. "There's Black Jack and Stillwater Willie and Claude Terry and Charlie Haw."

Eagerly I looked in. The men were wearied, their faces haggard and ghastly pale. Quickly and coolly they fingered the cards, but in their hollow eyes burned the fever of the game, a game where golden eagles were the chips and thousand-dollar jackpots were unremarkable. No doubt they had lost and won greatly, but they gave no sign. What did it matter? In the dumps waiting to be cleaned up were hundreds of thousands more; while in the ground were millions, millions.

All but Locasto were medium-sized men. Stillwater Willie was in evening-dress. He wore a red tie in which glittered a huge diamond pin, and yellow tan boots covered with mud.

"How did he get his name?" I asked.

"Well, you see, they say he was the only one that funked the Whitehorse Rapids. He's a high flier, all right."

The other two were less striking. Haw was a sandy-haired man with shifty, uneasy eyes; Terry of a bulldog type, stocky and powerful. But it was Locasto who gripped and riveted my attention.

He was a massive man, heavy of limb and brutal in strength. There was a great spread to his shoulders and a conscious power in his every movement. He had a square, heavy chin, a grim, sneering mouth, a falcon nose, black eyes that were as cold as the water in a deserted shaft. His hair was raven dark, and his skin betrayed the Mexican strain in his blood. Above the others he towered, strikingly masterful, and I felt somehow the power that emanated from the man, the brute force, the remorseless purpose.

Then the waiter returned with a tray of drinks and the door was closed.

"Well, you've seen him now," said Chester of the Police. "Your only plan, if you want to speak to him, is to wait till the game breaks up. When poker interferes with your business, to the devil with your business. They won't be interrupted. Well, old man, if you can't be good, be careful; and if you want me any time, ring up the town station. Bye, bye."

He sauntered off. For a time I strolled from game to game, watching the expressions on the faces of the players, and trying to take an interest in the play. Yet my mind was ever on the closed door and my ear strained to hear the click of chips. I heard the hoarse murmurs of their voices, an occasional oath or a yawn of fatigue. How I wished they would come out! Women went to the door, peered in cautiously, and beat a hasty retreat to the tune of reverberated curses. The big guns were busy; even the ladies must await their pleasure.

Oh, the weariness of that waiting! In my longing for Berna I had worked myself up into a state that bordered on distraction. It seemed as if a cloud was in my brain, obsessing me at all times.

I felt I must question this man, though it raised my gorge even to speak of her in his presence. In that atmosphere of corruption the thought of the girl was intolerably sweet, as of a ray of sunshine penetrating a noisome dungeon.

It was in the young morn when the game broke up. The outside air was clear as washed gold; within it was foul and fetid as a drunkard's breath. Men with pinched and pallid faces came out and inhaled the breeze, which was buoyant as champagne. Beneath the perfect blue of the spring sky the river seemed a shimmer of violet, and the banks dipped down with the green of chrysoprase.

Already a boy was sweeping up the dirty, nicotine-frescoed sawdust from the floor. (It was his perquisite, and from the gold he panned out he ultimately made enough to put him through college.) Then the inner door opened and Black Jack appeared.

* * * * *

CHAPTER III

He was wan and weary. Around his sombre eyes were chocolate-coloured hollows. His thick raven hair was disordered. He had lost heavily, and, bidding a curt good-bye to the others, he strode off. In a moment I had followed and overtaken him.

"Mr. Locasto."

He turned and gave me a stare from his brooding eyes. They were vacant as those of a dope-fiend, vacant with fatigue.

"Jack Locasto's my name," he answered carelessly.

I walked alongside him.

"Well, sir," I said, "my name's Meldrum, Athol Meldrum."

"Oh, I don't care what the devil your name is," he broke in petulantly. "Don't bother me just now. I'm tired."

"So am I," I said, "infernally tired; but it won't hurt you to listen to my name."

"Well, Mr. Athol Meldrum, good-day."

His voice was cold, his manner galling in its indifference, and a sudden anger glowed in me.

"Hold on," I said; "just a moment. You can very easily do me an immense favour. Listen to me."

"Well, what do you want," he demanded roughly; "work?"

"No," I said, "I just want a scrap of information. I came into the country with some Jews the name of Winklestein. I've lost track of them and I think you may be able to tell me where they are."

He was all attention now. He turned half round and scrutinised me with deliberate intensity. Then, like a flash, his rough manner changed. He was the polished gentleman, the San Francisco clublounger, the man of the world.

He rasped the stubble on his chin; his eyes were bland, his voice smooth as cream.

"Winklestein," he echoed reflectively, "Winklestein; seems to me I do remember the name, but for the life of me I can't recall where."

He was watching me like a cat, and pretending to think hard.

"Was there a girl with them?"

"Yes," I said eagerly, "a young girl."

"A young girl, ah!" He seemed to reflect hard again. "Well, my friend, I'm afraid I can't help you. I remember noticing the party on the way in, but what became of them I can't think. I don't usually bother about that kind of people. Well, good-night, or good-morning rather. This is my hotel."

He had half entered when he paused and turned to me. His face was urbane, his voice suave to sweetness; but it seemed to me there was a subtle mockery in his tone.

"I say, if I should hear anything of them, I'll let you know. Your name? Athol Meldrum—all right, I'll let you know. Good-bye."

He was gone and I had failed. I cursed myself for a fool. The man had baffled me. Nay, even I had hurt myself by giving him an inkling of my search. Berna seemed further away from me than ever. Home I went, discouraged and despairful.

Then I began to argue with myself. He must know where they were, and if he really had designs on the girl and was keeping her in hiding my interview with him would alarm him. He would take the first opportunity of warning the Winklesteins. When would he do it? That very night in all likelihood. So I reasoned; and I resolved to watch.

I stationed myself in a saloon from where I could command a view of his hotel, and there I waited. I think I must have watched the place for three hours, but I know it was a weariful business, and I was heartsick of it. Doggedly I stuck to my post. I was beginning to think he must have evaded me, when suddenly coming forth alone from the hotel I saw my man.

It was about midnight, neither light nor dark, but rather an absence of either quality, and the Northern sky was wan and ominous. In the crowded street I saw Locasto's hat overtopping all others, so that I had no difficulty in shadowing him. Once he stopped to speak to a woman, once to light a cigar; then he suddenly turned up a side street that ran through the red-light district.

He was walking swiftly and he took a path that skirted the swamp behind the town. I had no doubt of his mission. My heart began to beat with excitement. The little path led up the hill, clothed with fresh foliage and dotted with cabins. Once I saw him pause and look round. I had barely time to dodge behind some bushes, and feared for a moment he had seen me. But no! on he went again faster than ever.

I knew now I had divined his errand. He was at too great pains to cover his tracks. The trail had plunged among a maze of slender cotton-woods, and twisted so that I was sore troubled to keep him in view. Always he increased his gait and I followed breathlessly. There were few cabins hereabouts; it was a lonely place to be so near to town, very quiet and thickly screened from sight. Suddenly he seemed to disappear, and, fearing my pursuit was going to be futile, I rushed forward.

I came to a dead stop. There was no one to be seen. He had vanished completely. The trail climbed steeply up, twisty as a corkscrew. These cursed poplars, how densely they grew! Blindly I blundered forward. Then I came to a place where the trail forked. Panting for breath I hesitated which way to take, and it was in that moment of hesitation that a heavy hand was laid on my shoulder.

"Where away, my young friend?" It was Locasto. His face was Mephistophelian, his voice edged with irony. I was startled I admit, but I tried to put a good face on it.

"Hello," I said; "I'm just taking a stroll."

His black eyes pierced me, his black brows met savagely. The heavy jaw shot forward, and for a moment the man, menacing and terrible, seemed to tower above me.

"You lie!" like explosive steam came the words, and wolf-like his lips parted, showing his powerful teeth. "You lie!" he reiterated. "You followed me. Didn't I see you from the hotel? Didn't I determine to decoy you away? Oh, you fool! you fool! who are you that would pit your weakness against my strength, your simplicity against my cunning? You would try to cross me, would you? You would champion damsels in distress? You pretty fool, you simpleton, you meddler—"

Suddenly, without warning, he struck me square on the face, a blinding, staggering blow that brought me to my knees as falls a pole-axed steer. I was stunned, swaying weakly, trying vainly to get on my feet. I stretched out my clenched hands to him. Then he struck me again, a bitter, felling blow.

I was completely at his mercy now and he showed me none. He was like a fiend. Rage seemed to rend him. Time and again he kicked me, brutally, relentlessly, on the ribs, on the chest, on the head. Was the man going to do me to death? I shielded my head. I moaned in agony. Would he never stop? Then I became unconscious, knowing that he was still kicking me, and wondering if I would ever open my eyes again.

* * * * *

CHAPTER IV

"Long live the cold-feet tribe! Long live the soreheads!"

It was the Prodigal who spoke. "This outfit buying's got gold-mining beaten to a standstill. Here I've been three weeks in the burg and got over ten thousand dollars' worth of grub cached away. Every pound of it will net me a hundred per cent. profit. I'm beginning to look on myself as a second John D. Rockefeller."

"You're a confounded robber," I said. "You're working a cinch-game. What's your first name? Isaac?"

He turned the bacon he was frying and smiled gayly.

"Snort away all you like, old sport. So long as I get the mon you can call me any old name you please."

He was very sprightly and elate, but I was in no sort of mood to share in his buoyancy. Physically I had fully recovered from my terrible manhandling, but in spirit I still writhed at the outrage of it. And the worst was I could do nothing. The law could not help me, for there were no witnesses to the assault. I could never cope with this man in bodily strength. Why was I not a stalwart? If I had been as tall and strong as Garry, for instance. True, I might shoot; but there the Police would take a hand in the game, and I would lose out badly. There seemed to be nothing for it but to wait and pray for some means of retaliation.

Yet how bitterly I brooded over the business. At times there was even black murder in my heart. I planned schemes of revenge, grinding my teeth in impotent rage the while; and my feelings were complicated by that awful gnawing hunger for Berna that never left me. It was a perfect agony of heart, a panic-fear, a craving so intense that at times I felt I would go distracted with the pain of it.

Perhaps I am a poor sort of being. I have often wondered. I either feel intensely, or I am quite indifferent. I am a prey to my emotions, a martyr to my moods. Apart from my great love for Berna it seemed to me as if nothing mattered. All through these stormy years it was like that—nothing else mattered. And now that I am nearing the end of my life I can see that nothing else has ever mattered. Everything that happened appealed to me in its relation to her. It seemed to me as if I saw all the world through the medium of my love for her, and that all beauty, all truth, all good was but a setting for this girl of mine.

"Come on," said Jim; "let's go for a walk in the town."

The "Modern Gomorrah" he called it, and he was never tired of expatiating on its iniquity.

"See that man there?" he said, pointing to a grey-haired pedestrian, who was talking to an emphatic blonde. "That man's a lawyer. He's got a lovely home in Los Angeles, an' three of the sweetest girls you ever saw. A young fellow needed to have his credentials O. K.'d by the Purity Committee before he came butting round that man's home. Now he's off to buy wine for Daisy of the Deadline."

The grey-haired man had turned into a saloon with his companion.

"Yes, that's Dawson for you. We're so far from home. The good old moralities don't apply here. The hoary old Yukon won't tell on us. We've been a Sunday School Superintendent for ten years. For fifty more we've passed up the forbidden fruit. Every one else is helping themselves. Wonder what it tastes like? Wine is flowing like water. Money's the cheapest thing in sight. Cut loose, drink up. The orchestra's a-goin'. Get your partners for a nice juicy two-step. Come on, boys!"

He was particularly bitter, and it really seemed in that general lesion of the moral fibre that civilisation was only a makeshift, a veneer of hypocrisy.

"Why should we marvel," I said, "at man's brutality, when but an æon ago we all were apes?"

Just then we met the Jam-wagon. He had mushed in from the creeks that very day. Physically he looked supreme. He was berry-brown, lean, muscular and as full of suppressed energy as an unsprung bear-trap. Financially he was well ballasted. Mentally and morally he was in the state of a volcano before an eruption.

You could see in the quick breathing, in the restlessness of this man, a pent-up energy that clamoured to exhaust itself in violence and debauch. His fierce blue eyes were wild and roving, his lips twitched nervously. He was an atavism; of the race of those white-bodied, ferocious sea-kings that drank deep and died in the din of battle. He must live in the white light of excitement, or sink in the gloom of despair. I could see his fine nostrils quiver like those of a charger that scents the smoke of battle, and I realised that he should have been a soldier still, a leader of forlorn hopes, a partner of desperate hazards.

As we walked along, Jim did most of the talking in his favourite morality vein. The Jam-wagon puffed silently at his briar pipe, while I, very listless and downhearted, thought largely of my own troubles. Then, in the middle of the block, where most of the music-halls were situated, suddenly we met Locasto.

When I saw him my heart gave a painful leap, and I think my face must have gone as white as paper. I had thought much over this meeting, and had dreaded it. There are things which no man can overlook, and, if it meant death to me, I must again try conclusions with the brute.

He was accompanied by a little bald-headed Jew named Spitzstein, and we were almost abreast of them when I stepped forward and arrested them. My teeth were clenched; I was all a-quiver with passion; my heart beat violently. For a moment I stood there, confronting him in speechless excitement.

He was dressed in that miner's costume in which he always looked so striking. From his big Stetson to his high boots he was typically the big, strong man of Alaska, the Conqueror of the Wild. But his mouth was grim as granite, and his black eyes hard and repellent as those of a toad.

"Oh, you coward!" I cried. "You vile, filthy coward!"

He was looking down on me from his imperious height, very coolly, very cynically.

"Who are you?" he drawled; "I don't know you."

"Liar as well as coward," I panted. "Liar to your teeth. Brute, coward, liar—"

"Here, get out of my way," he snarled; "I've got to teach you a lesson."

Once more before I could guard he landed on me with that terrible right-arm swing, and down I went as if a sledgehammer had struck me. But instantly I was on my feet, a thing of blind passion, of desperate fight. I made one rush to throw myself on this human tower of brawn and muscle, when some one pinioned me from behind. It was Jim.

"Easy, boy," he was saying; "you can't fight this big fellow."

Spitzstein was looking on curiously. With wonderful quickness a crowd had collected, all avidly eager for a fight. Above them towered the fierce, domineering figure of Locasto. There was a breathless pause, then, at the psychological moment, the Jam-wagon intervened.

The smouldering fire in his eye had brightened into a fierce joy; his twitching mouth was now grim and stern as a prison door. For days he had been fighting a dim intangible foe. Here at last was something human and definite. He advanced to Locasto.

"Why don't you strike some one nearer your own size?" he demanded. His voice was tense, yet ever so quiet.

Locasto flashed at him a look of surprise, measuring him from head to foot.

"You're a brute," went on the Jam-wagon evenly; "a cowardly brute."

Black Jack's face grew dark and terrible. His eyes glinted sparks of fire.

"See here, Englishman," he said, "this isn't your scrap. What are you butting in about?"

"It isn't," said the Jam-wagon, and I could see the flame of fight brighten joyously in him. "It isn't, but I'll soon make it mine. There!"

Quick as a flash he dealt the other a blow on the cheek, an open-handed blow that stung like a whiplash.

"Now, fight me, you coward."

There and then Locasto seemed about to spring on his challenger. With hands clenched and teeth bared, he half bent as if for a charge. Then, suddenly, he straightened up.

"All right," he said softly; "Spitzstein, can we have the Opera House?"

"Yes, I guess so. We can clear away the benches."

"Then tell the crowd to come along; we'll give them a free show."

* * * * *

I think there must have been five hundred men around that ring. A big Australian pugilist was umpire. Some one suggested gloves, but Locasto would not hear of it.

"No," he said, "I want to mark the son of a dog so his mother will never know him again."

He had become frankly brutal, and prepared for the fray exultantly. Both men fought in their underclothing.

Stripped down, the Jam-wagon was seen to be much the smaller man, not only in height, but in breadth and weight. Yet he was a beautiful figure of a fighter, clean, well-poised, firm-limbed, with a body that seemed to taper from the shoulders down. His fair hair glistened; his eyes were wary and cool, his lips set tightly. In the person of this living adversary he was fighting an unseen one vastly more dread and terrific.

Locasto looked almost too massive. His muscles bulged out. The veins in his forearms were cord-like. His great chest seemed as broad as a door. His legs were statuesque in their size and strength. In that camp of strong men probably he was the most powerful.

And nowhere in the world could a fight have been awaited with greater zest. These men, miners, gamblers, adventurers of all kinds, pushed and struggled for a place. A great joy surged through them at the thought of the approaching combat. Keen-eyed, hard-breathing, a-thrill with expectation, the crowd packed closer and closer. Outside, people were clamouring for admission. They climbed on the stage, and into the boxes. They hung over the galleries. All told, there must have been a thousand of them.

As the two men stood up it was like the lithe Greek athlete compared with the brawny Roman gladiator. "Three to one on Locasto," some one shouted. Then a great hush came over the house, so that it might have been empty and deserted. Time was called. The fight began.

* * * * *

CHAPTER V

With one tiger-rush Locasto threw himself on his man. There was no preliminary fiddling here; they were out for blood, and the sooner they wallowed in it the better. Right and left he struck with mighty swings that would have felled an ox, but the Jam-wagon was too quick for him. Twice he ducked in time to avoid a furious blow, and, before Locasto could recover, he had hopped out of reach. The big man's fist swished through the empty air. He almost overbalanced with the force of his effort, but he swung round quickly, and there was the Jam-wagon, cool and watchful, awaiting his next attack.

Locasto's face grew fiendish in its sinister wrath; he shot forth a foul imprecation, and once more he hurled himself resistlessly on his foe. This time I thought my champion must go down, but no! With a dexterity that seemed marvellous, he dodged, ducked and side-stepped; and once more Locasto's blows went wide and short. Jeers began to go up from the throng. "Even money on the little fellow," sang out a voice with the flat twang of a banjo.

Locasto glared round on the crowd. He was accustomed to lord it over these men, and the jeers goaded him like banderilleros goad a bull. Again and again he repeated his tremendous rushes, only to find his powerful arms winnowing the empty air, only to see his agile antagonist smiling at him in mockery from the centre of the ring. Not one of his sledgehammer smashes reached their mark, and the round closed without a blow having landed.

From the mob of onlookers a chorus of derisive cheers went up. The little man with the banjo voice was holding up a poke of dust. "Even money on the little one." A hum of eager conversation broke forth.

I was at the ring-side. At the beginning I had been in an agony of fear for the Jam-wagon. Looking at the two men, it seemed as if he could hardly hope to escape terrible punishment at the hands of one so massively powerful, and every blow inflicted on him would have been like one inflicted on myself. But now I took heart and looked forward with less anxiety.

Again time was called, and Locasto sprang up, seemingly quite refreshed by his rest. Once more he plunged after his man, but now I could see his rushes were more under control, his smashing blows better timed, his fierce jabs more shrewdly delivered. Again I began to quake for the Jam-wagon, but he showed a wonderful quickness in his footwork, darting in and out, his hands swinging at his sides, a smile of mockery on his lips. He was deft as a dancing-master; he twinkled like a gleam of light, and amid that savage thresh of blows he was as cool as if he were boxing in the school gymnasium.

"Who is he?" those at the ring-side began to whisper. Time and again it seemed as if he were cornered, but in a marvellous way he wormed himself free. I held my breath as he evaded blow after blow, some of which seemed to miss him by a mere hair's breadth. He was taking chances, I thought, so narrowly did he permit the blows to miss him. I was all keyed up, on edge with excitement, eager for my man to strike, to show he was not a mere ring-tactician. But the Jam-wagon bided his time.

And so the round ended, and it was evident that the crowd was of the same opinion as myself. "Why don't he mix up a little?" said one. "Give him time," said another. "He's all right: there's some class to that work."

Locasto came up for the third round looking sobered, subdued, grimly determined. Evidently he had made up his mind to force his opponent out of his evasive tactics. He was wary as a cat. He went cautiously. Yet again he assumed the aggressive, gradually working the Jam-wagon into a corner. A collision was inevitable; there was no means of escape for my friend; that huge bulk, with its swinging, flail-like arms, menaced him hopelessly.

Suddenly Locasto closed in. He swooped down on the Jam-wagon. He had him. He shortened his right arm for a jab like the crash of a pile-driver. The arm shot out, but once again the Jam-wagon was not there. He ducked quickly, and Locasto's great fist brushed his hair.

Then, like lightning, the two came to a clinch. Now, thought I, it's all off with the Jam-wagon. I saw Locasto's eyes dilate with ferocious joy. He had the other in his giant arms; he could crush him in a mighty hug, the hug of a grizzly, crush him like an eggshell. But, quick as the snap of a trap, the Jam-wagon had pinioned his arms at the elbow, so that he was helpless. For a moment he held him, then, suddenly releasing his arms, he caught him round the body, shook him with a mighty side-heave, gave him the cross-buttock, and, before he could strike a single blow, threw him in the air and dashed him to the ground.

"Time!" called the umpire. It was all done so quickly it was hard for the eye to follow, but a mighty cheer went up from the house. "Two to one on the little fellow," called the banjo-voice. Suddenly Locasto rose to his feet. He was shamed, angered beyond all expression. Heaving and panting, he lurched to his corner, and in his eyes there was a look that boded ill for his adversary.

Time again. With the lightness of a panther the Jam-wagon sprang into the centre of the ring. More than halfway he met Locasto, and now his intention seemed to be to draw his man on rather than to avoid him. I watched his every movement with a sense of thrilling fascination. He had resumed his serpentine movements, advancing and retreating with shadow-like quickness, feinting, side-stepping, pawing the air till he had his man baffled and bewildered. Yet he never struck a blow.

All this seemed to be getting on Locasto's nerves. He was going steadily enough, trying by every means in his power to get the other man to "mix it up." He shouted the foulest abuse at him. "Stand up like a man, you son of a dog, and fight." The smile left the Jam-wagon's lips, and he settled down to business.

I saw him edging up to Locasto. He feinted wildly, then, stepping in closely, he swung a right and left to Black Jack's face. A moment later he was six feet away, with a bitter smile on his lips.

With a fierce bellow of rage Locasto, forgetting all his caution, charged him. He smashed his heavy right with all its might for the other's face, but, quick as the quiver of a bow-string, the Jam-wagon side-stepped and the blow missed. Then the Jam-wagon shifted and brought his left, full-weight, crash on Locasto's mouth.

At that fierce triumphant blow there was the first dazzling blood-gleam, and the crowd screeched with excitement. In a wild whirlwind of fury Locasto hurled himself on the Jam-wagon, his arms going like windmills. Any one of these blows, delivered in a vital spot, would have meant death, but his opponent was equal to this blind assault. Dodging, ducking, side-stepping, blocking, he foiled the other at every turn, and, just before the round ended, drove his left into the pit of the big man's stomach, with a thwack that resounded throughout the building.

Once more time was called. The Jam-wagon was bleeding about the knuckles. Several of Locasto's teeth had been loosened, and he spat blood frequently. Otherwise he looked as fit as ever. He pursued his man with savage determination, and seemed resolved to get in a deadly body-blow that would end the fight.

It was pretty to see the Jam-wagon work. He was sprightly as a ballet dancer, as, weaving in and out, he dodged the other's blows. His arms swung at his sides, and he threw his head about in a manner insufferably mocking and tantalising. Then he took to landing light body-blows, that grew more frequent till he seemed to be beating a regular tattoo on Locasto's ribs. He was springy as a panther, elusive as an eel. As for Locasto, his face was sober now, strained, anxious, and he seemed to be waiting with menacing eyes to get in that vital smash that meant the end.

The Jam-wagon began to put more force into his arms. He drove in a short-arm left to the stomach, then brought his right up to the other's chin. Locasto swung a deadly knock-out blow at the Jam-wagon, which just grazed his jaw, and the Jam-wagon retaliated with two lightning rights and a nervous left, all on the big man's face.

Then he sprang back, for he was excited now. In and out he wove. Once more he landed a hard left on Locasto's heaving stomach, and then, rushing in, he rained blow after blow on his antagonist. It was a furious mix-up, a whirling storm of blows, brutal, savage and murderous. No two men could keep up such a gait. They came into a clinch, but this time the Jam-wagon broke away, giving the deadly kidney blow as they parted. When time was called both men were panting hard, bruised and covered with blood.

How the house howled with delight! All the primordial brute in these men was glowing in their hearts. Nothing but blood could appease it. Their throats were parched, their eyes wild.

Round six. Locasto sprang into the centre of the ring. His face was hideously disfigured. Only in that battered, blood-stained mask could I recognise the black eyes gleaming deadly hatred. Rushing for the Jam-wagon, he hurled him across the ring. Again charging, he overbore him to the floor, but failed to hold him.

Then in the Jam-wagon there awoke the ancient spirit of the Berserker. He cared no more for punishment. He was insensible to pain. He was the sea-pirate again, mad with the lust of battle. Like a fiend he tore himself loose, and went after his man, rushing him with a swift, battering hail of blows around the ring. Like a tiger he was, and the violent lunges of Locasto only infuriated him the more.

Now they were in a furious mix-up, and suddenly Locasto, seizing him savagely, tried to whip him smashing to the floor. Then the wonderful agility of the Englishman was displayed. In a distance of less than a two-foot drop he turned completely like a cat. Leaping up, he was free, and, getting a waist-hold with a Cornish heave, he bore Locasto to the floor. Quickly he changed to a crotch-lock, and, lastly, holding Locasto's legs, he brought him to a bridge and worked his weight up on his body.

Black Jack, with a mighty heave, broke away and again regained his feet. This seemed to enrage the Jam-wagon the more, for he tore after his man like a maddened bull. Getting a hold with incredible strength, he lifted him straight up in the air and hurled him to the ground with sickening force.

Locasto lay there. His eyes were closed. He did not move. Several men rushed forward. "He's all right," said a medical-looking individual; "just stunned. I guess you can call the fight over."

The Jam-wagon slowly put on his clothes. Once more, in the person of Locasto, he had successfully grappled with "Old Man Booze." He was badly bruised about the body, but not seriously hurt in any way. Shudderingly I looked down at Locasto's face, beaten to a pulp, his body livid from head to foot. And then, as they bore him off to the hospital, I realised I was revenged.

"Did you know that man Spitzstein was charging a dollar for admission?" queried the Prodigal.

"No!"

"That's right. That darned little Jew netted nearly a thousand dollars."

* * * * *

CHAPTER VI

"Let me introduce you," said the Prodigal, "to my friend the 'Pote.'"

"Glad to meet you," said the Pote cheerfully, extending a damp hand. "Just been having a dishwashing bee. Excuse my dishybeel."

He wore a pale-blue undershirt, white flannel trousers girt round the waist with a red silk handkerchief, very gaudy moccasins, and a rakish Panama hat with a band of chocolate and gold.

"Take a seat, won't you?" Through his gold-rimmed spectacles his eyes shone benevolently as he indicated an easy-looking chair. I took it. It promptly collapsed under me.

"Ah, excuse me," he said; "you're not onto the combination of that chair. I'll fix it."

He performed some operation on it which made it less unstable, and I sat down gingerly.

I was in a little log-cabin on the hill overlooking the town. Through the bottle window the light came dimly. The walls showed the bark of logs and tufts of intersecting moss. In the corner was a bunk over which lay a bearskin robe, and on the little oblong stove a pot of beans was simmering.

The Pote finished his dishwashing and joined us, pulling on an old Tuxedo jacket.

"Whew! Glad that job's over. You know, I guess I'm fastidious, but I can't bear to use a plate for more than three meals without passing a wet rag over it. That's the worst of having refined ideas, they make life so complex. However, I mustn't complain. There's a monastic simplicity about this joint that endears it to me. And now, having immolated myself on the altar of cleanliness, I will solace my soul with a little music."

He took down a banjo from the wall and, striking a few chords, began to sing. His songs seemed to be original, even improvisations, and he sang them with a certain quaintness and point that made them very piquant. I remember one of the choruses. It went like this:

> "In the land of pale blue snow
> Where it's ninety-nine below,
> And the polar bears are dancing on the plain,
> In the shadow of the pole,
> Oh, my Heart, my Life, my Soul,
> I will meet thee when the ice-worms nest again."

Every now and then he would pause to make some lively comment.

"You've never heard of the blue snow, Cheechako? The rabbits have blue fur, and the ptarmigans' feathers are a bright azure. You've never had an ice-worm cocktail? We must remedy that. Great dope. Nothing like ice-worm oil for salads. Oh, I forgot, didn't give you my card."

I took it. It was engraved thus:

OLLIE GABOODLER.
Poetic Expert.

Turning it over, I read:

Graduate of the University of Hard Knocks.
All kinds of verse made to order with efficiency and dispatch.
Satisfaction guaranteed or money returned.
A trial solicited.
In Memoriam Odes a specialty.
Ballads, Rondeaux and Sonnets at modest prices.
Try our lines of Love Lyrics.
Leave orders at the Comet Saloon.

I stared at him curiously. He was smoking a cigarette and watching me with shrewd, observant eyes. He was a blond, blue-eyed, cherubic youth, with a whimsical mouth that seemed to alternate between seriousness and fun.

He laughed merrily at my look of dismay.

"Oh, you think it's a josh, but it's not. I've been a 'ghost' ever since I could push a pen. You know Will Wilderbush, the famous novelist? Well, Bill died six years ago from over-assiduous cultivation of John Barleycorn, and they hushed it up. But every year there's a new novel comes from his pen. It's 'ghosts.' I was Bill number three. Isn't it rummy?"

I expressed my surprise.

"Yes, it's a great joke this book-faking. Wouldn't Thackeray have lambasted the best sellers? A fancy picture of a girl on the cover, something doing all the time, and a happy ending—that's the recipe. Or else be as voluptuous as velvet. Wait till my novel, 'Three Minutes,' comes out. Order in advance."

"Indeed I will," I said.

He suddenly became grave.

"If I only could take the literary game seriously I might make good. But I'm too much of a 'farceur.' Well, one day we'll see. Maybe the North will inspire me. Maybe I'll yet become the Spokesman of the Frozen Silence, the Avatar of the Great White Land."

He strutted up and down, inflating his chest.

"Have you framed up any dope lately?" asked the Prodigal.

"Why, yes; only this morning, while I was eating my beans and bacon, I dashed off a few lines. I always write best when I'm eating. Want to hear them?"

He drew from his pocket an old envelope.

"They were written to the order of Stillwater Willie. He wants to present them to one of the Labelle Sisters. You know—that fat lymphatic blonde, Birdie Labelle. It is short and sweet. He wants to have it engraved on a gold-backed hand-mirror he's giving her.

"I see within my true love's eyes
The wide blue spaces of the skies;
I see within my true love's face

> The rose and lily vie in grace;
> I hear within my true love's voice
> The songsters of the Spring rejoice.
> Oh, why need I seek Nature's charms—

I hold my true love in my arms.

"How'll that hit her? There's such a lot of natural beauty about Birdie."

"Do you get much work?" I asked.

"No, it's dull. Poetry's rather a drug on the market up here. It's just a side-line. For a living I clean shoes at the 'Elight' Barbershop—I, who have lingered on the sunny slopes of Parnassus, and quenched my soul-thirst at the Heliconian spring—gents' tans a specialty."

"Did you ever publish a book?" I asked.

"Sure! Did you never read my 'Rhymes of a Rustler'? One reviewer would say I was the clear dope, the genuine eighteen-carat, jewelled-movement article; the next would aver I was the rankest dub that ever came down the pike. They said I'd imitated people, people I'd never read, people I'd never heard of, people I never dreamt existed. I was accused of imitating over twenty different writers. Then the pedants got after me, said I didn't conform to academic formulas, advised me to steep myself in tradition. They talked about form, about classic style and so on. As if it matters so long as you get down the thing itself so that folks can see it, and feel it go right home to their hearts. I can write in all the artificial verse forms, but they're mouldy with age, back numbers. Forget them. Quit studying that old Greek dope: study life, modern life, palpitating with colour, crying for expression. Life! Life! The sunshine of it was in my heart, and I just naturally tried to be its singer."

"I say," said the Prodigal from the bunk where he was lounging, in a haze of cigarette smoke, "read us that thing you did the other day, 'The Last Supper.'"

The Pote's eyes twinkled with pleasure.

"All right," he said. Then, in a clear voice, he repeated the following lines:

"THE LAST SUPPER.

Marie Vaux of the Painted Lips,
And the mouth so mocking gay;
A wanton you to the finger tips,
That break men's hearts in play;
A thing of dust I have striven for,
Honour and Manhood given for,
Headlong for ruin driven for—
And this is the last, you say:

Drinking your wine with dainty sips,
Marie Vaux of the Painted Lips.

Marie Vaux of the Painted Lips,
Long have you held your sway;
I have laughed at your merry quips,
Now is my time to pay.
What we sow we must reap again;
When we laugh we must weep again;
So to-night we will sleep again,
Nor wake till the Judgment Day.

'Tis a prison wine that your palate sips,
Marie Vaux of the Painted Lips.

Marie Vaux of the Painted Lips,
Down on your knees and pray;
Pray your last ere the moment slips,
Pray ere the dark and the terror grips,
And the bright world fades away:
Pray for the good unguessed of us,
Pray for the peace and rest of us.
Here comes the Shape in quest of us,
Now must we go away—

You and I in the grave's eclipse,
Marie Vaux of the Painted Lips."

Just as he finished there came a knock at the door, and a young man entered. He had the broad smiling face of a comedian, and the bulgy forehead of a Baptist Missionary. The Pote introduced him to me.

"The Yukon Yorick."

"Hello," chuckled the newcomer, "how's the bunch? Don't let me stampede you. How d'ye do, Horace! Glad to meet you." (He called everybody Horace.) "Just come away from a meeting of my creditors. What's that? Have a slab of booze? Hardly that, old fellow, hardly that. Don't tempt me, Horace, don't tempt me. Remember I'm only a poor working-girl."

He seemed brimming over with jovial acceptance of life in all its phases. He lit a cigar.

"Say, boys, you know old Dingbats the lawyer. Ha, yes. Well, met him on Front Street just now. Says I: 'Horace, that was a pretty nifty spiel you gave us last night at the Zero Club.' He looked at me all tickled up the spine. Ha, yes. He was pleased as Punch. 'Say, Horace,' I says, 'I'm on, but I won't give you away. I've got a book in my room with every word of that speech in it.' He looked flabbergasted. So I have—ha, yes, the dictionary."

He rolled his cigar unctuously in his mouth, with many chuckles and a histrionic eye.

"No, don't tempt me, Horace. Remember, I'm only a poor working-girl. Thanks, I'll just sit down on this soap-box. Knew a man once, Jobcroft was his name, Charles Alfred Jobcroft, sat down on a custard pie at a pink tea; was so embarrassed he wouldn't get up. Just sat on till every one else was gone. Every one was wondering why he wouldn't budge: just sat tight."

"I guess he *cussed hard*," ventured the Prodigal.

"Oh, Horace, spare me that! Remember I'm only a poor working-girl. Hardly that, old fellow. Say, hit me with a slab of booze quick. Make things sparkle, boys, make things sparkle."

He drank urbanely of the diluted alcohol that passed for whisky.

"Hit me easy, boys, hit me easy," he said, as they refilled his glass. "I can't hold my hootch so well as I could a few summers ago—and many hard Falls. Talking about holding your 'hooch,' the best I ever saw was a man called Podstreak, Arthur Frederick Podstreak. You couldn't get that man going. The way he could lap up the booze was a caution. He would drink one bunch of boys under the table, then leave them and go on to another. He would start in early in the morning and keep on going till the last thing at night. And he never got hilarious even; it didn't seem to phase him; he was as sober after the twentieth drink as when he started. Gee! but he was a wonder."

The others nodded their heads appreciatively.

"He was a fine, healthy-looking chap, too; the booze didn't seem to hurt him. Never saw such a constitution. I often watched him, for I suspected him of 'sluffing,' but no! He always had a bigger drink than every one else, always drank whisky, always drank it neat, and always had a chaser of water after. I said to myself: 'What's your system?' and I got to studying him hard. Then, one day, I found him out."

"What was it?"

"Well, one day I noticed something. I noticed he always held his glass in a particular way when he drank, and at the same time he pressed his stomach in the region of the 'solar plexus.' So that night I took him aside.

"'Look here, Podstreak,' I said, 'I'm next to you.' I really wasn't, but the bluff worked. He grew white.

"'For Heaven's sake, don't give me away,' he cried; 'the boys'll lynch me.'

"'All right,' I said; 'if you'll promise to quit.'

"Then he made a full confession, and showed me how he did it. He had an elastic rubber bag under his shirt, and a tube going up his arm and down his sleeve, ending in a white nozzle inside his cuff. When he went to empty his glass of whisky he simply pressed some air out of the rubber bag, put the nozzle in the glass, and let it suck up all the whisky. At night he used to empty all the liquor out of the bag and sell it to a saloon-keeper. Oh, he was a phoney piece of work.

"'I've been a total abstainer (in private) for seven years,' he told me. 'Yes,' I said, 'and you'll become one in public for another seven.' And he did."

Several men had dropped in to swell this Bohemian circle. Some had brought bottles. There was a painter who had been "hung," a Mus Bac., an ex-champion amateur pugilist, a silver-tongued orator, a man who had "suped" for Mansfield, and half a dozen others. The little cabin was crowded, the air hazy with smoke, the conversation animated. But mostly it was a monologue by the inimitable Yorick.

Suddenly the conversation turned to the immorality of the town.

"Now, I have a theory," said the Pote, "that the regeneration of Dawson is at hand. You know Good is the daughter of Evil, Virtue the offspring of Vice. You know how virtuous a man feels after a jag. You've got to sin to feel really good. Consequently, Sin must be good to be the means of good, to be the raw material of good, to be virtue in the making, mustn't it? The dance-halls are a good foil to the gospel-halls. If we were all virtuous, there would be no virtue in virtue, and if we were all bad no one would be bad. And because there's so much bad in this old burg of ours, it makes the good seem unnaturally good."

The Pote had the floor.

"A friend of mine had a beautiful pond of water-lilies. They painted the water exultantly and were a triumphant challenge to the soul. Folks came from far and near to see them. Then, one winter, my friend thought he would clean out his pond, so he had all the nasty, slimy mud scraped away till you could see the silver gravel glimmering on the bottom. But the lilies, with all their haunting loveliness, never came back."

"Well, what are you driving at, you old dreamer?"

"Oh, just this: in the nasty mud and slime of Dawson I saw a lily-girl. She lives in a cabin by the Slide along with a Jewish couple. I only caught a glimpse of her twice. They are unspeakable, but she is fair and sweet and pure. I would stake my life on her goodness. She looks like a young Madonna—"

He was interrupted by a shout of cynical laughter.

"Oh, get off your foot! A Madonna in Dawson—Ra! Ra!"

He shut up abashed, but I had my clue. I waited until the last noisy roisterer had gone.

"In the cabin by the Slide?" I asked.

He started, looked at me searchingly: "You know her?"

"She means a good deal to me."

"Oh, I understand. Yes, that long, queer cabin highest up the hill."

"Thanks, old chap."

"All right, good luck." He accompanied me to the door, staring at the marvel of the glamorous Northern midnight.

"Oh, for a medium to express it all! Your pedantic poetry isn't big enough; prose isn't big enough. What we want is something between the two, something that will interpret life, and stir the great heart of the people. Good-night."

* * * * *

CHAPTER VII

Very softly I approached the cabin, for a fear of encountering her guardians was in my heart. It was in rather a lonely place, perched at the base of that vast mountain abrasion they call the Slide, a long, low cabin, quiet and dark, and surrounded by rugged boulders. Carefully I reconnoitered, and soon, to my infinite joy, I saw the Jewish couple come forth and make their way townward. The girl was alone.

How madly beat my heart! It was a glooming kind of a night, and the cabin looked woefully bleak and solitary. No light came through the windows, no sound through the moss-chinked walls. I drew near.

Why this wild commotion of my being? What was it? Anxiety, joy, dread? I was poised on the pinnacle of hope that overhangs the abyss of despair. Fearfully I paused. I was racked with suspense, conscious of a longing so poignant that the thought of disappointment became insufferable pain. So violent was my emotion that a feeling almost of nausea overcame me.

I knew now that I cared for this girl more than I had ever thought to care for woman. I knew that she was dearer to me than all the world else; I knew that my love for her would live as long as life is long.

I knocked at the door. No answer.

"Berna," I cried in a faltering whisper.

Came the reply: "Who is there?"

"Love, love, dear; love is waiting."

Then, at my words, the door was opened, and the girl was before me. I think she had been lying down, for her soft hair was a little ruffled, but her eyes were far too bright for sleep. She stood gazing at me, and a little fluttering hand went up to her heart as if to still its beating.

"Oh, my dear, I knew you were coming."

A great radiance of joy seemed to descend on her.

"You knew?"

"I knew, yes, I knew. Something told me you were come at last. And I've waited—how I've waited! I've dreamed, but it's not a dream now, is it, dear; it's you?"

"Yes, it's me. I've tried so hard to find you. Oh, my dear, my dear!"

I seized the sweet, soft hand and covered it with kisses. At that moment I could have kissed the shadow of that little hand; I could have fallen before her in speechless adoration; I could have made my heart a footstool for her feet; I could have given her, O, so gladly, my paltry life to save her from a moment's sorrow—I loved her so, I loved her so!

"High and low I've sought you, beloved. Morning, noon and night you've been in my brain, my heart, my soul. I've loved you every moment of my life. It's been desire feeding despair, and, O, the agony of it! Thank God, I've found you, dear! thank God! thank God!"

O Love, look down on us and choir your harmonies! Transported was I, speaking with whirling words of sweetest madness, tremulous, uplifted with rapture, scarce conscious of my wild, impassioned metaphors. It was she, most precious of all creation; she, my beloved. And there, in the doorway, she poised, white as a lily, lustrous-eyed, and with hair soft as sunlit foam. O Divinity of Love, look down on us thy children; fold us in thy dove-soft wings; illumine us in thy white radiance; touch us with thy celestial hands. Bless us, Love!

How vastly alight were the grey eyes! How ineffably tender the sweet lips! A faint glow had come into her cheeks.

"O, it's you, really, really you at last," she cried again, and there was a tremor, the surface ripple of a sob in that clear voice. She fetched a deep sigh: "And I thought I'd lost you forever. Wait a moment. I'll come out."

Endlessly long the moment seemed, yet wondrously irradiate. The shadow had lifted from the world; the skies were alight with gladness; my heart was heaven-aspiring in its ecstasy. Then, at last, she came.

She had thrown a shawl around her shoulders, and coaxed her hair into charming waves and ripples.

"Come, let us go up the trail a little distance. They won't be back for nearly an hour."

She led the way along that narrow path, looking over her shoulder with a glorious smile, sometimes extending her hand back to me as one would with a child.

Along the brow of the bluff the way wound dizzily, while far below the river swept in a giant eddy. For a long time we spoke no word. 'Twas as if our hearts were too full for utterance, our happiness too vast for expression. Yet, O, the sweetness of that silence! The darkling gloom had silvered into lustrous light, the birds were beginning again their mad midnight melodies. Then, suddenly turning a bend in the narrow trail, a blaze of glory leapt upon our sight.

"Look, Berna," I cried.

The swelling river was a lake of saffron fire; the hills a throne of rosy garnet; the sky a dazzling panoply of rubies, girdled with flames of gold. We almost cringed, so gorgeous was its glow, so fierce its splendour.

Then, when we had seated ourselves on the hillside, facing the conflagration, she turned to me.

"And so you found me, dear. I knew you would, somehow. In my heart I knew you would not fail me. So I waited and waited. The time seemed pitilessly long. I only thought of you once, and that was always. It was cruel we left so suddenly, not even time to say good-bye. I can't tell you how bad I felt about it, but I could not help myself. They dragged me away. They began to be afraid of you, and he bade them leave at once. So in the early morning we started."

"I see, I see." I looked into the pools of her eyes; I sheathed her white hands in my brown ones, thrilling greatly at the contact of them.

"Tell me about it, child. Has he bothered you?"

"Oh, not so much. He thinks he has me safe enough, trapped, awaiting his pleasure. But he's taken up with some woman of the town just now. By-and-bye he'll turn his attention to me."

"Terrible! Terrible! Berna, you wring my heart. How can you talk of such things in that matter-of-fact way—it maddens me."

An odd, hard look ridged the corners of her mouth.

"I don't know. Sometimes I'm surprised at myself how philosophical I'm getting."

"But, Berna, surely nothing in this world would ever make you yield? O, it's horrible! horrible!"

She leaned to me tenderly. She put my arms around her neck; she looked at me till I saw my face mirrored in her eyes.

"Nothing in the world, dear, so long as I have you to love me and help me. If ever you fail me, well, then it wouldn't matter much what became of me."

"Even then," I said, "it would be too awful for words. I would rather drag your body from that river than see you yield to him. He's a monster. His very touch is profanation. He could not look on a woman without cynical lust in his heart."

"I know, my boy, I know. Believe me and trust me. I would rather throw myself from the bluff here than let him put a hand on me. And so long as I have your love, dear, I'm safe enough. Don't fear. O, it's been terrible not seeing you! I've craved for you ceaselessly. I've never been out since we came here. They wouldn't let me. They kept in themselves. He bade them. He has them both under his thumb. But now, for some reason, he has relaxed. They're going to open a restaurant downtown, and I'm to wait on table."

"No, you're not!" I cried, "not if I have anything to say in the matter. Berna, I can't bear to think of you in that garbage-heap of corruption down there. You must marry me—now."

"Now," she echoed, her eyes wide with surprise.

"Yes, right away, dear. There's nothing to prevent us. Berna, I love you, I want you, I need you. I'm just distracted, dear. I never know a moment's peace. I cannot take an interest in anything. When I speak to others I'm thinking of you, you all the time. O, I can't bear it, dearest; have pity on me: marry me now."

In an agony of suspense I waited for her answer. For a long time she sat there, thoughtful and quiet, her eyes cast down. At last she raised them to me.

"You said one year."

"Yes, but I was sorry afterwards. I want you now. I can't wait."

She looked at me gravely. Her voice was very soft, very tender.

"I think it better we should wait, dear. This is a blind, sudden desire on your part. I mustn't take advantage of it. You pity me, fear for me, and you have known so few other girls. It's generosity, chivalry, not love for poor little me. O, we mustn't, we mustn't. And then—you might change."

"Change! I'll never, never change," I pleaded. "I'll always be yours, absolutely, wholly yours, little girl; body and soul, to make or to mar, for ever and ever and ever."

"Well, it seems so sudden, so burning, so intense, your love, dear. I'm afraid, I'm afraid. Maybe it's not the kind that lasts. Maybe you'll tire. I'm not worth it, indeed I'm not. I'm only a poor ignorant girl. If there were others near, you would never think of me."

"Berna," I said, "if you were among a thousand, and they were the most adorable in all the world, I would pass over them all and turn with joy and gratitude to you. Then, if I were an Emperor on a throne, and you the humblest in all that throng, I would raise you up beside me and call you 'Queen.'"

"Ah, no," she said sadly, "you were wise once. I saw it afterwards. Better wait one year."

"Oh, my dearest," I reproached her, "once you offered yourself to me under any conditions. Why have you changed?"

"I don't know. I'm bitterly ashamed of that. Never speak of it again."

She went on very quietly, full of gentle patience.

"You know, I've been thinking a great deal since then. In the long, long days and longer nights, when I waited here in misery, hoping always you would come to me, I had time to reflect, to weight your words. I remember them all: 'love that means life and death, that great dazzling light, that passion that would raise to heaven or drag to hell.' You have awakened the woman in me; I must have a love like that."

"You have, my precious; you have, indeed."

"Well, then, let me have time to test it. This is June. Next June, if you have not made up your mind you were foolish, blind, hasty, I will give myself to you with all the love in the world."

"Perhaps *you* will change."

She smiled a peculiar little smile.

"Never, never fear that. I will be waiting for you, longing for you, loving you more and more every day."

I was bitterly cast down, crestfallen, numbed with the blow of her refusal.

"Just now," she said, "I would only be a drag on you. I believe in you. I have faith in you. I want to see you go out and mix in the battle of life. I know you will win. For my sake, dear, win. I would handicap you just now. There are all kinds of chances. Let us wait, boy, just a year."

I saw the pathetic wisdom of her words.

"I know you fear something will happen to me. No! I think I will be quite safe. I can withstand him. After a while he will leave me alone. And if it should come to the worst I can call on you. You mustn't go too far away. I will die rather than let him lay a hand on me. Till next June, dear, not a day longer. We will both be the better for the wait."

I bowed my head. "Very well," I said huskily; "and what will I do in the meantime?"

"Do! Do what you would have done otherwise. Do not let a woman divert the current of your life; let her swim with it. Go out on the creeks! Work! It will be better for you to go away. It will make it easier for me. Here we will both torture each other. I, too, will work and live quietly, and long for you. The time will pass quickly. You will come and see me sometimes?"

"Yes," I answered. My voice choked with emotion.

"Now we must go home," she said; "I'm afraid they will be back."

She rose, and I followed her down the narrow trail. Once or twice she turned and gave me a bright, tender look. I worshipped her more than ever. Was there ever maid more sweet, more gentle, more quick with anxious love? "Bless her, O bless her," I sighed. "Whatever comes, may she be happy." I adored her, but a great sadness filled my heart, and never a word I spoke.

We reached the cabin, and on the threshold she paused. The others had not yet returned. She held out both hands to me, and her eyes were glittering with tears.

"Be brave, my dearest; it's all for my sake—if you love me."

"I love you, my darling; anything for your sake. I'll go to-morrow."

"We're betrothed now, aren't we, dearest?"

"We're betrothed, my love."

She swayed to me and seemed to fit into my arms as a sword fits into its sheath. My lips lay on hers, and I kissed her with a passionate joy. She took my face between her hands and gazed at me long and earnestly.

"I love you, I love you," she murmured; "next June, my darling, next June."

Then she gently slipped away from me, and I was gazing blankly at the closed door.

"Next June," I heard a voice echo; and there, looking at me with a smile, was Locasto.

* * * * *

CHAPTER VIII

It comes like a violent jar to be awakened so rudely from a trance of love, to turn suddenly from the one you care for most in all the world, and behold the one you have best reason to hate. Nevertheless, it is not in human nature to descend rocket-wise from the ethereal heights of love. I was still in an exalted state of mind when I turned and confronted Locasto. Hate was far from my heart, and when I saw the man himself was regarding me with no particular unfriendliness, I was disposed to put aside for the moment all feelings of enmity. The generosity of the victor glowed within me.

As he advanced to me his manner was almost urbane in its geniality.

"You must forgive me," he said, not without dignity, "for overhearing you; but by chance I was passing and dropped upon you before I realised it."

He extended his hand frankly.

"I trust my congratulations on your good luck will not be entirely obnoxious. I know that my conduct in this affair cannot have impressed you in a very favourable light; but I am a badly beaten man. Can't you be generous and let by-gones be by-gones? Won't you?"

I had not yet come down to earth. I was still soaring in the rarefied heights of love, and inclined to a general amnesty towards my enemies.

As he stood there, quiet and compelling, there was an assumption of frankness and honesty about this man that it was hard to withstand. For the nonce I was persuaded of his sincerity, and weakly I surrendered my hand. His grip made me wince.

"Yes, again I congratulate you. I know and admire her. They don't make them any better. She's pure gold. She's a little queen, and the man she cares for ought to be proud and happy. Now, I'm a man of the world, I'm cynical about woman as a rule. I respect my mother and my sisters—beyond that—" He shrugged his shoulders expressively.

"But this girl's different. I always felt in her presence as I used to feel twenty-five years ago when I was a youth, with all my ideals untarnished, my heart pure, and woman holy in my sight."

He sighed.

"You know, young man, I've never told it to a soul before, but I'd give all I'm worth—a clear million—to have those days back. I've never been happy since."

He drew away quickly from the verge of sentiment.

"Well, you mustn't mind me taking an interest in your sweetheart. I'm old enough to be her father, you know, and she touches me strangely. Now, don't distrust me. I want to be a friend to you both. I want to help you to be happy. Jack Locasto's not such a bad lot, as you'll find when you know him. Is there anything I can do for you? What are you going to do in this country?"

"I don't quite know yet," I said. "I hope to stake a good claim when the chance comes. Meantime I'm going to get work on the creeks."

"You are?" he said thoughtfully; "do you know any one?"

"No."

"Well, I'll tell you what: I've got laymen working on my Eldorado claim; I'll give you a note to them if you like."

I thanked him.

"Oh, that's all right," he said. "I'm sorry I played such a mean part in the past, and I'll do anything in my power to straighten things out. Believe me, I mean it. Your English friend gave me the worst drubbing of my life, but three days after I went round and shook hands with him. Fine fellow that. We opened a case of wine to celebrate the victory. Oh, we're good friends now. I always own up when I'm beaten, and I never bear ill-will. If I can help you in any way, and hasten your marriage to that little girl there, well, you can just bank on Jack Locasto: that's all."

I must say the man could be most conciliating when he chose. There was a gravity in his manner, a suave courtesy in his tone, the heritage of his Spanish forefathers, that convinced me almost in spite of my better judgment. No doubt he was magnetic, dominating, a master of men. I thought: there are two Locastos, the primordial one, the Indian, who had assaulted me; and the dignified genial one, the Spaniard, who was willing to own defeat and make amends. Why should I not take him as I found him?

So, as he talked entertainingly to me, my fears were dissipated, my suspicions lulled. And when we parted we shook hands cordially.

"Don't forget," he said; "if you want help bank on me. I mean it now, I mean it."

* * * * *

'Twas early in the bright and cool of the morning when we started for Eldorado, Jim and I. I had a letter from Locasto to Ribwood and Hoofman, the laymen, and I showed it to Jim. He frowned.

"You don't mean to say you've palled up with that devil," he said.

"Oh, he's not so bad," I expostulated. "He came to me like a man and offered me his hand in friendship. Said he was ashamed of himself. What could I do? I've no reason to doubt his sincerity."

"Sincerity be danged. He's about as sincere as a tame rattlesnake. Put his letter in the creek."

But no! I refused to listen to the old man.

"Well, go your own gait," he said; "but don't say that I didn't warn you."

We had crossed over the Klondike to its left limit, and were on a hillside trail beaten down by the feet of miners and packers. Cabins clustered on the flat, and from them plumes of violet smoke mounted into the golden air. Already the camp was astir. Men were chopping their wood, carrying their water. The long, long day was beginning.

Following the trail, we struck up Bonanza, a small muddy stream in a narrow valley. Down in the creek-bed we could see ever-increasing signs of an intense mining activity. On every claim were dozens of cabins, and many high cones of greyish muck. We saw men standing on raised platforms turning windlasses. We saw buckets come up filled with the same dark grey dirt, to be dumped over the edge of the platform. Sometimes, where the dump had gradually arisen around man and windlass, the platform in the centre of that dark-greyish cone was twenty feet high.

Every mile the dumps grew more numerous, till some claims seemed covered with them. Looking down from the trail, they were like innumerable anthills blocking up the narrow channel, and around them swarmed the little ant-men in never-resting activity. The golden valley opened out to us in a vista of green curves, and the cleft of it was packed with tents, cabins, dumps and tailing piles, all bedded in a blue haze of wood fires.

"Look at that great centipede striding across the valley," I said.

"Yes," said Jim, "it's a long line of sluice-boxes. See the water a-shinin' in the sun. Looks like some big golden-backed caterpillar."

The little ants were shovelling into it from one of their heaps, and from that point it swirled on into the stream, a current of mud and stone.

"Seems to me that stream would wash away all the gold," I said. "I know it's all caught in the riffles, but I think if that dump was mine I would want sluice-boxes a mile long and about sixteen hundred riffles. But I guess they know what they are doing."

About noon we descended into the creek-bed and came to the Forks. It was a little town, a Dawson in miniature, with all its sordid aspects infinitely accentuated. It had dance-halls, gambling dens and many saloons: every convenience to ease the miner of the plethoric poke. There in the din and daze and dirt we tarried awhile; then, after eating heartily, we struck up Eldorado.

Here was the same feverish activity of gold-getting. Every claim was valued at millions, and men who had rarely owned enough to buy a decent coat were crying in the saloons because life was not long enough to allow them to spend their sudden wealth. Nevertheless, they were making a good stab at it. At the Forks I enquired regarding Ribwood and Hoofman: "Goin' to work for them, are you? Well, they've got a blamed hard name. If you get a job elsewhere, don't turn it down."

Jim left me; he would work on no claim of Locasto's, he said. He had a friend, a layman, who was a good man, belonged to the Army. He would try him. So we parted.

Ribwood was a tall, gaunt Cornishman, with a narrow, jutting face and a gloomy air; Hoofman, a burly, beet-coloured Australian with a bulging stomach.

"Yes, we'll put you to work," said Hoofman, reading the letter. "Get your coat off and shovel in."

So, right away, I found myself in the dump-pile, jamming a shovel into the pay-dirt and swinging it into a sluice-box five feet higher than my head. Keeping at this hour after hour was no fun, and if ever a man desisted for a moment the hard eyes of Hoofman were upon him, and the gloomy Ribwood had snatched up a shovel and was throwing in the muck furiously.

"Come on, boys," he would shout; "make the dirt fly. 'Taint every part of the world you fellers can make your ten bucks a day."

And it can be said that never labourer proved himself more worthy of his hire than the pick-and-shovel man of those early days. Few could stand it long without resting. They were lean as wolves those men of the dump and drift, and their faces were gouged and grooved with relentless toil.

Well, for three days I made the dirt fly; but towards quitting time, I must say, its flight was a very uncertain one. Again I suffered all the tortures of becoming toil-broken, the old aches and pains of the tunnel and the gravel-pit. Towards evening every shovelful of dirt seemed to weigh as much as if it was solid gold; indeed, the stuff seemed to get richer and richer as the day advanced, and during the last half-hour I judged it must be nearly all nuggets. The constant hoisting into the overhead sluice-box somehow worked muscles that had never gone into action before, and I ached elaborately.

In the morning the pains were fiercest. How I groaned until the muscles became limber. I found myself using very rough language, groaning, gritting my teeth viciously. But I stayed with the work and held up my end, while the laymen watched us sedulously, and seemed to grudge us even a moment to wipe the sweat out of our blinded eyes.

I was glad, indeed, when, on the evening of the third day, Ribwood came to me and said:

"I guess you'd better work up at the shaft to-morrow. We want a man to wheel muck."

They had a shaft sunk on the hillside. They were down some forty feet and were drifting in, wheeling the pay-dirt down a series of planks placed on trestles to the dump. I gripped the handles of a wheelbarrow loaded to overspilling, and steered it down that long, unsteady gangway full of uneven joins and sudden angles. Time and again I ran off the track, but after the first day I became quite an expert at the business. My spirits rose. I was on the way of becoming a miner.

* * * * *

CHAPTER IX

Turning the windlass over the shaft was a little, tough mud-rat, who excited in me the liveliest sense of aversion. Pat Doogan was his name, but I will call him the "Worm."

The Worm was the foulest-mouthed specimen I have yet met. He had the lowest forehead I have ever seen in a white man, and such a sharp, ferrety little face. His reddish hair had the prison clip, and his little reddish eyes were alive with craft and cruelty. I noticed he always regarded me with a peculiarly evil grin, that wrinkled up his cheeks and revealed his hideously blackened teeth. From the first he gave me a creepy feeling, a disgust as if I were near some slimy reptile.

Yet the Worm tried to make up to me. He would tell me stories blended of the horrible and the grotesque. One in particular I remember.

"Youse wanta know how I lost me last job. I'll tell youse. You see, it was like dis. Dere was two Blackmoor guys dat got into de country dis Spring; came by St. Michaels; Hindoos dey was. One of dem 'Sicks' (an' dey looked sick, dey was so loose an' weary in der style) got a job from old man Gustafson down de shaft muckin' up and fillin' de buckets.

"Well, dere was dat Blackmoor down in de deep hole one day when I comes along, an' strikes old Gus for a job. So, seein' as de man on de windlass wanted to quit, he passed it up to me, an' I took right hold an' started in.

"Say, I was feelin' powerful mean. I'd just finished up a two weeks' drunk, an' you tink de booze wasn't workin' in me some. I was seein' all kinds of funny t'ings. Why, as I was a-turnin' away at dat ol' windlass dere was red spiders crawlin' up me legs. But I was wise. I wouldn't look at dem, give dem de go-by. Den a yeller rat got gay wid me an' did some stunts on me windlass. But still I wouldn't let on. Den dere was some green snakes dat wriggled over de platform like shiny streaks on de water. Sure, I didn't like dat one bit, but I says, 'Dere ain't no snakes in de darned country, Pat, and you knows it. It's just a touch of de horrors, dat's all. Just pass 'em up, boy; don't take no notice of dem.'

"Well, dis went on till I begins to get all shaky an' jumpy, an' I was mighty glad when de time came to quit, an' de boys down below gives me de holler to pull dem up.

"So I started hoistin' wid dose snakes an' spiders an' rats jus' cavortin' round me like mad, when all to once who should I hoist outa de bowels of de earth but de very devil himself.

"His face was black. I could see de whites of his eyes, an' he had a big dirty towel tied round his head. Well, say, it was de limit. At de sight of dat ferocious monster comin' after old Pat I gives one yell, drops de crank-handle of de windlass, an' makes a flyin' leap down de dump. I hears an awful shriek, an' de bucket an' de devil goes down smash to de bottom of de shaft, t'irty-five feet. But I kep' on runnin'. I was so scared.

"Well, how was I to know dey had a Blackmoor down dere? He was a stiff when dey got him up, but how was I to know? So I lost me job."

On another occasion he told me:

"Say, kid, youse didn't know as I was liable to fits, did youse? Dat's so; eppylepsy de doctor tells me. Dat's what I am scared of. You see, it's like dis: if one of dem fits should hit me when I'm hoistin' de boys outer de shaft, den it would be a pity. I would sure lose me job like de oder time."

He was the most degraded type of man I had yet met on my travels, a typical degenerate, dirty, drunken, diseased. He had three suits of underclothing, which he never washed. He would wear through all three in succession, and when the last got too dirty for words he would throw it under his trunk and sorrowfully go back to the first, keeping up this rotation, till all were worn out.

One day Hoofman told me he wanted me to go down the shaft and work in the drift. Accordingly, next morning I and a huge Slav, by name Dooley Rileyvich, were lowered down into the darkness.

The Slav initiated me. Every foot of dirt had to be thawed out by means of wood fires. We built a fire at the far end of the drift every night, covering the face we were working. First we would lay kindling, then dry spruce lying lengthways, then a bank of green wood standing on end to keep in the heat and shed the dirt that sloughed down from the roof. In the morning our fire would be burned out, and enough pay-dirt thawed to keep us picking all day.

Down there I found it the hardest work of all. We had to be careful that the smoke had cleared from the drift before we ventured in, for frequently miners were asphyxiated. Indeed, the bad air never went entirely away. It made my eyes sore, my head ache. Yet, curiously enough, so long as you were below it did not affect you so much. It was when you stepped out of the bucket and struck the pure outer air that you reeled and became dizzy. It was blinding, too. Often at supper have my eyes been so blurred and sore I had to grope around uncertainly for the sugar bowl and the tin of cream.

In the drift it was always cool. The dirt kept sloughing down on us, and we had really gone in too far for our own safety, but the laymen cared little for that. At the end of the drift the roof was so low we were bent almost double, picking at the face in all kinds of cramped positions, and dragging after us the heavy bucket. To the big Slav it was all in the day's work, but to me it was hard, hard.

The shaft was almost forty feet deep. For the first ten feet a ladder ran down it, then stopped suddenly as if the excavators had decided to abandon it. I often looked at this useless bit of ladder and wondered why it had been left unfinished.

Every morning the Worm hoisted us down into the darkness, and at night drew us up. Once he said to me:

"Say, wouldn't it be de tough luck if I was to take a fit when I was hoistin' youse up? Such a nice bit of a boy, too, an' I guess I'd lose my job over de head of it."

I said: "Cut that out, or you'll have me so scared I won't go down."

He grinned unpleasantly and said nothing more. Yet somehow he was getting on my nerves terribly.

It was one evening we had banked our fires and were ready to be hoisted up. Dooley Rileyvich went first, and I watched him blot out the bit of blue for a while. Then, slowly, down came the bucket for me.

I got in. I was feeling uneasy all of a sudden, and devoutly wished I were anywhere else but in that hideous hole. I felt myself leave the ground and rise steadily. The walls of the shaft glided past me. Up, up I went. The bit of blue sky grew bigger, bigger. There was a star shining there. I watched it. I heard the creak, creak of the windlass crank. Somehow it seemed to have a sinister sound. It seemed to say: "Have a care, have a care, have a care." I was now ten feet from the top. The bucket was rocking a little, so I put out my hand and grasped the lowest rung of the ladder to steady myself.

Then, at that instant, it seemed the weight of the bucket pressing up against my feet was suddenly removed, and my arm was nigh jerked out of its socket. There I was hanging desperately on the lowest rung of the ladder, while, with a crash that made my heart sick, the bucket dashed to the bottom. At last, I realised, the Worm had had his fit.

Quickly I gripped with both hands. With a great effort I raised myself rung by rung on the ladder. I was panic-stricken, faint with fear; but some instinct had made me hold on desperately. Dizzily I hung all a-shudder, half-sobbing. A minute seemed like a year.

Ah! there was the face of Dooley looking down on me. He saw me clinging there. He was anxiously shouting to me to come up. Mastering an overpowering nausea I raised myself. At last I felt his strong arm around me, and here I swear it on a stack of Bibles that brutish Slav seemed to me like one of God's own angels.

I was on firm ground once more. The Worm was lying stiff and rigid. Without a word the stalwart Slav took him on his brawny shoulder. The creek was downhill but fifty yards. Ere we reached it the Worm had begun to show signs of reviving consciousness. When we got to the edge of the icy water he was beginning to groan and open his eyes in a dazed way.

"Leave me alone," he says to Rileyvich; "you Slavonian swine, lemme go."

Not so the Slav. Holding the wriggling, writhing little man in his powerful arms he plunged him heels over head in the muddy current of the creek.

"I guess I cure dose fits anyway," he said grimly.

Struggling, spluttering, blaspheming, the little man freed himself at last and staggered ashore. He cursed Rileyvich most comprehensively. He had not yet seen me, and I heard him wailing:

"Sure de boy's a stiff. Just me luck; I've lost me job."

* * * * *

CHAPTER X

"You'd better quit," said the Prodigal.

It was the evening of my mishap, and he had arrived unexpectedly from town.

"Yes, I mean to," I answered. "I wouldn't go down there again for a farm. I feel as weak as a sick baby. I couldn't stay another day."

"Well, that goes," said he. "It just fits in with my plans. I'm getting Jim to come in, too. I've realised on that stuff I bought, made over three thousand clear profit, and with it I've made a dicker for a property on the bench above Bonanza, Gold Hill they call it. I've a notion it's all right. Anyway, we'll tunnel in and see. You and Jim will have a quarter share each for your work, while I'll have an extra quarter for the capital I've put in. Is it a go?"

I said it was.

"Thought it would be. I've had the papers made out; you can sign right now."

So I signed, and next day found us all three surveying our claim. We put up a tent, but the first thing to do was to build a cabin. Right away we began to level off the ground. The work was pleasant, and conducted in such friendship that the time passed most happily. Indeed, my only worry was about Berna. She had never ceased to be at the forefront of my mind. I schooled myself into the belief that she was all right, but, thank God, every moment was bringing her nearer to me.

One morning, when we were out in the woods cutting timber for the cabin, I said to Jim:

"Did you ever hear anything more about that man Mosely?"

He stopped chopping, and lowered the axe he had poised aloft.

"No, boy; I've had no mail at all. Wait awhile."

He swung his axe with viciously forceful strokes. His cheery face had become so downcast that I bitterly blamed myself for my want of tact. However, the cloud soon passed.

About two days after that the Prodigal said to me:

"I saw your little guttersnipe friend to-day."

"Indeed, where?" I asked; for I had often thought of the Worm, thought of him with fear and loathing.

"Well, sir, he was just getting the grandest dressing-down I ever saw a man get. And do you know who was handing it to him—Locasto, no less."

He lit a cigarette and inhaled the smoke.

"I was just coming along the trail from the Forks when I suddenly heard voices in the bush. The big man was saying:

"'Lookee here, Pat, you know if I just liked to say half a dozen words I could land you in the penitentiary for the rest of your days.'

"Then the little man's wheedling voice:

"'Well, I did me best, Jack. I know I bungled the job, but youse don't want to cast dem t'ings up to me. Dere's more dan me orter be in de pen. Dere's no good in de pot callin' de kettle black, is dere?'

"Then Black Jack flew off the handle. You know he's got a system of manhandling that's near the record in these parts. Well, he just landed on the little man. He got him down and started to lambast the Judas out of him. He gave him the 'leather,' and then some. I guess he'd have done him to a finish hadn't I been Johnnie on the spot. At sight of me he gives a curse, jumps on his horse and goes off at a canter. Well, I propped the little man against a tree, and then some fellows came along, and we got him some brandy. But he was badly done up. He kept saying: 'Oh, de devil, de big devil, sure I'll give him his before I get t'rough.' Funny, wasn't it?"

"Yes, it's strange;" and for some time I pondered over the remarkable strangeness of it.

"That reminds me," said Jim; "has any one seen the Jam-wagon?"

"Oh yes," answered the Prodigal; "poor beggar! he's down and out. After the fight he went to pieces, every one treating him, and so on. You remember Bullhammer?"

"Yes."

195

"Well, the last I saw of the Jam-wagon—he was cleaning cuspidors in Bullhammer's saloon."

* * * * *

We had hauled the logs for the cabin, and the foundation was laid. Now we were building up the walls, placing between every log a thick wadding of moss. Every day saw our future home nearer completion.

One evening I spied the saturnine Ribwood climbing the hill to our tent. He hailed me:

"Say, you're just the man I want."

"What for?" I asked; "not to go down that shaft again?"

"No. Say! we want a night watchman up at the claim to go on four hours a night at a dollar an hour. You see, there's been a lot of sluice-box robberies lately, and we're scared for our clean-up. We're running two ten-hour shifts now and cleaning up every three days; but there's four hours every night the place is deserted, and Hoofman proposed we should get you to keep watch."

"Yes," I said; "I'll run up every evening if the others don't object."

They did not; so the next night, and for about a dozen after that, I spent the darkest hours watching on the claim where previously I had worked.

There was never any real darkness down there in that narrow valley, but there was dusk of a kind that made everything grey and uncertain. It was a vague, nebulous atmosphere in which objects merged into each other confusedly. Bushes came down to within a few feet of where we were working, dense-growing alder and birch that would have concealed a whole regiment of sluice-robbers.

It was the dimmest and most uncertain hour of the four, and I was sitting at my post of guard. As the night was chilly I had brought along an old grey blanket, similar in colour to the mound of the pay-dirt. There had been quite a cavity dug in the dump during the day, and into this I crawled and wrapped myself in my blanket. From my position I could see the string of boxes containing the riffles. Over me brooded the vast silence of the night. By my side lay a loaded shot-gun.

"If the swine comes," said Ribwood, "let him have a clean-up of lead instead of gold."

Lying there, I got to thinking of the robberies. They were remarkable. All had been done by an expert. In some cases the riffles had been extracted and the gold scooped out; in others a quantity of mercury had been poured in at the upper end of the boxes, and, as it passed down, the "quick" had gathered up the dust. Each time the robbers had cleaned up from two to three thousand dollars, and all within the past month. There was some mysterious master-crook in our midst, one who operated swiftly and surely, and left absolutely no clue of his identity.

It was strange, I thought. What nerve, what cunning, what skill must this midnight thief be possessed of! What desperate chances was he taking! For, in the miners' eyes, cache-stealing and sluice-box robbing were in the same category, and the punishment was—well, a rope and the nearest tree of size. Among those strong, grim men justice would be stern and swift.

I was very quiet for a while, watching dreamily the dark shadows of the dusk.

Hist! What was that? Surely the bushes were moving over there by the hillside. I strained my eyes. I was right: they were.

I was all nerves and excitement now, my heart beating wildly, my eyes boring through the gloom. Very softly I put out my hand and grasped the shot-gun.

I watched and waited. A man was parting the bushes. Stealthily, very stealthily, he peered around. He hesitated, paused, peered again, crouched on all-fours, crept forward a little. Everything was quiet as a grave. Down in the cabins the tired men slept peacefully; stillness and solitude.

Cautiously the man, crawling like a snake, worked his way to the sluice-boxes. None but a keen watcher could have seen him. Again and again he paused, peered around, listened intently. Very carefully, with my eyes fixed on him, I lifted the gun.

Now he had gained the shadow of the nearest sluice-box. He clung to the trestle-work, clung so closely you could scarce tell him apart from it. He was like a rat, dark, furtive, sinister. Slowly I lifted the gun to my shoulder. I had him covered.

I waited. Somehow I was loath to shoot. My nerves were a-quiver. Proof, more proof, I said. I saw him working busily, lying flat alongside the boxes. How crafty, how skilful he was! He was disconnecting the boxes. He would let the water run to the ground; then, there in the exposed riffles, would be his harvest. Would I shoot... now... now...

Then, in the midnight hush, my gun blazed forth. With one scream the man tumbled down, carrying along with him the disconnected box. The water rushed over the ground in a deluge. I must capture him. There he lay in that pouring stream... Now I had him.

In that torrent of icy water I grappled with my man. Over and over we rolled. He tried to gouge me. He was small, but oh, how strong! He held down his face. Fiercely I wrenched it up to the light. Heavens! it was the Worm.

I gave a cry of surprise, and my clutch on him must have weakened, for at that moment he gave a violent wrench, a cat-like twist, and tore himself free. Men were coming, were shouting, were running in from all directions.

"Catch him!" I cried. "Yonder he goes."

But the little man was shooting forward like a deer. He was in the bushes now, bursting through everything, dodging and twisting up the hill. Right and left ran his pursuers, mistaking each other for the robber in the semi-gloom, yelling frantically, mad with the excitement of a man-hunt. And in the midst of it all I lay in a pool of mud and water, with a sprained wrist and a bite on my leg.

"Why didn't you hold him?" shouted Ribwood.

"I couldn't," I answered. "I saved your clean-up, and he got some of the lead. Besides, I know who he is."

"You don't! Who is he?"

"Pat Doogan."

"You don't say. Well, I'm darned. You're sure?"

"Dead sure."

"Swear it in Court?"

"I will."

"Well, that's all right. We'll get him. I'll go into town first thing in the morning and get out a warrant for him."

He went, but the next evening back he returned, looking very surly and disgruntled.

"Well, what about the warrant?" said Hoofman.

"Didn't get it."

"Didn't get—"

"No, didn't get it," snapped Ribwood. "Look here, Hoofman, I met Locasto. Black Jack says Pat was cached away, dead to all the world, in the backroom of the Omega Saloon all night. There's two loafers and the barkeeper to back him up. What can we do in the face of that? Say, young feller, I guess you mistook your man."

"I guess I did not," I protested stoutly.

They both looked at me for a moment and shrugged their shoulders.

* * * * *

CHAPTER XI

Time went on and the cabin was quietly nearing completion. The roof of poles was in place. It only remained to cover it with moss and thawed-out earth to make it our future home. I think these were the happiest days I spent in the North. We were such a united trio. Each was eager to do more than the other, and we vied in little acts of mutual consideration.

Once again I congratulated myself on my partners. Jim, though sometimes bellicosely evangelical, was the soul of kindly goodness, cheerfulness and patience. It was refreshing to know among so many sin-calloused men one who always rang true, true as the gold in the pan. As for the Prodigal, he was a Prince. I often thought that God at the birth of him must have reached out to the sunshine and crammed a mighty handful of it into the boy. Surely it is better than all the riches in the world to have a temperament of eternal cheer.

As for me, I have ever been at the mercy of my moods, easily elated, quickly cast down. I have always been abnormally sensitive, affected by sunshine and by shadows, vacillating, intense in my feelings. I was truly happy in those days, finding time in the long evenings to think of the scenes of stress and sorrow I had witnessed, reconstructing the past, and having importune me again and again the many characters in my life drama.

Always and always I saw the Girl, elusively sweet, almost unreal, a thing to enshrine in that ideal alcove of our hearts we keep for our saints. (And God help us always to keep shining there a great light.)

Many others importuned me: Pinklove, Globstock, Pondersby, Marks, old Wilovich, all dead; Bullhammer, the Jam-wagon, Mosher, the Winklesteins, plunged in the vortex of the gold-born city; and lastly, looming over all, dark and ominous, the handsome, bold, sinister face of Locasto. Well, maybe I would never see any of them again.

Yet more and more my dream hours were jealously consecrated to Berna. How ineffably sweet were they! How full of delicious imaginings! How pregnant of high hope! O, I was born to love, I think, and I never loved but one. This story of my life is the story of Berna. It is a thing of words and words and words, yet every word is Berna, Berna. Feel the heartache behind it all. Read between the lines, Berna, Berna.

Often in the evenings we went to the Forks, which was a lively place indeed. Here was all the recklessness and revel of Dawson on a smaller scale, and infinitely more gross. Here were the dance-hall girls, not the dazzling creatures in diamonds and Paris gowns, the belles of the Monte Carlo and the Tivoli, but drabs self-convicted by their coarse, puffy faces. Here the men, fresh from their day's work, the mud of the claim hardly dry on their boot-tops, were buying wine with nuggets they had filched from sluice-box, dump and drift.

There was wholesale robbery going on in the gold-camp. On many claims where the owners were known to be unsuspicious, men would work for small wages because of the gold they were able to filch. On the other hand, many of the operators were paying their men in trade-dust valued at sixteen dollars an ounce, yet so adulterated with black sand as to be really worth about fourteen. All these things contributed to the low morale of the camp. Easy come, easy go with money, a wild intoxication of success in the air; gold gouged in glittering heaps from the ground during the day, and at night squandered in a carnival of lust and sin.

The Prodigal was always "snooping" around and gleaning information from most mysterious sources. One evening he came to us.

"Boys, get ready, quick. There's a rumour of a stampede for a new creek, Ophir Creek they call it, away on the other side of the divide somewhere. A prospector went down ten feet and got fifty-cent dirt. We've got to get in on this. There's a mob coming from Dawson, but we'll get there before the rush."

Quickly we got together blankets and a little grub, and, keeping out of sight, we crawled up the hill under cover of the brush. Soon we came to a place from which we could command a full view of the valley. Here we lay down, awaiting developments.

It was at the hour of dusk. Scarfs of smoke wavered over the cabins down in the valley. On the far slope of Eldorado I saw a hawk soar upwards. Surely a man was moving amid the brush, two men, a dozen men, moving in single file very stealthily. I pointed them out.

"It's the stampede," whispered Jim. "We've got to get on to the trail of that crowd. Travel like blazes. We can cut them off at the head of the valley."

So we struck into the stampede gait, a wild, jolting, desperate pace, that made the wind pant in our lungs like bellows, and jarred our bones in their sockets. Through brush and scrub timber we burst. Thorny vines tore at us detainingly, swampy niggerheads impeded us; but the excitement of the stampede was in our blood, and we plunged down gulches, floundered over marshes, climbed steep ridges and crashed through dense masses of underwood.

"Throw away your blankets, boys," said the Prodigal. "Just keep a little grub. Eldorado was staked on a stampede. Maybe we're in on another Eldorado. We must connect with that bunch if we break our necks."

It was hours after when we overtook them, about a dozen men, all in the maddest hurry, and casting behind them glances of furtive apprehension. When they saw us they were hugely surprised. Ribwood was one of the party.

"Hello," he says roughly; "any more coming after you boys?"

"Don't see them," said the Prodigal breathlessly. "We spied you and cottoned on to what was up, so we made a fierce hike to get in on it. Gee, I'm all tuckered out."

"All right, get in line. I guess there's lots for us all. You're in on a good thing, all right. Come along."

So off we started again. The leader was going like one possessed. We blundered on behind. We were on the other side of the divide looking into another vast valley. What a magnificent country it was! What a great manœuvring-ground it would make for an army! What splendid open spaces, and round smooth hills, and dimly blue valleys, and silvery winding creeks! It was veritably a park of the Gods, and enclosing it was the monstrous, corrugated palisade of the Rockies.

But there was small time to look around. On we went in the same mad, heart-breaking hurry, mile after mile, hour after hour.

"This is going to be a banner creek, boys," the whisper ran down the line. "We're in luck. We'll all be Klondike Kings yet."

Cheering, wasn't it? So on we went, hotter than ever, content to follow the man of iron who was guiding us to the virgin treasure.

We had been pounding along all night, up hill and down dale. The sun rose, the dawn blossomed, the dew dried on the blueberry; it was morning. Still we kept up our fierce gait. Would our leader never come to his destination? By what roundabout route was he guiding us? The sun climbed up in the blue sky, the heat quivered; it was noon. We panted as we pelted on, parched and weary, faint and footsore. The excitement of the stampede had sustained us, and we scarcely had noted the flight of time. We had been walking for fourteen hours, yet not a man faltered. I was ready to drop with fatigue; my feet were a mass of blisters, and every step was intolerable pain to me. But still our leader kept on.

"I guess we'll fool those trying to follow us," snapped Ribwood grimly.

Suddenly the Prodigal said to me: "Say, you boys will have to go on without me. I'm all in. Go ahead, I'll follow after I'm rested up."

He dropped in a limp heap on the ground and instantly fell asleep. Several of the others had dropped out too. They fell asleep where they gave up, utterly exhausted. We had now been going sixteen hours, and still our leader kept on.

"You're pretty tough for a youngster," growled one of them to me. "Keep it up, we're almost there."

So I hobbled along painfully, though the desire to throw myself down was becoming imperative. Just ahead was Jim, sturdily holding his own. The others were reduced to a bare half-dozen.

It was about four in the afternoon when we reached the creek. Up it our leader plunged, till he came to a place where a rude shaft had been dug. We gathered around him. He was a typical prospector, a child of hope, lean, swarthy, clear-eyed.

"Here it is, boys," he said. "Here's my discovery stake. Now you fellows go up or down, anywhere you've a notion to, and put in your stakes. You all know what a lottery it is. Maybe you'll stake a million-dollar claim, maybe a blank. Mining's all a gamble. But go ahead, boys. I wish you luck."

So we strung out, and, coming in rotation, Jim and I staked seven and eight below discovery.

"Seven's a lucky number for me," said Jim; "I've a notion this claim's a good one."

"I don't care," I said, "for all the gold in the world. What I want is sleep, sleep, rest and sleep."

So I threw myself down on a bit of moss, and, covering my head with my coat to ward off the mosquitoes, in a few minutes I was dead to the world.

* * * * *

CHAPTER XII

I was awakened by the Prodigal.

"Rouse up," he was saying; "you've slept right round the clock. We've got to get back to town and record those claims. Jim's gone three hours ago."

It was five o'clock of a crystal Yukon morning, with the world clear-cut and fresh as at the dawn of Things. I was sleep-stupid, sore, stiff in every joint. Racking pains made me groan at every movement, and the chill night air had brought on twinges of rheumatism. I looked at my location stake, beside which I had fallen.

"I can't do it," I said; "my feet are out of business."

"You must," he insisted. "Come, buck up, old man. Bathe your feet in the creek, and then you'll feel as fit as a fighting-cock. We've got to get into town hot-foot. They've got a bunch of crooks at the gold office, and we're liable to lose our claims if we are late."

"Have you staked, too?"

"You bet. I've got thirteen below. Hurry up. There's a wild bunch coming from town."

I groaned grievously, yet felt mighty refreshed by a dip in the creek. Then we started off once more. Every few moments we would meet parties coming post-haste from town. They looked worn and jaded, but spread eagerly up and down. There must have been several hundred of them, all sustained by the mad excitement of the stampede.

We did not take the circuitous route of the day before, but one that shortened the distance by some ten miles. We travelled a wild country, crossing unknown creeks that have since proved gold-bearing, and climbing again the high ridge of the divide. Then once more we dropped down into the Bonanza basin, and by nightfall we had reached our own cabin.

We lay down for a few hours. It seemed my weary head had just touched the pillow when once more the inexorable Prodigal awakened me.

"Come on, kid, we've got to get to Dawson when the recording office opens." So once more we pelted down Bonanza. Fast as we had come, we found many of those who had followed us were ahead. The North is the land of the musher. In that pure, buoyant air a man can walk away from himself. Any one of us thought nothing of a fifty-mile tramp, and one of eighty was scarcely considered notable.

It was about nine in the morning when we got to the gold office. Already a crowd of stampeders were waiting. Foremost in the crowd I saw Jim. The Prodigal looked thoughtful.

"Look here," he said, "I guess it's all right to push in with that bunch, but there's a slicker way of doing it for those that are 'next.' Of course, it's not according to Hoyle. There's a little side-door where you can get in ahead of the gang. See that fellow, Ten-Dollar Jim they call him; well, they say he can work the oracle for us."

"No," I said, "you can pay him ten dollars if you like. I'll take my chance in the regulation way."

So the Prodigal slipped away from me, and presently I saw him admitted at the side entrance. Surely, thought I, there must be some mistake. The public would not "stand for" such things.

There was quite a number ahead of me, and I knew I was in for a long wait. I will never forget it. For three days, with the exception of two brief sleep-spells, I had been in a fierce helter-skelter of excitement, and I had eaten no very satisfying food. As I stood in that sullen crowd I swayed with weariness, and my legs were doubling under me. Invisible hands were dragging me down, throwing dust in my eyes, hypnotising me with soporific gestures. I staggered forward and straightened up suddenly. On the outskirts of the crowd I saw the Prodigal trying to locate me. When he saw me he waved a paper.

"Come on, you goat," he shouted; "have a little sense. I'm all fixed up."

I shook my head. An odd sense of fair play in me made me want to win the game squarely. I would wait my turn. Noon came. I saw Jim coming out, tired but triumphant.

"All right," he megaphoned to me; "I'm through. Now I'll go and sleep my head off."

How I envied him. I felt I, too, had a "big bunch" of sleep coming to me. I was moving forward slowly. Bit by bit I was wedging nearer the door. I watched man after man push past the coveted threshold. They were all miners, brawny, stubble-chinned fellows with grim, determined faces. I was certainly the youngest there.

"What have you got?" asked a thick-set man on my right.

"Eight below," I answered.

"Gee! you're lucky."

"What'll you take for it?" asked a tall, keen-looking fellow on my left.

"Five thousand."

"Give you two."

"No."

"Well, come round and see me to-morrow at the Dominion, and we'll talk it over. My name's Gunson. Bring your papers."

"All right."

Something like dizziness seized me. Five thousand! The crowd seemed to be composed of angels and the sunshine to have a new and brilliant quality of light and warmth. Five thousand! Would I take it? If the claim was worth a cent it ought to be worth fifty thousand. I soared on rosy wings of optimism. I revelled in dreams. My claim! Mine! Eight below! Other men had bounded into affluence. Why not I?

No longer did I notice the flight of time. I was ready to wait till doomsday. A new lease of strength came to me. I was near the wicket now. Only two were ahead of me. A clerk was recording their claims. One had thirty-four above, the other fifty-two below. The clerk looked flustered, fatigued. His dull eyes were pursy with midnight debauches; his flesh sagged. In contrast with the clean, hard, hawk-eyed miners, he looked blotched and unwholesome.

Crossly he snatched from the other two their miner's certificates, made the entries in his book, and gave them their receipts. It was my turn now. I dashed forward eagerly. Then I stopped, for the man with the bleary eyes had shut the wicket in my face.

"Three o'clock," he snapped.

"Couldn't you take mine?" I faltered; "I've been waiting now these seven hours."

"Closing time," he ripped out still more tartly; "come again to-morrow."

There was a growling thunder from the crowd behind, and the weary, disappointed stampeders slouched away.

Body and soul of me craved for sleep. Beyond an overwhelming desire for rest, I was conscious of nothing else. My eyelids were weighted with lead. I lagged along dejectedly. At the hotel I saw the Prodigal.

"Get fixed up?"

"No, too late."

"You'd better take advantage of the general corruption and the services of Ten-Dollar Jim."

I was disheartened, disgusted, desperate.

"I will," I said. Then, throwing myself on the bed, I launched on a dreamless sea of sleep.

* * * * *

CHAPTER XIII

Next morning bright and early found me at the side-door, and the tall man admitted me. I slipped a ten-dollar gold piece into his palm, and presently found myself waiting at the yet unopened wicket. Outside I could see the big crowd gathering for their weary wait. I felt a sneaking sense of meanness, but I did not have long to enjoy my despicable sensations.

The recording clerk came to the wicket. He was very red-faced and watery-eyed. Involuntarily I turned my head away at the reek of his breath.

"I want to record eight below on Ophir," I said.

He looked at me curiously. He hesitated.

"What name?" he asked.

I gave it. He turned up his book.

"Eight below, you say. Why, that's already recorded."

"Can't be," I retorted. "I just got down from there yesterday after planting my stakes."

"Can't help it. It's recorded by some one else, recorded early yesterday."

"Look here," I exclaimed; "what kind of a game are you putting up on me? I tell you I was the first on the ground. I alone staked the claim."

"That's strange," he said. "There must be some mistake. Anyway, you'll have to move on and let the others get up to the wicket. You're blocking the way. All I can do is to look into the matter for you, and I've got no time now. Come back to-morrow. Next, please."

The next man pushed me aside, and there I stood, gaping and gasping. A man in the waiting line looked at me pityingly.

"It's no use, young fellow; you'd better make up your mind to lose that claim. They'll flim-flam you out of it somehow. They've sent some one out now to stake over you. If you kick, they'll say you didn't stake proper."

"But I have witnesses."

"It don't matter if you call the Angel Gabriel to witness, they're going to grab your claim. Them government officials is the crookedest bunch that ever made fuel for hell-fire. You won't get a square deal; they're going to get the fat anyhow. They've got the best claims spotted, an' men posted to jump them at the first chance. Oh, they're feathering their nests all right. They're like a lot of greedy pike just waiting to gobble down all they can. A man can't buy wine at twenty dollars per, and make dance-hall Flossies presents of diamond tararas on a government salary. That's what a lot of them are doing. Wine and women, and their wives an' daughters outside thinkin' they're little tin gods. Somehow they've got to foot the bill. Oh, it's a great country."

I was stunned with disappointment.

"What you want," he continued, "is to get a pull with some of the officials. Why, there's friends of mine don't need to go out of town to stake a claim. Only the other day a certain party known to me, went to—well, I mustn't mention names, anyway, he's high up in the government, and a friend of Quebec Suzanne's,—and says to him,'I want you to get number so and so on Hunker recorded for me. Of course I haven't been able to get out there, but—'

"The government bug puts his hands to his ears. 'Don't give me any unnecessary information,' he says; 'you want so and so recorded, Sam. Well, that's all right. I'll fix it.'

"That was all there was to it, and when next day a man comes in post-haste claiming to have staked it, it was there recorded in Sam's name. Get a stand-in, young fellow."

"But surely," I said, "somehow, somewhere there must be justice. Surely if these facts were represented at Ottawa and proof forthcoming—"

"Ottawa!" He gave a sniffing laugh. "Ottawa! Why, it's some of the big guns at Ottawa that's gettin' the cream of it all. The little fellows are just lapping up the drips. Look at them big concessions they're selling for a song, good placer ground that would mean pie to the poor miner, closed tight and everlastingly tied up. How is it done? Why, there's some politician at the bottom of the whole business. Look at the liquor permits—crude alcohol sent into the country by the thousand gallons, diluted to six times its bulk, and sold to the poor prospector for whisky at a dollar a drink. An' you can't pour your own drinks at that."

"Well," I said, "I'm not going to be cheated out of my claim. If I've got to move Heaven and earth—"

"You'll do nothing of the kind. If you get sassy there's the police to put the lid on you. You can talk till you're purple round the gills. It won't cut no figure. They've got us all cinched. We've just got to take our medicine. It's no use goin' round bellyaching. You'd better go away and sit down."

And I did.

* * * * *

CHAPTER XIV

I had to see Berna at once. Already I had paid a visit to the Paragon Restaurant, that new and glittering place of resort run by the Winklesteins, but she was not on duty. I saw Madam, resplendent in her false jewellery, with her beetle-black hair elaborately coiffured, and her large, bold face handsomely enamelled. She looked the picture of fleshy prosperity, a big handsome Jewess, hawk-eyed and rapacious. In the background hovered Winklestein, his little, squeezed-up, tallowy face beaded with perspiration. But he was dressed quite superbly, and his moustache was more wondrously waxed than ever.

I mingled with the crowd of miners, and in my rough garb, swarthy and bearded as I was, the Jewish couple did not know me. As I paid her, Madam gave me a sharp glance. But there was no recognisant gleam in her eyes.

In the evening I returned. I took a seat in one of the curtained boxes. At the long lunch-counter rough-necked fellows perched on tripod stools were guzzling food. The place was brilliantly lit up, many-mirrored and flashily ornate in gilt and white. The bill of fare was elaborate, the prices exalted. In the box before me a white-haired lawyer was entertaining a lady of easy virtue; in the box behind, a larrikin quartette from the Pavilion Theatre were holding high revelry. There was no mistaking the character of the place. In the heart of the city's tenderloin it was a haunt of human riff-raff, a palace of gilt and guilt, a first scene in the nightly comedy of "The Lobster."

I was feeling profoundly depressed, miserable, disgusted with everything. For the first time I began to regret ever leaving home. Out on the creeks I was happy. Here in the town the glaring corruption of things jarred on my nerves.

And it was in this place Berna worked. She waited on these wantons; she served those swine. She heard their loose talk, their careless oaths. She saw them foully drunk, staggering off to their shameful assignations. She knew everything. O, it was pitiful; it sickened me to the soul. I sat down and buried my face in my hands.

"Order, please."

I knew that sweet voice. It thrilled me, and I looked up suddenly. There was Berna standing before me.

She gave a quick start, then recovered herself. A look of delight came into her eyes, eager, vivid delight.

"My, how you frightened me, I wasn't expecting you. Oh, I am so glad to see you again."

I looked at her. I was conscious of a change in her, and the consciousness came with a sense of shearing pain.

"Berna," I said, "what are you doing with that paint on your face?"

"Oh, I'm sorry." She was rubbing distressfully at a dab of rouge on her cheek. "I knew you would be cross, but I had to; they made me. They said I looked like a spectre at the feast with my chalk face; I frightened away the customers. It's just a little pink,— all the women do it. It makes me look happier, and it doesn't hurt me any."

"What I want is to see in your cheeks, dear, the glow of health, not the flush of a cosmetic. However, never mind. How are you?"

"Pretty well—" hesitatingly.

"Berna," boomed the rough, contumacious voice of Madam, "attend to the customers."

"All right," I said; "get me anything. I just wanted to see you."

She hurried away. I saw her go behind the curtains of one of the closed boxes carrying a tray of dishes. I heard coarse voices chaffing her. I saw her come out, her cheeks flushed, yet not with rouge. A miner had tried to detain her. Somehow it all made me writhe, agitated me so that I could hardly keep my seat.

Presently she came hurrying round, bringing me some food.

"When can I see you, girl?" I asked.

"To-night. See me home. I'm off at midnight."

"All right. I'll be waiting."

She was kept very busy, and, though once or twice a tipsy roysterer ventured on some rough pleasantry, I noticed with returning satisfaction that most of the big, bearded miners treated her with chivalrous respect. She was quite friendly with them. They called her by name, and seemed to have a genuine affection for her. There was a protective manliness in the manner of these men that reassured me. So I swallowed my meal and left the place.

"That's a good little girl," said a grizzled old fellow to me, as he stood picking his teeth energetically outside the restaurant. "Straight as a string, and there ain't many up here you can say that of. If any one was to try any monkey business with that little girl, sir, there's a dozen of the boys would make him a first-rate case for the hospital ward. Yes, siree, that's a jim-dandy little girl. I just wish she was my darter."

In my heart I blessed him for his words, and pressed on him a fifty-cent cigar.

Again I wandered up and down the now familiar street, but the keen edge of my impression had been blunted. I no longer took the same interest in its sights. More populous it was, noisier, livelier than ever. In the gambling-annex of the Paystreak Saloon was Mr. Mosher shuffling and dealing methodically. Everywhere I saw flushed and excited miners, each with his substantial poke of dust. It was usually as big as a pork-sausage, yet it was only his spending-poke. Safely in the bank he had cached half a dozen of them ten times as big.

These were the halcyon days. Success was in the air. Men were drunk with it; carried off their feet, delirious. Money! It had lost its value. Every one you met was "lousy" with it; threw it away with both hands, and fast as they emptied one pocket it filled up the others. Little wonder a mad elation, a semi-frenzy of prodigality prevailed, for every day the golden valley was pouring into the city a seemingly exhaustless stream of treasure.

I saw big Alec, one of the leading operators, coming down the street with his men. He carried a Winchester, and he had a pack-train of burros, each laden down with gold. At the bank flushed and eager mobs were clamouring to have their pokes weighed. In buckets, coal-oil cans, every kind of receptacle, lay the precious dust. Sweating clerks were handling it as carelessly as a grocer handles sugar. Goldsmiths were making it into wonders of barbaric jewellery. There seemed no limit to the camp's wealth. Every one was mad, and the demi-mondaine was queen of all.

I saw Hewson and Mervin. They had struck it rich on a property they had bought on Hunker. Fortune was theirs.

"Come and have a drink," said Hewson. Already he had had many. His face was relaxed, flushed, already showing signs of a flabby degeneration. In this man of iron sudden success was insidiously at work, enervating his powers.

Mervin, too. I caught a glimpse of him, in the doorway of the Green Bay Tree. The Maccaroni Kid had him in tow, and he was buying wine.

I looked in vain for Locasto. He was on a big debauch, they told me. Viola Lennoir had "got him going."

At midnight, at the door of the Paragon, I was waiting in a fever of impatience when Berna came out.

"I'm living up at the cabin," she said; "you can walk with me as far as that. That is, if you want to," she added coquettishly.

She was very bright and did most of the talking. She showed a vast joy at seeing me.

"Tell me what you've been doing, dear—everything. Have you made a stake? So many have. I have prayed you would, too. Then we'll go away somewhere and forget all this. We'll go to Italy, where it's always beautiful. We'll just live for each other. Won't we, honey?"

She nestled up to me. She seemed to have lost much of her shyness. I don't know why, but I preferred my timid, shrinking Berna.

"It will take a whole lot to make me forget this," I said grimly.

"Yes, I know. Isn't it frightful? Somehow I don't seem to mind so much now. I'm getting used to it, I suppose. But at first—O, it was terrible! I thought I never could stand it. It's wonderful how we get accustomed to things, isn't it?"

"Yes," I answered bitterly.

"You know, those rough miners are good to me. I'm a queen among them, because they know I'm—all right. I've had several offers of marriage, too, really, really good ones from wealthy claim-owners."

"Yes," still more bitterly.

"Yes, young man; so you want to make a strike and take me away to Italy. Oh, how I plan and plan for us two. I don't care, my dearest, if you haven't got a cent in the world, I'm yours, always yours."

"That's all right, Berna," I said. "I'm going to make good. I've just lost a fifty-thousand dollar claim, but there's more coming up. By the first of June next I'll come to you with a bank account of six figures. You'll see, my little girl. I'm going to make this thing stick."

"You foolish boy," she said; "it doesn't matter if you come to me a beggar in rags. Come to me anyway. Come, and do not fail."

"What about Locasto?" I asked.

"I've scarcely seen anything of him. He leaves me alone. I think he's interested elsewhere."

"And are you sure you're all right, dear, down there?"

"Quite sure. These men would risk their lives for me. The other kind know enough to leave me alone. Besides, I know better now how to take care of myself. You remember the frightened cry-baby I used to be—well, I've learned to hold my own."

She was extraordinarily affectionate, full of unexpected little ways of endearment, and clung to me when we parted, making me promise to return very soon. Yes, she was my girl, devoted to me, attached to me by every tendril of her being. Every look, every word, every act of her expressed a bright, fine, radiant love. I was satisfied, yet unsatisfied, and once again I entreated her.

"Berna, are you sure, quite sure, you're all right in that place among all that folly and drunkenness and vice? Let me take you away, dear."

"Oh, no," she said very tenderly; "I'm all right. I would tell you at once, my boy, if I had any fear. That's just what a poor girl has to put up with all the time; that's what I've had to put up with all my life. Believe me, boy, I'm wonderfully blind and deaf at times. I don't think I'm very bad, am I?"

"You're as good as gold."

"For your sake I'll always try to be," she answered.

As we were kissing good-bye she asked timidly:

"What about the rouge, dear? Shall I cease to use it?"

"Poor little girl! Oh no, I don't suppose it matters. I've got very old-fashioned ideas. Good-bye, darling."

"Good-bye, beloved."

I went away treading on sunshine, trembling with joy, thrilled with love for her, blessing her anew.

Yet still the rouge stuck in my crop as if it were the symbol of some insidious decadence.

* * * * *

CHAPTER XV

It was about two months later when I returned from a flying visit to Dawson.

"Lots of mail for you two," I cried, exultantly bursting into the cabin.

"Mail? Hooray!"

Jim and the Prodigal, who were lying on their bunks, leapt up eagerly. No one longs for his letters like your Northern exile, and for two whole months we had not heard from the outside.

"Yes, I got over fifty letters between us three. Drew about a dozen myself, there's half a dozen for you, Jim, and the balance for you, old sport."

I handed the Prodigal about two dozen letters.

"Ha! now we'll have the whole evening just to browse on them. My, what a stack! How was it you had a time getting them?"

"Well, you see, when I got into town the mail had just been sorted, and there was a string of over three hundred men waiting at the general delivery wicket. I took my place at the tail-end of the line, and every newcomer fell in behind me. My! but it was such weary waiting, moving up step by step; but I'd just about got there when closing-time came. They wouldn't give out any more mail—after my three hours' wait, too."

"What did you do?"

"Well, it seems every one gives way to the womenfolk. So I happened to see a girl friend of mine, and she said she would go round first thing in the morning and enquire if there were any letters for us. She brought me this bunch."

I indicated the pile of letters.

"I'm told lots of women in town make a business of getting letters for men, and charge a dollar a letter. It's awful how hard it is to get mail. Half of the clerks seem scarcely able to read the addresses on the envelopes. It's positively sad to watch the faces of the poor wretches who get nothing, knowing, too, that the chances are there is really something for them sorted away in a wrong box."

"That's pretty tough."

"Yes, you should have seen them; men just ravenous to hear from their families; a clerk carelessly shuffling through a pile of letters. 'Beachwood, did you say? Nope, nothing for you.' 'Hold on there! what's that in your hand? Surely I know my wife's writing.' 'Beachwood—yep, that's right. Looked like Peachwood to me. All right. Next there.' Then the man would go off with his letter, looking half-wrathful, half-radiant. Well, I enjoyed my trip, but I'm glad I'm home."

I threw myself on my bunk voluptuously, and began re-reading my letters. There were some from Garry and some from Mother. While still unreconciled to the life I was leading, they were greatly interested in my wildly cheerful accounts of the country. They were disposed to be less censorious, and I for my part was only too glad Mother was well enough to write, even if she did scold me sometimes. So I was able to open my mail without misgivings.

But I was still aglow with memories of the last few hours. Once more I had seen Berna, spent moments with her of perfect bliss, left her with my mind full of exaltation and bewildered gratitude. She was the perfect answer to my heart's call, a mirror that seemed to flash back the challenge of my joy. I saw the love mists gather in her eyes, I felt her sweet lips mould themselves to mine, I thrilled with the sheathing ardour of her arms. Never in my fondest imaginings had I conceived that such a wealth of affection would ever be for me. Buoyant she was, brave, inspiring, and always with her buoyancy so wondrous tender I felt that willingly would I die for her.

Once again I told her of my fear, my anxiety for her safety among those rough men in that cesspool of iniquity. Very earnestly she strove to reassure me.

"Oh, my dear, it is in those rough men, the uncouth, big-hearted miners, that I place my trust. They know I'm a good girl. They wouldn't say a coarse thing before me for the world. You've no idea the chivalrous respect they show for me, and the rougher they are the finer their instincts seem to be. It's the others, the so-called gentlemen, who would like to take advantage of me if they could."

She looked at me with bright, clear eyes, fearless in their scorn of sham and pretence.

"Then there are the women. It's strange, but no matter how degraded they are they try to shield and protect me. Only last week Kimona Kate made a fearful scene with her escort because he said something bad before me. I'm getting tolerant. Oh, you've no idea until you know them what good qualities some of these women have. Often their hearts are as big as all outdoors; they would nurse you devotedly if you were sick; they would give you their last dollar if you were in want. Many of them have old mothers and little children they're supporting outside, and they would rather die than that their dear ones should know the life they are living. It's the men, the men that are to blame."

I shook my head sadly.

"I don't like it, Berna, I don't like it at all. I hate you to know the like of such people, such things. I just want you to be again the dear, sweet little girl I first knew, all maidenly modesty and shuddering aversion of evil."

"I'm afraid, dear, I shall never be that again," she said sorrowfully; "but am I any the worse for knowing? Why should you men want to keep all such knowledge to yourselves? Is our innocence simply to be another name for ignorance?"

She put her arms round my neck and kissed me fervently.

"Oh, no, my dear, my dear. I have seen the vileness of things, and it only makes me more in love with love and beauty. We'll go, you and I, to Italy very soon, and forget, forget. Even if we have to toil like peasants in the vineyards we'll go, far, far away."

So I felt strengthened, stimulated, gladdened, and, as I lay on my bunk listening to the merry crackle of the wood fire, I was in a purring lethargy of content. Then I remembered something.

"Oh, say, boys, I forgot to tell you. I met McCrimmon down the creek. You remember him on the trail, the Halfbreed. He was asking after you both; then all at once he said he wanted to see us on important business. He has a proposal to make, he says, that would be greatly to our advantage. He's coming along this evening.—What's the matter, Jim?"

Jim was staring blankly at one of the letters he had received. His face was a picture of distress, misery, despair. Without replying, he went and knelt down by his bed. He sighed deeply. Slowly his face grew calm again; then I saw that he was praying. We were silent in respectful sympathy, but when, in a little, he got up and went out, I followed him.

"Had bad news, old man?"

"I've had a letter that's upset me. I'm in a terrible position. If ever I wanted strength and guidance, I want it now."

"Heard about that man?"

"Yes, it's him, all right; it's Mosher. I suspicioned it all along. Here's a letter from my brother. He says there's no doubt that Mosher is Moseley."

His eyes were stormy, his face tragic in its bitterness.

"Oh, you don't know how I worshipped that woman, trusted her, would have banked my life on her; and when I was away making money for her she ups and goes away with that slimy reptile. In the old days I would have torn him to pieces, but now—"

He sighed distractedly.

"What am I to do? What am I to do? The Good Book says forgive your enemies, but how can I forgive a wrong like that? And my poor girl—he deserted her, drove her to the streets. Ugh! if I could kill him by slow torture, gloat over his agony—but I can't, can I?"

"No, Jim, you can't do anything. Vengeance is the Lord's."

"Yes, I know, I know. But it's hard, it's hard. O my girl, my girl!"

Tears overran his cheeks. He sat down on a log, burying his face in his hands.

"O God, help and sustain me in this my hour of need."

I was at a loss how to comfort him, and it was while I was waiting there that suddenly we saw the Halfbreed coming up the trail.

"Better come in, Jim," I said, "and hear what he's got to say."

* * * * *

CHAPTER XVI

We made McCrimmon comfortable. We kept no whisky in the cabin, but we gave him some hot coffee, which he drank with great satisfaction. Then he twisted a cigarette, lit it, and looked at us keenly. On his brown, flattish face were remarkable the impassivity of the Indian and the astuteness of the Scot. We were regarding him curiously. Jim had regained his calm, and was quietly watchful. The Prodigal seemed to have his ears cocked to listen. There was a feeling amongst us as if we had reached a crisis in our fortunes.

The Halfbreed lost no time in coming to the point.

"I like you boys. You're square and above-board. You're workers, and you don't drink—that's the main thing.

"Well, to get right down to cases. I'm a bit of a mining man. I've mined at Cassiar and Caribou, and I know something of the business. Now I've got next to a good thing.—I don't know how good yet, but I'll swear to you it's a tidy bit. There may be only ten thousand in it, and there may be one hundred and ten. It's a gambling proposition, and I want pardners, pardners that'll work like blazes and keep their faces shut. Are you on?"

"That's got us kodaked," said the Prodigal. "We're that sort, and if the proposition looks good to us we're with you. Anyway, we're clams at keeping our food-traps tight."

"All right; listen. You know the Arctic Transportation Co. have claims on upper Bonanza—well, a month back I was working for them. We were down about twenty feet and were drifting in. They set me to work in the drift. The roof kept sloughing in on me, and it was mighty dangerous. So far we hadn't got pay-dirt, but their mining manager wanted us to drift in a little further. If we didn't strike good pay in a few more feet we were to quit.

"Well, one morning I went down and cleaned away the ash of my fire. The first stroke of my pick on the thawed face made me jump, stare, stand stock-still, thinking hard. For there, right in the hole I had made, was the richest pocket I ever seen."

"You don't say! Are you sure?"

"Why, boys, as I'm alive there was nuggets in it as thick as raisins in a Christmas plum-duff. I could see the yellow gleam where the pick had grazed them, and the longer I looked the more could I see."

"Good Lord! What did you do?"

"What did I do! I just stepped back and picked at the roof for all I was worth. A big bunch of muck came down, covering up the face. Then, like a crazy man, I picked wherever the dirt seemed loose all the way down the drift. Great heaps of dirt caved in on me. I was stunned, nearly buried, but I did the trick. There were tons of dirt between me and my find."

We gasped with amazement.

"The rest was easy. I went up the shaft groaning and cursing. I pretended to faint. I told them the roof of the drift had fallen in on me. It was rotten stuff, anyway, and they knew it. They didn't mind me risking my life. I cursed them, said I would sue the Company, and went off looking too sore for words. The Manager was disgusted, he went down and took a look at things; declared he would throw up the work at that place; the ground was no good. He made that report to the Company."

The Halfbreed looked round triumphantly.

"Now, here's the point. We can get a lay on that ground. One of you boys must apply for it. They mustn't know I'm in with you, or they would suspect right away. They're none too scrupulous themselves in their dealings."

He paused impressively.

"You cinch that lay agreement. Get it signed right away. We'll go in and work like Old Nick. We'll make a big clean-up by Spring. I'll take you right to the gold. There's thousands and thousands lying snug in the ground just waiting for us. It's right in our mit. Oh, it's a cinch, a cinch!"

The Halfbreed almost grew excited. Bending forward, he eyed us keenly. In a breathless silence we stared at each other.

"Well," I objected, "seems to be putting up rather a job on the Company."

Jim was silent, but the Prodigal cut in sharply:

"Job nothing—it's a square proposition. We don't know for certain that gold's there. Maybe it's only a piffling pocket, and we'll get souped for our pains. No, it seems to me it's a fair gambling proposition. We're taking all kinds of chances. It means awful hard work; it means privation and, maybe, bitter disappointment. It's a gamble, I tell you, and are we going to be such poor sports as turn it down? I for one am strongly in favour of it. What do you say? A big sporting chance—are you there, boys, are you there?"

He almost shouted in his excitement.

"Hush! Some one might hear you," warned the Halfbreed.

"Yes, that's right. Well, it looks mighty good to me, and if you boys are willing we'll just draw up papers and sign an agreement right away. Is it a go?"

We nodded, so he got ink and paper and drew up a form of partnership.

"Now," said he, his eyes dancing, "now, to secure that lay before any one else cuts in on us. Gee! but it's getting dark and cold outdoors these days. Snow falling; well, I must mush to Dawson to-night."

He hurried on some warm, yet light, clothing, all the time talking excitedly of the chance that fortune had thrown in our way, and gleeful as a schoolboy.

"Now, boys," he says, "hope I'll have good luck. Jim, put in a prayer for me. Well, see you all to-morrow. Good-bye."

* * * * *

It was late next night when he returned. We were sitting in the cabin, anxious and expectant, when he threw open the door. He was tired, wet, dirty, but irrepressibly jubilant.

"Hurrah, boys!" he cried. "I've cinched it. I saw Mister Manager of the big Company. He was very busy, very important, very patronising. I was the poor miner seeking a lay. I played the part well. He began by telling me he didn't want to give any lays at present; just wanted to stand me off, you know; make me more keen. I spoke about some of their ground on Hunker. He didn't seem enthusiastic. Then, at last, as if in despair, I mentioned this bit on Bonanza. I could see he was itching to let me have it, but he was too foxy to show it. He actually told me it was an extra rich piece of ground, when all the time he knew his own mining engineer had condemned it."

The Prodigal's eyes danced delightedly.

"Well, we sparred round a bit like two fake fighters. My! but he was wily, that old Jew. Finally he agreed to let me have it on a fifty-per-cent. basis. Don't faint, boys. Fifty per cent., I said. I'm sorry. It was the best I could do, and you know I'm not slow. That means they get half of all we take out. Oh, the old shark! the robber! I tried to beat him down, but he stood pat; wouldn't budge. So I gave in, and we signed the lay agreement, and now everything's in shape. Gee whiz! didn't I give a sigh of relief when I got outside! He thinks I'm the fall guy, and went off chuckling."

He raised his voice triumphantly.

"And now, boys, we've got the ground cinched, so get action on yourselves. Here's where we make our first real stab at fortune. Here's where we even up on the hard jabs she's handed us in the past; here's where we score a bull's-eye, or I miss my guess. The gold's there, boys, you can bank on that; and the harder we work the more we're going to get of it. Now, we're going to work hard. We're going to make ordinary hard work look like a Summer vacation. We're going to work for all we're worth—and then some. Are you there, boys, are you there?"

"We are," we shouted with one accord.

* * * * *

CHAPTER XVII

There was no time to lose. Every hour for us meant so much more of that precious pay-dirt that lay under the frozen surface. The Winter leapt on us with a swoop, a harsh, unconciliating Winter, that made out-door work an unmitigated hardship. But there was the hope of fortune nerving and bracing us, till we lost in it all thought of self. Nothing short of desperate sickness, death even, would drive us from our posts. It was with this dauntless spirit we entered on the task before us.

And, indeed, it was one that called for all in a man of energy and self-sacrifice. There was wood to get for the thawing of the ground; there was a cabin to be built on the claim; and, lastly, there was a vast dump to be taken out of the ground for the spring sluicing. We planned things so that no man would be idle for a moment, and so that every ounce of strength expended would show its result.

The Halfbreed took charge, and we, recognising it as his show, obeyed him implicitly. He decided to put down two holes to bed-rock, and, after much deliberation, selected the places. This was a matter for the greatest judgment and experience, and we were satisfied that he had both.

We ran up a little cabin and banked it nearly to the low eaves with snow. By-and-bye more fell on the roof to the depth of three feet, so that the place seemed like a huge white hummock. Only in front could you recognise it as a cabin by the low doorway, where we had always to stoop on entering. Within were our bunks, a tiny stove, a few boxes to sit on, a few dishes, our grub; that was all. Often we regretted our big cabin on the hill, with its calico-lined "den" and its separate kitchen. But in this little box of a home we were to put in many weary months.

Not that the time seemed long to us; we were too busy for that. Indeed, often we wished it were twice as long. Snow had fallen in September, and by December we were in an Arctic world of uncompromising harshness. Day after day the glass stood between forty and fifty below zero. It was hatefully, dangerously cold. It seemed as if the frost-fiend had a cruel grudge against us. It made us grim—and careful. We didn't talk much in those days. We just worked, worked, worked, and when we did talk it was of our work, our ceaseless work.

Would we strike it rich? It was all a gamble, the most exciting gamble in the world. It thrilled our day hours with excitement; it haunted our sleep; it lent strength to the pick-stroke and vigour to the windlass-crank. It made us forget the bitter cold, till some one would exclaim, and gently knead the fresh snow on our faces. The cold burned our cheeks a fierce brick-red, and a frostbite showed on them like a patch of white putty. The old scars, never healing, were like blotches of lamp-black.

But neither cold nor fatigue could keep us away from the shaft and the drift. We had gone down to bed-rock, and were tunnelling in to meet the hole the Halfbreed had covered up. So far we had found nothing. Every day we panned samples of the dirt, always getting colours, sometimes a fifty-cent pan, but never what we dreamed of, hoped for.

"Wait, boys, till we get a two-hundred-dollar pan, then we'll begin to whoop it up some."

Once the Company Manager came down on a dog-team. He looked over our shaft. He wore a coon coat, with a cap of beaver, and huge fur mits hung by a cord around his neck. He was massive and impassive. Spiky icicles bristled around his mouth.

"What luck, boys?" His breath came like steam.

"None, so far," we told him, wearily, and off he went into the frozen gloom, saying he hoped we would strike it before long.

"Wait a while."

We were working two men to a shaft, burning our ground over night. The Prodigal and I manned the windlasses, while the old miners went down the drifts. It was a cold, cold job standing there on that rugged platform turning the windlass-crank. Long before it was fairly light we got to our posts, and lowered our men into the hole. The air was warmer down there; but the work was harder, more difficult, more dangerous.

At noon there was no sunshine, only a wan, ashen light that suffused the sky. A deathlike stillness lay on the valley, not a quiver or movement in leaf or blade. The snow was a shroud, smooth save where the funeral pines pricked through. In that intensity of cold, that shivering agony of desolation, it seemed as if nature was laughing at us—the Cosmic Laugh.

Our meals were hurriedly cooked and bolted. We grudged every moment of our respite from toil. At night we often were far too weary to undress. We lost our regard for cleanliness; we neglected ourselves. Always we talked of the result of the day's panning and the chances of to-morrow. Surely we would strike it soon.

"Wait awhile."

Colder it grew and colder. Our kerosene flowed like mush. The water froze solid in our kettle. Our bread was full of icy particles. Everything had to be thawed out continually. It was tiresome, exasperating, when we were in such a devil of a hurry. It kept us back; it angered us, this pest of a cold. Our tempers began to suffer. We were short, taciturn. The strain was beginning to tell on us.

"Wait awhile."

Then, one afternoon, the Something happened. It was Jim who was the chosen one. About three o'clock he signalled to be hoisted up, and when he appeared he was carrying a pan of dirt. "Call the others," he said.

All together in the little cabin we stood round, while Jim washed out the pan in snow-water melt over our stove. I will never forget how eagerly we watched the gravel, and the whirling, dexterous movements of the old man. We could see gleams of yellow in the muddy water. Thrills of joy and hope went through us. We had got the thing, the big thing, at last.

"Hurry, Jim," I said, "or I'll die of suspense."

Patiently he went on. There it was at last in the bottom of the pan—sweeter to our eyes than to a woman the sight of her firstborn. There it lay, glittering, gleaming gold, fine gold, coarse gold, nuggety gold.

"Now, boys, you can whoop it up," said Jim quietly; "for there's many and many a pan like it down there in the drift."

But never a whoop. What was the matter with us? When the fortune we had longed for so eagerly came at last, we did not greet it even with a cheer. Oh, we were painfully silent.

Solemnly we shook hands all round.

* * * * *

CHAPTER XVIII

"Now to weigh it," said the Prodigal.

On the tiny pair of scales we turned it out—ninety-five dollars' worth.

Well, it was a good start, and we were all possessed with a frantic eagerness to go down in the drift. I crawled along the tunnel. There, in the face of it, I could see the gold shining, and the longer I looked the more I seemed to see. It was rich, rich. I picked out and burnished a nugget as large as a filbert. There were lots of others like it. It was a strike. The question was: how much was there of it? The Halfbreed soon settled our doubts on that score.

"It stands to reason the pay runs between where I first found it and where we've struck it now. That alone means a tidy stake for each of us. Say, boys, if you were to cover all that distance with twenty-dollar gold pieces six feet wide, and packed edge to edge, I wouldn't take them for our interest in that bit of ground. I see a fine big ranch in Manitoba for my share; ay, and hired help to run it. The only thing that sticks in my gullet is that fifty per cent. to the Company."

"Well, we can't kick," I said; "we'd never have got the lay if they'd had a hunch. My! won't they be sore?"

Sure enough, in a few days the news leaked out, and the Manager came post-haste.

"Hear you've struck it rich, boys."

"So rich that I guess we'll have to pack down gravel from the benches to mix in before we can sluice it," said the Prodigal.

"You don't say. Well, I'll have to have a man on the ground to look after our interests."

"All right. It means a good thing for you."

"Yes, but it would have meant a better if we had worked it ourselves. However, you boys deserve your luck. Hello, the devil—"

He turned round and saw the Halfbreed. He gave a long whistle and went away, looking pensive.

* * * * *

It was the night of the discovery when the Prodigal made us an address.

"Look here, boys; do you know what this means? It means victory; it means freedom, happiness, the things we want, the life we love. To me it means travel, New York, Paris, evening dress, the opera. To McCrimmon here it means his farm. To each according to his notion, it means the 'Things That Matter.'

"Now, we've just begun. The hardest part is to come, is to get out the fortune that's right under our feet. We're going to get every cent of it, boys. There's a little over three months to do it in, leaving about a month to make sluice-boxes and clean up the dirt. We've got to work like men at a burning barn. We've worked hard, but we've got to go some yet. For my part, I'm willing to do stunts that will make my previous record look like a plugged dime. I guess you boys all feel the same way."

"You bet we do."

"Well, nuf sed; let's get busy."

So, once more, with redoubled energy, we resumed our tense, unremitting round of toil. Now, however, it was vastly different. Every bucket of dirt meant money in our pockets, every stroke of the pick a dollar. Not that it was all like the first rich pocket we had struck. It proved a most erratic and puzzling paystreak—one day rich beyond our dreams, another too poor to pay for the panning. We swung on a pendulum of hope and despair. Perhaps this made it all the more exciting, and stimulated us unnaturally, and always we cursed that primitive method of mining that made every bucket of dirt the net result of infinite labor.

Every day our two dumps increased in size (for we had struck pay on the other shaft), and every day our assurance and elation increased correspondingly. It was bruited around that we had one of the richest bits of ground in the country, and many came to gaze at us. It used to lighten my labours at the windlass to see their looks of envy and to hear their awe-stricken remarks.

"That's one of them," they would say; "one of the lucky four, the lucky laymen."

So, as the facts, grossly exaggerated, got noised abroad, they came to call us the "Lucky Laymen."

Looking back, there will always seem to me something weird and incomprehensible in those twilight days, an unreality, a vagueness like some dreary, feverish dream. For three months I did not see my face in a mirror. Not that I wanted to, but I mention this just to show how little we thought of ourselves.

In like manner, never did I have a moment's time to regard my inner self in the mirror of consciousness. No mental analysis now; no long hours of retrospection, no tête-à-tête interviews with my soul. At times I felt as if I had lost my identity. I was a slave of the genie Gold, releasing it from its prison in the frozen bowels of the earth. I was an automaton turning a crank in the frozen stillness of the long, long night.

It was a life despotically objective, and now, as I look back, it seems as if I had never lived it at all. I seem to look down a long, dark funnel and see a little machine-man bearing my semblance, patiently, steadily, wearily turning the handle of a windlass in the clear, lancinating cold of those sombre, silent days.

I say "bearing my outward semblance," and yet I sometimes wonder if that rough-bearded figure in heavy woollen clothes looked the least like me. I wore heavy sweaters, mackinaw trousers, thick German socks and moccasins. From frequent freezing my cheeks were corroded. I was miserably thin, and my eyes had a wild, staring expression through the pupils dilating in the long darkness. Yes, mentally and physically I was no more like myself than a convict enduring out his life in the soulless routine of a prison.

The days were lengthening marvellously. We noted the fact with dull joy. It meant more light, more time, more dirt in the dump. So it came about that, from ten hours of toil, we went to twelve, to fourteen; then, latterly, to sixteen, and the tension of it was wearing us down to skin and bone.

We were all feeling wretched, overstrained, ill-nourished, and it was only voicing the general sentiment when, one day, the Prodigal remarked:

"I guess I'll have to let up for a couple of days. My teeth are all on the bum. I'm going to town to see a dentist."

"Let me look at them," said the Halfbreed.

He looked. The gums were sullen, unwholesome-looking.

"Why, it's a touch of scurvy, lad; a little while, and you'd be spitting out your teeth like orange pips; your legs would turn black, and when you squeezed your fingers into the flesh the hole would stay. You'd get rotten, then you'd mortify and die. But it's the easiest thing in the world to cure. Nothing responds to treatment so readily."

He made a huge brew of green-spruce tea, of which we all partook, and in a few days the Prodigal was fit again.

It was mid-March when we finished working out our ground. We had done well, not so well, perhaps, as we had hoped for, but still magnificently well. Never had men worked harder, never fought more desperately for success. There were our two dumps, pyramids of gold-permeated dirt at whose value we could only guess. We had wrested our treasure from the icy grip of the eternal frost. Now it remained—and O, the sweetness of it—to glean the harvest of our toil.

* * * * *

CHAPTER XIX

"The water's beginning to run, boys," said the Halfbreed. "A few more days and we'll be able to start sluicing."

The news was like a flood of sunshine to us. For days we had been fixing up the boxes and getting everything in readiness. The sun beat strongly on the snow, which almost visibly seemed to retreat before it. The dazzlingly white surface was crisp and flaky, and around the tree boles curving hollows had formed. Here and there brown earth peered nakedly through. Every day the hillside runnels grew in strength.

We were working at the mouth of a creek down which ran a copious little stream all through the Springtime. We tapped it some distance above us, and ran part of it along our line of sluice-boxes. These boxes went between our two dumps, so that it was easy to shovel in from both sides. Nothing could have been more convenient.

At last, after a day of hot sunshine, we found quite a freshet of water coming down the boxes, leaping and dancing in the morning light. I remember how I threw in the first shovelful of dirt, and how good it was to see the bright stream discolour as our friend the water began his magic work. For three days we shovelled in, and on the fourth we made a clean-up.

"I guess it's time," said Jim, "or those riffles will be gettin' choked up."

And, sure enough, when we ran off the water there were some of them almost full of the yellow metal, wet and shiny, gloriously agleam in the morning light.

"There's ten thousand dollars if there's an ounce," said the Company's man, and the weigh-up proved he was right. So the gold was packed in two long buckskin pokes and sent into town to be deposited in the bank.

Day after day we went on shovelling in, and about twice a week we made a clean-up. The month of May was half over when we had only a third of our dirt run through the boxes. We were terribly afraid of the water failing us, and worked harder than ever. Indeed, it was difficult to tell when to leave off. The nights were never dark now; the daylight was over twenty hours in duration. The sun described an ellipse, rising a little east of north and setting a little west of north. We shovelled in till we were too exhausted to lift another ounce. Then we lay down in our clothes and slept as soon as we touched the pillow.

"There's eighty thousand to our credit in the bank, and only a third of our dump's gone. Hooray, boys!" said the Prodigal.

About one o'clock in the morning the birds began to sing, and the sunset glow had not faded from the sky ere the sunrise quickened it with life once more. Who that has lived in the North will ever forget the charm, the witchery of those midnight skies, where the fires of the sun are banked and never cold? Surely, long after all else is forgotten, will linger the memory of those mystic nights with all their haunting spell of weird, disconsolate solitude.

One afternoon I was working on the dump, intent on shovelling in as much dirt as possible before supper, when, on looking up, who should greet me but Locasto. Since our last interview in town I had not seen him, and, somehow, this sudden sight of him came as a kind of a shock. Yet the manner of the man as he approached me was hearty in the extreme. He held out his great hand to me, and, as I had no desire to antagonise him, I gave him my own.

He was riding. His big, handsome face was bronzed, his black eyes clear and sparkling, his white teeth gleamed like mammoth ivory. He certainly was a dashing, dominant figure of a man, and, in spite of myself, I admired him.

His manner in his salutation was cordial, even winning.

"I've just been visiting some of my creek properties," he said. "I heard you fellows had made a good strike, and I thought I'd come down and congratulate you. It is pretty good, isn't it?"

"Yes," I said; "not quite so good as we expected, but we'll all have a tidy sum."

"I'm glad. Well, I suppose you'll go outside this Fall."

"No, I think I'll stay in. You see, we've the Gold Hill property, which looks promising; and then we have two claims on Ophir."

"Oh, Ophir! I don't think you'll ever take a fortune out of Ophir. I bought a claim there the other day. The man pestered me, so I gave him five thousand for it, just to get rid of him. It's eight below."

"Why," I said, "that's the claim I staked and got beaten out of."

"You don't say so. Well, now, that's too bad. I bought it from a man named Spankiller; his brother's a clerk in the gold office. Tell you what I'll do. I'll let you have it for the five thousand I gave for it."

"No," I answered, "I don't think I want it now."

"All right; think it over, anyway. If you should change your mind, let me know. Well, I must go. I've got to get into town to-night. That's my mule-train back there on the trail. I've got pretty nearly ten thousand ounces over there."

I looked and saw the mules with the gold-packs slung over their backs. There were four men to guard them, and it seemed to me that in one of these men I recognised the little wizened figure of the Worm.

I shivered.

"Yes, I've done pretty well," he continued; "but it don't make any difference. I spend it as fast as I get it. A month ago I didn't have enough ready cash to pay my cigar bill, yet I could have gone to the bank and borrowed a hundred thousand. It was there in the dump. Oh, it's a rum business this mining. Well, good-bye."

He was turning to go when, suddenly, he stopped.

"Oh, by the way, I saw a friend of yours before I left. No need to mention names, you lucky dog. When's the big thing coming off? Well, I must congratulate you again. She looks sweeter than ever. By-by."

He was off, leaving a very sinister impression on my mind. In his parting smile there was a trace of mockery that gravely disquieted me. I had thought much of Berna during the past few months, but as the gold fever took hold of me I put her more and more from my mind. I told myself that all this struggle was for her. In the thought that she was safe I calmed all anxious fear. Sometimes by not thinking so much of dear ones, one can be more thoughtful of them. So it was with me. I knew that all my concentration of effort was for her sake, and would bring her nearer to me. Yet at Locasto's words all my old longing and heartache vehemently resurged.

In spite of myself, I was the prey of a growing uneasiness. Things seemed vastly different, now success had come to me. I could not bear to think of her working in that ambiguous restaurant, rubbing shoulders with its unspeakable habitués. I wondered how I had ever deceived myself into thinking it was all right. I began to worry, so that I knew only a trip into Dawson would satisfy me. Accordingly, I hired a big Swede to take my place at the shovel, and set out once more on the hillside trail for town.

* * * * *

CHAPTER XX

I found the town more animated than ever, the streets more populous, the gaiety more unrestrained. Everywhere were flaunting signs of a plethoric wealth. The anxious Cheechako had vanished from the scene, and the victorious miner masqueraded in his place. He swaggered along in the glow of the Spring sunshine, a picture of perfect manhood, bronzed and lean and muscular. He was brimming over with the exuberance of health. He had come into town to "live" things, to transmute this yellow dust into happiness, to taste the wine of life, to know the lips of flame.

It was the day of the Man with the Poke. He was King. The sheer animalism of him overflowed in midnight roysterings, in bacchanalian revels, in debauches among the human débris of the tenderloin.

Every one was waiting for him, to fleece him, rob him, strip him. It was also the day of the man behind the bar, of the gambler, of the harpy.

My strange, formless fears for Berna were soon set at rest. She was awaiting me. She looked better than I had ever seen her, and she welcomed me with an eager delight that kindled me to rapture.

"Just think of it," she said, "only two weeks, and we'll be together for always. It seems too good to be true. Oh, my dear, how can I ever love you enough? How happy we are going to be, aren't we?"

"We're going to be happier than any two people ever were before," I assured her.

We crossed the Yukon to the green glades of North Dawson, and there, on a little rise, we sat down, side by side. How I wish I could put into words the joy that filled my heart! Never was lad so happy as I. I spoke but little, for love's silences are sweeter than all words. Well, well I mind me how she looked: just like a picture, her hands clasped on her lap, her eyes star-bright, angel-sweet, mother-tender. From time to time she would give me a glance so full of trust and love that my heart would leap to her, and wave on wave of passionate tenderness come sweeping over me.

It may be there was something humble in my stintless adoration; it may be I was like a child for the pleasure of her nearness; it may be my eyes told all too well of the fire that burned within me, but O, the girl was kind, gentler than forgiveness, sweeter than all heaven. Caressingly she touched my hair. I kissed her fingers, kissed them again and again; and then she lifted my hand to her lips, and I felt her kiss fall upon it. How wondrously I tingled at the touch. My hand seemed mine no longer—a consecrated thing. Proud, happy me!

"Yes," she went on, "doesn't it seem as if we were dreaming? You know, I always thought it was a dream, and now it's coming true. You'll take me away from this place, won't you, boy?—far, far away. I'll tell you now, dear, I've borne it all for your sake, but I don't think I could bear it any longer. I would rather die than sink in the mire, and yet you can't imagine how this life affects one. It's sad, sad, but I don't get shocked at things in the way I used to. You know, I sometimes think a girl, no matter how good, sweet, modest to begin with, placed in such surroundings could fall gradually."

I agreed with her. Too well I knew I was becoming calloused to the evils around me. Such was the insidious corruption of the gold-camp, I now regarded with indifference things that a year ago I would have shrunk from with disgust.

"Well, it will be all over very soon, won't it, dear? I don't know what I'd have done if it hadn't been for the rough miners. They've been so kind to me. When they saw I was straight and honest they couldn't be good enough. They shielded me in every way, and kept back the other kind of men. Even the women have been my friends and helped me."

She looked at me archly.

"And, you know, I've had ever so many offers of marriage, too, from honest, rough, kindly men—and I've refused them ever so gracefully."

"Has Locasto ever made any more overtures?"

Her face grew grave.

"Yes, about a month ago he besieged me, gave me no rest, made all kinds of proposals and promises. He wanted to divorce his 'outside' wife and marry me. He wanted to settle a hundred thousand dollars on me. He tried everything in his power to force me to his will. Then, when he saw it was no use, he turned round and begged me to let him be my friend. He spoke so nicely of you. He said he would help us in any way he could. He's everything that's kind to me now. He can't do enough for me. Yet, somehow, I don't trust him."

"Well, my precious," I assured her, "all danger, doubt, despair, will soon be over. Locasto and the rest of them will be as shadows, never to haunt my little girl again. The Great, Black North will fade away, will dissolve into the land of sunshine and flowers and song. You will forget it."

"The Great Black North.—I will never forget it, and I will always bless it. It has given me my love, the best love in all the world."

"O my darling, my Life, I'll take you away from it all soon, soon. We'll go to my home, to Garry, to Mother. They will love you as I love you."

"I'm sure I will love them. What you have told me of them makes them seem very real to me. Will you not be ashamed of me?"

"I will be proud, proud of you, my girl."

Ah, would I not! I looked at that flower-like face the sunshine glorified so, the pretty, bright hair falling away from her low brow in little waves, the lily throat, the delicately patrician features, the proud poise of her head. Who would not have been proud of her? She awoke all that was divine in me. I looked as one might look on a vision, scarce able to believe it real.

Suddenly she pointed excitedly.

"Look, dear, look at the rainbow. Isn't it wonderful? Isn't it beautiful?"

I gazed in rapt admiration. Across the river a shower had fallen, and the clouds, clearing away abruptly, had left there a twin rainbow of matchless perfection. Its double arch was poised as accurately over the town as if it had been painted there. Each hoop was flawless in form, lovely in hue, tenderly luminous, exquisite in purity. Never had I seen the double iris so immaculate in colouring, and, with its bases resting on the river, it curved over the gold-born city like a frame of ethereal beauty.

"Does it not seem, dear, like an answer to our prayer, an omen of good hope, a promise for the future?"

"Yes, beloved, our future, yours and mine. The clouds are rolling away. All is bright with sunshine once again, and God sends His rainbow to cheer and comfort us. It will not be long now. On the first day of June, beloved, I will come to you, and we will be made man and wife. You will be waiting for me, will you not?"

"Yes, yes, waiting ever so eagerly, my lover, counting every hour, every minute."

I kissed her passionately, and we held each other tightly for a moment. I saw come into her eyes that look which comes but once into the eyes of a maid, that look of ineffable self-surrender, of passionate abandonment. Life is niggard of such moments, yet can our lives be summed up in them.

She rested her head on my shoulder; her lips lay on mine, and they moved faintly.

"Yes, lover, yes, the first of June. Don't fail me, honey, don't fail me."

We parted, buoyant with hope, in an ecstasy of joy. She was for me, this beautiful, tender girl, for me. And the time was nigh when she should be mine, mine to adore until the end. Always would she be by my side; daily could I plot and plan to give her pleasure; every hour by word and look and act could I lavish on her the exhaustless measure of my love. Ah! life would be too short for me. Could aught in this petty purblind existence of ours redeem it and exalt it so: her love, this pure sweet girl's, and mine. Let nations grapple, let Mammon triumph, let pestilence o'erwhelm; what matter, we love, we love. O proud, happy me!

* * * * *

I got back to the claim. Everything was going merrily, but I felt little desire to resume my toil. I was strangely wearied, worn out somehow. Yet I took up my shovel again with a body that rebelled in every tissue. Never had I felt like this before. Something was wrong with me. I was weak. At night I sweated greatly. I cared not to eat.

* * * * *

"Well," said the Prodigal, "it's all over but the shouting. From my calculations we've cleaned up two hundred and six thousand dollars. That's a hundred and three between us four. It's cost us about three to get out the stuff; so there will be, roughly speaking, about twenty-five thousand for each of us."

How jubilant every one was looking—every one but me. Somehow I felt as if money didn't matter just then, for I was sick, sick.

"Why, what's the matter?" said the Prodigal, staring at me curiously. "You look like a ghost."

"I feel like one, too," I answered. "I'm afraid I'm in for a bad spell. I want to lie down awhile, boys . . . I'm tired . . . The first of June, I've got a date on the first of June. I must keep it, I must . . . Don't let me sleep too long, boys. I mustn't fail. It's a matter of life and death. The first of June . . ."

Alas, on the first of June I lay in the hospital, raving and tossing in the clutches of typhoid fever.

* * * * *

CHAPTER XXI

I was lying in bed, and a heavy weight was pressing on me, so that, in spite of my struggles, I could not move. I was hot, insufferably hot. The blood ran boiling through my veins. My flesh was burning up. My brain would not work. It was all cobwebs, murky and stale as a charnel-house. Yet at times were strange illuminations, full of terror and despair. Blood-red lights and purple shadows alternated in my vision. Then came the dreams.

* * * * *

There was always Berna. Through a mass of grimacing, greed-contorted faces gradually there formed and lingered her sweet and pensive one. We were in a strange costume, she and I. It seemed like that of the early Georges. We were running away, fleeing from some one. For her sake a great fear and anxiety possessed me. We were eloping, I fancied.

There was a marsh to cross, a hideous quagmire, and our pursuers were close. We started over the quaking ground, then, suddenly, I saw her sink. I rushed to aid her, and I, too, sank. We were to our necks in the soft ooze, and there on the bank, watching us, was the foremost of our hunters. He laughed at our struggles; he mocked us; he rejoiced to see us drown. And in my dream the face of the man seemed strangely like Locasto.

* * * * *

We were in a bower of roses, she and I. It was still further back in history. We seemed to be in the garden of a palace. I was in doublet and hose, and she wore a long, flowing kirtle. The air was full of fragrance and sunshine. Birds were singing. A fountain scattered a shower of glittering diamonds on the breeze. She was sitting on the grass, while I reclined by her side, my head lying on her lap. Above me I could see her face like a lily bending over me. With dainty fingers she crumpled a rose and let the petals snow down on me.

Then, suddenly, I was seized, torn away from her by men in black, who roughly choked her screams. I was dragged off, thrown into a foul cell, left many days. Then, one night, I was dragged forth and brought before a grim tribunal in a hall of gloom and horror. They pronounced my doom—Death. The chief Inquisitor raised his mask, and in those gloating features I recognised—Locasto.

* * * * *

Again it seemed as if I were still further back in history, in some city under the Roman rule. I was returning from the Temple with my bride. How fair and fresh and beautiful she was, garlanded with flowers and radiantly happy. Again it was Berna.

Suddenly there are shouts, the beating of drums, the clash of cymbals. The great Governor of the Province is coming. He passes with his retinue. Suddenly he catches sight of her whom I have but newly wed. He stops. He asks who is the maid. They tell him. He looks at me with haughty contempt. He gives a sign. His servants seize her and drag her screaming away. I try to follow, to kill him. I, too, am seized, overpowered. They bind me, put out my eyes. The Roman sees them do it. He laughs as the red-hot iron kisses my eye-balls. He mocks me, telling me what a dainty feast awaits him in my bride. Again I see Locasto.

* * * * *

Then came another phase of my delirium, in which I struggled to get to her. She was waiting for me, wanting me, breaking her heart at my delay. O, Berna, my soul, my life, since the beginning of things we were fated. 'Tis no flesh love, but something deeper, something that has its source at the very core of being. It is not for your sweet face, your gentle spirit, my own, that you are dearer to me than all else: it is because—you are you. If all the world were to turn against you, flout you, stone you, then would I rush to your side, shield you, die with you. If you were attainted with leprosy, I would enter the lazar-house for your sake.

"O Berna, I must see you, I must, I must. Let me go to her . . . now . . . dear! She's calling me. She's in trouble. Oh, for the love of God, let me go . . . let me go, I say . . . Curse you, I will. She's in trouble. You can't hold me. I'm stronger than you all when she calls . . . Let me . . . let me . . . Oh, oh, oh . . . you're hurting me so. I'm weak, yes, weak as a baby . . . Berna, my child, my poor little girl, I can do nothing. There's a mountain weighing me down. There's a slab of gold on my chest. They're burning me up. My veins are on fire. I can't come . . . I can't, dear . . . I'm tired . . ."

Then the fever, the ravings, the wild threshing of my pillow, all passed away, and I was left limp, weak, helpless, resigned to my fate.

I was on the sunny slope of convalescence. The Prodigal had remained with me as long as I was in danger, but now that I had turned the corner, he had gone back to the creeks, so that I was left with only my thoughts for company. As I turned and twisted on my narrow cot it seemed as if the time would never pass. All I wanted was to get better fast, and to get out again. Then, I thought, I would marry Berna and go "outside." I was sick of the country, of everything.

I was lying thinking over these things, when I became aware that the man in the cot to the right was trying to attract my attention. He had been brought in that very morning, said to have been kicked by a horse. One of his ribs was broken, and his face badly smashed. He was in great pain, but quite conscious, and he was making stealthy motions to me.

"Say, mate," he said, "I piped you off soon's I set me lamps on you. Don't youse know me?"

I looked at the bandaged face wonderingly.

"Don't you spot de man dat near let youse down de shaft?"

Then, with a great start, I saw it was the Worm.

"'Taint no horse done me up," he said in a hoarse whisper; "'twas a man. You know de man, de worst devil in all Alaska, Black Jack. Bad luck to him! He knocked me down and give me de leather. But I'm goin' to get even some day. I'm just laying for him. I wouldn't be in his shoes for de richest claim in de Klondike."

The man's eyes glittered vengefully between the white bandages.

"'Twas all on account of de little girl he done it. You know de girl I mean. Black Jack's dead stuck on her, an' de furder she stands him off de more set he is to get her. Youse don't know dat man. He's never had de cold mit yet."

"Tell me what's the matter, for Heaven's sake."

"Well, when youse didn't come, de little girl she got worried. I used to be doin' chores round de restaurant, an' she asks me to take a note up to you. So I said I would. But I got on a drunk dat day, an' for a week after I didn't draw a sober breath. When I gets around again I told her I'd seen you an' given you de note an' you was comin' in right away."

"Heaven forgive you for that."

Then, as I hung half in, half out of the window, he clutched me by the throat

"Yep, dat's what I say now. But it's all too late. Well, a week went on an' you never showed up, an' meantime Locasto was pesterin' her cruel. She got mighty peaked like, pale as a ghost, an' I could see she cried most all her nights. Den she gives me anudder note. She gives me a hundred dollars to take dat note to you. I said she could lay on me dis time. I was de hurry-up kid, an' I starts off. But Black Jack must have cottoned on, for he meets me back of de town an' taxes me wid takin' a message. Den he sets on me like a wild beast an' does me up good and proper. But I'll fix him yet."

"Where are the notes?" I cried.

"In de pocket of me coat. Tell de nurse to fetch in me clothes, an' I'll give dem to youse."

The nurse brought the clothes, but the little man was too sore to move.

"Feel in de inside pocket."

There were the notes, folded very small, and written in pencil. There was a strange faintness at my heart, and my fingers trembled as I opened them. Fear, fear was clutching me, compressing me in an agonising grip.

Here was the first.

"My Darling Boy: Why didn't you come? I was all ready for you. O, it was such a terrible disappointment. I've cried myself to sleep every night since. Has anything happened to you, dear? For Heaven's sake write or send a message. I can't bear the suspense.

"Your loving
"Berna."

Blankly, dully, almost mechanically, I read the second.

"O, come, my dear, at once. I'm in serious danger. He's grown desperate. Swears if he can't get me by fair means he'll have me by foul. I'm terribly afraid. Why ar'n't you here to protect me? Why have you failed me? O, my darling, have pity on your poor little girl. Come quickly before it is too late."

It was unsigned.

Heavens! I must go to her at once. I was well enough. I was all right again. Why would they not let me go to her? I would crawl on my hands and knees if need be. I was strong, so strong now.

Ha! there were the Worm's clothes. It was after midnight. The nurse had just finished her rounds. All was quiet in the ward.

Dizzily I rose and slipped into the frayed and greasy garments. There were the hospital slippers. I must wear them. Never mind a hat.

I was out in the street. I shuffled along, and people stared at me, but no one delayed me. I was at the restaurant now. She wasn't there. Ah! the cabin on the hill.

I was weaker than I had thought. Once or twice in a half-fainting condition I stopped and steadied myself by holding a sapling tree. Then the awful intuition of her danger possessed me, and gave me fresh strength. Many times I stumbled, cutting myself on the sharp boulders. Once I lay for a long time, half-unconscious, wondering if I would ever be able to rise. I reeled like a drunken man. The way seemed endless, yet stumbling, staggering on, there was the cabin at last.

A light was burning in the front room. Some one was at home at all events. Only a few steps more, yet once again I fell. I remember striking my face against a sharp rock. Then, on my hands and knees, I crawled to the door.

I raised myself and hammered with clenched fists. There was silence within, then an agitated movement. I knocked again. Was the door ever going to be opened? At last it swung inward, with a suddenness that precipitated me inside the room.

The Madam was standing over me where I had fallen. At sight of me she screamed. Surprise, fear, rage, struggled for mastery on her face. "It's him," she cried, "*him*." Peering over her shoulder, with ashy, horrified face, I saw her trembling husband.

"Berna," I gasped hoarsely. "Where is she? I want Berna. What are you doing to her, you devils? Give her to me. She's mine, my promised bride. Let me go to her, I say."

The woman barred the way.

All at once I realised that the air was heavy with a strange odour, the odour of *chloroform*. Frenzied with fear, I rushed forward.

Then the Amazon roused herself. With a cry of rage she struck me. Savagely both of them came for me. I struggled, I fought; but, weak as I was, they carried me before them and threw me from the door. I heard the lock shoot; I was outside; I was impotent. Yet behind those log walls . . . Oh, it was horrible! horrible! Could such things be in God's world? And I could do nothing.

I was strong once more. I ran round to the back of the cabin. She was in there, I knew. I rushed at the window and threw myself against it. The storm frame had not been taken off. Crash! I burst through both sheets of glass. I was cruelly cut, bleeding in a dozen places, yet I was half into the room. There, in the dirty, drab light, I saw a face, the fiendish, rage-distorted face of my dream. It was Locasto.

He turned at the crash. With a curse he came at me. Then, as I hung half in, half out of the window, he clutched me by the throat. Using all his strength, he raised me further into the room, then he hurled me ruthlessly out onto the rocks outside.

I rose, reeling, covered with blood, blind, sick, speechless. Weakly I staggered to the window. My strength was leaving me. "O God, sustain me! Help me to save her."

Then I felt the world go blank. I swayed; I clutched at the walls; I fell.

There I lay in a ghastly, unconscious heap.

I had lost!

* * * * *

BOOK IV

THE VORTEX

He burned a hole in the frozen muck;
He scratched the icy mould;
And there in six-foot dirt he struck
A sack or so of gold.

> He burned a hole in the Decalogue,
> And then it came about—
> For Fortune's only a lousy rogue—
> His "pocket" petered out.

And lo! it was but a year all told,
When there in the shadow grim,
But six feet deep in the icy mould,
They burned a hole for him.

—"The Yukoner."

CHAPTER I

"No, no, I'm all right. Really I am. Please leave me alone. You want me to laugh? Ha! Ha! There! Is that all right now?"

"No, it isn't all right. It's very far from all right, my boy; and this is where you and your little uncle here are going to have a real heart to heart talk."

It was in the big cabin on Gold Hill, and the Prodigal was addressing me. He went on:

"Now, look here, kid, when it comes to expressing my feelings I'm in the kindergarten class; when it comes to handing out the high-toned dope I drop my cue every time; but when I'm needed to do the solid pardner stunt then you don't need to holler for me—I'm there. Well, I'm giving you a straight line of talk. Ever since the start I've taken a strong notion to you. You've always been ace-high with me, and there never will come the day when you can't eat on my meal-ticket. We tackled the Trail of Trouble together. You were always wanting to lift the heavy end of the log, and when the God of Cussedness was doing his best to rasp a man down to his yellow streak, you showed up white all through. Say, kid, we've been in tight places together; we've been stacked up against hard times together: and now I'll be gol-darned if I'm going to stand by and see you go downhill, while the devil oils the bearings."

"Oh, I'm all right," I protested.

"Yes, you're all right," he echoed grimly. "In an impersonation of an 'all-right' man it's the hook for yours. I've seen 'all-right' men like you hitting the hurry trail for the boneyard before now. You're 'all right'! Why, for the last two hours you've been sitting with that 'just-break-the-news-to mother' expression of yours, and paying no more heed to my cheerful brand of conversation than if I had been a measly four-flusher. You don't eat more than a sick sparrow, and often you don't bat an eye all night. You're looking worse than the devil in a gale of wind. You've lost your grip, my boy. You don't care whether school keeps or not. In fact, if it wasn't for your folks, you'd as lief take a short cut across the Great Divide."

"You're going it a little strong, old man."

"Oh no, I'm not. You know you're sick of everything. Feel as if life's a sort of penitentiary, and you've just got to do time. You don't expect to get any more fun out of it. Look at me. Every day's my sunshine day. If the sky's blue I like it; if it's grey I like it just as well. I never worry. What's the use? Yesterday's a dead one; to-morrow's always to-morrow. All we've got's the 'now,' and it's up to us to live it for all we're worth. You can use up more human steam to the square inch in worrying than you can to the square yard in hard work. Eliminate worry and you've got the only system."

"It's all very well for you to preach," I said, "you forget I've been a pretty sick man."

"That's no nursemaid's dream. You almost cashed in. Typhoid's a serious proposition at the best; but when you take a crazy streak on top of it, make a midnight getaway from the sick-ward and land up on the Slide looking as if you'd been run through a threshing machine, well, you're sure letting death get a short option on you. And you gave up. You didn't want to fight. You shirked, but your youth and constitution fought for you. They healed your wounds, they soothed your ravings, they cooled your fever. They were a great team, and they pulled you through. Seems as if they'd pulled you through a knot-hole, but they were on to their job. And you weren't one bit grateful—seemed to think they had no business to butt in."

"My hurts are more than physical."

"Yes, I know; there was that girl. You seemed to have a notion that that was the only girl on God's green brush-pile. As I camped there by your bedside listening to your ravings, and getting a strangle-hold on you when you took it into your head to get funny, you blabbed out the whole yarn. Oh, sonny, why didn't you tell your uncle? Why didn't you put me wise? I could have given you the right steer. Have you ever known me handle a job I couldn't make good at? I'm a whole matrimonial bureau rolled into one. I'd have had you prancing to the tune of the wedding march before now. But you kept mum as a mummy. Wouldn't even tell your old pard. Now you've lost her."

"Yes, I've lost her."

"Did you ever see her after you came out of the hospital?"

"Once, once only. It was the first day. I was as thin as a rail, as white as the pillow from which I had just raised my head. Death's reprieve was written all over me. I dragged along wearily, leaning on a stick. I was thinking of her, thinking, thinking always. As I scanned the faces of the crowds that thronged the streets, I thought only of her face. Then suddenly she was before me. She looked like a ghost, poor little thing; and for a fluttering moment we stared at each other, she and I, two wan, wearful ghosts."

"Yes, what did she say?"

"Say! she said nothing. She just looked at me. Her face was cold as ice. She looked at me as if she wanted to *pity* me. Then into her eyes there came a shadow of bitterness, of bitterness and despair such as might gloom the eyes of a lost soul. It unnerved me. It seemed as if she was regarding me almost with horror, as if I were a sort of a leper. As I stood there, I thought she was going to faint. She seemed to sway a moment. Then she drew a great, gasping breath, and turning on her heel she was gone."

"She cut you?"

"Yes, cut me dead, old fellow. And my only thought was of love for her, eternal love. But I'll never forget the look on her face as she turned away. It was as if I had lashed her with a whip. My God!"

"And you've never seen her since?"

"No, never. That was enough, wasn't it? She didn't want to speak to me any more, never wanted to set eyes on me any more. I went back to the ward; then, in a little, I came on here. My body was living, but my heart was dead. It will never live again."

"Oh, rot! You mustn't let the thing down you like that. It's going to kill you in the end. Buck up! Be a man! If you don't care to live for yourself, live for others. Anyway, it's likely all for the best. Maybe love had you locoed. Maybe she wasn't really good. See now how she lives openly with Locasto. They call her the Madonna; they say she looks more like a virgin-martyr than the mistress of a dissolute man."

I rose and looked at him, conscious that my face was all twisted with the pain of the thought.

"Look here," I said, "never did God put the breath of life into a better girl. There's been foul play. I know that girl better than any one in the world, and if every living being were to tell me she wasn't good I would tell them they lied, they lied. I would burn at the stake upholding that girl."

"Then why did she turn you down so cruelly?"

"I don't know; I can't understand it. I know so little about women. I have not wavered a moment. To-day in my loneliness and heartbreak I care and hunger for her more than ever. She's always here, right here in my head, and no power can drive her out. Let them say of her what they will, I would marry her to-morrow. It's killing me. I've aged ten years in the last few months. Oh, if I only could forget."

He looked at me thoughtfully.

"I say, old man, do you ever hear from your old lady?"

"Every mail."

"You've often told me of your home. Say! just give us a mental frame-up of it."

"Glengyle? Yes. I can see the old place now, as plainly as a picture: the green, dimpling hills all speckled with sheep; the grey house nestling snugly in a grove of birch; the wild water of the burn leaping from black pool to pool, just mad with the joy of life; the midges dancing over the water in the still sunshine, and the trout jumping for them—oh, it's the bonny, bonny place. You would think so too. You would like it, tramping knee-deep in the heather, to see the moorcock rise whirring at your feet; you would like to set sail with the fisher folk after the silver herring. It would make you feel good to see the calm faces of the shepherds, the peace in the eyes of the women. Ay, that was the best of it all, the Rest of it, the calm of it. I was pretty happy in those days."

"You were happy—then why not go back? That's your proper play; go back to your Mother. She wants you. You're pretty well heeled now. A little money goes a long way over there. You can count on thirty thousand. You'll be comfortable; you'll devote yourself to the old lady; you'll be happy again. Time's a regular steam-roller when it comes to smoothing out the rough spots in the past. You'll forget it all, this place, this girl. It'll all seem like the after effects of a midnight Welsh rabbit. You've got mental indigestion.

I hate to see you go. I'm really sorry to lose you; but it's your only salvation, so go, go!"

Never had I thought of it before. Home! how sweet the word seemed. Mother! yes, Mother would comfort me as no one else could. She would understand. Mother and Garry! A sudden craving came over me to see them again. Maybe with them I could find relief from this awful agony of heart, this thing that I could scarce bear to think of, yet never ceased to think of. Home! that was the solution of it all. Ah me! I would go home.

"Yes," I said, "I can't go too soon; I'll start to-morrow."

So I rose and proceeded to gather together my few belongings. In the early morning I would start out. No use prolonging the business of my going. I would say good-bye to those two partners of mine, with a grip of the hand, a tear in the eye, a husky: "Take care of yourself." That would be all. Likely I would never see them again.

Jim came in and sat down quietly. The old man had been very silent of late. Putting on his spectacles, he took out his well-worn Bible and opened it. Back in Dawson there was a man whom he hated with the hate that only death can end, but for the peace of his soul he strove to conquer it. The hate slumbered, yet at times it stirred, and into the old man's eyes there came the tiger-look that had once made him a force and a fear. Woe betide his enemy if that tiger ever woke.

"I've been a-thinkin' out a scheme," said Jim suddenly, "an' I'm a-goin' to put all of that twenty-five thousand of mine back into the ground. You know us old miners are gamblers to the end. It's not the gold, but the gettin' of it. It's the excitement, the hope, the anticipation of one's luck that counts. We're fighters, an' we've just got to keep on fightin'. We can't quit. There's the ground, and there's the precious metals it's a-tryin' to hold back on us. It's up to us to get them out. It's for the good of humanity. The miner an' the farmer rob no one. They just get down to that old ground an' coax it an' beat it an' bully it till it gives up. They're working for the good of humanity—the farmer an' the miner." The old man paused sententiously.

"Well, I can't quit this minin' business. I've just got to go on so long's I've got health an' strength; an' I'm a-goin' to shove all

I've got once more into the muck. I stand to make a big pile, or lose my wad."

"What's your scheme, Jim?"

"It's just this: I'm goin' to install a hydraulic plant on my Ophir Creek claim, I've got a great notion of that claim. It's an out-of-sight proposition for workin' with water. There's a little stream runs down the hill, an' the hill's steep right there. There's one hundred feet of fall, an' in Spring a mighty powerful bunch of water comes a-tumblin' down. Well, I'm goin' to dam it up above, bring it down a flume, hitch on a little giant, an' turn it loose to rip an' tear at that there ground. I'm goin' to begin a new era in Klondike minin'."

"Bully for you, Jim."

"The values are there in the ground, an' I'm sick of the old slow way of gettin' them out. This looks mighty good to me. Anyway, I'm a-goin' to give it a trial. It's just the start of things; you'll see others will follow suit. The individual miner's got to go; it's only a matter of time. Some day you'll see this whole country worked over by them big power dredges they've got down in Californy. You mark my words, boys; the old-fashioned miner's got to go."

"What are you going to do?"

"Well, I've written out for piping an' a monitor, an' next Spring I hope I'll have the plant in workin' order. The stuff's on the way now. Hullo! Come in!"

The visitors were Mervin and Hewson on their way to Dawson. These two men had been successful beyond their dreams. It was just like finding money the way fortune had pushed it in front of their noses. They were offensively prosperous; they reeked of success.

In both of them a great change had taken place, a change only too typical of the gold-camp. They seemed to have thawed out; they were irrepressibly genial; yet instead of that restraint that had formerly distinguished them, there was a grafted quality of weakness, of flaccidity, of surrender to the enervating vices of the town.

Mervin was remarkably thin. Dark hollows circled his eyes, and a curious nervousness twisted his mouth. He was "a terror for the women," they said. He lavished his money on them faster than he made it. He was vastly more companionable than formerly, but somehow you felt his virility, his fighting force had gone.

In Hewson the change was even more marked. Those iron muscles had couched themselves in easy flesh; his cheeks sagged; his eyes were bloodshot and untidy. Nevertheless he was more of a good fellow, talked rather vauntingly of his wealth, and affected a patronising manner. He was worth probably two hundred thousand, and he drank a bottle of brandy a day.

In the case of these two men, as in the case of a thousand others in the gold-camp, it seemed as if easy, unhoped-for affluence was to prove their undoing. On the trail they had been supreme; in fen or forest, on peak or plain, they were men among men, fighting with nature savagely, exultantly. But when the fight was over their arms rested, their muscles relaxed, they yielded to sensuous pleasures. It seemed as if to them victory really meant defeat.

As I went on with my packing I paid but little heed to their talk. What mattered it to me now, this babble of dumps and dust, of claims and clean-ups? I was going to thrust it all behind me, blot it clean out of my memory, begin my life anew. It would be a larger, more luminous life. I would live for others. Home! Mother! again how exquisitely my heart glowed at the thought of them.

Then all at once I pricked up my ears. They were talking of the town, of the men and women who were making it famous (or rather infamous), when suddenly they spoke the name of Locasto.

"He's gone off," Mervin was saying; "gone off on a big stampede. He got pretty thick with some of the Peel River Indians, and found they knew of a ledge of high-grade, free-milling quartz somewhere out there in the Land Back of Beyond. He had a sample of it, and you could just see the gold shining all through it. It was great stuff. Jack Locasto's the last man to turn down a chance like that. He's the worst gambler in the Northland, and no amount of wealth will ever satisfy him. So he's off with an Indian and one companion, that little Irish satellite of his, Pat Doogan. They have six months' grub. They'll be away all winter."

"What's become of that girl of his?" asked Hewson, "the last one he's been living with? You remember she came in on the boat with us. Poor little kid! Blast that man anyway. He's not content with women of his own kind, he's got to get his clutches on the best of them. That was a good little girl before he got after her. If she was a friend of mine I'd put a bullet in his ugly heart."

Hewson growled like a wrathful bear, but Mervin smiled his cynical smile.

"Oh, you mean the Madonna," he said; "why, she's gone on the dance-halls."

They continued to talk of other things, but I did not hear them any more. I was in a trance, and I only aroused when they rose to go.

"Better say good-bye to the kid here," said the Prodigal; "he's going to the old country to-morrow."

"No, I'm not," I answered sullenly; "I'm just going as far as Dawson."

He stared and expostulated, but my mind was made up. I would fight, fight to the last.

* * * * *

CHAPTER II

Berna on the dance-halls—words cannot convey all that this simple phrase meant to me. For two months I had been living in a dull apathy of pain, but this news galvanised me into immediate action.

For although there were many degrees of dance-hall depravity, at the best it meant a brand of ineffaceable shame. She had lived with Locasto, had been recognised as his mistress—that was bad enough; but the other—to be at the mercy of all, to be classed with the harpies that preyed on the Man with the Poke, the vampires of the gold-camp. Berna—Oh, it was unspeakable! The thought maddened me. The needle-point of suffering that for weeks had been boring into my brain seemed to have pierced its core at last.

When the Prodigal expostulated with me I laughed—a bitter, mirthless laugh.

"I'm going to Dawson," I said, "and if it was hell itself, I'd go there for that girl. I don't care what any one thinks. Home, society, honour itself, let them all go; they don't matter now. I was a fool to think I could ever give her up, a fool. Now I know that as long as there's life and strength in my body, I'll fight for her. Oh, I'm not the sentimentalist I was six months ago. I've lived since then. I can hold my own now. I can meet men on their own level. I can fight, I can win. I don't care any more, after what I've gone through. I don't set any particular value on my life. I'll throw it away as recklessly as the best of them. I'm going to have a fierce fight for that girl, and if I lose there'll be no more 'me' left to fight. Don't try to reason with me. Reason be damned! I'm going to Dawson, and a hundred men couldn't hold me."

"You seem to have some new stunts in your repertoire," he said, looking at me curiously; "you've got me guessing. Sometimes I think you're a candidate for the dippy-house, then again I think you're on to yourself. There's a grim set to your mouth and a hard look in your eyes that I didn't use to see. Maybe you can hold up your end. Well, anyway, if you will go I wish you good luck."

So, bidding good-bye to the big cabin, with my two partners looking ruefully after me, I struck off down Bonanza. It was mid-October. A bitter wind chilled me to the marrow. Once more the land lay stark beneath its coverlet of snow, and the sky was wan and ominous. I travelled fast, for a painful anxiety gripped me, so that I scarce took notice of the improved trail, of the increased activity, of the heaps of tailings built up with brush till they looked like walls of a fortification. All I thought of was Dawson and Berna.

How curious it was, this strange new strength, this indifference to self, to physical suffering, to danger, to public opinion! I thought only of the girl. I would make her marry me. I cared nothing for what had happened to her. I might be a pariah, an outcast for the rest of my days; at least I would save her, shield her, cherish her. The thought uplifted me, exalted me. I had suffered beyond expression. I had rearranged my set of ideas; my concept of life, of human nature, had broadened and deepened. What did it matter if physically they had wronged her? Was not the pure, virgin soul of her beyond their reach?

I was just in time to see the last boat go out. Already the river was "throwing ice," and every day the jagged edges of it crept further towards midstream. An immense and melancholy mob stood on the wharf as the little steamer backed off into the channel. There were uproarious souls on board, and many women of the town screaming farewells to their friends. On the boat all was excited, extravagant joy; on the wharf, a sorry attempt at resignation.

The last boat! they watched her as her stern paddle churned the freezing water; they watched her forge her slow way through the ever-thickening ice-flakes; they watched her in the far distance battling with the Klondike current; then, sad and despondent, they turned away to their lonely cabins. Never had their exile seemed so bitter. A few more days and the river would close tight as a drum. The long, long night would fall on them, and for nigh on eight weary months they would be cut off from the outside world.

Yet soon, very soon, a mood of reconciliation would set in. They would begin to make the best of things. To feed that great Octopus, the town, the miners would flock in from the creeks with treasure hoarded up in baking-powder tins; the dance-halls and gambling-places would absorb them; the gaiety would go on full swing, and there would seem but little change in the glittering abandon of the gold-camp. As I paced its sidewalks once more I marvelled at its growth. New streets had been made; the stores boasted expensive fittings and gloried in costly goods; in the bar-rooms were splendid mirrors and ornate woodwork; the restaurants offered European delicacies; all was on a new scale of extravagance, of garish display, of insolent wealth.

Everywhere the man with the fat "poke" was in evidence. He came into town unshorn, wild-looking, often raggedly clad, yet always with the same wistful hunger in his eyes. You saw that look, and it took you back to the dark and dirt and drudgery of the claim, the mirthless months of toil, the crude cabin with its sugar barrel of ice behind the door, its grease light dimly burning, its rancid smell of stale food. You saw him lying smoking his strong pipe, looking at that can of nuggets on the rough shelf, and dreaming of what it would mean to him—out there where the lights glittered and the gramophones blared. Surely, if patience, endurance, if grim, unswerving purpose, if sullen, desperate toil deserved a reward, this man had a peckful of pleasure for his due.

And always that hungry, wistful look. The women with the painted cheeks knew that look; the black-jack boosters knew it; the barkeeper with his knock-out drops knew it. They waited for him; he was their "meat."

Yet in a few days your wild and woolly man is transformed, and no longer does your sympathy go out towards him. Shaven and shorn, clad in silken underwear, with patent leather shoes, and a suit in New York style, you absolutely fail to recognise him as your friend of the moccasins and mackinaw coat. He is smoking a dollar Laranago, he has half a dozen whiskies "under his belt," and later on he has a "date" with a lady singer of the Pavilion Theatre. He is having a "whale" of a good time, he tells you; you wonder how long he will last.

Not for long. Sharp and short and sweet it is. He is brought up with a jerk, and the Dago Queen, for whom he has bought so much wine at twenty dollars a bottle, has no recognition for him in her flashing eyes. He has been "taken down the line," "trimmed to a finish" by an artist in the business. Ruefully he turns his poke inside out—not a "colour." He cannot even command the price of a penitential three-fingers of rye. Such is one of the commonest phases of life in the gold-camp.

As I strolled the streets I saw many a familiar face. Mosher I saw. He had grown very fat, and was talking to a diminutive woman with heavy blond hair (she must have weighed about ninety-five pounds, I think). They went off together.

A knife-edged wind was sweeping down from the north, and men in bulging coonskin coats filled up the sidewalks. At the Aurora corner I came across the Jam-wagon. He was wearing a jacket of summer flannels, and, as if to suggest extra warmth, he had turned up its narrow collar. In his trembling fingers he held an emaciated cigarette, which he inhaled avidly. He looked wretched, pinched with hunger, peaked with cold, but he straightened up when he saw me into a semblance of well-being. Then, in a little, he sagged forward, and his eyes went dull and abject. It was a business of the utmost delicacy to induce him to accept a small loan. I knew it would only plunge him more deeply into the mire; but I could not bear to see him suffer.

I went into the Parisian Restaurant. It was more glittering, more raffish, more clamant of the tenderloin than ever. There were men waiters in the conventional garb of waiterdom, and there was Madam, harder looking and more vulturish. You wondered if such a woman could have a soul, and what was the end and aim of her being. There she sat, a creature of rapacity and sordid lust. I marched up to her and asked abruptly:

"Where's Berna?"

She gave a violent start. There was a quality of fear in her bold eyes. Then she laughed, a hard, jarring laugh.

"In the Tivoli," she said.

Strange again! Now that the worst had come to pass, and I had suffered all that it was in my power to suffer, this new sense of strength and mastery had come to me. It seemed as if some of the iron spirit of the land had gotten into my blood, a grim, insolent spirit that made me fearless; at times a cold cynical spirit, a spirit of rebellion, of anarchy, of aggression. The greatest evil had befallen me. Life could do no more to harm me. I had everything to gain and nothing to lose. I cared for no man. I despised them, and, to back me in my bitterness, I had twenty-five thousand dollars in the bank.

I was still weak from my illness and my long mush had wearied me, so I went into a saloon and called for drinks. I felt the raw whisky burn my throat. I tingled from head to foot with a strange, pleasing warmth. Suddenly the bar, with its protecting rod of brass, seemed to me a very desirable place, bright, warm, suggestive of comfort and good-fellowship. How agreeably every one was smiling! Indeed, some were laughing for sheer joy. A big, merry-hearted miner called for another round, and I joined in.

Where was that bitter feeling now? Where that morbid pain at my heart? As I drank it all seemed to pass away. Magical change! What a fool I was! What was there to make such a fuss about? Take life easy. Laugh alike at the good and bad of it. It was all a farce anyway. What would it matter a hundred years from now? Why were we put into this world to be tortured? I, for one, would protest. I would writhe no more in the strait-jacket of existence. Here was escape, heartsease, happiness—here in this bottled impishness. Again I drank.

What a rotten world it all was! But I had no hand in the making of it, and it wasn't my task to improve it. I was going to get the best I could out of it. Eat, drink and be merry, that was the last word of philosophy. Others seemed to be able to extract all kinds of happiness from things as they are, so why not I? In any case, here was the solution of my troubles. Better to die happily drunk than miserably sober. I was not drinking from weakness. Oh no! I was drinking with deliberate intent to kill pain.

How wonderfully strong I felt! I smashed my clenched fist against the bar. My knuckles were bruised and bleeding, but I felt no pain. I was so light of foot, I imagined I could jump over the counter. I ached to fight some one. Then all at once came the thought of Berna. It came with tragical suddenness, with poignant force. Intensely it smote me as never before. I could have burst into maudlin tears.

"What's the matter, Slim?" asked a mouldy mannikin, affectionately hanging on to my arm.

Disgustedly I looked at him.

"Take your filthy paws off me," I said.

His jaw dropped and he stared at me. Then, before he could draw on his fund of profanity, I burst through the throng and made for the door.

I was drunk, deplorably drunk, and I was bound for the Tivoli.

* * * * *

CHAPTER III

I wish it to be understood that I make no excuses for myself at this particular stage of my chronicle. I am only conscious of a desire to tell the truth. Many of the stronger-minded will no doubt condemn me; many of those inclined to a rigid system of morality will be disgusted with me; but, however it may be, I will write plainly and without reserve.

When I reeled out of the Grubstake Saloon I was in a peculiar state of exaltation. No longer was I conscious of the rasping cold, and it seemed to me I could have couched me in the deep snow as cosily as in a bed of down. Surpassingly brilliant were the lights. They seemed to convey to me a portentous wink. They twinkled with jovial cheer. What a desirable place the world was, after all!

With an ebullient sense of eloquence, of extravagant oratory, I longed for a sympathetic ear. An altruistic emotion pervaded me. Who would suspect, thought I, as I walked a little too circumspectly amid the throng, that my heart was aglow, that I was tensing my muscles in the pride of their fitness, that my brain was a bewildering kaleidoscope of thoughts and images?

Gramophones were braying in every conceivable key. Brazen women were leering at me. Potbellied men regarded me furtively. Alluringly the gambling-dens and dancing-dives invited me. The town was a giant spider drawing in its prey, and I was the prey, it seemed. Others there were in plenty, men with the eager, wistful eyes; but who was there so eager and wistful as I? And I didn't care any more. Strike up the music! On with the dance! Only one life have we to live. Ah! there was the Tivoli.

To the right as I entered was a palatial bar set off with burnished brass, bevelled mirrors and glittering, vari-coloured pyramids of costly liqueurs. Up to the bar men were bellying, and the bartenders in white jackets were mixing drinks with masterly dexterity. It was a motley crowd. There were men in broadcloth and fine linen, men in blue shirts and mud-stiffened overalls, grey-bearded elders and beardless boys. It was a noisy crowd, laughing, brawling, shouting, singing. Here was the foam of life, with never a hint of the muddy sediment underneath.

To the left I had a view of the gambling-room, a glimpse of green tables, of spinning balls, of cool men, with shades over their eyes, impassively dealing. There were huge wheels of fortune, keno tables, crap outfits, faro layouts, and, above all, the dainty, fascinating roulette. Everything was in full swing. Miners with flushed faces and a wild excitement in their eyes were plunging recklessly; others, calm, alert, anxious, were playing cautiously. Here and there were the fevered faces of women. Gold coin was stacked on the tables, while a man with a pair of scales was weighing dust from the tendered pokes.

In front of me was a double swing-door painted in white and gold, and, pushing through this, for the first time I found myself in a Dawson dance-hall.

I remember being struck by the gorgeousness of it, its glitter and its glow. Who would have expected, up in this bleak-visaged North, to find such a fairyland of a place? It was painted in white and gold, and set off by clusters of bunched lights. There was much elaborate scroll-work and ornate decoration. Down each side, raised about ten feet from the floor, and supported on gilt pillars, were little private boxes hung with curtains of heliotrope silk. At the further end of the hall was a stage, and here a vaudeville performance was going on.

I sat down on a seat at the very back of the audience. Before me were row after row of heads, mostly rough, rugged and unwashed. Their faces were eager, rapt as those of children. They were enjoying, with the deep satisfaction of men who for many a weary month had been breathing the free, unbranded air of the Wild. The sensuous odour of patchouli was strangely pleasant to them; the sight of a woman was thrillingly sweet; the sound of a song was ravishing. Looking at many of those toil-grooved faces one could see that there was no harm in their hearts. They were honest, uncouth, simple; they were just like children, the children of the Wild.

A woman of generous physique was singing in a shrill, nasal voice a pathetic ballad. She sang without expression, bringing her hands with monotonous gestures alternately to her breast. Her squat, matronly figure, beef from the heels up, looked singularly absurd in her short skirt. Her face was excessively over-painted, her mouth good-naturedly large, and her eyes out of their slit-like lids leered at the audience.

"Ain't she great?" said a tall bean-pole of a man on my right, as she finished off with a round of applause. "There's some class to her work."

He looked at me in a confidential way, and his pale-blue eyes were full of rapturous appreciation. Then he did something that surprised me. He tugged open his poke and, dipping into it, he produced a big nugget. Twisting this in a scrap of paper, he rose up, long, lean and awkward, and with careful aim he threw it on the stage.

"Here ye are, Lulu," he piped in his shrill voice. The woman, turning in her exit, picked up the offering, gave her admirer a wide, gold-toothed smile, and threw him an emphatic kiss. As the man sat down I could see his mouth twisting with excitement, and his watery blue eyes snapped with pleasure.

"By heck," he said, "she's great, ain't she? Many's the bottle of wine I've opened for that there girl. Guess she'll be glad when she hears old Henry's in town again. Henry's my name, Hard-pan Henry they call me, an' I've got a claim on Hunker. Many's the wallopin' poke have I toted into town an' blowed in on that there girl. An' I just guess this one'll go the same gait. Well, says I, what's the odds? I'm havin' a good time for my money. When it's gone there's lots more in the ground. It ain't got no legs. It can't run away."

He chuckled and hefted his poke in a horny hand. There was a flutter of the heliotrope curtains, and the face of Lulu, peeping over the plush edge of a box, smiled bewitchingly upon him. With another delighted chuckle the old man went to join her.

"Darned old fool," said a young man on my left. He looked as if his veins were chuckful of health; his skin was as clear as a girl's, his eye honest and fearless. He was dressed in mackinaw, and wore a fur cap with drooping ear-flaps.

"He's the greatest mark in the country," the Youth went on. "He's got no more brains than God gave geese. All the girls are on to him. Before he can turn round that old bat up there will have him trimmed to a finish. He'll be doing flip-flaps, and singing "Way Down on the Suwanee River' standing on his head. Then the girl will pry him loose from his poke, and to-morrow he'll start off up the creek, teetering and swearing he's had a dooce of a good time. He's the easiest thing on earth."

The Youth paused to look on a new singer. She was a soubrette, trim, dainty and confident. She wore a blond wig, and her eyes in their pits of black were alluringly bright. Paint was lavished on her face in violent dabs of rose and white, and the inevitable gold teeth gleamed in her smile. She wore a black dress trimmed with sequins, stockings of black, a black velvet band around her slim neck. She was greeted with much applause, and she began to sing in a fairly sweet voice.

"That's Nellie Lestrange," said the Youth. "She's a great rustler—Touch-the-button-Nell, they call her. They say that when she gets a jay into a box it's all day with him. She's such a nifty wine-winner the end of her thumb's calloused pressing the button for fresh bottles."

Touch-the-button-Nell was singing a comic ditty of a convivial order. She put into it much vivacity, appealing to the audience to join in the chorus with a pleading, "Now all together, boys." She had tripping steps and dainty kicks that went well with the melody. When she went off half a dozen men rose in their places, and aimed nuggets at her. She captured them, then, with a final saucy flounce of her skirt, made her smiling exit.

"By Gosh!" said the Youth, "I wonder these fellows haven't got more savvy. You wouldn't catch *me* chucking away an ounce on one of those fairies. No, sir! Nothing doing! I've got a five-thousand-dollar poke in the bank, and to-morrow I'll be on my way outside with a draft for every cent of it. A certain little farm 'way back in Vermont looks pretty good to me, and a little girl that don't know the use of face powder, bless her. She's waiting for me."

The excitement of the liquor had died away in me, and what with the heat and smoke of the place, I was becoming very drowsy. I was almost dozing off to sleep when some one touched me on the arm. It was a negro waiter I had seen dodging in and out of the boxes, and known as the Black Prince.

"Dey's a lady up'n de box wants to speak with yuh, sah," he said politely.

"Who is it?" I asked in surprise.

"Miss Labelle, sah, Miss Birdie Labelle."

I started. Who in the Klondike had not heard of Birdie Labelle, the eldest of the three sisters, who married Stillwater Willie? A thought flashed through me that she could tell me something of Berna.

"All right," I said; "I'll come."

I followed him upstairs, and in a moment I was ushered into the presence of the famous soubrette.

"Hullo, kid!" she exclaimed, "sit down. I saw you in the audience and kind-a took a notion to your face. How d'ye do?"

She extended a heavily bejewelled hand. She was plump, pleasant-looking, with a piquant smile and flaxen hair. I ordered the waiter to bring her a bottle of wine.

"I've heard a lot about you," I said tentatively.

"Yes, I guess so," she answered. "Most folks have up here. It's a sort of reflected glory. I guess if it hadn't been for Bill I'd never have got into the limelight at all."

She sipped her champagne thoughtfully.

"I came in here in '97, and it was then I met Bill. He was there with the coin all right. We got hitched up pretty quick, but he was such a mut I soon got sick of him. Then I got skating round with another guy. Well, an egg famine came along. There was only nine hundred samples of hen fruit in town, and one store had a corner on them. I went down to buy some. Lord! how I wanted them eggs. I kept thinking how I'd have them done, shipwrecked, two on a raft or sunny side up, when who should come along but Bill. He sees what I want, and quick as a flash what does he do but buy up the whole bunch at a dollar apiece! 'Now,' says he to me, 'if you want eggs for breakfast just come home where you belong.'

"Well, say, I was just dying for them eggs, so I comes to my milk like a lady. I goes home with Bill."

She shook her head sadly, and once more I filled up her glass.

She prattled on with many a gracious smile, and I ordered another bottle of wine. In the next box I could hear the squeaky laugh of Hard-pan Henry and the teasing tones of his inamorata. The visits of the Black Prince to this box with fresh bottles had been fast and furious, and at last I heard the woman cry in a querulous voice: "Say, that black man coming in so often gives me a pain. Why don't you order a case?"

Then the man broke in with his senile laugh:

"All right, Lulu, whatever you say goes. Say, Prince, tote along a case, will you?"

Surely, thought I, there's no fool like an old fool.

A little girl was singing, a little, winsome girl with a sweet childish voice and an innocent face. How terribly out of place she looked in that palace of sin. She sang a simple, old-world song full of homely pathos and gentle feeling. As she sang she looked down on those furrowed faces, and I saw that many eyes were dimmed with tears. The rough men listened in rapt silence as the childish treble rang out:

> "Darling, I am growing old;
> Silver threads among the gold
> Shine upon my brow to-day;
> Life is fading fast away."

Then from behind the scenes a pure alto joined in and the two voices, blending in exquisite harmony, went on:

> "But, my darling, you will be, will be,
> Always young and fair to me.
> Yes, my darling, you will be
> Always young and fair to me."

As the last echo died away the audience rose as one man, and a shower of nuggets pelted on the stage. Here was something that touched their hearts, stirred in them strange memories of tenderness, brought before them half-forgotten scenes of fireside happiness.

"It's a shame to let that kid work in the halls," said Miss Labelle. There were tears in her eyes, too, and she hurriedly blinked them away.

Then the curtain fell. Men were clearing the floor for the dance, so, bidding the lady adieu, I went downstairs.

* * * * *

CHAPTER IV

I found the Youth awaiting me.

"Say, pardner," said he, "I was just getting a bit anxious about you. I thought sure that fairy had you in tow for a sucker. I'm going to stay right with you, and you're not going to shake me. See!"

"All right," I said; "come on and we'll watch the dance."

So we got in the front row of spectators, while behind us the crowd packed as closely as matches in a box. The champagne I had taken had again aroused in me that vivid sense of joy and strength and colour. Again the lights were effulgent, the music witching, the women divine. As I swayed a little I clutched unsteadily at the Youth. He looked at me curiously.

"Brace up, old man," he said. "Guess you're not often in town. You're not much used to the dance-hall racket."

"No," I assured him.

"Well," he continued, "it's the rottenest game ever. I've seen more poor beggars put plumb out of business by the dance-halls than by all the saloons and gambling-joints put together. It's the game of catching the sucker brought to the point of perfection, and there's very few cases where it fails."

He perceived I was listening earnestly, and he warmed up to his subject.

"You see, the boys get in after they've been out on the claim for six months at a stretch, and town looks mighty good to them. The music sounds awful nice, and the women, well, they look just like angels. The boys are all right, but they've got that mad craving for the sight of a woman a man gets after he's been off out in the Wild, and these women have got the captivation of men down to a fine art. Once one of them gets to looking at you with eyes that eat right into you, and soft white hands, and pretty coaxing ways, well, it's mighty hard to hold back. A man's a fool to come near these places if he's got a poke—'cept, like me, he knows the ropes and he's right onto himself."

The Youth said this with quite a complacent air. He went on:

"These girls work on a percentage basis. You'll notice every time you buy them a drink the waiter gives them a check. That means that when the night's over they cash in and get twenty-five per cent, of the money you've spent on them. That's how they're so keen on ordering fresh bottles. Sometimes they'll say a bottle's gone flat before it's empty, and have you order another. Or else they'll pour half of it into the cuspidor when you're not looking. Then, when you get too full to notice the difference, they'll run in ginger ale on you. Or else they'll get you ordering by the case, and have half a dozen dummy bottles in it. Oh, there's all kinds of schemes these box rustlers are on to. When you pay for a drink you toss over your poke, and they take the price out. Do you think they're particular to a quarter ounce or so? No, sir! and you always get the short end of it. It's a bad game to go up against."

The Youth looked at me as though proud of his superior sophistication.

The floor was cleared. Girls were now coming from behind the stage, preening themselves and chaffing with the crowd. The orchestra struck up some jubilant ragtime that set the heart dancing and the heels tapping in tune. Brighter than ever seemed the lights; more dazzling the white and gilt of the walls. Some of the girls were balancing lightly to a waltz rhythm. There was a witching grace in their movements, and the Youth watched them intently. He looked down at his feet clad in old moccasins.

"Gee, I'd like just to have one spin," he said; "just one before I leave the darned old country for good. I was always crazy about dancing. I'd ride thirty miles to attend a dance back home."

His eyes grew very wistful. Suddenly the music stopped and the floor-master came forward. He was a tall, dark man with a rich and vibrant baritone voice.

"That's the best spieler in the Yukon," said the Youth.

"Come on, boys," boomed the spieler. "Look alive there. Don't keep the ladies waiting. Take your hands out of your pockets and get in the game. Just going to begin, a dreamy waltz or a nice juicy two-step, whichever you prefer. Hey, professor, strike up that waltz!"

Once more the music swelled out.

"How's that, boys? Doesn't that make your feet like feathers? Come on, boys! Here you are for the nice, glossy floor and the nice, flossy girls. Here you are! Here you are! That's right, select your partners! Swing your honeys! Hurry up there! Just a-goin' to begin. What's the matter with you fellows? Wake up! a dance won't break you. Come on! don't be a cheap skate. The girls are fine, fit and fairy-like, the music's swell and the floor's elegant. Come on, boys!"

There was a compelling power in his voice, and already a number of couples were waltzing round. The women were exquisite in their grace and springy lightness. They talked as they danced, gazing with languishing eyes and siren smiles at the man of the moment.

Some of them, who had not got partners, were picking out individuals from the crowd and coaxing them to come forward. A drunken fellow staggered onto the floor and grabbed a girl. She was young, dainty and pretty, but she showed no repugnance for him. Round and round he cavorted, singing and whooping, a wild, weird object; when, suddenly, he tripped and fell, bringing her down with him. The crowd roared; but the girl good-naturedly picked him up, and led him off to the bar.

A man in a greasy canvas suit with mucklucks on his feet had gone onto the floor. His hair was long and matted, his beard wild and rank. He was dancing vehemently, and there was the glitter of wild excitement in his eyes. He looked as if he had not bathed for years, but again I could see no repulsion in the face of the handsome brunette with whom he was waltzing. Dance after dance they had together, locked in each other's arms.

"That's a 'live one,'" said the Youth. "He's just come in from Dominion with a hundred ounces, and it won't last him over the night. Amber, there, will get it all. She won't let the other girls go near. He's her game."

Between dances the men promenaded to the bar and treated their companions to a drink. In the same free, trusting way they threw over their pokes to the bartender and had the price weighed out. The dances were very short, and the drinks very frequent.

Madder and madder grew the merriment. The air was hot; the odour of patchouli mingled with the stench of stale garments and the reek of alcohol. Men dripping with sweat whirled round in wild gyrations. Some of them danced beautifully; some merely shuffled over the floor. It did not make any difference to the girls. They were superbly muscular and used to the dragging efforts of novices. After a visit to the bar back they came once more, licking their lips, and fell to with fresh energy.

There was no need to beg the crowd now. A wave of excitement seemed to have swept over them. They clamoured to get a dance. The "live one" whooped and pranced on his wild career, while Amber steered him calmly through the mazes of the waltz. Touch-the-button-Nell was talking to a tall fair-moustached man whom I recognised as a black-jack booster. Suddenly she left him and came over to us. She went up to the Youth.

She had discarded her blond wig, and her pretty brown hair parted in the middle and rippled behind her ears. Her large violet-blue eyes had a devouring look that would stir the pulse of a saint. She accosted the Youth with a smile of particular witchery.

"Say, kid, won't you come and have a two-step with me? I've been looking at you for the last half-hour and wishing you'd ask me."

The Youth had advised me: "If any of them asks you, tell them to go to the devil;" but now he looked at her and his boyish face flushed.

"Nothing doing," he said stoutly.

"Oh, come now," she pleaded; "honest to goodness, kid, I've turned down the other fellow for you. You won't refuse me, will you? Come on; just one, sweetheart."

She was holding the lapels of his coat and dragging him gently forward. I could see him biting his lip in embarrassment.

"No, thanks, I'm sorry," he stammered. "I don't know how to dance. Besides, I've got no money."

She grew more coaxing.

"Never mind about the coin, honey. Come on, have one on me. Don't turn me down, I've taken such a notion to you. Come on now; just one turn."

I watched his face. His eyes clouded with emotion, and I knew the psychology of it. He was thinking:

"Just one—surely it wouldn't hurt. Surely I'm man enough to trust myself, to know when to quit. Oh, lordy, wouldn't it be sweet just to get my arm round a woman's waist once more! The sight of them's honey to me; surely it wouldn't matter. One round and I'll shake her and go home."

The hesitation was fatal. By an irresistible magnetism the Youth was drawn to this woman whose business it ever was to lure and beguile. By her siren strength she conquered him as she had conquered many another, and as she led him off there was a look of triumph on her face. Poor Youth! At the end of the dance he did not go home, nor did he "shake" her. He had another and another and another. The excitement began to paint his cheeks, the drink to stoke wild fires in his eyes. As I stood deserted I tried to attract him, to get him back; but he no longer heeded me.

"I don't see the Madonna to-night," said a little, dark individual in spectacles. Somehow he looked to me like a newspaper man "chasing" copy.

"No," said one of the girls; "she ain't workin'. She's sick; she don't take very kindly to the business, somehow. Don't seem to get broke in easy. She's funny, poor kid."

Carelessly they went on to talk of other things, while I stood there gasping, staring, sick at heart. All my vinous joy was gone, leaving me a haggard, weary wretch of a man, disenchanted and miserable to the verge of—what? I shuddered. The lights seemed to have gone blurred and dim. The hall was tawdry, cheap and vulgar. The women, who but a moment before had seemed creatures of grace and charm, were now nothing more than painted, posturing harridans, their seductive smiles the leers of shameless sin.

And this was a Dawson dance-hall, the trump card in the nightly game of despoliation. Dance-halls, saloons, gambling-dens, brothels, the heart of the town was a cancer, a hive of iniquity. Here had flocked the most rapacious of gamblers, the most beautiful and unscrupulous women on the Pacific slope. Here in the gold-born city they waited for their prey, the Man with the Poke. Back there in the silent Wild, with pain and bloody sweat, he toiled for them. Sooner or later must he come within reach of their talons to be fleeced, flouted and despoiled. It was an organised system of sharpers, thugs, harpies, and birds of prey of every kind. It was a blot on the map. It was a great whirlpool, and the eddy of it encircled the furthest outpost of the golden valley. It was a vortex of destruction, of ruin and shame. And here was I, hovering on its brink, likely to be soon sucked down into its depths.

I pressed my way to the door, and stood there staring and swaying, but whether with wine or weakness I knew not. In the vociferous and flamboyant street I could hear the raucous voices of the spielers, the jigging tunes of the orchestras, the click of ivory balls, the popping of corks, the hoarse, animal laughter of men, the shrill, inane giggles of women. Day and night the game went on without abatement, the game of despoliation.

And I was on the verge of the vortex. Memories of Glengyle, the laughing of the silver-scaled sea, the tawny fisher-lads with their honest eyes, the herring glittering like jewels in the brown nets, the women with their round health-hued cheeks and motherly eyes. Oh, Home, with your peace and rest and content, can you not save me from this?

And as I stood there wretchedly a timid little hand touched my arm.

* * * * *

CHAPTER V

It is odd how people who have been parted a weary while, yet who have thought of each other constantly, will often meet with as little show of feeling as if they had but yesterday bid good-bye. I looked at her and she at me, and I don't think either of us betrayed any emotion. Yet must we both have been infinitely moved.

She was changed, desperately, pitifully changed. All the old sweetness was there, that pathetic sweetness which had made the miners call her the Madonna; but alas, forever gone from her was the fragrant flower of girlhood. Her pallor was excessive, and the softness had vanished out of her face, leaving there only lines of suffering. Sorrow had kindled in her grey eyes a spiritual lustre, a shining, tearless brightness. Ah me, sad, sad, indeed, was the change in her!

So she looked at me, a long and level look in which I could see neither love nor hate. The bright, grey eyes were clear and steady, and the pinched and pitiful lips did not quiver. And as I gazed on her I felt that nothing ever would be the same again. Love could no more be the radiant spirit of old, the prompter of impassioned words, the painter of bewitching scenes. Never again could we feel the world recede from us as we poised on bright wings of fancy; never again compare our joy with that of the heaven-born; never again welcome that pure ideal that comes to youth alone, and that pitifully dies in the disenchantment of graver days. We could sacrifice all things for each other; joy and grieve for each other; live and die for each other,—but the Hope, the Dream, the exaltation of love's dawn, the peerless white glory of it—had gone from us forever and forever.

Her lips moved:

"How you have changed!"

"Yes, Berna, I have been ill. But you, you too have changed."

"Yes," she said very slowly. "I have been—dead."

There was no faltering in her voice, never a throb of pathos. It was like the voice of one who has given up all hope, the voice of one who has arisen from the grave. In that cold mask of a face I could see no glimmer of the old-time joy, the joy of the season when wild roses were aglow. We both were silent, two pitifully cold beings, while about us the howling bedlam of pleasure-plotters surged and seethed.

"Come upstairs where we can talk," said she. So we sat down in one of the boxes, while a great freezing shadow seemed to fall and wrap us around. It was so strange, this silence between us. We were like two pale ghosts meeting in the misty gulfs beyond the grave.

"And why did you not come?" she asked.

"Come—I tried to come."

"But you did not." Her tone was measured, her face averted.

"I would have sold my soul to come. I was ill, desperately ill, nigh to death. I was in the hospital. For two weeks I was delirious, raving of you, trying to get to you, making myself a hundred times worse because of you. But what could I do? No man could have been more helpless. I was out of my mind, weak as a child, fighting for my life. That was why I did not come."

When I began to speak she started. As I went on she drew a quick, choking breath. Then she listened ever so intently, and when I had finished a great change came over her. Her eyes stared glassily, her head dropped, her hands clutched at the chair, she seemed nigh to fainting. When she spoke her voice was like a whisper.

"And they lied to me. They told me you were too eager gold-getting to think of me; that you were in love with some other woman out there; that you cared no more for me. They lied to me. Well, it's too late now."

She laughed, and the once tuneful voice was harsh and grating. Still were her eyes blank with misery. Again and again she murmured: "Too late, too late."

Quietly I sat and watched her, yet in my heart was a vast storm of agony. I longed to comfort her, to kiss that face so white and worn and weariful, to bring tears to those hopeless eyes. There seemed to grow in me a greater hunger for the girl than ever before, a longing to bring joy to her again, to make her forget. What did it all matter? She was still my love. I yearned for her. We both had suffered, both been through the furnace. Surely from it would come the love that passeth understanding. We would rear no lily walls, but out of our pain would we build an abiding place that would outlast the tomb.

"Berna," I said, "it is not too late."

There was a desperate bitterness in her face. "Yes, yes, it is. You do not understand. You—it's all right for you, you are blameless; but I—"

"You too are blameless, dear. We have both been miserably duped. Never mind, Berna, we will forget all. I love you, Oh how much I never can tell you, girl! Come, let us forget and go away and be happy."

It seemed as if my every word was like a stab to her. The sweet face was tragically wretched.

"Oh no," she answered, "it can never be. You think it can, but it can't. You could not forget. I could not forget. We would both be thinking; always, always torturing each other. To you the thought would be like a knife thrust, and the more you loved me the deeper would pierce its blade. And I, too, can you not realise how fearfully I would look at you, always knowing you were thinking of THAT, and what an agony it would be to me to watch your agony? Our home would be a haunted one, a place of ghosts. Never again can there be joy between you and me. It's too late, too late!"

She was choking back the sobs now, but still the tears did not come.

"Berna," I said gently, "I think I could forget. Please give me a chance to prove it. Other men have forgotten. I know it was not your fault. I know that spiritually you are the same pure girl you were before. You are an angel, dear; my angel."

"No, I was not to blame. When you failed to come I grew desperate. When I wrote you and still you failed to come I was almost distracted. Night and day he was persecuting me. The others gave me no peace. If ever a poor girl was hounded to dishonour I was. Yet I had made up my mind to die rather than yield. Oh, it's too horrible."

She shuddered.

"Never mind, dear, don't tell me about it."

"When I awoke to life sick, sick for many days, I wanted to die, but I could not. There seemed to be nothing for it but to stay on there. I was so weak, so ill, so indifferent to everything that it did not seem to matter. That was where I made my mistake. I should have killed myself. Oh, there's something in us all that makes us cling to life in spite of shame! But I would never let him come near me again. You believe me, don't you?"

"I believe you."

"And though, when he went away, I've gone into this life, there's never been any one else. I've danced with them, laughed with them, but that's all. You believe me?"

"Yes, dear."

"Thank God for that! And now we must say good-bye."

"*Good-bye?*"

"I said—good-bye. I would not spoil your life. You know how proud I am, how sensitive. I would not give you such as I. Once I would have given myself to you gladly, but now—please go away."

"Impossible."

"No, the other is impossible. You don't know what these things mean to a woman. Leave me, please."

"Leave you—to what?"

"To death, ruin—I don't know what. If I'm strong enough I will die. If I am weak I will sink in the mire. Oh, and I am only a girl too, a young girl!"

"Berna, will you marry me?"

"No! No! No!"

"Berna, I will never leave you. Here I tell you frankly, plainly, I don't know whether or not you still love me—you haven't said a word to show it—but I know I love you, and I will love you as long as life lasts. I will never leave you. Listen to me, dear: let us go away, far, far away. You will forget, I will forget. It will never be the same, but perhaps it will be better, greater than before. Come with me, O my love! Have pity on me, Berna, have pity. Marry me. Be my wife."

She merely shook her head, sitting there cold as a stone.

"Then," I said, "if you call yourself dishonoured, I too will become dishonoured. If you choose to sink in the mire, I too will sink. We will go down together, you and I. Oh, I would rather sink with you, dear, than rise with the angels. You have chosen—well, I too have chosen. We stand on the edge of the vortex, now will we plunge down. You will see me steep myself in shame, then when I am a hundred shades blacker than you can ever hope to be, my angel, you will stoop and pity me. Oh, I don't care any more. I've played the fool too long; now I'll play the devil, and you'll stand by and watch me. Sometimes it's nice to make those we love suffer, isn't it? I would break my arm to make you feel sorry for me. But now you'll see me in the vortex. We'll go down together, dear. Hand in hand hell-ward we'll go down, we'll go down."

She was looking at me in a frightened way. A madness seemed to have gotten into me.

"Berna, you're on the dance-halls. You're at the mercy of the vilest wretch that's got an ounce of gold in his filthy poke. They can buy you as they buy white flesh everywhere on earth. You must dance with them, drink with them, go away with them. Berna, I can buy you. Come, dance with me, drink with me. We'll live, live. We'll eat, drink and be merry. On with the dance! Oh, for the joy of life! Since you'll not be my love you'll be my light-of-love. Come, Berna, come!"

I paused. With her head lying on the cushioned edge of the box she was crying. The plush was streaky with her tears.

"Will you come?" I asked again.

She did not move.

"Then," said I, "there are others, and I have money, lots of it. I can buy them. I am going down into the vortex. Look on and watch me."

I left her crying.

* * * * *

CHAPTER VI

It is with shame I write the following pages. Would I could blot them out of my life. To this day there must be many who remember my meteoric career in the firmament of fast life. It did not last long, but in less than a week I managed to squander a small fortune.

Those were the days when Dawson might fitly have been called the dissolute. It was the régime of the dance-hall girl, and the taint of the tenderloin was over the town. So far there were few decent women to be seen on the streets. Respectable homes were being established, but even there social evils were discussed with an astonishing frankness and indifference. In the best society men were welcomed who were known to be living in open infamy. A general callousness to social corruption prevailed.

For Dawson was at this time the Mecca of the gambler and the courtesan. Of its population probably two-thirds began their day when most people finished it. It was only towards nightfall that the town completely roused up, that the fever of pleasure providing began. Nearly every one seemed to be affected by the spirit of degeneracy. On the faces of many of the business men could be seen the stamp of the pace they were going. Cases in Court had to be adjourned because of the debauches of lawyers. Bank tellers stepped into their cages sleepless from all-night orgies. Government officials lived openly with wanton women. High and low were attainted by the corruption. In those days of headstrong excitement, of sudden fortune, of money to be had almost for the picking up, when the gold-camp was a reservoir into which poured by a thousand channels the treasure of the valley, few were those among the men who kept a steady head, whose private records were pure and blameless.

No town of its size has ever broken up more homes. Men in the intoxication of fast-won wealth in that far-away land gave way to excesses of every kind. Fathers of families paraded the streets arm in arm with demi-mondaines. To be seen talking to a loose woman was unworthy of comment, not to have a mistress was not to be in the swim. Words cannot express the infinite and general degradation. It is scarcely possible to exaggerate it. That teeming town at the mouth of the Klondike set a pace in libertinism that has never been equalled.

I would divide its population into three classes: the sporting fraternity, whose business it was to despoil and betray; the business men, drawn more or less into the vortex of dissipation; the miners from the creeks, the Man with the Poke, here to-day, gone, to-morrow, and of them all the most worthy of respect. He was the prop and mainstay of the town. It was like a vast trap set to catch him. He would "blow in" brimming with health and high spirits; for a time he would "get into the game;" sooner or later he would cut loose and "hit the high places"; then, at last, beggared and broken, he would crawl back in shame and sorrow to the claim. O, that grey city! could it ever tell its woes and sorrows the great, white stars above would melt into compassionate tears.

Ah well, to the devil with all moralising! A short life and a merry one. Switch on the lights! Ring up the curtain! On with the play!

* * * * *

In the casino a crowd is gathering round the roulette wheel. Three-deep they stand. A woman rushes out from the dance-hall and pushes her way through the throng. She is very young, very fair and redundant of life. A man jostles her. From frank blue eyes she flashes a look at him, and from lips sweet as those of a child there comes the remonstrance: "Curse you; take care."

The men make way for her, and she throws a poke of dust on the red. "A hundred dollars out of that," she says. The coupier nods; the wheel spins round; she loses.

"Give me another two hundred in chips," she cries eagerly. The dealer hands them to her, and puts her poke in a drawer. Again and again she plays, placing chips here and there round the table.

Sometimes she wins, sometimes she loses. At last she has quite a pile of chips before her. She laughs gleefully. "I guess I'll cash in now," she says. "That's good enough for to-night."

The man hands her back her poke, writes out a cheque for her winnings, and off she goes like a happy child.

"Who's that?" I ask.

"That? that's Blossom. She's a 'bute,' she is. Want a knockdown? Come on round to the dance-hall."

* * * * *

Once more I see the Youth. He is nearing the end of his tether. He borrows a few hundred dollars from me. "One more night," he says with a bitter grin, "and the hog goes back to wallow in the mire. They've got you going too—Oh, Lord, it's a great game! Ha! ha!"

He goes off unsteadily; then from out of the luminous mists there appears the Jam-wagon. In a pained way he looks at me. "Here, chuck it, old man," he says; "come home to my cabin and straighten up."

"All right," I answer; "just one drink more."

One more means still one more. Poor old Jam-wagon! It's the blind leading the blind.

Mosher haunts me with his gleaming bald head and his rat-like eyes. He is living with the little ninety-five-pound woman, the one with the mop of hair.

Oh, it is a hades of a life I am steeped in! I drink and I drink. It seems to me I am always drinking. Rarely do I eat. I am one of half a dozen spectacular "live ones." All the camp is talking of us, but it seems to me I lead the bunch in the race to ruin. I wonder what Berna thinks of it all. Was there ever such a sensitive creature? Where did she get that obstinate pride? Child of misfortune! She minded me of a delicate china cup that gets mixed in with the coarse crockery of a hash joint.

Remonstrantly the Prodigal speeds to town.

"Are you crazy?" he cries. "I don't mind you making an ass of yourself, but lushing around all that coin the way you're doing—it's wicked; it makes me sick. Come home at once."

"I won't," I say. "What if I am crazy? Isn't it my money? I've never sown my wild oats yet. I'm trying to catch up, that's all. When the money's done I'll quit. I'm having the time of my life. Don't come spoiling it with your precepts. What a lot of fun I've missed by being good. Come along; 'listen to the last word of human philosophy—have a drink.'"

He goes away shaking his head. There's no fear of him ever breaking loose. He, with his smile of sunshine, would make misfortune pay. He is a rolling stone that gathers no moss, but manages to glue itself to greenbacks at every turn.

* * * * *

I am in a box at the Palace Grand. The place is packed with rowdy men and ribald women. I am at the zenith of my shame. Right and left I am buying wine. Like vultures at a feast they bunch into the box. Like carrion flies they buzz around me. That is what I feel myself to be—carrion.

How I loathe myself! but I think of Berna, and the thought goads me to fresh excesses. I will go on till flesh and blood can stand it no longer, till I drop in my tracks. I realise that somehow I must make her pity me, must awake in her that guardian angel which exists in every woman. Only in that way can I break down the barrier of her pride and arouse the love latent in her heart.

There are half a dozen girls in the box, a bevy of beauties, and I buy a case of wine for each, over a thousand dollars' worth. Screaming with laughter they toss it in bottles down to their friends in the audience. It is a scene of riotous excitement. The audience roars, the girls shriek, the orchestra tries to make itself heard. Madder and madder grows the merriment. The fierce fever of it scorches in my veins. I am mad to spend, to throw away money, to outdo all others in bitter, reckless prodigality. I fling twenty-dollar gold pieces to the singers. I open bottle after bottle of wine. The girls are spraying the crowd with it, the floor of the box swims with it. I drop my pencil signing a tab, and when I look down it is floating in a pool of champagne.

Then comes the last. The dance has begun. Men in fur caps, mackinaw coats and mucklucks are waltzing with women clad in Paris gowns and sparkling with jewels. The floor is thronged. I have a large, hundred-ounce poke of dust, and I unloose the thong. Suddenly with a mad shout I scatter its contents round the hall. Like a shower of golden rain it falls on men and women alike. See how they grovel for it, the brutes, the vampires! How they fight and grab and sprawl over it! How they shriek and howl and curse! It is like an arena of wild beasts; it is pandemonium. Oh, how I despise them! My gorge rises, but—to the end, to the end. I must play my part.

* * * * *

Always amid that lurid carnival of sin floats the figure of Blossom, Blossom with her child-face of dazzling fairness, her china-blue eyes, her round, smooth cheeks. How different from the pinched pallid face of Berna! Poor, poor Berna! I never see her, but amid all the saturnalia she haunts me. The thought of her is agony, agony. I cannot bear to think of her. I know she watches me. If she would only stoop and save me now! Or have I not fallen low enough? What a faith I have in that deep mother-love of hers that will redeem me in the end. I must go deeper yet. Faster and faster must I swirl into the vortex.

Oh, these women, how in my heart I loathe them! I laugh with them, I quaff with them, I let them rob me; but that's all.

* * * * *

In all that fierce madness of debauch, thank God, I retained my honour. They beguiled me, they tried to lure me into their rooms; but at the moment I went to enter I recoiled. It was as if an invisible arm stretched across the doorway and barred me out.

And Blossom, she, too, tried so hard to lure me, and because I resisted it inflamed her. Half angel, half devil was Blossom, a girl in years, but woefully wise, a soft siren when pleased, a she-devil when roused. She made me her special quarry. She fought for me. She drove off all the other girls. We talked together, we drank together, we "played the tables" together, but nothing more. She would coax me with the prettiest gestures, and cajole me with the sweetest endearments; then, when I steadfastly resisted her, she would fly into a fury and flout me with the foulness of the stews. She was beautiful, but born to be bad. No power on heaven or earth could have saved her. Yet in her badness she was frank, natural and untroubled as a child.

It was in one of the corridors of the dance-hall in the early hours of the morning. The place was deserted, strewed with débris of the night's debauch. The air was fetid, and from the gambling-hall down below arose the shouts of the players. We were up there, Blossom and I. I was in a strange state of mind, a state bordering on frenzy. Not much longer, I felt, could I keep up this pace. Something had to happen, and that soon.

She put her arms around me. I could feel her cheek pressed to mine. I could see her bosom rise and fall.

"Come," she said.

She led me towards her room. No longer was I able to resist. My foot was on the threshold and I was almost over when—

"Telegram, sir."

It was a messenger. Confusedly I took the flimsy envelope and tore it open. Blankly I stared at the line of type. I stared like a man in a dream. I was sober enough now.

"Ain't you coming?" said Blossom, putting her arms round me.

"No," I said hoarsely, "leave me, please leave me. Oh, my God!"

Her face changed, became vindictive, the face of a fury.

"Curse you!" she hissed, gnashing her teeth. "Oh, I knew. It's that other, that white-faced doll you care for. Look at me! Am I not better than her? And you scorn me. Oh, I hate you. I'll get even with you and her. Curse you, curse you—"

She snatched up an empty wine bottle. Swinging it by the neck she struck me square on the forehead. I felt a stunning blow, a warm rush of blood. Then I fell limply forward, and all the lights seemed to go out.

There I lay in a heap, and the blood spurting from my wound soaked the little piece of paper. On it was written:

"*Mother died this morning. Garry.*"

* * * * *

CHAPTER VII

"Where am I?"

"Here, with me."

Low and sweet and tender was the voice. I was in bed and my head was heavily bandaged, so that the cloths weighed upon my eyelids. It was difficult to see, and I was too weak to raise myself, but I seemed to be in semi-darkness. A lamp burning on a small table nearby was turned low. By my bedside some one was sitting, and a soft, gentle hand was holding mine.

"Where is *here*?" I asked faintly.

"Here—my cabin. Rest, dear."

"Is that you, Berna?"

"Yes, please don't talk."

I thrilled with a sudden sweetness of joy. A flood of sunshine bathed me. It was all over, then, the turmoil, the storm, the shipwreck. I was drifting on a tranquil ocean of content. Blissfully I closed my eyes. Oh, I was happy, happy!

In her cabin, with her, and she was nursing me—what had happened? What new turn of events had brought about this wonderful thing? As I lay there in the quiet, trying to recall the something that went before, my poor sick brain groped but feebly amid a murk of sinister shadows.

"Berna," I said, "I've had a bad dream."

"Yes, dear, you've been sick, very sick. You've had an attack of fever, brain fever. But don't try to think, just rest quietly."

So for a while longer I lay there, thrilled with a strange new joy, steeped in the ineffable comfort of her presence, and growing better, stronger with every breath. Memories came thronging back, memories that made me cringe and wince, and shudder with the shame of them. Yet ever the thought that she was with me was like a holy blessing. Surely it was all good since it had ended in this.

Yet there was something else, some memory darker than the others, some shadow of shadows that baffled me. Then as I battled with a growing terror and suspense, it all came back to me, the telegram, the news, my collapse. A great grief welled up in me, and in my agony I spoke to the girl.

"Berna, tell me, is it true? Is my Mother dead?"

"Yes, it's true, dear. You must try to bear it bravely."

I could feel her bending over me, could feel her hand holding mine, could feel her hair brush my cheek, yet I forgot even her just then. I thought only of Mother, of her devotion and of how little I had done to deserve it. So this was the end: a narrow grave, a rending grief and the haunting spectre of reproach.

I saw my Mother sitting at that window that faced the west, her hands meekly folded on her lap, her eyes wistfully gazing over the grey sea. I knew there was never a day of her life when she did not sit thus and think of me. I could guess at the heartache that gentle face would not betray, the longing those tender lips would not speak, the grief those sweet eyes studied to conceal. As, sitting there in the strange clouded sunset of my native land, she let her knitting drop on her lap, I knew she prayed for me. Oh, Mother! Mother!

My sobs were choking me, and Berna was holding my hand very tightly. Yet in a little I grew calmer.

"Berna," I said, "I've only got you now, only you, little girl. So you must love me, you mustn't leave me."

"I'll never leave you—if you want me to stay."

"God bless you, dear. I can't tell you the comfort you are to me. I'll try to be quiet now."

I will always remember those days as I grew slowly well again. The cot in which I lay stood in the sitting-room of the cabin, and from the window I could overlook the city. Snow had fallen, the days were diamond bright, and the smoke ascended sharply in the glittering air. The little room was papered with a design of wild roses that minded me of the Whitehorse Rapids. On the walls were some little framed pictures; the floor was carpeted in dull brown, and a little heater gave out a pleasant warmth. Through a doorway draped with a curtain I could see her busy in her little kitchen.

She left me much alone, alone with my thoughts. Often when all was quiet I knew she was sitting there beyond the curtain, sitting thinking, just as I was thinking. Quiet was the keynote of our life, quiet and sunshine. That little cabin might have been a hundred miles from the gold-born city, it was so quiet. Here drifted no echo of its abandoned gaiety, its glory of demoralisation. How sweet she looked in her spotless home attire, her neat waist, her white apron with bib and sleeves, her general air of a little housewife. And never was there so devoted a nurse.

Sometimes she would read to me from one of the few books I had taken everywhere on my travels, a page or two from my beloved Stevenson, a poem from my great-hearted Henley, a luminous passage from my Thoreau. How those readings brought back the time when, tired of flicking the tawny pools, I would sit on the edge of the boisterous little burn and read till the grey shadows sifted down! I was so happy then, and I did not know it. Now everything seemed changed. Life had lost its zest. Its savour was no longer sweet. Its very success was more bitter than failure. Would I ever get back that old-time rapture, that youthful joy, that satisfaction with all the world?

It was sweet prolonging my convalescence, yet the time came when I could no longer let her wait upon me. What was going to happen to us? I thought of that at all times, and she knew I thought of it. Sometimes I could see a vivid colour in her cheeks, an eager brightness in her eye. Was ever a stranger situation? She slept in the little kitchen, and between us there was but that curtain. The faintest draught stirred it. There I lay through the long, long night in that quiet cabin. I heard her breathing. Sometimes even I heard her murmur in her sleep. I knew she was there, within a few yards of me. I thought of her always. I loved her beyond all else on earth. I was gaining daily in health and strength, yet not for the wealth of the world would I have passed that little curtain. She was as safe there as if she were guarded with swords. And she knew it.

Once when I was in agony I called to her in the night, and she came to me. She came with a mother's tenderness, with exquisite endearments, with the great love shining in her eyes. She leaned over me, she kissed me. As she bent over my bed I put my arm round her. There in the darkness were we, she and I, her kisses warm upon my lips, her hair brushing my brow, and a great love devouring us. Oh, it was hard, but I released her, put her from me, told her to go away.

"I'll play the game fair," I said to myself. I must be very, very careful. Our position was full of danger. So I forced myself to be cold to her, and she looked both surprised and pained at the change in me. Then she seemed to put forth special efforts to please me. She changed the fashion of her hair, she wore pretty bows of ribbon. She talked brightly and lightly in a febrile way. She showed little coquettish tricks of manner that were charming to my mind. Ever she looked at me with wistful concern. Her heart was innocent, and she could not understand my sudden coldness. Yet that night had given me a lightning glimpse of my nature that frightened me. The girl was winsome beyond words, and I knew I had but to say it and she would come to me. Yet I checked myself. I retreated behind a barrier of reserve. "Play the game," I said; "play the game."

So as I grew better and stronger she seemed to lose her cheerfulness. Always she had that anxious, wistful look. Once came a sound from the kitchen like stifled sobbing, and again in the night I heard her cry. Then the time came when I was well enough to get up, to go away.

I dressed, looking like the cadaverous ghost I felt myself to be. She was there in the kitchen, sitting quietly, waiting.

"Berna," I called.

She came, with a smile lighting up her face.

"I'm going."

The smile vanished, and left her with that high proud look, yet behind it was a lurking fear.

"You're going?" she faltered.

"Yes," I said roughly, "I'm going."

She did not speak.

"Are you ready?" I went on.

"Ready?"

"Yes, you're going, too."

"Where?"

I took her suddenly in my arms.

"Why, you dear little angel, to get married, of course. Come on, Berna, we'll find the nearest parson. We won't lose any more precious time."

Then a great rush of tears came into her eyes. But still she hung back. She shook her head.

"Why, Berna, what's the matter? Won't you come?"

"I think not."

"In Heaven's name, what is wrong, dear? Don't you love me?"

"Yes, I love you. It's because I love you I won't come."

"Won't you marry me?"

"No, no, I can't. You know what I said before. I haven't changed any. I'm still the same—dishonoured girl. You could never give me your name."

"You're as pure as the driven snow, little one."

"No one thinks so but you, and it's that that makes all the difference. Everybody knows. No, I could never marry you, never take your name, never bind you to me."

"Well, what's to be done?"

"You must go away, or—stay."

"Stay?"

"Yes. You've been living alone with me for a month. I picked you up that night in the dance-hall. I had you brought here. I nursed you. Do you think people don't give us credit for the worst? We are as innocent as children, yet do you think I have a shred of reputation left? Already I am supposed to be your mistress. Everybody knows; nobody cares. There are so many living that way here. If you told them we were innocent they would scoff at us. If you go they will say you have discarded me."

"What shall I do?"

"Just stay. Oh, why can't we go on as we've been doing? It's been so like home. Don't leave me, dear. I don't want to bind you. I just want to be of some use to you, to help you, to be with you always. Love me for a little, anyway. Then when you're tired of me you can go, but don't go now."

I was dazed, but she went on.

"What does the ceremony matter? We love each other. Isn't that the real marriage? It's more; it's an ideal. We'll both be free to go if we wish. There will be no bonds but those of love. Is not that beautiful, two people cleaving together for love's sake, living for each other, sacrificing for each other, yet with no man-made law to tell them: 'This must ye do'? Oh, stay, stay!"

Her arms were round my neck. The grey eyes were full of pleading. The sweet lips had the old, pathetic droop. I yielded to the empery of love.

"Well," I said, "we will go on awhile, on one condition—that by-and-bye you marry me."

"Yes, I will, I will; I promise. If you don't tire of me; if you are sure beyond all doubt you will never regret it, then I will marry you with the greatest joy in the world."

So it came about that I stayed.

* * * * *

CHAPTER VIII

In this infernal irony of an existence why do the good things of life always come when we no longer have the same appetite to enjoy them? The year following, in which Berna and I kept house, was not altogether a happy one. Somehow we had both just missed something. We had suffered too much to recover our poise very easily. We were sick, not in body, but in mind. The thought of her terrible experience haunted her. She was as sensitive as the petal of a delicate flower, and often would I see her lips quiver and a look of pain come into her eyes. Then I knew of what she was thinking. I knew, and I, too, suffered.

I tried to make her forget, yet I could not succeed; and even in my most happy moments there was always a shadow, the shadow of Locasto; there was always a fear, the fear of his return. Yes, it seemed at times as if we were two unfortunates, as if our happiness had come too late, as if our lives were irretrievably shipwrecked.

Locasto! where was he? For near a year had he been gone, somewhere in that wild country at the Back of Beyond. Somewhere amid the wilder peaks and valleys of the Rockies he fought his desperate battle with the Wild. There had been sinister rumours of two lone prospectors who had perished up in that savage country, of two bodies that lay rotting and half buried by a landslide. I had a sudden, wild hope that one of them might be my enemy; for I hated him and I would have joyed at his death. When I loved Berna most exquisitely, when I gazed with tender joy upon her sweetness, when, with glad, thankful eyes, I blessed her for the sympathy and sunshine of her presence, then between us would come a shadow, dark, menacing and mordant. So the joy-light would vanish from my eyes and a great sadness fall upon me.

What would I do if he returned? I wondered. Perhaps if he left us alone I might let by-gones be by-gones; but if he ever came near her again—well, I oiled the chambers of my Colt and heard its joyous click as it revolved. "That's for him," I said, "that's for him, if by look, by word, or by act he ever molests her again." And I meant it, too. Suffering had hardened me, made me dangerous. I would have killed him.

Then, as the months went past and the suspicion of his fate deepened almost to a certainty, I began to breathe more freely. I noticed, too, a world of difference in Berna. She grew light-hearted. She sang and laughed a good deal. The sunshine came back to her eyes, and the shadow seldom lingered there. Sometimes the thought that we were not legally married troubled me, but on all sides were men living with their Klondike wives, either openly or secretly, and where this domestic ménage was conducted in quietness there was little comment on it. We lived to ourselves, and for ourselves. We left our neighbours alone. We made few friends, and in the ferment of social life we were almost unnoticed.

Of course, the Prodigal expostulated with me in severe terms. I did not attempt to argue with him. He would not have understood my point of view. There are heights and depths in life to which he with his practical mind could never attain. Yet he became very fond of Berna, and often visited us.

"Why don't you go and get churched decently, if you love her?" he demanded.

"So I will," I answered calmly; "give me a little time. Wait till we get more settled."

And, indeed, we were up to our necks in business these days. Our Gold Hill property had turned out well. We had a gang of men employed there, and I made frequent trips out to Bonanza. We had given the Halfbreed a small interest, and installed him as manager. The Jam-wagon, too, we had employed as a sort of assistant foreman. Jim was busy installing his hydraulic plant on Ophir Creek, and altogether we had enough to think about. I had set my heart on making a hundred thousand dollars, and as things were looking it seemed as if two more years would bring me to that mark.

"Then," said I to Berna, "we'll go and travel all over the world, and do it in style."

"Will we, dear?" she answered tenderly. "But I don't want money much now, and I don't know that I care so much about travel either. What I would like would be to go to your home, and settle down and live quietly. What I want is a nice flower garden, and a pony to drive into town, and a home to fuss about. I would embroider, and read, and play a little, and cook things, and—just be with you."

She was greatly interested in my description of Glengyle. She never tired of questioning me about it. Particularly was she interested in my accounts of Garry, and rather scoffed at my enthusiastic description of him.

"Oh, that wonderful brother of yours! One would think he was a small god, to hear you talk. I declare I'm half afraid of him. Do you think he would like me?"

"He would love you, little girl; any one would."

"Don't be foolish," she chided me. And then she drew my head down and kissed me.

I think we had the prettiest little cabin in all Dawson. The big logs were peeled smooth, and the ends squarely cut. The chinks were filled in with mortar. The whole was painted a deep rich crimson. The roof was covered with sheet-iron, and it, too, was painted crimson. There was a deep porch to it. It was the snuggest, neatest little home in the world.

Windows hung with dainty lace curtains peeped through its clustering greenery of vines, but the glory of it all was the flower garden. There was a bewildering variety of flowers, but mostly I remember stocks and pinks, Iceland poppies, marguerites, asters, marigolds, verbenas, hollyhocks, pansies and petunias, growing in glorious profusion. Even the roughest miner would stand and stare at them as he tramped past on the board sidewalk.

They were a mosaic of glowing colour, yet the crowning triumph was the poppies and sweet peas. Set in the centre of the lawn was a circle that was a leaping glow of poppies. Of every shade were they, from starry pink to luminous gold, from snowy white to passionate crimson. Like vari-coloured lamps they swung, and wakened you to wonder and joy with the exultant challenge of their beauty. And the sweet peas! All up the south side of the cabin they grew, overtopping the eaves in their riotous perfection. They rivalled the poppies in the radiant confusion of their colour, and they were so lavish of blossom we could not pick them fast enough. I think ours was the pioneer garden of the gold-born city, and awakened many to the growth-giving magic of the long, long day.

And it was the joy and pride of Berna's heart. I would sit on the porch of a summer's evening when down the mighty Yukon a sunset of vast and violent beauty flamed and languished, and I would watch her as she worked among her flowers. I can see her flitting figure in a dress of dainty white as she hovered over a beautiful blossom. I can hear her calling me, her voice like the music of a flute, calling me to come and see some triumph of her skill. I have a picture of her coming towards me with her arms full of flowers, burying her face lovingly among the velvet petals, and raising it again, the sweetest flower of all. How radiantly outshone her eyes, and her face, delicate as a cameo, seemed to have stolen the fairest tints of the lily and the rose.

Starry vines screened the porch, and everywhere were swinging baskets of silver birch, brimming over with the delicate green of smilax or clouded in an amethystine mist of lobelias. I can still see the little sitting-room with its piano, its plenitude of cushions, its book-rack, its Indian corner, its tasteful paper, its pictures, and always and everywhere flowers, flowers. The air was heavy with the fragrance of them. They glorified the crudest corner, and made our home like a nook in fairyland.

I remember one night as I sat reading she came to me. Never did I see her look so happy. She was almost childlike in her joy. She sat down by my chair and looked up at me. Then she put her arms around me.

"Oh, I'm so happy," she said with a sigh.

"Are you, dearest?" I caressed the soft floss of her hair.

"Yes, I just wish we could live like this forever;" and she nestled up to me ever so fondly.

Aye, she was happy, and I will always bless the memory of those days, and thank God I was the means of bringing a little gladness into her marred life. She was happy, and yet we were living in what society would call sin. Conventionally we were not man and wife, yet never were man and wife more devoted, more self-respecting. Never were man and wife endowed with purer ideals, with a more exalted conception of the sanctity of love. Yet there were many in the town not half so delicate, so refined, so spiritual, who would have passed my little lady like a pariah. But what cared we?

And perhaps it was the very greatness of my love for her that sometimes made me fear; so that often in the ecstasy of a moment I would catch my breath and wonder if it all could last. And when the poplars turned to gold, and up the valley stole a shuddering breath of desolation, my fear grew apace. The sky was all resplendent with the winter stars, and keen and hard their facets sparkled. And I knew that somewhere underneath those stars there slept Locasto. But was it the sleep of the living or of the dead? Would he return?

* * * * *

CHAPTER IX

Two men were crawling over the winter-locked plain. In the aching circle of its immensity they were like little black ants. One, the leader, was of great bulk and of a vast strength; while the other was small and wiry, of the breed that clings like a louse to life while better men perish.

On all sides of the frozen lake over which they were travelling were hills covered with harsh pine, that pricked funereally up to the boulder-broken snows. Above that was a stormy and fantastic sea of mountains baring many a fierce peak-fang to the hollow heavens. The sky was a waxen grey, cold as a corpse-light. The snow was an immaculate shroud, unmarked by track of bird or beast. Death-sealed the land lay in its silent vastitude, in its despairful desolation.

The small man was breaking trail. Down almost to his knees in the soft snow, he sank at every step; yet ever he dragged a foot painfully upward, and made another forward plunge. The snowshoe thong, jagged with ice, chafed him cruelly. The muscles of his legs ached as insistently as if clamped in a vice. He lurched forward with fatigue, so that he seemed to be ever stumbling, yet recovering himself.

"Come on there, you darned little shrimp; get a move on you," growled the big man from within the frost-fringed hood of his parka.

The little man started as if galvanised into sudden life. His breath steamed and almost hissed as it struck the icy air. At each raw intake of it his chest heaved. He beat his mittened hands on his breast to keep them from freezing. Under the hood of his parka great icicles had formed, hanging to the hairs of his beard, walrus-like, and his eyes, thickly wadded with frost, glared out with the furtive fear of a hunted beast.

"Curse him, curse him," he whimpered; but once more he lifted those leaden snowshoes and staggered on.

The big man lashed fiercely at the dogs, and as they screamed at his blows he laughed cruelly. They were straining forward in the harness, their bellies almost level with the ground, their muscles standing out like whalebone. Great, gaunt brutes they were, with ribs like barrel-staves, and hip-bones sharp as stakes. Their woolly coats were white with frost, their sly, slit-eyed faces ice-sheathed, their feet torn so that they left a bloody track on the snow at every step.

"Mush on there, you curs, or I'll cut you in two," stormed the big man, and once again the heavy whip fell on the yelling pack. They were pulling for all they were worth, their heads down, their shoulders squared. Their breath came pantingly, their tongues gleamed redly, their white teeth shone. They were fighting, fighting for life, fighting to placate a cruel master in a world where all was cruelty and oppression.

For there in the Winter Wild pity was not even a name. It was the struggle for life, desperate and never-ending. The Wild abhorred life, abhorred most of all these atoms of heat and hurry in the midst of her triumphant stillness. The Wild would crush those defiant pigmies that disputed the majesty of her invincible calm.

A dog was hanging back in the harness. It whined; then as the husky following snapped at it savagely, it gave a lurch and fell. The big man shot forward with a sudden fury in his eyes. Swinging the heavy-thonged whip, again and again he brought it down on the writhing brute. Then he twisted the thong around his hand and belaboured its hollow ribs with the butt. It screamed for a while, but soon it ceased to scream; it only moaned a little. With glistening fangs and ears up-pricked the other dogs looked at their fallen comrade. They longed to leap on it, to rend its gaunt limbs apart, to tear its quivering flesh; but there was the big man with his murderous whip, and they cowered before him.

The big man kicked the fallen dog repeatedly. The little man paused in his painful progress to look on apathetically.

"You'll stave in its ribs," he remarked presently; "and then we'll never make timber by nightfall."

The big man had failed in his efforts to rouse the dog. There in that lancinating cold, in an ecstasy of rage, despairfully he poised over it.

"Who told you to put in your lip?" he snarled. "Who's running this show, you or I? I'll stave in its ribs if I choose, and I'll hitch you to the sled and make you pull your guts out, too."

The little man said no more. Then, the dog still refusing to rise, the big man leapt over the harness and came down on the animal with both feet. There was a scream of pitiful agony, and the snap of breaking bones. But the big man slipped and fell. Down he came, and like a flash the whole pack piled onto him.

For a moment there was a confused muddle of dogs and master. This was the time for which they had waited, these savage semi-wolves. This man had beaten them, had starved them, had been a devil to them, and now he was down and at their mercy. Ferociously they sprang on him, and their white fangs snapped like traps in his face. They fought to get at his throat. They tore at his parka. Oh, if they could only make their teeth meet in his warm flesh! But no; they were all tangled up in the harness, and the man was fighting like a giant. He had the leader by the throat and was using her as a shield against the others. His right hand swung the whip with flail-like blows. Foiled and confused the dogs fell to fighting among themselves, and triumphantly the man leapt to his feet.

He was like a fiend now. Fiercely he raged among the snarling pack, kicking, clubbing, cursing, till one and all he had them beaten into cowering subjection.

He was still panting from his struggle. His face was deathly pale, and his eyes were glittering. He strode up to the little man, who had watched the performance stolidly.

"Why didn't you help me, you dirty little whelp?" he hissed. "You wanted to see them chew me up; you know you did. You'd like to have them rip me to ribbons. You wouldn't move a finger to save me. Oh, I know, I know. I've had enough of you this trip to last me a lifetime. You've bucked me right along. Now, blast your dirty little soul, I hate you, and for the rest of the way I'm going to make your life hell. See! Now I'll begin."

The little man was afraid. He seemed to grow smaller, while over him towered the other, dark, fierce and malignant. The little man was desperate. Defensively he crouched, yet the next instant he was overthrown. Then, as he lay sprawling in the snow, the big man fell to lashing him with the whip. Time after time he struck, till the screams of his victim became one long, drawn-out wail of agony. Then he desisted. Jerking the other on his feet once more, he bade him go on breaking trail.

Again they struggled on. The light was beginning to fail, and there was no thought in their minds but to reach that dark belt of timber before darkness came. There was no sound but the crunch of their snowshoes, the panting of the dogs, the rasping of the sleigh. When they paused the silence seemed to fall on them like a blanket. There was something awful in the quality of this deathly silence. It was as if something material, something tangible, hovered over them, closed in on them, choked them, throttled them. It was almost like a Presence.

Weary and worn were men and dogs as they struggled onwards in the growing gloom, but because of the feeling in his heart the little man no longer was conscious of bodily pain. It was black murder that raged there.

With straining sinews and bones that cracked, the dogs bent to a heavy pull, while at the least sign of shirking down swished the relentless whip. And the big man, as if proud of his strength, gazed insolently round on the Wild. He was at home in this land, this stark wolf-land, so callous, so cruel. Was he not cruel, too? Surely this land cowered before him. Its hardships could not daunt him, nor its terrors dismay. As he urged on his bloody-footed dogs, he exulted greatly. Of all Men of the High North was he not king?

At last they reached the forest fringe, and after a few harsh directions he had the little man making camp. The little man worked with a strange willingness. All his taciturnity had gone. As he gathered the firewood and filled the Yukon stove, he hummed a merry air. He had the water boiling and soon there was the fragrance of tea in the little tent. He produced sourdough bread (which he fried in bacon fat), and some dried moose-meat.

To men of the trail this was a treat. They ate ravenously, but they did not speak. Yet the little man was oddly cheerful. Time and again the big man looked at him suspiciously. Outside it was a steely night, with an icicle of a moon. The cold leapt on one savagely. To step from the tent was like plunging into icy water, yet within those canvas walls the men were warm and snug. The stove crackled its cheer. A grease-light sputtered, and by its rays the little man was mending his ice-stiffened moccasins. He hummed an Irish air, and he seemed to be tickled with some thought he had.

"Stop that tune," growled the other. "If you don't know anything else, cut it out. I'm sick of it."

The little man shut up meekly. Again there was silence, broken by a whining and a scratching outside. It was the five dogs crying for their supper, crying for the frozen fish they had earned so well. They wondered why it was not forthcoming. When they received it they would lie on it, to warm it with the heat of their bodies, and then gnaw off the thawed portions. They were very wise, these dogs. But to-night there was no fish, and they whined for it.

"Dog feed all gone?"

"Yep," said the small man.

"Hell! I'll silence these brutes anyway."

He went to the door and laid onto them so that they slunk away into the shadows. But they did not bury themselves in the snow and sleep. They continued to prowl round the tent, hunger-mad and desperate.

"We've only got enough grub left for ourselves now," said the big man; "and none too much at that. I guess I'll put you on half-rations."

He laughed as if it was the hugest joke. Then rolling himself in a robe, he lay down and slept.

The little man did not sleep. He was still turning over the thought that had come to him. Outside in the atrocious cold the whining malamutes crept nearer and nearer. Savage were they, Indian raised and sired by a wolf. And now, in the agonies of hunger, they cried for fish, and there was none for them, only kicks and curses. Oh, it was a world of ghastly cruelty! They howled their woes to the weary moon.

"Short rations, indeed," mumbled the little man. He crawled into his sleeping bag, but he did not close his eyes. He was watching.

About dawn he rose. An evil dawn it was, sallow, sinister and askew.

The little man selected the heavy-handled whip for the job. Carefully he felt its butt, then he struck. It was a shrewd blow and a neatly delivered, for the little man had been in the business before. It fell on the big man's head, and he crumpled up. Then the little man took some rawhide thongs and trussed up his victim. There lay the big man, bound and helpless, with a clotted blood-hole in his black hair.

Then the little man gathered up the rest of the provisions. He looked around carefully, as if fearful of leaving anything behind. He made a pack of the food and lashed it on his back. Now he was ready to start. He knew that within fifty miles, travelling to the south, he would strike a settlement. He was safe.

He turned to where lay the unconscious body of his partner. Again and again he kicked it; he cursed it; he spat on it. Then, after a final look of gloating hate, he went off and left the big man to his fate.

At last, at long last, the Worm had turned.

* * * * *

CHAPTER X

The dogs! The dogs were closing in. Nearer and nearer they drew, headed by a fierce Mackenzie River bitch. They wondered why their master did not wake; they wondered why the little tent was so still; why no plume of smoke rose from the slim stovepipe. All was oddly quiet and lifeless. No curses greeted them; no whiplash cut into them; no strong arm jerked them over the harness. Perhaps it was a primordial instinct that drew them on, that made them strangely bold. Perhaps it was only the despair of their hunger, the ache of empty bellies. Closer and closer they crept to the silent tent.

Locasto opened his eyes. Within a foot of his face were the fangs of a malamute. At his slight movement it drew back with a snarl, and retreated to the door. Locasto could see the other dogs crouching and eyeing him fixedly. What could be the matter? What had gotten into the brutes? Where was the Worm? Where were the provisions? Why was the tent flap open and the stove stone-cold? Then with a dawning comprehension that he had been deserted, Locasto uttered a curse and tried to rise.

At first he thought he was stiff with cold, but a downward glance showed him his condition. He was helpless. He grew sick at the pit of his stomach, and glared at the dogs. They were drawing in on him. They seemed to bulk suddenly, to grow huge and menacing. Their gleaming teeth snapped in his face. He could fancy these teeth stripping the flesh from his body, gnawing at his bones with drooling jaws. Violently he shuddered. He must try to free himself, so that at least he could fight.

Grimly the Worm had done his work, but he had hardly reckoned on the strength of this man. With a vast throe of fear Locasto tried to free himself. Tenser, tenser grew the thongs; they strained, they bit into his flesh, but they would not break. Yet as he relaxed it seemed to him they were less tight. Then he rested for another effort.

Once again the gaunt, grey bitch was crawling up. He remembered how often he had starved it, clubbed it until it could barely stand. Now it was going to get even. It would snap at his throat, rip out his windpipe, bury its fangs in his bleeding flesh. He cursed it in the old way. With a spring it backed out again and stood with the others. He made another giant effort. Once again he felt the thongs strain and strain; then, when he ceased, he imagined they were still looser.

The dogs seemed to have lost all fear. They stood in a circle within a few feet of him, regarding him intently. They smelled the blood on his head, and a slaver ran from their jaws. Again he cursed them, but this time they did not move. They seemed to realise he could not harm them. With their evilly-slanted eyes they watched his struggles. Strange, wise, uncanny brutes, they were biding their time, waiting to rush in on him, to rend him.

Again he tried to get free. Now he fancied he could move his arm a little. He must hurry, for every instant the malamutes were growing bolder. Another strain and a wrench. Ha! he was able to squeeze his right arm from under the rawhide.

He felt the foul breath of the dogs on his face, and quickly he struck at them. They jumped back, then, as if at a signal, they sprang in again. There was no time to lose. They were attacking him in earnest. Quickly he wrenched out his other arm. He was just in time, for the dogs were upon him.

He struggled to his knees and shielded his head with his arms. Wildly he swung at the nearest dog. Full on the face he struck it, and it shot back as if hit by a bullet. But the others were on him. They had him down, snarling and ripping, a mad ferment of fury. Two of them were making for his face. As he lay on his back he gripped each by the throat. His hands were torn and bleeding, but he had them fast. In his grip of steel they struggled to free themselves in vain. They backed, they writhed, they twisted in a bow. With his huge hands he was choking them, choking them to death, using them as a shield against the other three. Then slowly he worked himself into a sitting position. He hurled one of the dogs to the tent door. He swung bludgeon blows at the others. They fled yelping and howling. He still held the Mackenzie River bitch. Getting his knee on her body, he bent her almost into a circle, bent her till her back broke with a snap.

Then he rose and freed himself from the remaining thongs. He was torn and cut and bleeding, but he had triumphed.

"Oh, the devil!" he growled, grinding his teeth. "He would have me chewed to rags by malamutes."

He stared around.

"He's taken everything, the scum! left me to starve. Ha! one thing he's forgotten—the matches. At least I can keep warm."

He picked up the canister of matches and relit the stove.

"I'll kill him for this," he muttered. "Night and day I'll follow him. I'll camp on his trail till I find him. Then—I'll torture him; I'll strip him and leave him naked in the snow."

He slipped into his snowshoes, gave a last look around to see that no food had been left, and with a final growl of fury he started in pursuit.

* * * * *

Ahead of him, ploughing their way through the virgin snow, he could see the dragging track of the long snowshoes. He examined it, and noted that it was sharp and crisp at the edges.

"He's got a good five hours' start of me! Travelling fast, too, by the length of the track."

He had a thought of capturing the dogs and hitching them up; but, thoroughly terrified, they had retreated into the woods. To overtake this man, to glut his lust for revenge, he must depend on his own strength and endurance.

"Now, Jack Locasto," he told himself grimly, "you've got a fight on your hands, such a fight as you never had before. Get right down to it."

So, with head bowed and shoulders sloping forward, he darted on the track of the Worm.

"He's got to break trail, the viper! and that's where I score. I can make twice the time. Oh, just wait, you little devil! just wait!"

He ground his teeth vindictively, and put an inch more onto his stride. He was descending a long, open valley that seemed from its trackless snows to have been immemorially life-shunned and accursed. Black, witch-like pines sentinelled its flanks, and accentuated its desolation. And over all there was the silence of the Wild, that double-strong solution of silence from which all other silences are distilled, and spread out. Yet, as he gazed around him in this everlasting solitude, there was no fear in his heart.

"I can fight this accursed land and beat it out every time," he exulted. "It can't get any the better of me."

It was cold, so cold that it was difficult to imagine it could ever be warm again. To expose flesh was to feel instantly the sharp sting that heralds frostbite. As he ran, the sharp intake of icy air made his lungs seem to contract. His eyes smarted and tingled. The lashes froze closely. Ice formed in his nostrils and his nose began to bleed. He pulled up a moment.

"Curse this infernal country!"

He had not eaten and the icy air begot a ravenous hunger. He dreamed of food, but chiefly of bacon, fat, greasy bacon. How glorious it would be just to eat of it, raw, tallow bacon! He had nothing to eat. He would have nothing till he had overtaken the Worm. On! On!

He came to where the Worm had made a camp. There were the ashes of a fire.

"Curse him; he's got some matches after all," he said with bitter chagrin. Eagerly he searched all around in the snow to see if he could not find even a crumb of food. There was nothing. He pushed on. Night fell and he was forced to make camp.

Oh, he was hungry! The night was vastly resplendent, a spendthrift night scattering everywhere its largess of stars. The cold had a crystalline quality and the trees detonated strangely in the silence. He built a huge fire: that at least he could have, and through eighteen hours of darkness he crouched by it, afraid to sleep for fear of freezing.

"If I only had a tin to boil water in," he muttered; "there's lots of reindeer moss, and I could stew some of my mucklucks. Ah! I'll try and roast a bit of them."

He cut a strip from the Indian boots he was wearing, and held it over the fire. The hair singed away and the corners crisped and charred. He put it in his mouth. It was pleasantly warm, but even his strong teeth refused to meet in it. However, he tore it into smaller pieces, and bolted them.

At last the dawn came, that evil, sneaking, corpse-like dawn, and Locasto flung himself once more on the trail. He was not feeling so fit now. Hunger and loss of blood had weakened him so that his stride insensibly shortened, and his step had lost its spring. However, he plodded on doggedly, an incarnation of vengeance and hate. Again he examined the snowshoe trail ever stretching in front, and noticed how crisped and hard was its edge. He was not making the time he had reckoned on. The Worm must be a long way ahead.

Still he did not despair. The little man might rest a day, or oversleep, or strain a sinew, then—Locasto pictured with gloating joy the terror of the Worm as he awoke to find himself overtaken. Oh, the snake! the vermin! On! On!

Beyond a doubt he was growing weaker. Once or twice he stumbled, and the last time he lay a few moments before rising. He wanted to rest badly. The cold was keener than ever; it was merciless; it was excruciating. He no longer had the vitality to withstand it. It stabbed and stung him whenever he exposed bare flesh. He pulled the parka hood very close, so that only his eyes peered out. So he moved through the desolation of the Arctic Wild, a dark, muffled figure, a demon of vengeance, fierce and menacing.

He stood on a vast, still plateau. The sky was like a great grotto of ice. The land lay in a wan apathy of suffering, dumb, hopeless, drear. Icy land and icy sky met in a trap, a trap that held him fast; and over all, vast, titanic, terrible, the Spirit of the Wild seemed to brood. It laughed at him, a laugh of derision, of mockery, of callous gloating triumph. Locasto shuddered. Then night came and he built another giant fire.

Again he bolted down some roasted muckluck. Overhead the stars glittered vindictively. They were green and blue and red, and they had spiny rays like starfish on which they danced. This night he had to make tremendous efforts to keep from sleeping. Several times he drowsed forward, and almost fell into the fire. As he crouched there his beard was singeing and his face scorched, but his back seemed as if it was cased in ice. Often he would turn and warm it at the fire, but not for long. He hated to face the terror of the silence and the dark, the shadow where waited Death. Better the crackling cheer of the spruce flame.

At dawn the sky was leaden and the cold less despotic. Stretching interminably ahead was that lonely snowshoe trail. Locasto was puzzled.

"Where in creation is the little devil going to, anyway?" he said, knitting his brows. "I figured he'd make direct for Dawson, but he's either changed his mind or got a wrong steer. By Heavens, that's it—the little varmint's lost his way."

Locasto had an Indian's unerring sense of location.

"I guess I can't afford to follow him any more," he reflected. "I've gone too far already. I'm all petered out. I'll have to let him go in the meantime. It's save yourself, Jack Locasto, while there's yet time. Me for Dawson."

He struck off almost at right angles to the trail he had been following, over a low range of hills. It was evil going, and as he broke through the snow-crust mile after wearing mile, he felt himself grow weaker and weaker. "Buck up, old man," he adjured himself fiercely. "You've got to fight, fight."

There was a strange stillness in the air, not the natural stillness of the Wild, but an unhealthy one, as of a suspension of something, of a vacuum, of bated breath. It was curiously full of terror. More and more he felt like a trapped animal, caught in a vast cage. The sky to the north was glooming ominously. Every second the horizon grew blacker, more bodeful, and Locasto stared at it, with a sudden quake at his heart.

"Blizzard, by thunder!" he gasped.

Was that a breath of wind that stung his cheek? Was it a snowflake that drifted along with it? Denser and denser grew the gloom, and now there was a roaring as of a great wind. King Blizzard was come.

"I guess I'm done for," he hissed through clenched teeth. "But I'll fight to the finish. I'll die game."

* * * * *

CHAPTER XI

It was on him now with a swoop and a roar. He was in the thick of a mud-grey darkness, a bitter, blank darkness full of whirling wind-eddies and vast flurries of snow. He could not see more than a few feet before him. The stinging flakes blinded him; the coal-black night engulfed him. In that seething turmoil of the elements he was as helpless as a child.

"I guess you're on your last trail, Jack Locasto," he muttered grimly.

Nevertheless he lowered his head and butted desperately into the heart of the storm. He was very faint from lack of food, but despair had given him a new strength, and he plunged through drift and flurry with the fury of a goaded bull.

The night had fallen black as the pit. He was in an immensity of darkness, a darkness that packed close up to him, and hugged him, and enfolded him like a blanket. And in the black void winds were raging with an insane fury, whirling aloft mountains of snow and hurling them along plain and valley. The forests shrieked in fear; the creatures of the Wild cowered in their lairs, but the solitary man stumbled on and on. As if by magic barriers of snow piled up before him, and almost to his shoulders he floundered through them. The wind had a hatchet edge that pierced his clothes and hacked him viciously. He knew his only plan was to keep moving, to stumble, stagger on. It was a fight for life.

He had forgotten his hunger. Those wild visions of gluttony had gone from him. He had forgotten his thirst for revenge, forgotten everything but his own dire peril.

"Keep moving, keep moving for God's sake," he urged himself hoarsely. "You'll freeze if you let up a moment. Don't let up, don't!"

But oh, how hard it was not to rest! Every muscle in his body seemed to beg and pray for rest, yet the spirit in him drove them to work anew. He was making a certain mad headway, travelling, always travelling. He doubted not he was doomed, but instinct made him fight on as long as an atom of strength remained.

He floundered to his armpits in a snowdrift. He struggled out and staggered on once more. In the mad buffoonery of that cutting wind he scarce could stand upright. His parka was frozen stiff as a board. He could feel his hands grow numb in his mits. From his fingers the icy cold crept up and up. Long since he had lost all sensation in his feet. From the ankles down they were like wooden clogs. He had an idea they were frozen. He lifted them, and watched them sink and disappear in the clinging snow. He beat his numb hands against his breast. It was of no use—he could not get back the feeling in them. A craving to lie down in the snow assailed him.

Life was so sweet. He had visions of cities, of banquets, of theatres, of glittering triumphs, of glorious excitements, of women he had loved, conquered and thrown aside. Never again would he see that world. He would die here, and they would find him rigid and brittle, frozen so hard they would have to thaw him out before they buried him. He fancied he saw himself frozen in a grotesque position. There would be ice-crystals in the very centre of his heart, that heart that had glowed so fiercely with the lust of life. Yes, life was sweet. A vast self-pity surged over him. Well, he had done his best; he could struggle no more.

But struggle he did, another hour, two hours, three hours. Where was he going? Maybe round in a circle. He was like an automaton now. He did not think any more, he just kept moving. His feet clumped up and down. He lifted himself out of snowpits; he staggered a few steps, fell, crawled on all fours in the darkness, then in a lull of the furious wind rose once more to his feet. The night was abysmal; closer and closer it hugged him. The wind was charging him from all points, baffling him like a merry monster, beating him down. The snow whirled around him in a narrow eddy, and he tried to grope out of it and failed. Oh, he was tired, tired!

He must give up. It was too bad. He was so strong, and capable of so much for good or bad. Alas! it had been all for bad. Oh, if he had but another chance he might make his life tell a different tale! Well, he wasn't going to whine or cower. He would die game.

His feet were frozen; his arms were frozen. Here he would lie down and—quit. It would soon be over, and it was a pleasant death, they said. One more look he gave through the writhing horror of the darkness; one more look before he closed his eyes to the horror of the Greater Darkness . . .

Ha! what was that? He fancied he saw a dim glow just ahead. It could not be. It was one of those cheating dreams that came to a dying man, an illusion, a mockery. He closed his eyes. Then he opened them again—the glow was still there.

Surely it must be real! It was steady. As he fell forward it seemed to grow more bright. On hands and knees he crawled to it. Brighter and brighter it grew. It was but a few feet away. Oh, God! could it be?

Then there was a lull in the storm, and with a final plunge Locasto fell forward, fell towards a lamp lighted in a window, fell against the closed door of a little cabin.

* * * * *

The Worm suffered acutely from the intense cold. He cursed it in his prolific and exhaustive way. He cursed the leaden weight of his snowshoes, and the thongs that chafed his feet. He cursed the pack he carried on his back, which momently grew heavier. He cursed the country; then, after a general debauch of obscenity, he decided it was time to feed.

He gathered some dry twigs and built a fire on the snow. He hurried, for the freezing process was going on in his carcase, and he was afraid. It was all ready. Now to light it—the matches.

Where in hell were the matches? Surely he could not have left them at the camp. With feverish haste he overturned his pack. No, they were not there. Could he have dropped them on the trail? He had a wild idea of going back. Then he thought of Locasto lying in the tent. He could never face that. But he must have a fire. He was freezing to death—right now. Already his fingers were tingling and stiffening.

Huh! maybe he had some matches in his pockets. No—yes, he had—one, two, three, four, five, that was all. Five slim sulphur matches, part of a block, and jammed in a corner of his waistcoat pocket. Eagerly he lit one. The twigs caught. The flame leapt up. Oh it was good! He had a fire, a fire.

He made tea, and ate some bread and meat. Then he felt his strength and courage return. He had four matches left. Four matches meant four fires. That would mean four more days' travel. By that time he would have reached the Dawson country.

That night he made a huge blaze, chopping down several trees and setting them alight. There, lying in his sleeping-bag, he rested well. In the early dawn he was afoot once more.

Was there ever such an atrocious soul-freezing cold! He cursed it with every breath he drew. At noon he felt a vast temptation to make another fire, but he refrained. Then that night he had bad luck, for one of his precious matches proved little more than a sliver tipped with the shadow of pink. In spite of his efforts it was abortive, and he was compelled to use another. He was down to his last match.

Well, he must travel extra hard. So next day in a panic of fear he covered a vast stretch of country. He must be getting near to one of the gold creeks. As he surmounted the crest of every ridge he expected to see the blue smoke of cabin fires, yet always was there the same empty desolation. Then night came and he prepared to camp.

Once more he chopped down some trees and piled them in a heap. He was very hungry, very cold, very tired. What a glorious blaze he would soon have! How gallantly the flames would leap and soar! He collected some dry moss and twigs. Never had he felt the cold so bitter. It was growing dusk. Above him the sky had a corpse-like glimmer, and on the snow strange bale-fires glinted. It was a weird, sardonic light that waited, keeping tryst with darkness.

He shuddered and his fingers trembled. Then ever so carefully he drew forth that most precious of things, the last match.

He must hurry; his fingers were tingling, freezing, stiffening fast. He would lie down on the snow, and strike it quickly . . . "O God!"

From his numb fingers the slim little match had dropped. There it lay on the snow. Gingerly he picked it up, with a wild hope that it would be all right. He struck it, but it doubled up. Again he struck it: the head came off—he was lost.

He fell forward on his face. His hands were numb, dead. He lay supported by his elbows, his eyes gazing blankly at the unlit fire. Five minutes passed; he did not rise. He seemed dazed, stupid, terror-stricken. Five more minutes passed. He did not move. He seemed to stiffen, to grow rigid, and the darkness gathered around him.

A thought came to his mind that he would straighten out, so that when they found him he would be in good shape to fit in a coffin. He did not want them to break his legs and arms. Yes, he would straighten out. He tried—but he could not, so he let it go at that.

Over him the Wild seemed to laugh, a laugh of scorn, of mockery, of exquisite malice.

And there in fifteen minutes the cold slew him. When they found him he lay resting on his elbows and gazing with blank eyes of horror at his unlit fire.

* * * * *

CHAPTER XII

"It's a beast of a night," said the Halfbreed.

He and I were paying a visit to Jim in the cabin he had built on Ophir. Jim was busy making ready for his hydraulic work of the coming Spring, and once in a while we took a run up to see him. I was much worried about the old man. He was no longer the cheerful, optimistic Jim of the trail. He had taken to living alone. He had become grim and taciturn. He cared only for his work, and, while he read his Bible more than ever, it was with a growing fondness for the stern old prophets. There was no doubt the North was affecting him strangely.

"Lord! don't it blow? Seems as if the wind had a spite against us, wanted to put us out of business. It minds me of the blizzards we have in the Northwest, only it seems ten times worse."

The Halfbreed went on to tell us of snowstorms he had known, while huddled round the stove we listened to the monstrous uproar of the gale.

"Why don't you chink your cabin better, Jim?" I asked; "the snow's sifting through in spots."

He shoved more wood into the stove, till it glowed to a dull red, starred with little sparks that came and went.

"Snow with that wind would sift through a concrete wall," he said. "It's part an' parcel of the awful land. I tell you there's a curse on this country. Long, long ago godless people have lived in it, lived an' sinned an' perished. An' for its wickedness in the past the Lord has put His everlasting curse on it."

Sharply I looked at him. His eyes were staring. His face was drawn into a knot of despair. He sat down and fell into a mood of gloomy silence.

How the storm was howling! The Half breed smoked his cigarette stolidly, while I listened and shuddered, mightily thankful that I was so safe and warm.

"Say, I wonder if there's any one out in this bedlam of a night?"

"If there is, God help him," said the Halfbreed. "He'll last about as long as a snowball in hell."

"Yes, fancy wandering round out there, dazed and desperate; fancy the wind knocking you down and heaping the snow on you; fancy going on and on in the darkness till you freeze stiff. Ugh!"

Again I shuddered. Then, as the other two sat in silence, my mind strayed to other things. Chiefly I thought of Berna, all alone in Dawson. I longed to be back with her again. I thought of Locasto. Where in his wild wanderings had he got to? I thought of Glengyle and Garry. How had he fared after Mother died? Why did he not marry? Once a week I got a letter from him, full of affection and always urging me to come home. In my letters I had never mentioned Berna. There was time enough for that.

Lord! a terrific gust of wind shook the cabin. It howled and screamed insanely through the heaving night. Then there came a lull, a strange, deep lull, deathlike after the mighty blast. And in the sudden quiet it seemed to me I heard a hollow cry.

"Hist! What was that?" whispered the Halfbreed.

Jim, too, was listening intently.

"Seems to me I heard a moan."

"Sounded like the cry of an outcast soul. Maybe it's the spirit of some poor devil that's lost away out in the night. I hate to open the door for nothing. It will make the place like an ice-house."

Once more we listened intently, holding our breath. There it was again, a low, faint moan.

"It's some one outside," gasped the Halfbreed. Horror-stricken, we stared at each other, then he rushed to the door. A great gust of wind came in on us.

"Hurry up, you fellows," he cried; "lend a hand. I think it's a man."

Frantically we pulled it in, an unconscious form that struck a strange chill to our hearts. Anxiously we bent over it.

"He's not dead," said the Halfbreed, "only badly frozen, hands and feet and face. Don't take him near the fire."

He had been peering inside the parka hood and suddenly he turned to me.

"Well, I'm darned—it's Locasto."

Locasto! I shrank back and stood there staring blankly. Locasto! all the old hate resurged into my heart. Many a time had I wished him dead; and even dying, never could I have forgiven him. As I would have shrank from a reptile, I drew back.

"No, no," I said hoarsely, "I won't touch him. Curse him! Curse him! He can die."

"Come on there," said Jim fiercely. "You wouldn't let a man die, would you? There's the brand of a dog on you if you do. You'll be little better than a murderer. It don't matter what wrong he's done you, it's your duty as a man to help him. He's only a human soul, an' he's like to die anyway. Come on. Get these mits off his hands."

Mechanically I obeyed him. I was dazed. It was as if I was impelled by a stronger will than my own. I began pulling off the mits. The man's hands were white as putty. I slit the sleeves and saw that the awful whiteness went clear up the arm. It was horrible.

Jim and the Halfbreed had cut open his mucklucks and taken off his socks, and there stretched out were two naked limbs, clay-white almost to the knees. Never did I see anything so ghastly. Tearing off his clothing we laid him on the bed, and forced some brandy between his lips.

At last heat was beginning to come back to the frozen frame. He moaned, and opened his eyes in a wild gaze. He did not know us. He was still fighting the blizzard. He raised himself up.

"Keep a-going, keep a-going," he panted.

"Keep that bucket a-going," said the Halfbreed. "Thank God, we've got plenty of ice-water. We've got to thaw him out."

Then for this man began a night of agony, such as few have endured. We lifted him onto a chair and put one of those clay-cold feet into the water. At the contact he screamed, and I could see ice crystallise on the edge of the bucket. I had forgotten my hatred of the man. I only thought of those frozen hands and feet, and how to get life into them once more. Our struggle began.

"The blood's beginning to circulate back," said the Halfbreed. "I guess that water feels scalding hot to him right now. We'll have to hold him down presently. Ugh—hold on, boys, for all you're worth."

He had not warned us any too soon. In a terrible spasm of agony Locasto threw us off quickly. We grasped him again. Now we were struggling with him. He fought like a demon. He was cursing us, praying us to leave him alone, raving, shrieking. Grimly we held on, yet, all three, it was as much as we could do to keep him down.

"One would think we were murdering him," said the Halfbreed. "Keep his foot in the bucket there. I wish we'd some kind of dope to give him. There's boiling lead running through his veins right now. Keep him down, boys; keep him down."

It was hard, but keep him down we did; though his cries of anguish deafened us through that awful night, and our muscles knotted as we gripped. Hour after hour we held him, plunging now a hand, now a foot in the ice-water, and holding it there. How long he fought! How strong he was! But the time came when he could fight no more. He was like a child in our hands.

There, at last it was done. We wrapped the tender flesh in pieces of blanket. We laid him moaning on the bed. Then, tired out with our long struggle, we threw ourselves down and slept like logs.

Next morning he was still unconscious. He suffered intense pain, so that Jim or the Halfbreed had to be ever by him. I, for my part, refused to go near. Indeed, I watched with a growing hatred his slow recovery. I was sorry, sorry. I wished he had died.

At last he opened his eyes, and feebly he asked where he was. After the Halfbreed had told him, he lay silent awhile.

"I've had a close call," he groaned. Then he went on triumphantly: "I guess the Wild hasn't got the bulge on me yet. I can give it another round."

He began to pick up rapidly, and there in that narrow cabin I sat within a few feet of him, and beheld him grow strong again. I suppose my face must have showed my bitter hate, for often I saw him watching me through half-closed eyes, as if he realised my feelings. Then a sneering smile would curve his lips, a smile of satanic mockery. Again and again I thought of Berna. Fear and loathing convulsed me, and at times a great rage burned in me so that I was like to kill him.

"Seems to me everything's healing up but that hand," said the Halfbreed. "I guess it's too far gone. Gangrene's setting in. Say, Locasto, looks like you'll have to lose it."

Locasto had been favouring me with a particularly sardonic look, but at these words the sneer was wiped out, and horror crowded into his eyes.

"Lose my hand—don't tell me that! Kill me at once! I don't want to be maimed. Lose my hand! Oh, that's terrible! terrible!"

He gazed at the discoloured flesh. Already the stench of him was making us sick, but this hand with its putrid tissues was disgusting to a degree.

"Yes," said the Halfbreed, "there's the line of the gangrene, and it's spreading. Soon mortification will extend all up your arm, then you'll die of blood poison. Locasto, better let me take off that hand. I've done jobs like that before. I'm a handy man, I am. Come, let me take it off."

"Heavens! you're a cold-blooded butcher. You're going to kill me, between you all. You're in a plot leagued against me, and that long-faced fool over there's at the bottom of it. Damn you, then, go on and do what you want."

"You're not very grateful," said the Halfbreed. "All right, lie there and rot."

At his words Locasto changed his tune. He became alarmed to the point of terror. He knew the hand was doomed. He lay staring at it, staring, staring. Then he sighed, and thrust its loathsomeness into our faces.

"Come on," he growled. "Do something for me, you devils, or I'll do it myself."

* * * * *

The hour of the operation was at hand. The Halfbreed got his jack-knife ready. He had filed the edge till it was like a rough saw. He cut the skin of the wrist just above the gangrene line, and raised it up an inch or so. It was here Locasto showed wonderful nerve. He took a large bite of tobacco and chewed steadily, while his keen black eyes watched every move of the knife.

"Hurry up and get the cursed thing off," he snarled.

The Halfbreed nicked the flesh down to the bone, then with the ragged jack-knife he began to saw. I could not bear to look. It made me deathly sick. I heard the grit, grit of the jagged blade. I will remember the sound to my dying day. How long it seemed to take! No man could stand such torture. A groan burst from Locasto's lips. He fell back on the bed. His jaws no longer worked, and a thin stream of brown saliva trickled down his chin. He had fainted.

Quickly the Halfbreed finished his work. The hand dropped on the floor. He pulled down the flaps of skin and sewed them together.

"How's that for home-made surgery?" he chuckled. He was vastly proud of his achievement. He took the severed hand upon a shovel and, going to the door, he threw it far out into the darkness.

* * * * *

CHAPTER XIII

"WHY don't you go outside?" I asked of the Jam-wagon.

I had rescued him from one of his periodical plunges into the cesspool of debauch, and he was peaked, pallid, penitent. Listlessly he stared at me a long moment, the dull, hollow-eyed stare of the recently regenerate.

"Well," he said at last, "I think I stay for the same reason many another man stays—pride. I feel that the Yukon owes me one of two things, a stake or a grave—and she's going to pay."

"Seems to me, the way you're shaping you're more liable to get the latter."

"Yes—well, that'll be all right."

"Look here," I remonstrated, "don't be a rotter. You're a man, a splendid one. You might do anything, be anything. For Heaven's sake stop slipping cogs, and get into the game."

His thin, handsome face hardened bitterly.

"I don't know. Sometimes I think I'm not fit to play the game; sometimes I wonder if it's all worth while; sometimes I'm half inclined to end it."

"Oh, don't talk nonsense."

"I'm not; I mean it, every word. I don't often speak of myself. It doesn't matter who I am, or what I've been. I've gone through a lot—more than most men. For years I've been a sort of a human derelict, drifting from port to port of the seven seas. I've sprawled in their mire; I've eaten of their filth; I've wallowed in their moist, barbaric slime. Time and time again I've gone to the mat, but somehow I would never take the count. Something's always saved me at the last."

"Your guardian angel."

"Maybe. Somehow I wouldn't be utterly downed. I'm a bit of a fighter, and every day's been a battle with me. Oh, you don't know, you can't believe how I suffer! Often I pray, and my prayer always is: 'O dear God, don't allow me to *think*. Lash me with Thy wrath; heap burdens on me, but don't let me *think*.' They say there's a hell hereafter. They lie: it's here, now."

I was astonished at his vehemence. His face was wrenched with pain, and his eyes full of remorseful misery.

"What about your friends?"

"Oh, them—I died long ago, died in the early '80's. In a little French graveyard there's a tombstone that bears my name, my real name, the name of the 'me' that was. Heart, soul and body, I died. My sisters mourned me, my friends muttered, 'Poor devil.' A few women cried, and a girl—well, I mustn't speak of that. It's all over long ago; but I must eternally do something, fight, drink, work like the devil—anything but think. I mustn't *think*."

"What about your guardian angel?"

"Yes, sometimes I think he's going to give me another chance. This is no life for a man like me, slaving in the drift, burning myself up in the dissipation of the town. A great, glad fight with a good sweet woman to fight for—that would save me. Oh, to get away from it all, get a clean start!"

"Well, I believe in you. I'm sure you'll be all right. Let me lend you the money."

"Thank you, a thousand thanks; but I cannot take it. There it is again—my pride. Maybe I'm all wrong. Maybe I'm a lost soul, and my goal's the potter's field. No; thanks! In a day or two I'll be fighting-fit again. I wouldn't have bored you with this talk, but I'm weak, and my nerve's gone."

"How much money have you got?" I asked.

He pulled a poor piece of silver from his pocket.

"Enough to do me till I join the pick-and-shovel gang."

"What are those tickets in your hand?"

He laughed carelessly.

"Chances in the ice pools. Funny thing, I don't remember buying them. Must have been drunk."

"Yes, and you seem to have had a 'hunch.' You've got the same time on all three: seven seconds, seven minutes past one, on the ninth—that's to-day. It's noon now. That old ice will have to hurry up if you're going to win. Fancy, if you did! You'd clean up over three thousand dollars. There would be your new start."

"Yes, fancy," he echoed mockingly. "Over five thousand betting, and the guesses as close as peas in a pod."

"Well, the ice may go out any moment. It's awful rotten."

With a curious fascination, we gazed down at the mighty river. Around us was a glow of spring sunshine, above us the renaissance of blue skies. Rags of snow still glimmered on the hills, and the brown earth, as if ashamed of its nakedness, was bursting greenly forth. On the slope overlooking the Klondike, girls in white dresses were gathering the wild crocus. All was warmth, colour, awakening life.

Surely the river ice could not hold much longer. It was patchy, netted with cracks, heaved up in ridges, mottled with slushy pools, corroded to the bottom. Decidedly it was rotten, rotten. Still it held stubbornly. The Klondike hammered it with mighty bergs, black and heavy as a house. Down the swift current they sped, crashing, grinding, roaring, to batter into the unbroken armour of the Yukon. And along its banks, watching even as we watched, were thousands of others. On every lip was the question—"The ice—when will it go out?" For to these exiles of the North, after eight months of isolation, the sight of open water would be like Heaven. It would mean boats, freedom, friendly faces, and a step nearer to that "outside" of their dreams.

Towards the centre of the vast mass of ice that belted in the city was a post, and on this lonely post thousands of eyes were constantly turning. For an electric wire connected it with the town, so that when it moved down a certain distance a clock would register the exact moment. Thus, thousands gazing at that solitary post thought of the bets they had made, and wondered if this year they would be the lucky ones. It is a unique incident in Dawson life, this gambling on the ice. There are dozens of pools, large and small, and both men and women take part in the betting, with an eagerness and excitement that is almost childish.

I sat on a bench on the N. C. trail overlooking the town, and watched the Jam-wagon crawl down the hill to his cabin. Poor fellow! How drawn and white was his face, and his long, clean frame—how gaunt and weary! I felt sorry for him. What would become of him? He was a splendid "misfit." If he only had another chance! Somehow I believed in him, and fervently I hoped he would have that good clean start again.

Up in the cold remoteness of the North are many of his kind—the black sheep, the undesirables, the discards of the pack.

Their lips are sealed; their eyes are cold as glaciers, and often they drink deep. Oh, they are a mighty company, the men you don't enquire about; but it is the code of the North to take them as you find them, so they go their way unregarded.

How clear the air was! It was like looking through a crystal lens—every leaf seemed to stand out vividly. Sounds came up to me with marvellous distinctness. Summer was coming, and with it the assurance of a new peace. Down there I could see our home, and on its veranda, hammock-swung, the white figure of Berna. How precious she was to me! How anxiously I watched over her! A look, a word meant more to me than volumes. If she was happy I was full of joy; if she was sad the sunshine paled, the flowers drooped, there was no gladness in the day. Often as she slept I watched her, marvelling at the fine perfection of her face. Always was she an object of wonder to me—something to be adored, to demand all that was fine and high in me.

Yet sometimes it was the very intensity of my love that made me fear; so that in the ecstasy of a moment I would catch my breath and wonder if it all could last. And always the memory of Locasto was a sinister shadow. He had gone "outside," terribly broken in health, gone cursing me hoarsely and vowing he would return. Would he?

Who that knows the North can ever deny its lure? Wherever you be, it will call and call to you. In the sluggish South you will hear it, will long for the keen tingle of its silver days, the vaster glory of its star-strewn nights. In the city's heart it will come to you till you hunger for its big, clean spaces, its racing rivers, its purple tundras. In the homes of the rich its voice will seek you out, and you will ache for your lonely camp-fire, a sunset splendouring to golden death, the night where the silence clutches and the heavens vomit forth white fire. Yes, you will hear it, and hear it, till a madness comes over you, till you leave the crawling men of the sticky pavements to seek it out once more, the sapphire of its lustrous lakes, the white yearning of its peaks to the myriad stars. Then, as a child comes home, will you come home. And I knew that some day to the land wherein he had reigned a conqueror, Locasto, too, would return.

As I looked down on the grey town, the wonder of its growth came over me. How changed from the muddle of tents and cabins, the boat-lined river, the swarming hordes of the Argonauts! Where was the niggerhead swamp, the mud, the unrest, the mad fever of '98? I looked for these things and saw in their stead fine residences, trim gardens, well-kept streets. I almost rubbed my eyes as I realised the magic of the transformation.

And great as was the city's outward change, its change of spirit was still greater. The day of dance-hall domination was over. Vice walked very circumspectly. No longer was it possible on the street to speak to a lady of easy virtue without causing comment.

The demireps of the deadline had been banished over the Klondike, where, in a colony reached by a crazy rope bridge, their red lights gleamed like semaphores of sin. The dance-halls were still running, but the picturesque impunity of the old muckluck days was gone forever. You looked in vain for the crude scenes where the wilder passions were unleashed, and human nature revealed itself in primal nakedness. Heroism, brutality, splendid achievement, unbridled license, the North seems to bring out all that is best and worst in a man. It breeds an exuberant vitality, a madness for action, whether it be for good or evil.

In the town, too, life was becoming a thing of more sober hues. Sick of slipshod morality, men were sending for their wives and children. The old ideals of home and love and social purity were triumphing. With the advent of the good woman, the dance-hall girl was doomed. The city was finding itself. Society divided into sets. The more pretentious were called Ping-pongs, while a majority rejoiced in the name of Rough-necks. The post-office abuses were remedied, the grafters ousted from the government offices. Rapidly the gold-camp was becoming modernised.

Yes, its spectacular days were over. No more would the "live one" disport himself in his wild and woolly glory. The delirium of '98 was fast becoming a memory. The leading actors in that fateful drama—where were they? Dead: some by their own hands; down and out many, drivelling sottishly of by-gone days; poor prospectors a few, dreaming of a new gold strike.

And, as I think of it, it comes over me that the thing is vastly tragic. Where are they now, these Klondike Kings, these givers of champagne baths, these plungers of the gold-camp? How many of those that stood out in the limelight of '98 can tell the tale to-day? Ladue is dead, leaving little behind. Big Alec MacDonald, after lavishing a dozen fortunes on his friends, dies at last, almost friendless and alone. Nigger Jim and Stillwater Willie—in what back slough of vicissitude do they languish to-day? Dick Low lies in a drunkard's grave. Skookum Jim would fain qualify for one. Dawson Charlie, reeling home from a debauch, drowns in the river. In impecunious despair, Harry Waugh hangs himself. Charlie Anderson, after squandering a fortune on a thankless wife, works for a labourer's hire.

So I might go on and on. Their stories would fill volumes. And as I sat on the quiet hillside, listening to the drowsy hum of the bees, the inner meaning of it all came home to me. Once again the great lone land was sifting out and choosing its own. Far-reaching was its vengeance, and it worked in divers ways. It fell on them, even as it had fallen on their brethren of the trail. In the guise of fortune it dealt their ruin. From the austere silence of its snows it was mocking them, beguiling them to their doom. Again it was the Land of the Strong. Before all it demanded strength, moral and physical strength. I was minded of the words of old Jim, "Where one wins ninety and nine will fail"; and time had proved him true. The great, grim land was weeding out the unfit, was rewarding those who could understand it, the faithful brotherhood of the high North.

Full of such thoughts as these, I raised my eyes and looked down the river towards the Moosehide Bluffs. Hullo! There, just below the town, was a great sheet of water, and even as I watched I saw it spread and spread. People were shouting, running from their houses, speeding to the beach. I was conscious of a thrill of excitement. Ever widening was the water, and now it stretched from bank to bank. It crept forward to the solitary post. Now it was almost there. Suddenly the post started to move. The vast ice-field was sliding forward. Slowly, serenely it went, on, on.

Then, all at once, the steam-whistles shrilled out, the bells pealed, and from the black mob of people that lined the banks there went up an exultant cheer. "The ice is going out—the ice is going out!"

I looked at my watch. Could I believe my eyes? Seven seconds, seven minutes past one—his "hunch" was right; his guardian angel had intervened; the Jam-wagon had been given his chance to make a new start.

* * * * *

CHAPTER XIV

The waters were wild with joy. From the mountain snows the sun had set them free. Down hill and dale they sparkled, trickling from boulders, dripping from mossy crannies, rioting in narrow runlets. Then, leaping and laughing in a mad ecstasy of freedom, they dashed into the dam.

Here was something they did not understand, some contrivance of the tyrant Man to curb them, to harness them, to make them his slaves. The waters were angry. They gloomed fearsomely. As they swelled higher in the broad basin their wrath grew apace. They chafed against their prison walls, they licked and lapped at the stolid bank. Higher and higher they mounted, growing stronger with every leap. More and more bitterly they fretted at their durance. Behind them other waters were pressing, just as eager to escape as they. They lashed and writhed in savage spite. Not much longer could these patient walls withstand their anger. Something must happen.

The "something" was a man. He raised the floodgate, and there at last was a way of escape. How joyously the eager waters rushed at it! They tumbled and tossed in their mad hurry to get out. They surged and swept and roared about the narrow opening.

But what was this? They had come on a wooden box that streaked down the slope as straight as an arrow from the bow. It was some other scheme of the tyrant Man. Nevertheless, they jostled and jammed to get into it. On its brink they poised a moment, then down, down they dashed.

Like a cataract they rushed, ever and ever growing faster. Ho! this was motion now, this was action, strength, power. As they shot down that steep hill they shrieked for very joy. Freedom, freedom at last! No more trickling feebly from snowbanks; no more boring devious channels in oozy clay, no more stagnating in sullen dams. They were alive, alive, swift, intense, terrific. They gloried in their might. They roared the raucous song of freedom, and faster and faster they charged. Like a stampede of maddened horses they thundered on. What power on earth could stop them? "We must be free! We must be free!" they cried.

Suddenly they saw ahead the black hole of a great pipe, a hollow shard of steel. Prison-like it looked, again some contrivance of the tyrant Man. They would fain have overleapt it, but it was too late. Countless other waters were behind them, forcing them forward with irresistible power. And, faster and faster still, they crashed into the shard of steel.

They were trapped, atrociously trapped, cabined, confined, rammed forward by a vast and remorseless pressure. Yet there was escape just ahead. It was a tiny point of light, an outlet. They must squeeze through it. They were crushed and pinioned in that prison of steel, and mightily they tried to burst it. No! there was only that orifice; they must pass through it. Then with that great force behind them, tortured, maddened, desperate, the waters crashed through the shard of steel, to serve the will of Man.

The man stood by his water-gun and from its nozzle, the gleaming terror leapt. At first it was only a slim volley of light, compact and solid as a shaft of steel. To pierce it would have splintered to pieces the sharpest sword. It was a core of water, round, glistening and smooth, yet in its mighty power it was a monster of destruction.

The man was directing it here and there on the face of the hill. It flew like an arrow from the bow, and wherever he aimed it the hillside seemed to reel and shudder at the shock. Great cataracts of gravel shot out, avalanches of clay toppled over; vast boulders were hurled into the air like heaps of fleecy wool.

Yes, the waters were mad. They were like an angry bull that gored the hillside. It seemed to melt and dissolve before them. Nothing could withstand that assault. In a few minutes they would reduce the stoutest stronghold to a heap of pitiful ruins.

There, where the waters shot forth in their fury, stood their conqueror. He was one man, yet he was doing the work of a hundred. As he battered at that bank of clay he exulted in his power. A little turn of the wrist and a huge mass of gravel crumbled into nothingness. He bored deep holes in the frozen muck, he hammered his way down to bed rock, he swept it clean as a floor. There, with the solid force of a battering-ram, he pounded at the heart of the hill.

The roar deafened him. He heard the crash of falling rock, but he was so intent on his work he did not hear another man approach. Suddenly he looked up and saw.

He gave a mighty start, then at once he was calm again. This was the meeting he had dreaded, longed for, fought against, desired. Primordial emotions surged within him, but outwardly he gave no sign. Almost savagely, and with a curious blaze in his eyes he redirected the little giant.

He waved his hand to the other man.

"Go away!" he shouted.

Mosher refused to budge. The generous living of Dawson had made him pursy, almost porcine. His pig eyes glittered, and he took off his hat to wipe some beads of sweat from the monumental baldness of his forehead. He caressed his coal-black beard with a podgy hand on which a large diamond sparkled. His manner was arrogance personified. He seemed to say, "I'll make this man dance to my music."

His rich, penetrating voice pierced through the roar of the "giant."

"Here, turn off your water. I want to speak to you. Got a business proposition to make."

Still Jim was dumb.

Mosher came close to him and shouted into his ear. The two men were very calm.

"Say, your wife's in town. Been there for the last year. Didn't you know it?"

Jim shook his head. He was particularly interested in his work just then. There was a great saddle of clay, and he scooped it up magically.

"Yes, she's in town—living respectable."

Jim redirected his giant with a savage swish.

"Say, I'm a sort of a philant'ropic guy," went on Mosher, "an' there's nothing I like better than doing the erring wife restitootion act. I think I could induce that little woman of yours to come back to you."

Jim gave him a swift glance, but the man went on.

"To tell the truth, she's a bit stuck on me. Not my fault, of course. Can't help it if a girl gets daffy on me. But say, I think I could get her switched on to you if you made it worth my while. It's a business proposition."

He was sneering now, frankly villainous. Jim gave no sign.

"What d'ye say? This is a likely bit of ground—give me a half-share in this ground, an' I'll guarantee to deliver that little piece of goods to you. There's an offer."

Again that smug look of generosity beamed on the man's face. Once more Jim motioned him to go, but Mosher did not heed. He thought the gesture was a refusal. His face grew threatening. "All right, if you won't," he snarled, "look out! I know you love her still. Let me tell you, I own that woman, body and soul, and I'll make life hell for her. I'll torture you through her. Yes, I've got a cinch. You'd better change your mind."

He had stepped back as if to go. Then, whether it was an accident or not no one will ever know—but the little giant swung round till it bore on him.

It lifted him up in the air. It shot him forward like a stone from a catapult. It landed him on the bank fifty feet away with a sickening crash. Then, as he lay, it pounded and battered him out of all semblance of a man.

The waters were having their revenge.

* * * * *

CHAPTER XV

"There's something the matter with Jim," the Prodigal 'phoned to me from the Forks; "he's gone off and left the cabin on Ophir, taken to the hills. Some prospectors have just come in and say they met him heading for the White Snake Valley. Seemed kind of queer, they say. Wouldn't talk much. They thought he was in a fair way to go crazy."

"He's never been right since the accident," I answered; "we'll have to go after him."

"All right. Come up at once. I'll get McCrimmon. He's a good man in the woods. We'll be ready to start as soon as you arrive."

So the following day found the three of us on the trail to Ophir. We travelled lightly, carrying very little food, for we thought to find game in the woods. On the evening of the following day we reached the cabin.

Jim must have gone very suddenly. There were the remains of a meal on the table, and his Bible was gone from its place. There was nothing for it but to follow and find him.

"By going to the headwaters of Ophir Creek," said the Halfbreed, "we can cross a divide into the valley of the White Snake, and there we'll corral him, I guess."

So we left the trail and plunged into the virgin Wild. Oh, but it was hard travelling! Often we would keep straight up the creek-bed, plunging through pools that were knee-deep, and walking over shingly bars. Then, to avoid a big bend of the stream, we would strike off through the bush. Every yard seemed to have its obstacle. There were windfalls and tangled growths of bush that defied our uttermost efforts to penetrate them. There were viscid sloughs, from whose black depths bubbles arose wearily, with grey tree-roots like the legs of spiders clutching the slimy mud of their banks. There were oozy bottoms, rankly speared with rush-grass.

There were leprous marshes spotted with unsightly niggerheads. Dripping with sweat, we fought our way under the hot sun. Thorny boughs tore at us detainingly. Fallen trees delighted to bar our way. Without let or cease we toiled, yet at the day's end our progress was but a meagre one.

Our greatest bane was the mosquitoes. Night and day they never ceased to nag us. We wore veils and had gloves on our hands, so that under our armour we were able to grin defiance at them. But on the other side of that netting they buzzed in an angry grey cloud. To raise our veils and take a drink was to be assaulted ferociously. As we walked we could feel them resisting our progress, and it seemed as if we were forcing our way through solid banks of them. If we rested, they alighted in such myriads that soon we appeared literally sheathed in tiny atoms of insect life, vainly trying to pierce the mesh of our clothing. To bare a hand was to have it covered with blood in a moment, and the thought of being at their mercy was an exquisitely horrible one. Night and day their voices blended in a vast drone, so that we ate, drank and slept under our veils.

In that rankly growing wilderness we saw no sign of life, not even a rabbit. It was all desolate and God-forsaken. By nightfall our packs seemed very heavy, our limbs very tired. Three days, four days, five days passed. The creek was attenuated and hesitating, so we left it and struck off over the mountains. Soon we climbed to where the timber growth was less obstructive. The hillside was steep, almost vertical in places, and was covered with a strange, deep growth of moss. Down in it we sank, in places to our knees, and beneath it we could feel the points of sharp boulders. As we climbed we plunged our hands deep into the cool cushion of the moss, and half dragged ourselves upward. It was like an Oriental rug covering the stony ribs of the hill, a rug of bizarre colouring, strangely patterned in crimson and amber, in emerald and ivory. Birch-trees of slim, silvery beauty arose in it, and aided us as we climbed.

So we came at last, after a weary journey, to a bleak, boulder-studded plateau. It was above timber-line, and carpeted with moss of great depth and gaudy hue. Suddenly we saw two vast pillars of stone upstanding on the aching barren. I think they must have been two hundred feet high, and, like monstrous sentinels in their lonely isolation, they overlooked that vast tundra. They startled us.

We wondered by what strange freak of nature they were stationed there.

Then we dropped down into a vast, hush-filled valley, a valley that looked as if it had been undisturbed since the beginning of time. Like a spirit-haunted place it was, so strange and still. It was loneliness made visible. It was stillness written in wood and stone. I would have been afraid to enter it alone, and even as we sank in its death-haunted dusk I shuddered with a horror of the place.

The Indians feared and shunned this valley. They said, of old, strange things had happened there; it had been full of noise and fire and steam; the earth had opened up, belching forth great dragons that destroyed the people. And indeed it was all like the vast crater of an extinct volcano, for hot springs bubbled forth and a grey ash cropped up through the shallow soil.

There was no game in the valley. In its centre was a solitary lake, black and bottomless, and haunted by a giant white water-snake, sluggish, blind and very old. Stray prospectors swore they had seen it, just at dusk, and its sightless, staring eyes were too terrible ever to forget.

And into this still, cobweb-hued hollow we dropped—dropped almost straight down over the flanks of those lean, lank mountains that fringed it so forlornly. Here, ringed all around by desolate heights, we were as remote from the world as if we were in some sallow solitude of the moon. Sometimes the valley was like a gaping mouth, and the lips of it were livid grey. Sometimes it was like a cup into which the sunset poured a golden wine and filled it quivering to the brim. Sometimes it was like a grey grave full of silence. And here in this place of shadows, where the lichen strangled the trees, and under-foot the moss hushed the tread, where we spoke in whispers, and mirth seemed a mockery, where every stick and stone seemed eloquent of disenchantment and despair, here in this valley of Dead Things we found Jim.

He was sitting by a dying camp-fire, all huddled up, his arms embracing his knees, his eyes on the fading embers. As we drew near he did not move, did not show any surprise, did not even raise his head. His face was very pale and drawn into a pucker of pain. It was the queerest look I ever saw on a man's face. It made me creep.

His eyes followed us furtively. Silently we squatted in a ring round his camp-fire. For a while we said no word, then at last the Prodigal spoke:

"Jim, you're coming back with us, aren't you?"

Jim looked at him.

"Hush!" says he, "don't speak so loud. You'll waken all them dead fellows."

"What d'ye mean?"

"Them dead fellows. The woods is full of them, them that can't rest. They're all around, ghosts. At night, when I'm a-sittin' over the fire, they crawl out of the darkness, an' they get close to me, closer, closer, an' they whisper things. Then I get scared an' I shoo them away."

"What do they whisper, Jim?"

"Oh say! they tell me all kinds of things, them fellows in the woods. They tell me of the times they used to have here in the valley; an' how they was a great people, an' had women an' slaves; how they fought an' sang an' got drunk, an' how their kingdom was here, right here where it's all death an' desolation. An' how they conquered all the other folks around an' killed the men an' captured the women. Oh, it was long, long ago, long before the flood!"

"Well, Jim, never mind them. Get your pack ready. We're going home right now."

"Goin' home?—I've no home any more. I'm a fugitive an' a vagabond in the earth. The blood of my brother crieth unto me from the ground. From the face of the Lord shall I be hid an' every one that findeth me shall slay me. I have no home but the wilderness. Unto it I go with prayer an' fastin'. I have killed, I have killed!"

"Nonsense, Jim; it was an accident."

"Was it? Was it? God only knows; I don't. Only I know the thought of murder was black in my heart. It was there for ever an' ever so long. How I fought against it! Then, just at that moment, everything seemed to come to a head. I don't know that I meant what I did, but I thought it."

"Come home, Jim, and forget it."

"When the rivers start to run up them mountain peaks I'll forget it. No, they won't let me forget it, them ghosts. They whisper to me all the time. Hist! don't you hear them? They're whispering to me now. 'You're a murderer, Jim, a murderer,' they say. 'The brand of Cain is on you, Jim, the brand of Cain.' Then the little leaves of the trees take up the whisper, an' the waters murmur it, an' the very stones cry out ag'in me, an' I can't shut out the sound. I can't, I can't."

"Hush, Jim!"

"No, no, the devil's a-hoein' out a place in the embers for me. I can't turn no more to the Lord. He's cast me out, an' the light of His countenance is darkened to me. Never again; oh, never again!"

"Oh come, Jim, for the sake of your old partners, come home."

"Well, boys, I'll come. But it's no good. I'm down an' out."

Wearily we gathered together his few belongings. He had been living on bread, and but little remained. Had we not reached him, he would have starved. He came like a child, but seemed a prey to acute melancholy.

It was indeed a sad party that trailed down that sad, dead valley. The trees were hung with a dreary drapery of grey, and the ashen moss muffled our footfalls. I think it was the *deadest* place I ever saw. The very air seemed dead and stale, as if it were eternally still, unstirred by any wind. Spiders and strange creeping things possessed the trees, and at every step, like white gauze, a mist of mosquitoes was thrown up. And the way seemed endless.

A great weariness weighed upon our spirits. Our feet flagged and our shoulders were bowed. As we looked into each other's faces we saw there a strange lassitude, a chill, grey despair. Our voices sounded hollow and queer, and we seldom spoke. It was as if the place was a vampire that was sucking the life and health from our veins.

"I'm afraid the old man's going to play out on us," whispered the Prodigal.

Jim lagged forlornly behind, and it was very anxiously we watched him. He seemed to know that he was keeping us back. His efforts to keep up were pitiful. We feigned an equal weariness, not to distress him, and our progress was slow, slow.

"Looks as if we'll have to go on half-rations," said the Halfbreed. "It's taking longer to get out of this valley than I figured on."

And indeed it was like a vast prison, and those peaks that brindled in the sunset glow were like bars to hold us in. Every day the old man's step was growing slower, so that at last we were barely crawling along. We were ascending the western slope of the valley, climbing a few miles a day, and every step we rose from that sumphole of the gods was like the lifting of a weight. We were tired, tired, and in the wan light that filtered through the leaden clouds our faces were white and strained.

"I guess we'll have to go on quarter-rations from now," said the Halfbreed, a few days later. He ranged far and wide, looking for game, but never a sign did he see. Once, indeed, we heard a shot. Eagerly we waited his return, but all he had got was a great, grey owl, which we cooked and ate ravenously.

* * * * *

CHAPTER XVI

At last, at last we had climbed over the divide, and left behind us forever the vampire valley. Oh, we were glad! But other troubles were coming. Soon the day came when the last of our grub ran out. I remember how solemnly we ate it. We were already more than three-parts starved, and that meal was but a mouthful.

"Well," said the Halfbreed, "we can't be far from the Yukon now. It must be the valley beyond this one. Then, in a few days, we can make a raft and float down to Dawson."

This heartened us, so once more we took up our packs and started. Jim did not move.

"Come on, Jim."

Still no movement.

"What's the matter, Jim? Come on."

He turned to us a face that was grey and deathlike.

"Go on, boys. Don't mind me. My time's up. I'm an old man. I'm only keeping you back. Without me you've got a chance; with me you've got none. Leave me here with a gun. I can shoot an' rustle grub. You boys can come back for me. You'll find old Jim spry an' chipper, awaitin' you with a smile on his face. Now go, boys. You'll go, won't you?"

"Go be darned!" said the Prodigal. "You know we'll never leave you, Jim. You know the code of the trail. What d'ye take us for—skunks? Come on, we'll carry you if you can't walk."

He shook his head pitifully, but once more he crawled after us. We ourselves were making no great speed. Lack of food was beginning to tell on us. Our stomachs were painfully empty and dead.

"How d'ye feel?" asked the Prodigal. His face had an arrestively hollow look, but that frozen smile was set on it.

"All right," I said, "only terribly weak. My head aches at times, but I've got no pain."

"Neither have I. This starving racket's a cinch. It's dead easy. What rot they talk about the gnawing pains of hunger, an' ravenous men chewing up their boot-tops. It's easy. There's no pain. I don't even feel hungry any more."

None of us did. It was as if our stomachs, in despair at not receiving any food, had sunk into apathy. Yet there was no doubt we were terribly weak. We only made a few miles a day now, and even that was an effort. The distance seemed to be elastic, to stretch out under our feet. Every few yards we had to help Jim over a bad place. His body was emaciated and he was getting very feeble. A hollow fire burned in his eyes. The Halfbreed persisted that beyond those despotic mountains lay the Yukon Valley, and at night he would rouse us up:

"Say, boys, I hear the 'toot' of a steamer. Just a few more days and we'll get there."

Running through the valley, we found a little river. It was muddy in colour and appeared to contain no fish. We ranged along it eagerly, hoping to find a few minnows, but without success. It seemed to me, as I foraged here and there for food, it was not hunger that impelled me so much as the instinct of self-preservation. I knew that if I did not get something into my stomach I would surely die.

Down the river we trailed forlornly. For a week we had eaten nothing. Jim had held on bravely, but now he gave up.

"For God's sake, leave me, boys! Don't make me feel guilty of your death. Haven't I got enough on my soul already? For God's pity, lads, save yourselves! Leave me here to die."

He pleaded brokenly. His legs seemed to have become paralysed. Every time we stopped he would pitch forward on his face, or while walking he would fall asleep and drop. The Prodigal and I supported him, but it was truly hard to support ourselves, and sometimes we collapsed, coming down all three together in a confused and helpless heap. The Prodigal still wore that set grin. His face was nigh fleshless, and, through the straggling beard, it sometimes minded me of a grinning skull. Always Jim moaned and pleaded:

"Leave me, dear boys, leave me!"

He was like a drunken man, and his every step was agony.

We threw away our packs. We no longer had the strength to bear them. The last thing to go was the Halfbreed's rifle. Several times it dropped out of his hand. He picked it up in a dazed way. Again and again it dropped, but at last the time came when he no longer picked it up. He looked at it for a stupid while, then staggered on without it.

At night we would rest long hours round the camp-fire. Often far into the day would we rest. Jim lay like a dead man, moaning continually, while we, staring into each other's ghastly faces, talked in jerks. It was an effort to hunt food. It was an effort to goad ourselves to continue the journey.

"Sure the river empties into the Yukon, boys," said the Halfbreed. "'Tain't so far, either. If we can just make a few miles more we'll be all right."

At night, in my sleep, I was a prey to the strangest hallucinations. People I had known came and talked to me. They were so real that, when I awoke, I could scarce believe I had been dreaming. Berna came to me often. She came quite close, with great eyes of pity that looked into mine. Her lips moved.

"Be brave, my boy. Don't despair," she pleaded. Always in my dreams she pleaded like that, and I think that but for her I would have given up.

The Halfbreed was the most resolute of the party. He never lost his head. At times we others raved a little, or laughed a little, or cried a little, but the Halfbreed remained cool and grim. Ceaselessly he foraged for food. Once he found a nest of grouse eggs, and, breaking them open, discovered they contained half-formed birds. We ate them just as they were, crunched them between our swollen gums. Snails, too, we ate sometimes, and grass roots and moss which we scraped from the trees. But our greatest luck was the decayed grouse eggs.

Early one afternoon we were all resting by a camp-fire on which was boiling some moss, when suddenly the Halfbreed pointed. There, in a glade down by the river's edge, were a cow moose and calf. They were drinking. Stupidly we gazed. I saw the Halfbreed's hand go out as if to clutch the rifle. Alas! his fingers closed on the empty air. So near they were we could have struck them with a stone. Taking his sheath knife in his mouth, the Halfbreed started to crawl on his belly towards them. He had gone but a few yards when they winded him. One look they gave, and in a few moments they were miles away. That was the only time I saw the Halfbreed put out. He fell on his face and lay there for a long time.

Often we came to sloughs that we could not cross, and we had to go round them. We tried to build rafts, but we were too weak to navigate them. We were afraid we would roll off into the deep black water and drown feebly. So we went round, which in one case meant ten miles. Once, over a slough a few yards wide, the Halfbreed built a bridge of willows, and we crawled on hands and knees to the other side.

From a certain point our trip seems like a nightmare to me. I can only remember parts of it here and there. We reeled like drunken men. We sobbed sometimes, and sometimes we prayed. There was no word from Jim now, not even a whimper, as we half dragged, half carried him on. Our eyes were large with fever, our hands were like claws. Long sickly beards grew on our faces. Our clothes were rags, and vermin overran us. We had lost all track of time. Latterly we had been travelling about half a mile a day, and we must have been twenty days without proper food.

The Halfbreed had crawled ahead a mile or so, and he came back to where we lay. In a voice hoarse almost to a whisper he told us a bigger river joined ours down there, and on the bar was an old Indian camp. Perhaps in that place some one might find us. It seemed on the route of travel. So we made a last despairing effort and reached it. Indians had visited it quite recently. We foraged around and found some putrid fish bones, with which we made soup.

There was a grave set high on stilts, and within it a body covered with canvas. The Halfbreed wrenched the canvas from the body, and with it he made a boat eight feet in length by six in breadth. It was too rotten to hold him up, and he nearly drowned trying to float it, so he left it lying on the edge of the bar. I remember this was a terrible disappointment to us, and we wept bitterly. I think that about this time we were all half-crazy. We lay on that bar like men already dead, with no longer hope of deliverance.

* * * * *

Then Jim passed in his checks. In the night he called me.

"Boy," he whispered, "you an' I'se been good pals, ain't we?"

"Yes, old man."

"Boy, I'm in agony. I'm suffering untold pain. Get the gun, for God's sake, an' put me out of my misery."

"There's no gun, Jim; we left it back on the trail."

"Then take your knife."

"No, no."

"Give me your knife."

"Jim, you're crazy. Where's your faith in God?"

"Gone, gone; I've no longer any right to look to Him. I've killed. I've taken life He gave. 'Vengeance is mine,' He said, an' I've taken it out of His hands. God's curse is on me now. Oh, let me die, let me die!"

I sat by him all night. He moaned in agony, and his passing was hard. It was about three in the morning when he spoke again:

"Say, boy, I'm going. I'm a useless old man. I've lived in sin, an' I've repented, an' I've backslid. The Lord don't want old Jim any more. Say, kid, see that little girl of mine down in Dawson gets what money's comin' to me. Tell her to keep straight, an' tell her I loved her. Tell her I never let up on lovin' her all these years. You'll remember that, boy, won't you?"

"I'll remember, Jim."

"Oh, it's all a hoodoo, this Northern gold," he moaned. "See what it's done for all of us. We came to loot the land an' it's a-takin' its revenge on us. It's accursed. It's got me at last, but maybe I can help you boys to beat it yet. Call the others."

I called them.

"Boys," said Jim, "I'm a-goin'. I've been a long time about it. I've been dying by inches, but I guess I'll finish the job pretty slick this time. Well, boys, I'm in possession of all my faculties. I want you to know that. I was crazy when I started off, but that's passed away. My mind's clear. Now, pardners, I've got you into this scrape. I'm responsible, an' it seems to me I'd die happier if you'd promise me one thing. Livin', I can't help you; dead, I can—*you know how*. Well, I want you to promise me you'll do it. It's a reasonable proposition. Don't hesitate. Don't let sentiment stop you. I wish it. It's my dying wish. You're starvin', an' I can help you, can give you strength. Will you promise, if it comes to the last pass, you'll do it?"

We were afraid to look each other in the face.

"Oh, promise, boys, promise!"

"Promise him anyway," said the Halfbreed. "He'll die easier."

So we nodded our heads as we bent over him, and he turned away his face, content.

'Twas but a little after he called me again.

"Boy, give me your hand. Say a prayer for me, won't you? Maybe it'll help some, a prayer for a poor old sinner that's backslid. I can never pray again."

"Yes, try to pray, Jim, try. Come on; say it after me: 'Our Father—'"

"'Our Father—'"

"'Which art in Heaven—'"

"'Which art in—'"

His head fell forward. "Bless you, my boy. Father, forgive, forgive—"

He sank back very quietly.

He was dead.

* * * * *

Next morning the Halfbreed caught a minnow. We divided it into three and ate it raw. Later on he found some water-lice under a stone. We tried to cook them, but they did not help us much. Then, as night fell once more, a thought came into our minds and stuck there. It was a hidden thought, and yet it grew and grew. As we sat round in a circle we looked into each other's faces, and there we read the same revolting thought. Yet did it not seem so revolting after all. It was as if the spirit of the dead man was urging us to this thing, so insistent did the thought become. It was our only hope of life. It meant strength again, strength and energy to make a raft and float us down the river. Oh, if only—but, no! We could not do it. Better, a hundred times better, die.

Yet life was sweet, and for twenty-three days we had starved. Here was a chance to live, with the dead man whispering in our ears to do it. You who have never starved a day in your lives, would you blame us? Life is sweet to you, too. What would you have done? The dead man was urging us, and life was sweet.

But we struggled, God knows we struggled. We did not give in without agony. In our hopeless, staring eyes there was the anguish of the great temptation. We looked in each other's death's-head faces. We clasped skeleton hands round our rickety knees, and swayed as we tried to sit upright. Vermin crawled over us in our weakness. We were half-crazy, and muttered in our beards.

It was the Halfbreed who spoke, and his voice was just a whisper:

"It's our only chance, boys, and we've promised him. God forgive me, but I've a wife and children, and I'm a-goin' to do it."

He was too weak to rise, and with his knife in his mouth he crawled to the body.

* * * * *

It was ready, but we had not eaten. We waited and waited, hoping against hope. Then, as we waited, God was merciful to us. He saved us from this thing.

"Say, I guess I've got a pipe-dream, but I think I see two men coming downstream on a raft."

"No, it's no dream," I said; "two men."

"Shout to them; I can't," said the Prodigal.

I tried to shout, but my voice came as a whisper. The Halfbreed, too, tried to shout. There was scarcely any sound to it. The men did not see us as we lay on that shingly bar. Faster and faster they came. In hopeless, helpless woe we watched them. We could do nothing. In a few moments they would be past. With eyes of terror we followed them, tried to make signals to them. O God, help us!

Suddenly they caught sight of that crazy boat of ours made of canvas and willows. They poled the raft in close, then one of them saw those three strange things writhing impotently on the sand. They were skeletons, they were in rags, they were covered with vermin.—* * * *

We were saved; thank God, we were saved!

* * * * *

CHAPTER XVII

"Berna, we must get married."

"Yes, dearest, whenever you wish."

"Well, to-morrow."

She smiled radiantly; then her face grew very serious.

"What will I wear?" she asked plaintively.

"Wear? Oh, anything. That white dress you've got on—I never saw you looking so sweet. You mind me of a picture I know of Saint Cecilia, the same delicacy of feature, the same pure colouring, the same grace of expression."

"Foolish one!" she chided; but her voice was deliciously tender, and her eyes were love-lit. And indeed, as she stood by the window holding her embroidery to the failing light, you scarce could have imagined a girl more gracefully sweet. In a fine mood of idealising, my eyes rested on her.

"Yes, fairy girl, that briar rose you are doing in the centre of your little canvas hoop is not more delicate in the tinting than are your cheeks; your hands that ply the needle so daintily are whiter than the May blossoms on its border; those coils of shining hair that crown your head would shame the silk you use for softness."

"Don't," she sighed; "you spoil me."

"Oh no, it's true, true. Sometimes I wish you were not so lovely. It makes me care so much for you that—it hurts. Sometimes I wish you were plain, then I would feel more sure of you. Sometimes I fear, fear some one will steal you away from me."

"No, no," she cried; "no one ever will. There will never be any one but you."

She came over to me, and knelt by my chair, putting her arms around me prettily. The pure, sweet face looked up into mine.

"We have been happy here, haven't we, boy?" she asked.

"Exquisitely happy. Yet I have always been afraid."

"Of what, dearest?"

"I don't know. Somehow it seems too good to last."

"Well, to-morrow we'll be married."

"Yes, we should have done that a year ago. It's all been a mistake. It didn't matter at first; nobody noticed, nobody cared. But now it's different. I can see it by the way the wives of the men look at us. I wonder do women resent the fact that virtue is only its own reward—they are so down on those who stray. Well, we don't care anyway. We'll marry and live our lives. But there are other reasons."

"Yes?"

"Yes. Garry talks of coming out. You wouldn't like him to find us living like this—without benefit of the clergy?"

"Not for the world!" she cried, in alarm.

"Well, he won't. Garry's old-fashioned and terribly conventional, but you'll take to him at once. There's a wonderful charm about him. He's so good-looking, yet so clever. I think he could win any woman if he tried, only he's too upright and sincere."

"What will he think of me, I wonder, poor, ignorant me? I believe I'm afraid of him. I wish he'd stay away and leave us alone. Yet for your sake, dear, I do wish him to think well of me."

"Don't fear, Berna. He'll be proud of you. But there's a second reason."

"What?"

I drew her up beside me on the great Morris-chair.

"Oh, my beloved! perhaps we'll not always be alone as we are now. Perhaps, perhaps some day there will be others—little ones—for their sakes."

She did not speak. I could feel her nestle closer to me. Her cheek was pressed to mine; her hair brushed my brow and her lips were like rose-petals on my own. So we sat there in the big, deep chair, in the glow of the open fire, silent, dreaming, and I saw on her lashes the glimmer of a glorious tear.

"Why do you cry, beloved?"

"Because I'm so happy. I never thought I could be so happy. I want it to last forever, I never want to leave this little cabin of ours. It will always be home to me. I love it; oh, how I love it!—every stick and stone of it! This dear little room—there will never be another like it in the world. Some day we may have a fine home, but I think I'll always leave some of my heart here in the little cabin."

I kissed away her tears. Foolish tears! I blessed her for them. I held her closer to me. I was wondrous happy. No longer did the shadow of the past hang over us. Even as children forget, were we forgetting. Outside the winter's day was waning fast. The ruddy firelight danced around us. It flickered on the walls, the open piano, the glass front of the bookcase. It lit up the Indian corner, the lounge with its cushions and brass reading-lamp, the rack of music, the pictures, the lace curtains, the gleaming little bit of embroidery. Yes, to me, too, these things were wistfully precious, for it seemed as if part of her had passed into them. It would have been like tearing out my heart-strings to part with the smallest of them.

"*Husband*, I'm so happy," she sighed.

"Wife, dear, dear wife, I too."

There was no need for words. Our lips met in passionate kisses, but the next moment we started apart. Some one was coming up the garden path—a tall figure of a man. I started as if I had seen a ghost. Could it be?—then I rushed to the door.

There on the porch stood Garry.

* * * * *

CHAPTER XVIII

As he stood before me once again it seemed as if the years had rolled away, and we were boys together. A spate of tender memories came over me, memories of the days of dreams and high resolves, when life rang true, when men were brave and women pure. Once more I stood upon that rock-envisaged coast, while below me the yeasty sea charged with a roar the echoing caves. The gulls were glinting in the sunshine, and by their little brown-thatched homes the fishermen were spreading out their nets. High on the hillside in her garden I could see my mother idling among her flowers. It all came back to me, that sunny shore, the whitewashed cottages, the old grey house among the birches, the lift of sheep-starred pasture, and above it the glooming dark of the heather hills.

And it was but three years ago. How life had changed! A thousand things had happened. Fortune had come to me, love had come to me. I had lived, I had learned. I was no longer a callow, uncouth lad. Yet, alas! I no longer looked futurewards with joy; the savour of life was no more sweet. It was another "me" I saw in my mirror that day, a "me" with a face sorely lined, with hair grey-flecked, with eyes sad and bitter. Little wonder Garry, as he stood there, stared at me so sorrowfully.

"How you've changed, lad!" said he at last.

"Have I, Garry? You're just about the same."

But indeed he, too, had changed, had grown finer than my fondest thoughts of him. He seemed to bring into the room the clean, sweet breath of Glengyle, and I looked at him with admiration in my eyes. Coming out of the cold, his colour was dazzling as that of a woman; his deep blue eyes sparkled; his fair silky hair, from the pressure of his cap, was moulded to the shape of his fine head. Oh, he was handsome, this brother of mine, and I was proud, proud of him!

"By all that's wonderful, what brought you here?"

His teeth flashed in that clever, confident smile.

"The stage. I just arrived a few minutes ago, and hurried here at once. Aren't you glad to see me?"

"Glad? Yes, indeed! I can't tell you how glad. But it's a shock to me your coming so suddenly. You might have let me know."

"Yes, it was a sudden resolve; I should have wired you. However, I thought I would give you a surprise. How are you, old man?"

"Me—oh, I'm all right, thanks."

"Why, what's the matter with you, lad? You look ten years older. You look older than your big brother now."

"Yes, I daresay. It's the life, it's the land. A hard life and a hard land."

"Why don't you go out?"

"I don't know, I don't know. I keep on planning to go out and then something turns up, and I put it off a little longer. I suppose I ought to go, but I'm tied up with mining interests. My partner is away in the East, and I promised to stay in and look after things. I'm making money, you see."

"Not sacrificing your youth and health for that, are you?"

"I don't know, I don't know."

There was a puzzled look in his frank face, and for my part I was strangely ill at ease. With all my joy at his coming, there was a sense of anxiety, even of fear. I had not wanted him to come just then, to see me there. I was not ready for him. I had planned otherwise.

He was fixing me with a clear, penetrating look. For a moment his eyes seemed to bore into me, then like a flash the charm came back into his face. He laughed that ringing laugh of his.

"Well, I was tired of roaming round the old place. Things are in good order now. I've saved a little money and I thought I could afford to travel a little, so I came up to see my wandering brother, and his wonderful North."

His gaze roved round the room. Suddenly it fell on the piece of embroidery. He started slightly and I saw his eyes narrow, his mouth set. His glance shifted to the piano with its litter of music. He looked at me again, in an odd, bewildered way. He went on speaking, but there was a queer constraint in his manner.

"I'm going to stay here for a month, and then I want you to come back with me. Come back home and get some of the old colour into your cheeks. The country doesn't agree with you, but we'll have you all right pretty soon. We'll have you flogging the trout pools and tramping over the heather with a gun. You remember how—whir-r-r—the black-cock used to rise up right at one's very feet. They've been very plentiful the last two years. Oh, we'll have the good old times over again! You'll see, we'll soon put you right."

"It's good of you, Garry, to think so much of me; but I'm afraid, I'm afraid I can't come just yet. I've got so much to do. I've got thirty men working for me. I've just got to stay."

He sighed.

"Well, if you stay I'll stay, too. I don't like the way you're looking. You're working too hard. Perhaps I can help you."

"All right; I'm afraid you'll find it rather awful, though. No one lives up here in winter if they possibly can avoid it. But for a time it will interest you."

"I think it will." And again his eyes stared fixedly at that piece of embroidery on its little hoop.

"I'm terribly, glad to see you anyway, Garry. There's no use talking, words can't express things like that between us two. You know what I mean. I'm glad to see you, and I'll do my best to make your visit a happy one."

Between the curtains that hung over the bedroom door I could see Berna standing motionless. I wondered if he could see her too. His eyes followed mine. They rested on the curtains and the strong, stern look came into his face. Yet again he banished it with a sunny smile.

"Mother's one regret was that you were not with her when she died. Do you know, old man, I think she was always fonder of you than of me? You were the sentimental one of the family, and Mother was always a gentle dreamer. I took more after Dad; dry and practical, you know. Well, Mother used to worry a good deal about you. She missed you dreadfully, and before she died she made me promise I'd always stand by you, and look after you if anything happened."

"There's not much need of that, Garry. But thanks all the same, old man. I've seen a lot in the past few years. I know something of the world now. I've changed. I'm sort of disillusioned. I seem to have lost my zest for things—but I know how to handle men, how to fight and how to win."

"It's not that, lad. You know that to win is often to lose. You were never made for the fight, my brother. It's all been a mistake. You're too sensitive, too high-strung for a fighting-man. You have too much sentiment in you. Your spirit urged you to fields of conquest and romance, yet by nature you were designed for the gentler life. If you could have curbed your impulse and only dreamed your adventures, you would have been the happier. Imagination's been a curse to you, boy. You've tortured yourself all these years, and now you're paying the penalty."

"What penalty?"

"You've lost your splendid capacity for happiness; your health's undermined; your faith in mankind is destroyed. Is it worth while? You've plunged into the fight and you've won. What does your victory mean? Can it compare with what you've lost? Here, I haven't a third of what you have, and yet I'm magnificently happy. I don't envy you. I am going to enjoy every moment of my life. Oh, my brother, you've been making a sad mistake, but it's not too late! You're young, young. It's not too late."

Then I saw that his words were true. I saw that I had never been meant for the fierce battle of existence. Like those high-strung horses that were the first to break their hearts on the trail, I was unsuited for it all. Far better would I have been living the sweet, simple life of my forefathers. My spirit had upheld me, but now I knew there was a poison in my veins, that I was a sick man, that I had played the game and won—at too great a cost. I was like a sprinter that breasts the tape, only to be carried fainting from the field. Alas! I had gained success only to find it was another name for failure.

"Now," said Garry, "you must come home. Back there on the countryside we can find you a sweet girl to marry. You will love her, have children and forget all this. Come."

I rose. I could no longer put it off.

"Excuse me one moment," I said. I parted the curtains and entered the bedroom.

She was standing there, white to the lips and trembling. She looked at me piteously.

"I'm afraid," she faltered.

"Be brave, little girl," I whispered, leading her forward. Then I threw aside the curtain.

"Garry," I said, "this is—this is Berna."

* * * * *

CHAPTER XIX

Garry, Berna—there they stood, face to face at last. Long ago I had visioned this meeting, planned for, yet dreaded it, and now with utter suddenness it had come.

The girl had recovered her calm, and I must say she bore herself well. In her clinging dress of simple white her figure was as slimly graceful as that of a wood-nymph, her head poised as sweetly as a lily on its stem. The fair hair rippled away in graceful lines from the fine brow, and as she gazed at my brother there was a proud, high look in her eyes.

And Garry—his smile had vanished. His face was cold and stern. There was a stormy antagonism in his bearing. No doubt he saw in her a creature who was preying on me, an influence for evil, an overwhelming indictment against me of sin and guilt. All this I read in his eyes; then Berna advanced to him with outstretched hand.

"How do you do? I've heard so much about you I feel as if I'd known you long ago."

She was so winning, I could see he was quite taken aback. He took the little white hand and looked down from his splendid height to the sweet eyes that gazed into his. He bowed with icy politeness.

"I feel flattered, I assure you, that my brother should have mentioned me to you."

Here he shot a dark look at me.

"Sit down again, Garry," I said. "Berna and I want to talk to you."

He complied, but with an ill grace. We all three sat down and a grave constraint was upon us. Berna broke the silence.

"What sort of a trip have you had?"

He looked at her keenly. He saw a simple girl, shy and sweet, gazing at him with a flattering interest.

"Oh, not so bad. Travelling sixty miles a day on a jolting stage gets monotonous, though. The road-houses were pretty decent as a rule, but some were vile. However, it's all new and interesting to me."

"You will stay with us for a time, won't you?"

He favoured me with another grim look.

"Well, that all depends—I haven't quite decided yet. I want to take Athol here home with me."

"Home—" There was a pathetic catch in her voice. Her eyes went round the little room that meant "home" to her.

"Yes, that will be nice," she faltered. Then, with a brave effort, she broke into a lively conversation about the North. As she talked an inspiration seemed to come to her. A light beaconed in her eyes. Her face, fine as a cameo, became eager, rapt. She was telling him of the magical summers, of the midnight sunsets, of the glorious largess of the flowers, of the things that meant so much to her. She was wonderfully animated. As I watched her I thought what a perfect little lady she was; and I felt proud of her.

He was listening carefully, with evident interest. Gradually his look of stern antagonism had given way to one of attention. Yet I could see he was not listening so much to her as he was studying her. His intent gaze never moved from her face.

Then I talked a while. The darkness had descended upon us, but the embers in the open fireplace lighted the room with a rosy glow. I could not see his eyes now, but I knew he was still watching us keenly. He merely answered "yes" and "no" to our questions, and his voice was very grave. Then, after a little, he rose to go.

"I'll return to the hotel with you," I said.

Berna gave us a pathetically anxious little look. There was a red spot on each cheek and her eyes were bright. I could see she wanted to cry.

"I'll be back in half an hour, dear," I said, while Garry gravely shook hands with her.

We did not speak on the way to his room. When we reached it he switched on the light and turned to me.

"Brother, who's this girl?"

"She's—she's my housekeeper. That's all I can say at present, Garry."

"Married?"

"No."

"Good God!"

Stormily he paced the floor, while I watched him with a great calm. At last he spoke.

"Tell me about her."

"Sit down, Garry; light a cigar. We may as well talk this thing over quietly."

"All right. Who is she?"

"Berna," I said, lighting my cigar, "is a Jewess. She was born of an unwed mother, and reared in the midst of misery and corruption."

He stared at me. His mouth hardened; his brow contracted.

"But," I went on, "I want to say this. You remember, Garry, Mother used to tell us of our sister who died when she was a baby. I often used to dream of my dead sister, and in my old, imaginative days I used to think she had never died at all, but she had grown up and was with us. How we would have loved her, would we not, Garry? Well, I tell you this—if our sister had grown up she could have been no sweeter, purer, gentler than this girl of mine, this Berna."

He smiled ironically.

"Then," he said, "if she is so wonderful, why, in the name of Heaven, haven't you married her?"

His manner towards her in the early part of the interview had hurt me, had roused in me a certain perversity. I determined to stand by my guns.

"Garry," I said, "this is—this is Berna"

"Marriage," said I, "isn't everything; often isn't anything. Love is, and always will be, the great reality. It existed long before marriage was ever thought of. Marriage is a good thing. It protects the wife and the children. As a rule, it enforces constancy. But there's a higher ideal of human companionship that is based on love alone, love so perfect, so absolute that legal bondage insults it; love that is its own justification. Such a love is ours."

The ironical look deepened to a sneer.

"And look you here, Garry," I went on; "I am living in Dawson in what you would call 'shame.' Well, let me tell you, there's not ninety-nine in a hundred legally married couples that have formed such a sweet, love-sanctified union as we have. That girl is purest gold, a pearl of untold price. There has never been a jar in the harmony of our lives. We love each other absolutely. We trust and believe in each other. We would make any sacrifice for each other. And, I say it again, our marriage is tenfold holier than ninety-nine out of a hundred of those performed with all the pomp of surplice and sacristy."

"Oh, man! man!" he said crushingly, "what's got into you? What nonsense, what clap-trap is this? I tell you that the old way, the way that has stood for generations, is the best, and it's a sorry day I find a brother of mine talking such nonsense. I'm almost glad Mother's dead. It would surely have broken her heart to know that her son was living in sin and shame, living with a—"

"Easy now, Garry," I cautioned him. We faced each other with the table between us.

"I'm going to have my say out. I've come all this way to say it, and you've got to hear me. You're my brother. God knows I love you. I promised I'd look after you, and now I'm going to save you if I can."

"Garry," I broke in, "I'm younger than you, and I respect you; but in the last few years I've grown to see things different from the way we were taught; broader, clearer, saner, somehow. We can't always follow in the narrow path of our forefathers. We must think and act for ourselves in these days. I see no sin and shame in what I'm doing. We love each other—that is our vindication. It's a pure, white light that dims all else. If you had seen and striven and suffered as I have done, you might think as I do. But you've got your smug old-fashioned notions. You gaze at the trees so hard you can't see the forest. Yours is an ideal, too; but mine is a purer, more exalted one."

"Balderdash!" he cried. "Oh, you anger me! Look here, Athol, I came all this way to see you about this matter. It's a long way to come, but I knew my brother was needing me and I'd have gone round the world for you. You never told me anything of this girl in your letters. You were ashamed."

"I knew I could never make you understand."

"You might have tried. I'm not so dense in the understanding. No, you would not tell me, and I've had letters, warning letters. It was left to other people to tell me how you drank and gambled and squandered your money; how you were like to a madman. They told me you had settled down to live with one of the creatures, a woman

359

who had made her living in the dance-halls, and every one knows no woman ever did that and remained straight. They warned me of the character of this girl, of your infatuation, of your callousness to public opinion. They told me how barefaced, how shameless you were. They begged me to try and save you. I would not believe it, but now I've come to see for myself, and it's all true, it's all true."

He bowed his head in emotion.

"Oh, she's good!" I cried. "If you knew her you would think so, too. You, too, would love her."

"Heaven forbid! Boy, I must save you. I must, for the honour of the old name that's never been tarnished. I must make you come home with me."

He put both hands on my shoulders, looking commandingly into my face.

"No, no," I said, "I'll never leave her."

"It will be all right. We can pay her. It can be arranged. Think of the honour of the old name, lad."

I shook him off. "Pay!"—I laughed ironically. "Pay" in connection with the name of Berna—again I laughed.

"She's good," I said once again. "Wait a little till you know her. Don't judge her yet. Wait a little."

He saw it was of no use to waste further words on me. He sighed.

"Well, well," he said, "have it your own way. I think she's ruining you. She's dragging you down, sapping your moral principles, lowering your standard of pure living. She must be bad, bad, or she wouldn't live with you like that. But have it your own way, boy; I'll wait and see."

* * * * *

CHAPTER XX

In the crystalline days that followed I did much to bring about a friendship between Garry and Berna. At first I had difficulty in dragging him to the house, but in a little while he came quite willingly. The girl, too, aided me greatly. In her sweet, shy way she did her best to win his regard, so that as the winter advanced a great change came over him. He threw off that stern manner of his as an actor throws off a part, and once again he was the dear old Garry I knew and loved.

His sunny charm returned, and with it his brilliant smile, his warm, endearing frankness. He was now twenty-eight, and if there was a handsomer man in the Northland I had yet to see him. I often envied him for his fine figure and his clean, vivid colour. It was a wonderfully expressive face that looked at you, firm and manly, and, above all, clever. You found a pleasure in the resonant sweetness of his voice. You were drawn irresistibly to the man, even as you would have been drawn to a beautiful woman. He was winning, lovable, yet back of all his charm there was that great quality of strength, of austere purpose.

He made a hit with every one, and I verily believe that half the women in the town were in love with him. However, he was quite unconscious of it, and he stalked through the streets with the gait of a young god. I knew there were some who for a smile would have followed him to the ends of the earth, but Garry was always a man's man. Never do I remember the time when he took an interest in a woman. I often thought, if women could have the man of their choice, a few handsome ones like Garry would monopolise them, while we common mortals would go wifeless. Sometimes it has seemed to me that love is but a second-hand article, and that our matings are at best only makeshifts.

I must say I tried very hard to reconcile those two. I threw them together on every opportunity, for I wanted him to understand and to love her. I felt he had but to know her to appreciate her at her true value, and, although he spoke no word to me, I was soon conscious of a vast change in him. Short of brotherly regard, he was everything that could be desired to her—cordial, friendly, charming. Once I asked Berna what she thought of him.

"I think he's splendid," she said quietly. "He's the handsomest man I've ever seen, and he's as nice as he's good-looking. In many ways you remind me of him—and yet there's a difference."

"I remind you of him—no, girl. I'm not worthy to be his valet. He's as much above me as I am above—say a siwash. He has all the virtues; I, all the faults. Sometimes I look at him and I see in him my ideal self. He is all strength, all nobility, while I am but a commonplace mortal, full of human weaknesses. He is the self I should have been if the worst had been the best."

"Hush! you are my sweetheart," she assured me with a caress, "and the dearest in the world."

"By the way, Berna," I said, "you remember something we talked about before he came? Don't you think that now—?"

"Now—?"

"Yes."

"All right." She flashed a glad, tender look at me and left the room. That night she was strangely elated.

Every evening Garry would drop in and talk to us. Berna would look at him as he talked and her eyes would brighten and her cheeks flush. On both of us he had a strangely buoyant effect. How happy we could be, just we three. It was splendid having near me the two I loved best on earth.

That was a memorable winter, mild and bright and buoyant. At last Spring came with gracious days of sunshine. The sleighing was glorious, but I was busy, very busy, so that I was glad to send Garry and Berna off together in a smart cutter, and see them come home with their cheeks like roses, their eyes sparkling and laughter in their voices. I never saw Berna looking so well and happy.

I was head over ears in work. In a mail just arrived I had a letter from the Prodigal, and a certain paragraph in it set me pondering. Here it was:

"You must look out for Locasto. He was in New York a week ago. He's down and out. Blood-poisoning set in in his foot after he got outside, and eventually he had to have it taken off. He's got a false mit for the one Mac sawed off. But you should see him. He's all shot to pieces with the 'hooch.' It's a fright the pace he's gone. I had an interview with him, and he raved and blasphemed horribly. Seemed to have a terrible pick at you. Seems you have copped out his best girl, the only one he ever cared a red cent for. Said he would get even with you if he swung for it. I think he's dangerous, even a madman. He is leaving for the North now, so be on your guard."

Locasto coming! I had almost forgotten his existence. Well, I no longer cared for him. I could afford to despise him. Surely he would never dare to molest us. If he did—he was a broken, discredited blackguard. I could crush him.

Coming here! He must even now be on the way. I had a vision of him speeding along that desolate trail, sitting in the sleigh wrapped in furs, and brooding, brooding. As day after day the spell of the great and gloomy land grew on his spirit, I could see the sombre eyes darken and deepen. I could see him in the road-house at night, gaunt and haggard, drinking at the bar, a desperate, degraded cripple. I could see him growing more reckless every day, every hour. He was coming back to the scene of his ruined fortunes, and God knows with what wild schemes of vengeance his heart was full. Decidedly I must beware.

As I sat there dreaming, a ring came to the 'phone. It was the foreman at Gold Hill.

"The hoisting machine has broken down," he told me. "Can you come out and see what is required?"

"All right," I replied. "I'll leave at once."

"Berna," I said, "I'll have to go out to the Forks to-night. I'll be back early to-morrow. Get me a bite to eat, dear, while I go round and order the horse."

On my way I met Garry and told him I would be gone over night. "Won't you come?" I asked.

"No, thanks, old man, I don't feel like a night drive."

"All right. Good-bye."

So I hurried off, and soon after, with a jingle of bells, I drove up to my door. Berna had made supper. She seemed excited. Her eyes were starry bright, her cheeks burned.

"Aren't you well, sweetheart?" I asked. "You look feverish."

"Yes, dear, I'm well. But I don't want you to go to-night. Something tells me you shouldn't. Please don't go, dear. Please, for my sake."

"Oh, nonsense, Berna! You know I've been away before. Get one of the neighbour's wives to sleep with you. Get in Mrs. Brooks."

"Oh, don't go, don't go, I beg you, dear. I don't want you to. I'm afraid, I'm afraid. Won't some one else do?"

"Nonsense, girl. You mustn't be so foolish. It's only for a few hours. Here, I'll ring up Mrs. Brooks and you can ask her."

She sighed. "No, never mind. I'll ring her up after you've gone."

She clung to me tightly, so that I wondered what had got into the girl. Then gently I kissed her, disengaged her hands, and bade her good-night.

As I was rattling off through the darkness, a boy handed me a note. I put it in my pocket, thinking I would read it when I reached Ogilvie Bridge. Then I whipped up the horse.

The night was crisp and exhilarating. I had one of the best trotters in the country, and the sleighing was superb. As I sped along, with a jingle of bells, my spirits rose. Things were looking splendid. The mine was turning out far better than we had expected. Surely we could sell out soon, and I would have all the money I wanted. Even then the Prodigal was putting through a deal in New York that would realise our fortunes. My life-struggle was nearly over.

Then again, I had reconciled Garry to Berna. When I told him of a certain secret I was hugging to my breast he would capitulate entirely. How happy we would all be! I would buy a small estate near home, and we would settle down. But first we would spend a few years in travel. We would see the whole world. What good times we would have, Berna and I! Bless her! It had all worked out beautifully.

Why was she so frightened, so loath to let me go? I wondered vaguely and flicked up the horse so that it plunged sharply forward. The vast blue-black sky was like an inverted gold-pan and the stars were flake colours adhering to it. The cold snapped at me till my cheeks tingled, and my eyes felt as if they could spark. Oh, life was sweet!

Bother! In my elation I had forgotten to get off at the Old Inn and read my note. Never mind, I would keep it till I reached the Forks.

As I spun along, I thought of how changed it all was from the Bonanza I first knew. How I remembered tramping along that hillside slope, packing a sack of flour over a muddy trail, a poor miner in muddy overalls! Now I was driving a smart horse on a fine road. I was an operator of a first-class mine. I was a man of business, of experience. Higher and higher my spirits rose.

How fast the horse flew! I would be at the Forks in no time. I flashed past cabin windows. I saw the solitary oil-lamp and the miner reading his book or filling his pipe. Never was there a finer, more intelligent man; but his day was passing. The whole country was falling into the hands of companies. Soon, thought I, one or two big combines would control the whole wealth of that land. Already they had their eyes on it. The gold-ships would float and roar where the old-time miner toiled with pick and pan. Change! Change!

I almost fancied I could see the monster dredges ploughing up the valley, where now men panted at the windlass. I could see vast heaps of tailings filling the creek-bed; I could hear the crash of the steel grizzlies; I could see the buckets scooping up the pay-dirt. I felt strangely prophetic. My imagination ran riot in all kinds of wonders, great power plants, quartz discoveries. Change! Change!

Yes, the stamp-mill would add its thunder to the other voices; the country would be netted with wires, and clamorous for far and wide. Man had sought out this land where Silence had reigned so long. He had awakened the echoes with the shot of his rifle and the ring of his axe. Silence had raised a startled head and poised there, listening. Then, with crack of pick and boom of blast, man had hurled her back. Further and further had he driven her. With his advancing horde, mad in their lust for the loot of the valley, he had banished her. His engines had frightened her with their canorous roar. His crashing giants had driven her cowering to the inviolate fastnesses of her hills. And there she broods and waits.

But Silence will return. To her was given the land that she might rule and have dominion over it forever. And in a few years the clamour will cease, the din will die away. In a few years the treasure will be exhausted, and the looters will depart. The engines will lie in rust and ruin; the wind will sweep through the empty homes; the tailing-piles lie pallid in the moon. Then the last man will strike the last blow, and Silence will come again into her own.

Yea, Silence will come home once more. Again will she rule despotic over peak and plain. She is only waiting, brooding in the impregnable desolation of her hills. To her has been given empery of the land, and hand in hand with Darkness will she return.

* * * * *

CHAPTER XXI

Ha! here I had reached the Forks at last. As I drew up at the hotel, the clerk came out to meet me.

"Gent wants to speak to you at the 'phone, sir."

It was Murray of Dawson, an old-timer, and rather a friend of mine.

"Hello!"

"Hello! Say, Meldrum, this is Murray speaking. Say, just wanted to let you know there's a stage due some time before morning. Locasto's on board, and they say he's heeled for you. Thought I'd better tell you so's you can get fixed up for him."

"All right," I answered. "Thank you. I'll turn and come right back."

So I switched round the horse, and once more I drove over the glistening road. No longer did I plan and exult. Indeed a grim fear was gripping me. Of a sudden the shadow of Locasto loomed up sinister and menacing. Even now he was speeding Dawsonward with a great hatred of me in his heart. Well, I would get back and prepare for him.

There came to my mind a comic perception of the awkwardness of returning to one's own home unexpectedly, in the dead of night. At first I decided I would go to a hotel, then on second thoughts I determined to try the house, for I had a desire to be near Berna.

I knocked gently, then a little louder, then at last quite loudly. Within all was still, dark as a sepulchre. Curious! she was such a light sleeper, too. Why did she not hear me?

Once more I decided to go to the hotel; once more that vague, indefinite fear assailed me and again I knocked. And now my fear was becoming a panic. I had my latch-key in my pocket, so very quietly I opened the door.

I was in the front room, and it was dark, very dark and quiet. I could not even hear her breathe.

"Berna," I whispered.

No reply.

That dim, nameless dread was clutching at my heart, and I groped overhead in the darkness for the drop-light. How hard it was to find! A dozen times my hand circled in the air before I knocked my knuckles against it. I switched it on.

Instantly the cabin was flooded with light. In the dining-room I could see the remains of our supper lying untidily. That was not like her. She had a horror of dirty dishes. I passed into the bedroom—Ah! the bed had never been slept on.

What a fool I was! It flashed on me she had gone over to Mrs. Brooks' to sleep. She was afraid of being alone. Poor little girl! How surprised she would be to see me in the morning!

Well, I would go to bed. As I was pulling off my coat, I found the note that had been given to me. Blaming myself for my carelessness, I pulled it out of my pocket and opened it. As I unfolded the sheet, I noticed it was written in what looked like a disguised hand. Strange! I thought. The writing was small and faint. I rubbed my eyes and held it up to the light.

Merciful God! What was this? Oh no, it could not be! My eyes were deceiving me. It was some illusion. Feverishly I read again. Yes, they were the same words. What could they mean? Surely, surely—Oh, horror on horrors! They could not mean THAT. Again I read them. Yes, there they were:

> "If you are fool enough to believe that Berna is faithful to you visit your brother's room to-night.
>
> "A Wellwisher."

Berna! Garry!—the two I loved. Oh, it could not be! It was monstrous! It was too horrible! I would not believe it; I would not. Curse the vile wretch that wrote such words! I would kill him. Berna! my Berna! she was as good as gold, as true as steel. Garry! I would lay my life on his honour. Oh, vile calumny! what devil had put so foul a thing in words? God! it hurt me so, it hurt me so!

Dazedly I sat down. A sudden rush of heat was followed by a sweat that pricked out of me and left me cold. I trembled. I saw a ghastly vision of myself in a mirror. I felt sick, sick. Going to the decanter on the bureau, I poured myself a stiff jolt of whisky.

Again I sat down. The paper lay on the hearthrug, and I stared at it hatefully. It was unspeakably loathsome, yet I was fascinated by it. I longed to take it up, to read it again. Somehow I did not dare. I was becoming a coward.

Well, it was a lie, a black devil's lie. She was with one of the neighbours. I trusted her. I would trust her with my life. I would go to bed. In the morning she would return, and then I would unearth the wretch who had dared to write such things. I began to undress.

Slowly I unfastened my collar—that cursed paper; there it lay. Again it fascinated me. I stood glaring at it. Oh, fool! fool! go to bed.

Wearily I took off my clothes—Oh, that devilish note! It was burning into my brain—it would drive me mad. In a frenzy of rage, I took it up as if it were some leprous thing, and dropped it in the fire.

There I lay in bed with the darkness enfolding me, and I closed my eyes to make a double darkness. Ha! right in the centre of my eyes, burned the fatal paper with its atrocious suggestion. I sprang up. It was of no use. I must settle this thing once and for all. I turned on the light and deliberately dressed again.

I was going to the hotel where Garry had his room. I would tell him I had come back unexpectedly and ask to share his room. I was not acting on the note! I did not suspect her. Heaven forbid! But the thing had unnerved me. I could not stay in this place.

The hotel was quiet. A sleepy night-clerk stared at me, and I pushed past him. Garry's rooms were on the third floor. As I climbed the long stairway, my heart was beating painfully, and when I reached his door I was sadly out of breath. Through the transom I could see his light was burning.

I knocked faintly.

There was a sudden stir.

Again I knocked.

Did my ears deceive me or did I hear a woman's startled cry? There was something familiar about it—Oh, my God!

I reeled. I almost fell. I clutched at the doorframe. I leaned sickly against the door for support. Heaven help me!

"I'm coming," I heard him say.

The door was unlocked, and there he stood. He was fully dressed. He looked at me with an expression on his face I could not define, but he was very calm.

"Come in," he said.

I went into his sitting-room. Everything was in order. I would have sworn I heard a woman scream, and yet no one was in sight. The bedroom door was slightly ajar. I eyed it in a fascinated way.

"I'm sorry to disturb you, Garry," I said, and I was conscious how strained and queer my voice sounded. "I got back suddenly, and there's no one at home. I want to stay here with you, if you don't mind."

"Certainly, old man; only too glad to have you."

His voice was steady. I sat down on the edge of a chair. My eyes were riveted on that bedroom door.

"Had a good drive?" he went on genially. "You must be cold. Let me give you some whisky."

My teeth were chattering. I clutched the chair. Oh, that door! My eyes were fastened on it. I was convinced I heard some one in there. He rose to get the whisky.

"Say when?"

I held the glass with a shaking hand:

"When."

"What's the matter, old man? You're ill."

I clutched him by the arm.

"Garry, there's some one in that room."

"Nonsense! there's no one there."

"There is, I tell you. Listen! Don't you hear them breathing?"

He was quiet. Distinctly I could hear the panting of human breath. I was going mad, mad. I could stand it no longer.

"Garry," I gasped, "I'm going to see, I'm going to see."

"Don't—"

"Yes, I must, I say. Let me go. I'll drag them out."

"Hold on—"

"Leave go, man! I'm going, I say. You won't hold me. Let go, I tell you, let go—Now come out, come out, whoever you are—Ah!"

It was a woman.

"Ha!" I cried, "I told you so, brother; a woman. I think I know her, too. Here, let me see—I thought so."

I had clutched her, pulled her to the light. It was Berna.

Her face was white as chalk, her eyes dilated with terror. She trembled. She seemed near fainting.

"I thought so."

Now that it seemed the worst was betrayed to me, I was strangely calm.

"Berna, you're faint. Let me lead you to a chair."

I made her sit down. She said no word, but looked at me with a wild pleading in her eyes. No one spoke.

There we were, the three of us: Berna faint with fear, ghastly, pitiful; I calm, yet calm with a strange, unnatural calmness, and Garry—he surprised me. He had seated himself, and with the greatest *sang-froid* he was lighting a cigarette.

A long tense silence. At last I broke it.

"What have you got to say for yourself, Garry?" I asked.

It was wonderful how calm he was.

"Looks pretty bad, doesn't it, brother?" he said gravely.

"Yes, it couldn't look worse."

"Looks as if I was a pretty base, despicable specimen of a man, doesn't it?"

"Yes, about as base as a man could be."

"That's so." He rose and turned up the light of a large reading-lamp, then coming to me he looked me square in the face. Abruptly his casual manner dropped. He grew sharp, forceful; his voice rang clear.

"Listen to me."

"I'm listening."

"I came out here to save you, and I'm going to save you. You wanted me to believe that this girl was good. You believed it. You were bewitched, befooled, blinded. I could see it, but I had to make you see it. I had to make you realise how worthless she was, how her love for you was a sham, a pretence to prey on you. How could I prove it? You would not listen to reason: I had to take other means. Now, hear me."

"I hear."

"I laid my plans. For three months I've tried to conquer her, to win her love, to take her from you. She was truer to you than I had bargained for; I must give her credit for that. She made a good fight, but I think I have triumphed. To-night she came to my room at my invitation."

"Well?"

"Well. You got a note. *Now, I wrote that note.* I planned this scene, this discovery. I planned it so that your eyes would be opened, so that you would see what she was, so that you would cast her from you—unfaithful, a wanton, a—"

"Hold on there," I broke in; "brother of mine or no, I won't hear you call her those names; no, not if she were ten times as unfaithful. You won't, I say. I'll choke the words in your throat. I'll kill you, if you utter a word against her. Oh, what have you done?"

"What have I done! Try to be calm, man. What have I done? Well, this is what I've done, and it's the lucky day for you I've done it. I've saved you from shame; I've freed you from sin; I've shown you the baseness of this girl."

He rose to his feet.

"Oh, my brother, I've stolen from you your mistress; that's what I've done."

"Oh, no, you haven't," I groaned. "God forgive you, Garry; God forgive you! She's not my—not what you think. She's my *wife*!"

* * * * *

CHAPTER XXII

I thought that he would faint. His face went white as paper and he shrank back. He gazed at me with wild, straining eyes.

"God forgive me! Oh, why didn't you tell me, boy? Why didn't you tell me?"

In his voice there was a note more poignant than a sob.

"You should have trusted me," he went on. "You should have told me. When were you married?"

"Just a month ago. I was keeping it as a surprise for you. I was waiting till you said you liked and thought well of her. Oh, I thought you would be pleased and glad, and I was treasuring it up to tell you."

"This is terrible, terrible!"

His voice was choked with agony. On her chair, Berna drooped wearily. Her wide, staring eyes were fixed on the floor in pitiful perplexity.

"Yes, it's terrible enough. We were so happy. We lived so joyously together. Everything was perfect, a heaven for us both. And then you came, you with your charm that would lure an angel from high heaven. You tried your power on my poor little girl, the girl that never loved but me. And I trusted you, I tried to make you and her friends. I left you together. In my blind innocence I aided you in every way—a simple, loving fool. Oh, now I see!"

"Yes, yes, I know. Your words stab me. It's all true, true."

"You came like a serpent, a foul, crawling thing, to steal her from me, to wrong me. She was loving, faithful, pure. You would have dragged her in the mire. You—"

"Stop, brother, stop, for Heaven's sake! You wrong me."

He held out his hand commandingly. A wonderful change had come over him. His face had regained its calm. It was proud, stern.

"You must not think I would have been guilty of that," he said quietly. "I've played a part I never thought to play; I've done a thing I never thought to have dirtied my hands in the doing, and I'm sorry and ashamed for it. But I tell you, Athol—that's all. As God's my witness, I've done you no wrong. Surely you don't think me as low as that? Surely you don't believe that of me? I did what I did for my very love for you, for your honour's sake. I asked her here that you might see what she was—but that's all, I swear it. She's been as safe as if in a cage of steel."

"I know it," I said; "I know it. You don't need to tell me that. You brought her here to expose her, to show me what a fool I was. It didn't matter how much it hurt me, the more the better, anything to save the name. You would have broken my heart, sacrificed me on the altar of your accursed pride. Oh, I can see plainly now! There's a thousand years of prejudice and bigotry concentrated in you. Thank God, I have a human heart!"

"I thought I was acting for the best!" he cried.

I laughed scornfully.

"I know it—according to your lights. You asked her here that I might see what she was. You tell me you have gained her love; you say she came here at your bidding; you swear she would have been unfaithful to me. Well, I tell you, brother of mine, in your teeth I tell you—*I don't believe you!*"

Suddenly the little, drooping figure on the chair had raised itself; the white, woe-begone face with the wide, staring eyes was turned towards me; the pitiful look had gone, and in its stead was one of wild, unspeakable joy.

"It's all right, Berna," I said; "I don't believe him, and if a million others were to say the same, if they were to thunder it in my ears down all eternity, I would tell them they lied, they lied!"

A heaven-lit radiance was in the grey eyes. She made as if to come to me, but she swayed, and I caught her in my arms.

"Don't be frightened, little girl. Give me your hand. See! I'll kiss it, dear. Now, don't cry; don't, honey."

Her arms were around me. She clung to me ever so tightly.

"Garry," I said, "this is my wife. When I have lost my belief in all else, I will believe in her. You have made us both suffer. As for what you've said—you're mistaken. She's a good, good girl. I will not believe that by thought, word or deed she has been untrue to me. She will explain everything. Now, good-bye. Come, Berna."

Suddenly she stopped me. Her hand was on my arm, and she turned towards Garry. She held herself as proudly as a queen.

"I want to explain now," she said, "before you both."

She pulled from her bosom a little crumpled note, and handed it to me. Then, as I read it, a great light burst on me. Here it was:

"Dear Berna:

"For heaven's sake be on your guard. Jack Locasto is on his way north again. I think he's crazy. I know he'll stick at nothing, and I don't want to see blood spilt. He says he means to wipe out all old scores. For your sake, and for the sake of one dear to you, be warned.

"In haste,
"Viola Lennoir."

"I got it two days ago," she said. "Oh, I've been distracted with fear. I did not like to show it to you. I've brought you nothing but trouble, and I've never spoken of him, never once. You understand, don't you?"

"Yes, little girl, I understand."

"I wanted to save you, no matter at what cost. To-night I tried to prevent you going out there, for I feared you might meet him. I knew he was very near. Then, when you had gone, my fear grew and grew. There I sat, thinking over everything. Oh, if I only had a friend, I thought; some one to help me. Then, as I sat, dazed, distracted, the 'phone rang. It was your brother."

"Yes, go on, dear."

"He told me he wanted to see me; he begged me to come at once. I thought of you, of your danger, of some terrible mishap. I was terrified. I went."

She paused a moment, as if the recital was infinitely painful to her, then she went on.

"I found my way to his room. My mind was full of you, of that man, of how to save you. I did not think of myself, of my position. At first I was too agitated to speak. He bade me sit down, compose myself. His manner was quiet, grave. Again I feared for you. He asked me to excuse him for a moment, and left the room. He seemed to be gone an age, while I sat there, trying to fight down my terror. The suspense was killing me. Then he came back. He closed and locked the door. All at once I heard a step outside, a knock. 'Hush! go in there,' he said. He opened the door. I heard him speaking to some one. I waited, then you burst in on me. You know the rest."

"Yes, yes."

"As for your brother, I've tried, oh, so hard, to be nice to him for your sake. I liked him; I wanted to be to him as a sister, but never an unfaithful thought has entered my head, never a wrong feeling sullied my heart. I've been true to you. You told me once of a love that gives all and asks for nothing; a love that would turn its back on friends and kindred for the sake of its beloved. You said: 'His smile will be your rapture, his frown your anguish. For him will you dare all, bear all. To him will you cling in sorrow, suffering and poverty. Living, you would follow him round the world; dying, you would desire but him.'—Well, I think I love you like that."

"Oh, my dear, my dear!"

"I want to bring you happiness, but I only bring you trouble, sorrow. Sometimes, for your sake, I wish we had never met."

She turned to Garry.

"As for you, you've done me a great wrong. I can never forget it. Will you go now, and leave us in peace?"

His head was bent, so that I could not see his face.

"Can you not forgive?" he groaned.

She shook her head sadly. "No, I am afraid I can never forgive."

"Can I do nothing to atone?"

"No, I'm afraid your punishment must be—that you can do nothing."

He said never a word. She turned to me:

"Come, my husband, we will go."

I was opening the door to leave him forever. Suddenly I heard a step coming up the stairs, a heavy, hurried tread. I looked down a moment, then I pushed her back into the room.

"Be prepared, Berna," I said quietly; "here comes Locasto."

* * * * *

CHAPTER XXIII

There we waited, Garry and I, and between us Berna. We heard that heavy tread come up, up the creaking stairway, stumble a moment, then pause on the landing. There was something ominous, something pregnant in that pause. The steps halted, wavered a little, then, inflexible as doom, on they came towards us. The next instant the door was thrown open, and Locasto stood in the entrance.

Even in that brief moment I was struck by the change in him. He seemed to have aged by twenty years. He was gaunt and lank as a starved timber wolf; his face was hollow almost as a death's head; his hair was long and matted, and his eyes burned with a strange, unnatural fire. In that dark, aquiline face the Indian was never more strongly revealed. He limped, and I noticed his left hand was gloved.

From under his bristling brows he glared at us. As he swayed there he minded me of an evil beast, a savage creature, a mad, desperate thing. He reeled in the doorway, and to steady himself put out his gloved hand. Then with a malignant laugh, the fleering laugh of a fiend, he stepped into the room.

"So! Seems as if I'd lighted on a pretty nest of love-birds. Ho! ho! my sweet! You're not satisfied with one lover, you must have two. Well, you are going to be satisfied with one from now on, and that's Jack Locasto. I've stood enough from you, you white-faced jade. You've haunted me, you've put some kind of a spell on me. You've lured me back to this land, and now I'm going to have you or die! You've played with me long enough. The jig's up. Stand out from between those two. Stand out, I say! March out of that door."

She only shrank back the farther.

"You won't come, curse you; you won't come, you milk-faced witch, with your great eyes that bore holes in me, that turn my heart to fire, that make me mad. You won't come. Stand back there, you two, and let the girl come."

We shielded her.

"Ha! that's it—you defy me. You won't let me get her. Well, it'll be all the worse for her. I'll make her life a hell. I'll beat her. You won't stand back. You, the dark one—don't I know you; haven't I hated you more than the devil hates a saint; hated you worse than bitter poison? These three black years you've balked me, you've kept her from me. Oh, I've itched to kill you times without number, and I've spared you. But now it's my call. Stand back there, stand back I say. Your time's come. Here's where I shoot."

His hand leapt up and I saw it gripped a revolver. He had me covered. His face was contorted with devilish triumph, and I knew he meant to kill. At last, at last my time had come. I saw his fingers twitching on the trigger, I gazed into the hollow horror of that barrel. My heart turned to ice. I could not breathe. Oh, for a respite, a moment—Ugh! . . . he pulled the trigger, and, *at the same instant, Garry sprang at him*!

What had happened? The shot rang in my ears. I was still standing there. I felt no wound. I felt no pain. Then, as I stared at my enemy, I heard a heavy fall. Oh, God! there at my feet lay Garry, lay in a huddled, quivering heap, lay on his face, and in his fair hair I saw a dark stain start and spread. Then, in a moment, I realised what my brother had done.

I fell on my knees beside him.

"Garry, Garry!" I moaned. I heard Berna scream, and I saw that Locasto was coming for me. He was a man no longer. He had killed. He was a brute, a fury, a devil, mad with the lust of slaughter. With a snarl he dashed at me. Again I thought he was going to shoot, but no! He raised the heavy revolver and brought it crashing down on my head. I felt the blow fall, and with it my strength seemed to shoot out of me. My legs were paralysed. I could not move. And, as I lay there in a misty daze, he advanced on Berna.

There she stood at bay, a horror-stricken thing, weak, panting, desperate. I saw him corner her. His hands were stretched out to clutch her; a moment more and he would have her in his arms, a moment—ah! With a suddenness that was like a flash she had raised the heavy reading-lamp and dashed it in his face.

I heard his shriek of fear; I saw him fall as the thing crashed between his eyes; I saw the flames spurt and leap. High in the air he rose, awful in his agony. He was in a shroud of fire; he was in a pool of flame. He howled like a dog and fell over on the bed.

Then suddenly the oil-soaked bedding caught. The curtains seemed to leap and change into flame. As he rolled and roared in his agony, the blaze ran up the walls, and caught the roof. Help, help! the room was afire, was burning up. Fire! Fire!

Out in the corridor I heard a great running about, shouting of men, screaming of women. The whole place seemed to be alive, panic-stricken, frenzied with fear. Everything was in flames now, burning fiercely, madly, and there was no stopping them. The hotel was burning, and I, too, must burn. What a horrible end! Oh, if I could only do something! But I could not move. From the waist down I was like a dead man. Where was Berna? Pray God she was safe. I could not cry for aid. The room was reeling round and round. I was faint, dizzy, helpless.

The hotel was ablaze. In the streets below crowds were gathering. People were running up and down the stairway, fighting to get free, mad with terror, leaping from the windows. Oh, it was awful, to burn, to burn! I seemed to be caged in flames that were darting at me savagely, spitefully. Would nobody save me?

Yes, some one was trying to save me, was dragging my body across the floor. Consciousness left me, and it seemed for ages I lay in a stupor. When I opened my eyes again some one was still tugging at me. We were going down the stairway, and on all sides of us were sheets of flapping flame. I was wrapped in a blanket. How had it got there? Who was that dark figure pulling at me so desperately, trying to lift me, staggering a few paces with me, stumbling blindly on? Brave one, noble one, whoever you be! Foolhardy one, reckless one, whoever you be! Save yourself while yet there is time. Leave me to my fate. But, oh, the agony of it to burn, to burn . . . !

* * * * *

Another desperate effort and we are almost at the door. Flames are darting at us like serpents, leaping kitten-like at our heels. Above us is a billowy canopy of fire soaring upward with a vast crackling roar. Fiery splinters shoot around us, while before us is a black pit of smoke. Smooth walls of fire uprear about us. We are in a cavern of fire, and in another moment it will engulf us. Oh, my rescuer, a last frenzied effort! We are almost at the door. Then I am lifted up and we both tumble out into the street. Not a second too soon, for, like a savage beast foiled of its prey, a blast of flame shoots after us, and the doorway is a gulf of blazing wrath.

* * * * *

I am lying in the snow, lying on a blanket, and some one holds my head.

"Berna, is that you?"

She nods. She does not speak. I shudder as I look at her. Her face is like a great burn, a black mask in which her eyes and teeth gleam whitely . . .

"Oh, Berna, Berna, and it was you that dragged me out . . . !"

* * * * *

My eyes go to the fiery hell in front. As I look the roof crashes in and we are showered by falling sparks. I see a fireman run back. He is swathed in flame. Madly he rolls in the snow. The hotel is like a cascade of flame; it spouts outward like water, beautiful golden water. In its centre is a wonderful whirlpool. I see the line of a black girder leap out, and hanging over it a limp, charred shape. A moment it hangs uncertainly, then plunges downward into the roasting heart of the pit. And I know it for Locasto.

* * * * *

Oh, Berna, Berna! I can't bear to look at her. Why did she do it? It's pitiful, pitiful . . .

The fire is spreading. Right and left it swings and leaps in giant strides. Sudden flames shoot out, curl over and roll like golden velvet down the black faces of the buildings. The fire leaps the street. All is pandemonium now. Mad with fear and excitement, men and women rave and curse and pray. Water! water! is the cry; but no water comes. Suddenly a mob of terror-goaded men comes surging down the street. They bring the long hose line that connects with the pump-station on the river. Hurrah! now they will soon have the flames under control. Water, water is coming.

The line is laid and a cry goes up to turn on the water. Hurry there! But no water comes. What can be the matter? Then the dread whisper goes round that the man in charge of the pumping-station has neglected his duty, and the engine fires are cold. A howl of fury and despair goes up to the lurid heavens. Women wring their hands and moan; men stand by in a stupor of hopeless agony. And the fire, as if it knew of its victory, leaps up in a roaring ecstasy of triumph.

There we watched, Berna and I, lying in the snow that melts all around us in the fierce, scorching glare. Through the lurid rift of smoke I can see the friendly stars. Against that curtain of blaze, strangely beautiful in its sinuous strength, I watch the black silhouettes of men running hither and thither like rats, gutting the houses, looting the stores, tearing the hearts out of the homes. The fire seems a great bird, and from its nest of furnace heat it spreads its flapping wings over the city.

Yes, there is no hope. The gold-born city is doomed. From where I lie the scene is one long vista of blazing gables, ribs and rafters hugged by tawny arms of fire. Squat cabins swirling in mad eddies of flame; hotels, dance-halls, brothels swathed and smothered in flame-rent blankets of swirling smoke. There is no hope. The fire is a vast avenger, and before its wrath the iniquity of the tenderloin is swept away. That flimsy hive of humanity, with its sins and secrets and sorrows, goes up in smoke and ashes to the silent stars.

The gold-born city is doomed. Yet, as I lay there, it seemed to me like a judgment, and that from its ruins would arise a new city, clean, upright, incorruptible. Yes, the gold-camp would find itself. Even as the gold, must it pass through the furnace to be made clean. And from the site where in the olden days the men who toiled for the gold were robbed by every device of human guile, a new city would come to be—a great city, proud and prosperous, beloved of homing hearts, and blessed in its purity and peace.

"Beloved," I sighed through a gathering mist of consciousness. I felt some hot tears falling on my face. I felt a kiss seal my lips. I felt a breathing in my ear.

"Oh, my dear, my dear!" she said. "I've only brought you sorrow and pain, but you've brought me love, that love that is a dazzling light, beside which the sunshine is as darkness."

"Berna!" I raised myself; I put out my arms to clasp her. They clasped the empty air. Wildly, wildly I looked around. She was gone!

"Berna!" Again I cried, but there was no reply. I was alone, alone. Then a great weakness came over me . . .

I never saw her again.

* * * * *

THE LAST

It is finished. I have written here the story of my life, or of that portion of it which means everything to me, for the rest means nothing. Now that it is done, I too have done, so I sit me down and wait. For what am I waiting? A divine miracle perhaps.

Somehow I feel I will see her again, somehow, somewhere. Surely God would not reveal to us the shining light of the Great Reality only to plunge us again into outer darkness? Love cannot be in vain. I will not believe it. Somehow, somewhere!

So in the glow of the great peat fire I sit me down and wait, and the faith grows in me that she will come to me again; that I will feel the soft caress of her hand upon my pillow, that I will hear her voice all tuned to tenderness, that I will see through my tear-blinded eyes her sweet compassionate face. Somehow, somewhere!

With the aid of my crutch I unlatch one of the long windows and step out onto the terrace. I peer through the darkness and once more I have a sense of that land of imperious vastitudes so unfathomably lonely. With an unspeakable longing in my heart, I try to pierce the shadows that surround me. From the cavernous dark the snowflakes sting my face, but the great night seems good to me, and I sink into a garden seat. Oh, I am tired, tired . . .

I am waiting, waiting. I close my eyes and wait. I know she will come. The snow is covering me. White as a statue, I sit and wait.

* * * * *

Ah, Berna, my dear, my dear! I knew you would return; I knew, I knew. Come to me, little one. I'm tired, so tired. Put your arms around me, girl; kiss me, kiss me. I'm weak and ill, but now you've come I'll soon be well again. You won't leave me any more; will you, honey? Oh, it's good to have you once again! It seems like a dream. Kiss me once more, sweetheart. It's all so cold and dark. Put your arms around me . . .

Oh, Berna, Berna, light of my life, I knew all would come right at last—beyond the mists, beyond the dreaming; at last, dear love, at last! . . .

BALLADS OF A BOHEMIAN

PRELUDE

Alas! upon some starry height,
The Gods of Excellence to please,
This hand of mine will never smite
The Harp of High Serenities.
Mere minstrel of the street am I,
To whom a careless coin you fling;
But who, beneath the bitter sky,
Blue-lipped, yet insolent of eye,
Can shrill a song of Spring;
A song of merry mansard days,
The cheery chimney-tops among;
Of rolics and of roundelays
When we were young . . . when we were young;
A song of love and lilac nights,
Of wit, of wisdom and of wine;
Of Folly whirling on the Heights,
Of hunger and of hope divine;
Of Blanche, Suzette and Celestine,
And all that gay and tender band
Who shared with us the fat, the lean,
The hazard of Illusion-land;
When scores of Philistines we slew
As mightily with brush and pen
We sought to make the world anew,
And scorned the gods of other men;
When we were fools divinely wise,
Who held it rapturous to strive;
When Art was sacred in our eyes,
And it was Heav'n to be alive . . .

O days of glamor, glory, truth,
To you to-night I raise my glass;
O freehold of immortal youth,
Bohemia, the lost, alas!
O laughing lads who led the romp,
Respectable you've grown, I'm told;
Your heads you bow to power and pomp,
You've learned to know the worth of gold.
O merry maids who shared our cheer,
Your eyes are dim, your locks are gray;
And as you scrub I sadly fear
Your daughters speed the dance to-day.
O windmill land and crescent moon!
O Columbine and Pierrette!
To you my old guitar I tune
Ere I forget, ere I forget . . .

So come, good men who toil and tire,
Who smoke and sip the kindly cup,
Ring round about the tavern fire
Ere yet you drink your liquor up;
And hear my simple songs of earth,
Of youth and truth and living things;
Of poverty and proper mirth,
Of rags and rich imaginings;
Of cock-a-hoop, blue-heavened days,
Of hearts elate and eager breath,
Of wonder, worship, pity, praise,
Of sorrow, sacrifice and death;
Of lusting, laughter, passion, pain,
Of lights that lure and dreams that thrall . . .
And if a golden word I gain,
Oh, kindly folks, God save you all!
And if you shake your heads in blame . . .
Good friends, God love you all the same.

BOOK ONE

SPRING

I

Montparnasse,

April 1914.
	All day the sun has shone into my little attic, a bitter sunshine that brightened yet did not warm. And so as I toiled and toiled doggedly enough, many were the looks I cast at the three faggots I had saved to cook my evening meal. Now, however, my supper is over, my pipe alight, and as I stretch my legs before the embers I have at last a glow of comfort, a glimpse of peace.

My Garret

Here is my Garret up five flights of stairs;
Here's where I deal in dreams and ply in fancies,
Here is the wonder-shop of all my wares,
My sounding sonnets and my red romances.
Here's where I challenge Fate and ring my rhymes,
And grope at glory—aye, and starve at times.

Here is my Stronghold: stout of heart am I,
Greeting each dawn as songful as a linnet;
And when at night on yon poor bed I lie
(Blessing the world and every soul that's in it),

Here's where I thank the Lord no shadow bars
My skylight's vision of the valiant stars.

Here is my Palace tapestried with dreams.
Ah! though to-night ten *sous* are all my treasure,
While in my gaze immortal beauty gleams,
Am I not dowered with wealth beyond all measure?
Though in my ragged coat my songs I sing,
King of my soul, I envy not the king.

Here is my Haven: it's so quiet here;
Only the scratch of pen, the candle's flutter;
Shabby and bare and small, but O how dear!
Mark you—my table with my work a-clutter,
My shelf of tattered books along the wall,
My bed, my broken chair—that's nearly all.

Only four faded walls, yet mine, all mine.
Oh, you fine folks, a pauper scorns your pity.
Look, where above me stars of rapture shine;
See, where below me gleams the siren city . . .
Am I not rich?—a millionaire no less,
If wealth be told in terms of Happiness.

Ten *sous* . . . I think one can sing best of poverty when one is holding it at arm's length. I'm sure that when I wrote these lines, fortune had for a moment tweaked me by the nose. To-night, however, I am truly down to ten *sous*. It is for that I have stayed in my room all day, rolled in my blankets and clutching my pen with clammy fingers. I must work, work, work. I must finish my book before poverty crushes me. I am not only writing for my living but for my life. Even to-day my Muse was mutinous. For hours and hours anxiously I stared at a paper that was blank; nervously I paced up and down my garret; bitterly I flung myself on my bed. Then suddenly it all came. Line after line I wrote with hardly a halt. So I made another of my Ballads of the Boulevards. Here it is:

Julot the *Apache*

You've heard of Julot the *apache*, and Gigolette, his *môme* . . .
Montmartre was their hunting-ground, but Belville was their home.
A little chap just like a boy, with smudgy black mustache,—
Yet there was nothing juvenile in Julot the *apache*.
From head to heel as tough as steel, as nimble as a cat,
With every trick of twist and kick, a master of *savate*.
And Gigolette was tall and fair, as stupid as a cow,
With three combs in the greasy hair she banged upon her brow.
You'd see her on the Place Pigalle on any afternoon,
A primitive and strapping wench as brazen as the moon.
And yet there is a tale that's told of Clichy after dark,
And two *gendarmes* who swung their arms with Julot for a mark.
And oh, but they'd have got him too; they banged and blazed away,
When like a flash a woman leapt between them and their prey.
She took the medicine meant for him; she came down with a crash . . .
"Quick now, and make your get-away, O Julot the *apache*!" . . .
But no! He turned, ran swiftly back, his arms around her met;
They nabbed him sobbing like a kid, and kissing Gigolette.

Now I'm a reckless painter chap who loves a jamboree,
And one night in Cyrano's bar I got upon a spree;
And there were trollops all about, and crooks of every kind,
But though the place was reeling round I didn't seem to mind.
Till down I sank, and all was blank when in the bleary dawn
I woke up in my studio to find—my money gone;
Three hundred francs I'd scraped and squeezed to pay my quarter's rent.
"Some one has pinched my wad," I wailed; "it never has been spent."
And as I racked my brains to seek how I could raise some more,
Before my cruel landlord kicked me cowering from the door:
A knock . . ."Come in," I gruffly groaned; I did not raise my head,
Then lo! I heard a husky voice, a swift and silky tread:

"You got so blind, last night, *mon vieux*, I collared all your cash—
Three hundred francs . . . There! *Nom de Dieu*," said Julot the *apache*.

And that was how I came to know Julot and Gigolette,
And we would talk and drink a *bock*, and smoke a cigarette.
And I would meditate upon the artistry of crime,
And he would tell of cracking cribs and cops and doing time;
Or else when he was flush of funds he'd carelessly explain
He'd biffed some bloated *bourgeois* on the border of the Seine.
So gentle and polite he was, just like a man of peace,
And not a desperado and the terror of the police.

Now one day in a *bistro* that's behind the Place Vendôme
I came on Julot the *apache*, and Gigolette his *môme*.
And as they looked so very grave, says I to them, says I,
"Come on and have a little glass, it's good to rinse the eye.
You both look mighty serious; you've something on the heart."
"Ah, yes," said Julot the *apache*, "we've something to impart.
When such things come to folks like us, it isn't very gay . . .
It's Gigolette—she tells me that a *gosse* is on the way."
Then Gigolette, she looked at me with eyes like stones of gall:
"If we were honest folks," said she, "I wouldn't mind at all.
But then . . . you know the life we lead; well, anyway I mean
(That is, providing it's a girl) to call her Angeline."
"Cheer up," said I; "it's all in life. There's gold within the dross.
Come on, we'll drink another *verre* to Angeline the *gosse*."

And so the weary winter passed, and then one April morn
The worthy Julot came at last to say the babe was born.
"I'd like to chuck it in the Seine," he sourly snarled, "and yet
I guess I'll have to let it live, because of Gigolette."
I only laughed, for sure I saw his spite was all a bluff,
And he was prouder than a prince behind his manner gruff.
Yet every day he'd blast the brat with curses deep and grim,
And swear to me that Gigolette no longer thought of *him*.
And then one night he dropped the mask; his eyes were sick with dread,

And when I offered him a smoke he groaned and shook his head:
"I'm all upset; it's Angeline . . . she's covered with a rash . . .
She'll maybe die, my little *gosse*," cried Julot the *apache*.

But Angeline, I joy to say, came through the test all right,
Though Julot, so they tell me, watched beside her day and night.
And when I saw him next, says he: "Come up and dine with me.
We'll buy a beefsteak on the way, a bottle and some *brie*."
And so I had a merry night within his humble home,
And laughed with Angeline the *gosse* and Gigolette the *mome*.
And every time that Julot used a word the least obscene,
How Gigolette would frown at him and point to Angeline:
Oh, such a little innocent, with hair of silken floss,
I do not wonder they were proud of Angeline the *gosse*.
And when her arms were round his neck, then Julot says to me:
"I must work harder now, *mon vieux*, since I've to work for three."
He worked so very hard indeed, the police dropped in one day,
And for a year behind the bars they put him safe away.

So dark and silent now, their home; they'd gone—I wondered where,
Till in a laundry near I saw a child with shining hair;
And o'er the tub a strapping wench, her arms in soapy foam;
Lo! it was Angeline the *gosse*, and Gigolette the *mome*.
And so I kept an eye on them and saw that all went right,
Until at last came Julot home, half crazy with delight.
And when he'd kissed them both, says he: "I've had my fill this time.
I'm on the honest now, I am; I'm all fed up with crime.
You mark my words, the page I turn is going to be clean,
I swear it on the head of her, my little Angeline."

And so, to finish up my tale, this morning as I strolled
Along the boulevard I heard a voice I knew of old.
I saw a rosy little man with walrus-like mustache . . .
I stopped, I stared . . . By all the gods! 'twas Julot the *apache*.
"I'm in the garden way," he said, "and doing mighty well;
I've half an acre under glass, and heaps of truck to sell.

Come out and see. Oh come, my friend, on Sunday, wet or shine . . .
Say!—*it's the First Communion of that little girl of mine.*"

II

Chez Moi, Montparnasse,

The same evening.

To-day is an anniversary. A year ago to-day I kicked over an office stool and came to Paris thinking to make a living by my pen. I was twenty then, and in my pocket I had twenty pounds. Of that, my ten *sous* are all that remain. And so to-night I am going to spend them, not prudently on bread, but prodigally on beer.

As I stroll down the Boul' Mich' the lingering light has all the exquisite tenderness of violet; the trees are in their first translucent green; beneath them the lamps are lit with purest gold, and from the Little Luxembourg comes a silver jangle of tiny voices. Taking the gay side of the street, I enter a cafe. Although it isn't its true name, I choose to call my cafe—

L'Escargot D'Or

O Tavern of the Golden Snail!
Ten *sous* have I, so I'll regale;
Ten *sous* your amber brew to sip
(Eight for the *bock* and two the tip),
And so I'll sit the evening long,
And smoke my pipe and watch the throng,
The giddy crowd that drains and drinks,
I'll watch it quiet as a sphinx;
And who among them all shall buy
For ten poor *sous* such joy as I?
As I who, snugly tucked away,
Look on it all as on a play,

A frolic scene of love and fun,
To please an audience of One.

O Tavern of the Golden Snail!
You've stuff indeed for many a tale.
All eyes, all ears, I nothing miss:
Two lovers lean to clasp and kiss;
The merry students sing and shout,
The nimble *garcons* dart about;
Lo! here come Mimi and Musette
With: *"S'il vous plait, une cigarette?"*
Marcel and Rudolf, Shaunard too,
Behold the old rapscallion crew,
With flowing tie and shaggy head . . .
Who says Bohemia is dead?
Oh shades of Murger! prank and clown,
And I will watch and write it down.

O Tavern of the Golden Snail!
What crackling throats have gulped your ale!
What sons of Fame from far and near
Have glowed and mellowed in your cheer!
Within this corner where I sit
Banville and Coppe/e clashed their wit;
And hither too, to dream and drain,
And drown despair, came poor Verlaine.
Here Wilde would talk and Synge would muse,
Maybe like me with just ten *sous*.
Ah! one is lucky, is one not?
With ghosts so rare to drain a pot!
So may your custom never fail,
O Tavern of the Golden Snail!

There! my pipe is out. Let me light it again and consider. I have no illusions about myself. I am not fool enough to think I am a poet, but I have a knack of rhyme and I love to make verses. Mine is a tootling, tin-whistle music. Humbly and afar I follow in the footsteps of Praed and Lampson, of Field and Riley, hoping that in time my Muse may bring me bread and butter. So far, however, it has been all kicks and no coppers. And to-night I am at the end of my tether. I wish I knew where to-morrow's breakfast was coming from. Well, since rhyming's been my ruin, let me rhyme to the bitter end.

It Is Later Than You Think

Lone amid the cafe's cheer,
Sad of heart am I to-night;
Dolefully I drink my beer,
But no single line I write.
There's the wretched rent to pay,
Yet I glower at pen and ink:
Oh, inspire me, Muse, I pray,
It is later than you think!

Hello! there's a pregnant phrase.
Bravo! let me write it down;
Hold it with a hopeful gaze,
Gauge it with a fretful frown;
Tune it to my lyric lyre . . .
Ah! upon starvation's brink,
How the words are dark and dire:
It is later than you think.

Weigh them well . . . Behold yon band,
Students drinking by the door,
Madly merry, *bock* in hand,
Saucers stacked to mark their score.
Get you gone, you jolly scamps;
Let your parting glasses clink;
Seek your long neglected lamps:
It is later than you think.

Look again: yon dainty blonde,
All allure and golden grace,
Oh so willing to respond
Should you turn a smiling face.
Play your part, poor pretty doll;

Feast and frolic, pose and prink;
There's the Morgue to end it all,
And it's later than you think.

Yon's a playwright—mark his face,
Puffed and purple, tense and tired;
Pasha-like he holds his place,
Hated, envied and admired.
How you gobble life, my friend;
Wine, and woman soft and pink!
Well, each tether has its end:
Sir, it's later than you think.

See yon living scarecrow pass
With a wild and wolfish stare
At each empty absinthe glass,
As if he saw Heaven there.
Poor damned wretch, to end your pain
There is still the Greater Drink.
Yonder waits the sanguine Seine . . .
It is later than you think.

Lastly, you who read; aye, you
Who this very line may scan:
Think of all you planned to do . . .
Have you done the best you can?
See! the tavern lights are low;
Black's the night, and how you shrink!
God! and is it time to go?
Ah! the clock is always slow;
It is later than you think;
Sadly later than you think;
Far, far later than you think.

Scarcely do I scribble that last line on the back of an old envelope when a voice hails me. It is a fellow free-lance, a short-story man called MacBean. He is having a feast of *Marennes* and he asks me to join him.

MacBean is a Scotsman with the soul of an Irishman. He has a keen, lean, spectacled face, and if it were not for his gray hair he might be taken for a student of theology. However, there is nothing of the Puritan in MacBean. He loves wine and women, and money melts in his fingers.

He has lived so long in the Quarter he looks at life from the Parisian angle. His knowledge of literature is such that he might be a Professor, but he would rather be a vagabond of letters. We talk shop.

We discuss the American short story, but MacBean vows they do these things better in France. He says that some of the *contes* printed every day in the *Journal* are worthy of Maupassant. After that he buys more beer, and we roam airily over the fields of literature, plucking here and there a blossom of quotation. A fine talk, vivid and eager. It puts me into a kind of glow.

MacBean pays the bill from a handful of big notes, and the thought of my own empty pockets for a moment damps me. However, when we rise to go, it is well after midnight, and I am in a pleasant daze. The rest of the evening may be summed up in the following jingle:

Noctambule

Zut! it's two o'clock.
See! the lights are jumping.
Finish up your *bock*,
Time we all were humping.
Waiters stack the chairs,
Pile them on the tables;
Let us to our lairs
Underneath the gables.

Up the old Boul' Mich'
Climb with steps erratic.
Steady . . . how I wish
I was in my attic!
Full am I with cheer;
In my heart the joy stirs;

Couldn't be the beer,
Must have been the oysters.

In obscene array
Garbage cans spill over;
How I wish that they
Smelled as sweet as clover!
Charing women wait;
Cafes drop their shutters;
Rats perambulate
Up and down the gutters.

Down the darkened street
Market carts are creeping;
Horse with wary feet,
Red-faced driver sleeping.
Loads of vivid greens,
Carrots, leeks, potatoes,
Cabbages and beans,
Turnips and tomatoes.

Pair of dapper chaps,
Cigarettes and sashes,
Stare at me, perhaps
Desperate *Apache\s*.
"Needn't bother me,
Jolly well you know it;
*Parceque je suis
Quartier Latin poe\te*.

"Give you villanelles,
Madrigals and lyrics;
Ballades and rondels,
Odes and panegyrics.
Poet pinched and poor,
Pricked by cold and hunger;
Trouble's troubadour,
Misery's balladmonger."

Think how queer it is!
Every move I'm making,
Cosmic gravity's
Center I am shaking;
Oh, how droll to feel
(As I now am feeling),
Even as I reel,
All the world is reeling.

Reeling too the stars,
Neptune and Uranus,
Jupiter and Mars,
Mercury and Venus;
Suns and moons with me,
As I'm homeward straying,
All in sympathy
Swaying, swaying, swaying.

Lord! I've got a head.
Well, it's not surprising.
I must gain my bed
Ere the sun be rising;
When the merry lark
In the sky is soaring,
I'll refuse to hark,
I'll be snoring, snoring.

Strike a sulphur match . . .
Ha! at last my garret.
Fumble at the latch,
Close the door and bar it.
Bed, you graciously
Wait, despite my scorning . . .
So, bibaciously
Mad old world, good morning.

III

My Garret, Montparnasse,

April.

Insomnia

Heigh ho! to sleep I vainly try;
Since twelve I haven't closed an eye,
And now it's three, and as I lie,
From Notre Dame to St. Denis
The bells of Paris chime to me;
"You're young," they say, "and strong and free."

I do not turn with sighs and groans
To ease my limbs, to rest my bones,
As if my bed were stuffed with stones,
No peevish murmur tips my tongue—
Ah no! for every sound upflung
Says: "Lad, you're free and strong and young."

And so beneath the sheet's caress
My body purrs with happiness;
Joy bubbles in my veins . . . Ah yes,
My very blood that leaps along
Is chiming in a joyous song,
Because I'm young and free and strong.

Maybe it is the springtide. I am so happy I am afraid. The sense of living fills me with exultation. I want to sing, to dance; I am dithyrambic with delight.

> I think the moon must be to blame:
> It fills the room with fairy flame;
> It paints the wall, it seems to pour
> A dappled flood upon the floor.
> I rise and through the window stare . . .
> Ye gods! how marvelously fair!
> From Montrouge to the Martyr's Hill,
> A silver city rapt and still;
> Dim, drowsy deeps of opal haze,
> And spire and dome in diamond blaze;
> The little lisping leaves of spring
> Like sequins softly glimmering;
> Each roof a plaque of argent sheen,
> A gauzy gulf the space between;
> Each chimney-top a thing of grace,
> Where merry moonbeams prank and chase;
> And all that sordid was and mean,
> Just Beauty, deathless and serene.
>
> O magic city of a dream!
> From glory unto glory gleam;
> And I will gaze and pity those
> Who on their pillows drowse and doze . . .
> And as I've nothing else to do,
> Of tea I'll make a rousing brew,
> And coax my pipes until they croon,
> And chant a ditty to the moon.

There! my tea is black and strong. Inspiration comes with every sip. Now for the moon.

> The moon peeped out behind the hill
> As yellow as an apricot;
> Then up and up it climbed until
> Into the sky it fairly got;

The sky was vast and violet;
The poor moon seemed to faint in fright,
And pale it grew and paler yet,
Like fine old silver, rinsed and bright.
And yet it climbed so bravely on
Until it mounted heaven-high;
Then earthward it serenely shone,
A silver sovereign of the sky,
A bland sultana of the night,
Surveying realms of lily light.

Moon Song

A child saw in the morning skies
The dissipated-looking moon,
And opened wide her big blue eyes,
And cried: "Look, look, my lost balloon!"
And clapped her rosy hands with glee:
"Quick, mother! Bring it back to me."

A poet in a lilied pond
Espied the moon's reflected charms,
And ravished by that beauty blonde,
Leapt out to clasp her in his arms.
And as he'd never learnt to swim,
Poor fool! that was the end of him.

A rustic glimpsed amid the trees
The bluff moon caught as in a snare.
"They say it do be made of cheese,"
Said Giles, "and that a chap bides there . . .
That Blue Boar ale be strong, I vow—
The lad's a-winkin' at me now."

Two lovers watched the new moon hold
The old moon in her bright embrace.
Said she: "There's mother, pale and old,
And drawing near her resting place."

Said he: "Be mine, and with me wed,"
Moon-high she stared . . . she shook her head.

A soldier saw with dying eyes
The bleared moon like a ball of blood,
And thought of how in other skies,
So pearly bright on leaf and bud
Like peace its soft white beams had lain;
Like Peace! . . . He closed his eyes again.

Child, lover, poet, soldier, clown,
Ah yes, old Moon, what things you've seen!
I marvel now, as you look down,
How can your face be so serene?
And tranquil still you'll make your round,
Old Moon, when we are underground.

"And now, blow out your candle, lad, and get to bed. See, the dawn is in the sky. Open your window and let its freshness rouge your cheek. You've earned your rest. Sleep."

Aye, but before I do so, let me read again the last of my *Ballads*.

The Sewing-Girl

The humble garret where I dwell
Is in that Quarter called the Latin;
It isn't spacious—truth to tell,
There's hardly room to swing a cat in.
But what of that! It's there I fight
For food and fame, my Muse inviting,
And all the day and half the night
You'll find me writing, writing, writing.

Now, it was in the month of May
As, wrestling with a rhyme rheumatic,
I chanced to look across the way,
And lo! within a neighbor attic,
A hand drew back the window shade,

And there, a picture glad and glowing,
I saw a sweet and slender maid,
And she was sewing, sewing, sewing.

So poor the room, so small, so scant,
Yet somehow oh, so bright and airy.
There was a pink geranium plant,
Likewise a very pert canary.
And in the maiden's heart it seemed
Some fount of gladness must be springing,
For as alone I sadly dreamed
I heard her singing, singing, singing.

God love her! how it cheered me then
To see her there so brave and pretty;
So she with needle, I with pen,
We slaved and sang above the city.
And as across my streams of ink
I watched her from a poet's distance,
She stitched and sang . . . I scarcely think
She was aware of my existence.

And then one day she sang no more.
That put me out, there's no denying.
I looked—she labored as before,
But, bless me! she was crying, crying.
Her poor canary chirped in vain;
Her pink geranium drooped in sorrow;
"Of course," said I, "she'll sing again.
Maybe," I sighed, "she will to-morrow."

Poor child; 'twas finished with her song:
Day after day her tears were flowing;
And as I wondered what was wrong
She pined and peaked above her sewing.
And then one day the blind she drew,
Ah! though I sought with vain endeavor
To pierce the darkness, well I knew
My sewing-girl had gone for ever.

        And as I sit alone to-night
        My eyes unto her room are turning . . .
        I'd give the sum of all I write
        Once more to see her candle burning,
        Once more to glimpse her happy face,
        And while my rhymes of cheer I'm ringing,
        Across the sunny sweep of space
        To hear her singing, singing, singing.

   Heigh ho! I realize I am very weary. It's nice to be so tired, and to know one can sleep as long as one wants. The morning sunlight floods in at my window, so I draw the blind, and throw myself on my bed . . .

IV

My Garret, Montparnasse,

April.

Hurrah! As I opened my eyes this morning to a hard, unfeeling world, little did I think what a surprise awaited me. A big blue envelope had been pushed under my door. Another rejection, I thought, and I took it up distastefully. The next moment I was staring at my first cheque.

It was an express order for two hundred francs, in payment of a bit of verse . . . So to-day I will celebrate. I will lunch at the D'Harcourt, I will dine on the Grand Boulevard, I will go to the theater.

Well, here's the thing that has turned the tide for me. It is somewhat in the vein of "Sourdough" Service, the Yukon bard. I don't think much of his stuff, but they say he makes heaps of money. I can well believe it, for he drives a Hispano-Suiza in the Bois every afternoon. The other night he was with a crowd at the Dome Cafe, a chubby chap who sits in a corner and seldom speaks. I was disappointed. I thought he was a big, hairy man who swore like a trooper and mixed brandy with his beer. He only drank Vichy, poor fellow!

Lucille

Of course you've heard of the *Nancy Lee*, and how she sailed away
On her famous quest of the Arctic flea, to the wilds of Hudson's Bay?
For it was a foreign Prince's whim to collect this tiny cuss,

And a golden quid was no more to him than a copper to coves like us.
So we sailed away and our hearts were gay as we gazed on the gorgeous scene;
And we laughed with glee as we caught the flea of the wolf and the wolverine;
Yea, our hearts were light as the parasite of the ermine rat we slew,
And the great musk ox, and the silver fox, and the moose and the caribou.
And we laughed with zest as the insect pest of the marmot crowned our zeal,
And the wary mink and the wily "link", and the walrus and the seal.
And with eyes aglow on the scornful snow we danced a rigadoon,
Round the lonesome lair of the Arctic hare, by the light of the silver moon.

But the time was nigh to homeward hie, when, imagine our despair!
For the best of the lot we hadn't got—the flea of the polar bear.

Oh, his face was long and his breath was strong, as the Skipper he says to me:
"I wants you to linger 'ere, my lad, by the shores of the Hartic Sea;
I wants you to 'unt the polar bear the perishin' winter through,
And if flea ye find of its breed and kind, there's a 'undred quid for you."
But I shook my head: "No, Cap," I said; "it's yourself I'd like to please,
But I tells ye flat I wouldn't do that if ye went on yer bended knees."
Then the Captain spat in the seething brine, and he says: "Good luck to you,
If it can't be did for a 'undred quid, supposin' we call it two?"
So that was why they said good-by, and they sailed and left me there—
Alone, alone in the Arctic Zone to hunt for the polar bear.

Oh, the days were slow and packed with woe, till I thought they would never end;
And I used to sit when the fire was lit, with my pipe for my only friend.
And I tried to sing some rollicky thing, but my song broke off in a prayer,
And I'd drowse and dream by the driftwood gleam; I'd dream of a polar bear;
I'd dream of a cloudlike polar bear that blotted the stars on high,
With ravenous jaws and flenzing claws, and the flames of hell in his eye.
And I'd trap around on the frozen ground, as a proper hunter ought,
And beasts I'd find of every kind, but never the one I sought.
Never a track in the white ice-pack that humped and heaved and flawed,
Till I came to think: "Why, strike me pink! if the creature ain't a fraud."
And then one night in the waning light, as I hurried home to sup,
I hears a roar by the cabin door, and a great white hulk heaves up.
So my rifle flashed, and a bullet crashed; dead, dead as a stone fell he,
And I gave a cheer, for there in his ear—Gosh ding me!—a tiny flea.

At last, at last! Oh, I clutched it fast, and I gazed on it with pride;
And I thrust it into a biscuit-tin, and I shut it safe inside;
With a lid of glass for the light to pass, and space to leap and play;
Oh, it kept alive; yea, seemed to thrive, as I watched it night and day.
And I used to sit and sing to it, and I shielded it from harm,
And many a hearty feed it had on the heft of my hairy arm.
For you'll never know in that land of snow how lonesome a man can feel;
So I made a fuss of the little cuss, and I christened it "Lucille".
But the longest winter has its end, and the ice went out to sea,
And I saw one day a ship in the bay, and there was the *Nancy Lee*.
So a boat was lowered and I went aboard, and they opened wide their eyes—

Yes, they gave a cheer when the truth was clear, and they saw my
    precious prize.
And then it was all like a giddy dream; but to cut my story short,
We sailed away on the fifth of May to the foreign Prince's court;
To a palmy land and a palace grand, and the little Prince was there,
And a fat Princess in a satin dress with a crown of gold on her
    hair.
And they showed me into a shiny room, just him and her and me,
And the Prince he was pleased and friendly-like, and he calls for
    drinks for three.
And I shows them my battered biscuit-tin, and I makes my modest
    spiel,
And they laughed, they did, when I opened the lid, and out there
    popped Lucille.

Oh, the Prince was glad, I could soon see that, and the Princess
    she was too;
And Lucille waltzed round on the tablecloth as she often used to
    do.
And the Prince pulled out a purse of gold, and he put it in my
    hand;
And he says: "It was worth all that, I'm told, to stay in that nasty
    land."
And then he turned with a sudden cry, and he clutched at his royal
    beard;
And the Princess screamed, and well she might—for Lucille had
    disappeared.

"She must be here," said his Noble Nibbs, so we hunted all
    around;
Oh, we searched that place, but never a trace of the little beast we
    found.
So I shook my head, and I glumly said: "Gol darn the saucy cuss!
It's mighty queer, but she isn't here; so . . . she must be on one of
    us.
You'll pardon me if I make so free, but—there's just one thing to
    do:
If you'll kindly go for a half a mo' I'll search me garments
    through."

Then all alone on the shiny throne I stripped from head to heel;
In vain, in vain; it was very plain that I hadn't got Lucille.
So I garbed again, and I told the Prince, and he scratched his august head;
"I suppose if she hasn't selected you, it must be me," he said.
So *he* retired; but he soon came back, and his features showed distress:
"Oh, it isn't you and it isn't me." . . . Then we looked at the Princess.
So *she* retired; and we heard a scream, and she opened wide the door;
And her fingers twain were pinched to pain, but a radiant smile she wore:
"It's here," she cries, "our precious prize. Oh, I found it right away . . ."
Then I ran to her with a shout of joy, but I choked with a wild dismay.
I clutched the back of the golden throne, and the room began to reel . . .
What she held to me was, ah yes! a flea, but . . . *it wasn't my Lucille.*

After all, I did not celebrate. I sat on the terrace of the Cafe Napolitain on the Grand Boulevard, half hypnotized by the passing crowd. And as I sat I fell into conversation with a god-like stranger who sipped some golden ambrosia. He told me he was an actor and introduced me to his beverage, which he called a "Suze-Anni". He soon left me, but the effect of the golden liquid remained, and there came over me a desire to write. *C'e/tait plus fort que moi.* So instead of going to the Folies Berge\re I spent all evening in the Omnium Bar near the Bourse, and wrote the following:

On the Boulevard

Oh, it's pleasant sitting here,
Seeing all the people pass;
You beside your *bock* of beer,
I behind my *demi-tasse*.
Chatting of no matter what.
You the Mummer, I the Bard;

Oh, it's jolly, is it not?—
Sitting on the Boulevard.

More amusing than a book,
If a chap has eyes to see;
For, no matter where I look,
Stories, stories jump at me.
Moving tales my pen might write;
Poems plain on every face;
Monologues you could recite
With inimitable grace.

(Ah! Imagination's power)
See yon *demi-mondaine* there,
Idly toying with a flower,
Smiling with a pensive air . . .
Well, her smile is but a mask,
For I saw within her muff
Such a wicked little flask:
Vitriol—ugh! the beastly stuff.

Now look back beside the bar.
See yon curled and scented *beau*,
Puffing at a fine cigar—
Sale espe\ce de maquereau.
Well (of course, it's all surmise),
It's for him she holds her place;
When he passes she will rise,
Dash the vitriol in his face.

Quick they'll carry him away,
Pack him in a Red Cross car;
Her they'll hurry, so they say,
To the cells of St. Lazare.
What will happen then, you ask?
What will all the sequel be?
Ah! Imagination's task
Isn't easy . . . let me see . . .

She will go to jail, no doubt,
For a year, or maybe two;
Then as soon as she gets out
Start her bawdy life anew.
He will lie within a ward,
Harmless as a man can be,
With his face grotesquely scarred,
And his eyes that cannot see.

Then amid the city's din
He will stand against a wall,
With around his neck a tin
Into which the pennies fall.
She will pass (I see it plain,
Like a cinematograph),
She will halt and turn again,
Look and look, and maybe laugh.

Well, I'm not so sure of that—
Whether she will laugh or cry.
He will hold a battered hat
To the lady passing by.
He will smile a cringing smile,
And into his grimy hold,
With a laugh (or sob) the while,
She will drop a piece of gold.

"Bless you, lady," he will say,
And get grandly drunk that night.
She will come and come each day,
Fascinated by the sight.
Then somehow he'll get to know
(Maybe by some kindly friend)
Who she is, and so . . . and so
Bring my story to an end.

How his heart will burst with hate!
He will curse and he will cry.
He will wait and wait and wait,

Till again she passes by.
Then like tiger from its lair
He will leap from out his place,
Down her, clutch her by the hair,
Smear the vitriol on her face.

(Ah! Imagination rare)
See . . . he takes his hat to go;
Now he's level with her chair;
Now she rises up to throw . . .
God! and she has done it too . . .
Oh, those screams; those hideous screams!
I imagined and . . . it's true:
How his face will haunt my dreams!

What a sight! It makes me sick.
Seems I am to blame somehow.
Garcon, fetch a brandy quick . . .
There! I'm feeling better now.
Let's collaborate, we two,
You the Mummer, I the Bard;
Oh, what ripping stuff we'll do,
Sitting on the Boulevard!

It is strange how one works easily at times. I wrote this so quickly that I might almost say I had reached the end before I had come to the beginning. In such a mood I wonder why everybody does not write poetry. Get a Roget's *Thesaurus*, a rhyming dictionary: sit before your typewriter with a strong glass of coffee at your elbow, and just click the stuff off.

Facility

So easy 'tis to make a rhyme,
That did the world but know it,
Your coachman might Parnassus climb,
Your butler be a poet.

Then, oh, how charming it would be
If, when in haste hysteric
You called the page, you learned that he
Was grappling with a lyric.

Or else what rapture it would yield,
When cook sent up the salad,
To find within its depths concealed
A touching little ballad.

Or if for tea and toast you yearned,
What joy to find upon it
The chambermaid had coyly laid
A palpitating sonnet.

Your baker could the fashion set;
Your butcher might respond well;
With every tart a triolet,
With every chop a rondel.

Your tailor's bill . . . well, I'll be blowed!
Dear chap! I never knowed him . . .
He's gone and written me an ode,
Instead of what I *owed* him.

So easy 'tis to rhyme . . . yet stay!
Oh, terrible misgiving!
Please do not give the game away . . .
I've got to make my living.

V

My Garret

May 1914.

Golden Days

Another day of toil and strife,
Another page so white,
Within that fateful Log of Life
That I and all must write;
Another page without a stain
To make of as I may,
That done, I shall not see again
Until the Judgment Day.

Ah, could I, could I backward turn
The pages of that Book,
How often would I blench and burn!
How often loathe to look!
What pages would be meanly scrolled;
What smeared as if with mud;
A few, maybe, might gleam like gold,
Some scarlet seem as blood.

O Record grave, God guide my hand
And make me worthy be,
Since what I write to-day shall stand
To all eternity;
Aye, teach me, Lord of Life, I pray,

As I salute the sun,
To bear myself that every day
May be a Golden One.

I awoke this morning to see the bright sunshine flooding my garret. No chamber in the palace of a king could have been more fair. How I sang as I dressed! How I lingered over my coffee, savoring every drop! How carefully I packed my pipe, gazing serenely over the roofs of Paris.

Never is the city so lovely as in this month of May, when all the trees are in the fullness of their foliage. As I look, I feel a freshness of vision in my eyes. Wonder wakes in me. The simplest things move me to delight.

The Joy of Little Things

It's good the great green earth to roam,
Where sights of awe the soul inspire;
But oh, it's best, the coming home,
The crackle of one's own hearth-fire!
You've hob-nobbed with the solemn Past;
You've seen the pageantry of kings;
Yet oh, how sweet to gain at last
The peace and rest of Little Things!

Perhaps you're counted with the Great;
You strain and strive with mighty men;
Your hand is on the helm of State;
Colossus-like you stride . . . and then
There comes a pause, a shining hour,
A dog that leaps, a hand that clings:
O Titan, turn from pomp and power;
Give all your heart to Little Things.

Go couch you childwise in the grass,
Believing it's some jungle strange,
Where mighty monsters peer and pass,
Where beetles roam and spiders range.
'Mid gloom and gleam of leaf and blade,

What dragons rasp their painted wings!
O magic world of shine and shade!
O beauty land of Little Things!

I sometimes wonder, after all,
Amid this tangled web of fate,
If what is great may not be small,
And what is small may not be great.
So wondering I go my way,
Yet in my heart contentment sings . . .
O may I ever see, I pray,
God's grace and love in Little Things.

So give to me, I only beg,
A little roof to call my own,
A little cider in the keg,
A little meat upon the bone;
A little garden by the sea,
A little boat that dips and swings . . .
Take wealth, take fame, but leave to me,
O Lord of Life, just Little Things.

Yesterday I finished my tenth ballad. When I have done about a score I will seek a publisher. If I cannot find one, I will earn, beg or steal the money to get them printed. Then if they do not sell I will hawk them from door to door. Oh, I'll succeed, I know I'll succeed. And yet I don't want an easy success; give me the joy of the fight, the thrill of the adventure. Here's my last ballad:

The Absinthe Drinkers

He's yonder, on the terrace of the Cafe de la Paix,
The little wizened Spanish man, I see him every day.
He's sitting with his Pernod on his customary chair;
He's staring at the passers with his customary stare.
He never takes his piercing eyes from off that moving throng,
That current cosmopolitan meandering along:
Dark diplomats from Martinique, pale Rastas from Peru,
An Englishman from Bloomsbury, a Yank from Kalamazoo;

A poet from Montmartre's heights, a dapper little Jap,
Exotic citizens of all the countries on the map;
A tourist horde from every land that's underneath the sun—
That little wizened Spanish man, he misses never one.
Oh, foul or fair he's always there, and many a drink he buys,
And there's a fire of red desire within his hollow eyes.
And sipping of my Pernod, and a-knowing what I know,
Sometimes I want to shriek aloud and give away the show.
I've lost my nerve; he's haunting me; he's like a beast of prey,
That Spanish man that's watching at the Cafe de la Paix.

Say! Listen and I'll tell you all . . . the day was growing dim,
And I was with my Pernod at the table next to him;
And he was sitting soberly as if he were asleep,
When suddenly he seemed to tense, like tiger for a leap.
And then he swung around to me, his hand went to his hip,
My heart was beating like a gong—my arm was in his grip;
His eyes were glaring into mine; aye, though I shrank with fear,
His fetid breath was on my face, his voice was in my ear:
"Excuse my *brusquerie*," he hissed; "but, sir, do you suppose—
That portly man who passed us had a *wen upon his nose?*"

And then at last it dawned on me, the fellow must be mad;
And when I soothingly replied: "I do not think he had,"
The little wizened Spanish man subsided in his chair,
And shrouded in his raven cloak resumed his owlish stare.
But when I tried to slip away he turned and glared at me,
And oh, that fishlike face of his was sinister to see:
"Forgive me if I startled you; of course you think I'm queer;
No doubt you wonder who I am, so solitary here;
You question why the passers-by I piercingly review . . .
Well, listen, my bibacious friend, I'll tell my tale to you.

"It happened twenty years ago, and in another land:
A maiden young and beautiful, two suitors for her hand.
My rival was the lucky one; I vowed I would repay;
Revenge has mellowed in my heart, it's rotten ripe to-day.
My happy rival skipped away, vamoosed, he left no trace;
And so I'm waiting, waiting here to meet him face to face;

For has it not been ever said that all the world one day
Will pass in pilgrimage before the Cafe de la Paix?"

"But, sir," I made remonstrance, "if it's twenty years ago,
You'd scarcely recognize him now, he must have altered so."
The little wizened Spanish man he laughed a hideous laugh,
And from his cloak he quickly drew a faded photograph.
"You're right," said he, "but there are traits (oh, this you must allow)
That never change; Lopez was fat, he must be fatter now.
His paunch is senatorial, he cannot see his toes,
I'm sure of it; and then, behold! that wen upon his nose.
I'm looking for a man like that. I'll wait and wait until . . ."
"What will you do?" I sharply cried; he answered me: "Why, kill!
He robbed me of my happiness—nay, stranger, do not start;
I'll firmly and politely put—a bullet in his heart."

And then that little Spanish man, with big cigar alight,
Uprose and shook my trembling hand and vanished in the night.
And I went home and thought of him and had a dreadful dream
Of portly men with each a wen, and woke up with a scream.
And sure enough, next morning, as I prowled the Boulevard,
A portly man with wenny nose roamed into my regard;
Then like a flash I ran to him and clutched him by the arm:
"Oh, sir," said I, "I do not wish to see you come to harm;
But if your life you value aught, I beg, entreat and pray—
Don't pass before the terrace of the Cafe de la Paix."
That portly man he looked at me with such a startled air,
Then bolted like a rabbit down the rue Michaudie\re.
"Ha! ha! I've saved a life," I thought; and laughed in my relief,
And straightway joined the Spanish man o'er his *ape/ritif.*
And thus each day I dodged about and kept the strictest guard
For portly men with each a wen upon the Boulevard.
And then I hailed my Spanish pal, and sitting in the sun,
We ordered many Pernods and we drank them every one.
And sternly he would stare and stare until my hand would shake,
And grimly he would glare and glare until my heart would quake.
And I would say: "Alphonso, lad, I must expostulate;
Why keep alive for twenty years the furnace of your hate?

Perhaps his wedded life was hell; and you, at least, are free . . ."
"That's where you've got it wrong," he snarled; "the fool she took
  was *me*.
My rival sneaked, threw up the sponge, betrayed himself a churl:
'Twas he who got the happiness, I only got—the girl."
With that he looked so devil-like he made me creep and shrink,
And there was nothing else to do but buy another drink.

Now yonder like a blot of ink he sits across the way,
Upon the smiling terrace of the Cafe de la Paix;
That little wizened Spanish man, his face is ghastly white,
His eyes are staring, staring like a tiger's in the night.
I know within his evil heart the fires of hate are fanned,
I know his automatic's ready waiting to his hand.
I know a tragedy is near. I dread, I have no peace . . .
Oh, don't you think I ought to go and call upon the police?
Look there . . . he's rising up . . . my God!
He leaps from out his place . . .
Yon millionaire from Argentine . . . the two are face to face . . .
A shot! A shriek! A heavy fall! A huddled heap! Oh, see
The little wizened Spanish man is dancing in his glee . . .
I'm sick . . . I'm faint . . . I'm going mad . . .
Oh, please take me away . . .
There's BLOOD upon the terrace of the Cafe de la Paix . . .

And now I'll leave my work and sally forth. The city is *en fete*. I'll join
  the crowd and laugh and sing with the best.

The sunshine seeks my little room
To tell me Paris streets are gay;
That children cry the lily bloom
All up and down the leafy way;
That half the town is mad with May,
With flame of flag and boom of bell:
For Carnival is King to-day;
So pen and page, awhile farewell.

BOOK TWO

EARLY SUMMER

I

Parc Montsouris

June 1914.

The Release

To-day within a grog-shop near
I saw a newly captured linnet,
Who beat against his cage in fear,
And fell exhausted every minute;
And when I asked the fellow there
If he to sell the bird were willing,
He told me with a careless air
That I could have it for a shilling.

And so I bought it, cage and all
(Although I went without my dinner),
And where some trees were fairly tall
And houses shrank and smoke was thinner,
The tiny door I open threw,
As down upon the grass I sank me:
Poor little chap! How quick he flew . . .
He didn't even wait to thank me.

> Life's like a cage; we beat the bars,
> We bruise our breasts, we struggle vainly;
> Up to the glory of the stars
> We strain with flutterings ungainly.
> And then—God opens wide the door;
> Our wondrous wings are arched for flying;
> We poise, we part, we sing, we soar . . .
> Light, freedom, love . . . Fools call it—Dying.

Yes, that wretched little bird haunted me. I had to let it go. Since I have seized my own liberty I am a fanatic for freedom. It is now a year ago I launched on my great adventure. I have had hard times, been hungry, cold, weary. I have worked harder than ever I did and discouragement has slapped me on the face. Yet the year has been the happiest of my life.

And all because I am free. By reason of filthy money no one can say to me: Do this, or do that. "Master" doesn't exist in my vocabulary. I can look any man in the face and tell him to go to the devil. I belong to myself. I am not for sale. It's glorious to feel like that. It sweetens the dry crust and warms the heart in the icy wind. For that I will hunger and go threadbare; for that I will live austerely and deny myself all pleasure. After health, the best thing in life is freedom.

Here is the last of my ballads. It is by way of being an experiment. Its theme is commonplace, its language that of everyday. It is a bit of realism in rhyme.

The Wee Shop

> She risked her all, they told me, bravely sinking
> The pinched economies of thirty years;
> And there the little shop was, meek and shrinking,
> The sum of all her dreams and hopes and fears.
> Ere it was opened I would see them in it,
> The gray-haired dame, the daughter with her crutch;
> So fond, so happy, hoarding every minute,
> Like artists, for the final tender touch.

The opening day! I'm sure that to their seeming
Was never shop so wonderful as theirs;
With pyramids of jam-jars rubbed to gleaming;
Such vivid cans of peaches, prunes and pears;
And chocolate, and biscuits in glass cases,
And bon-bon bottles, many-hued and bright;
Yet nothing half so radiant as their faces,
Their eyes of hope, excitement and delight.

I entered: how they waited all a-flutter!
How awkwardly they weighed my acid-drops!
And then with all the thanks a tongue could utter
They bowed me from the kindliest of shops.
I'm sure that night their customers they numbered;
Discussed them all in happy, breathless speech;
And though quite worn and weary, ere they slumbered,
Sent heavenward a little prayer for each.

And so I watched with interest redoubled
That little shop, spent in it all I had;
And when I saw it empty I was troubled,
And when I saw them busy I was glad.
And when I dared to ask how things were going,
They told me, with a fine and gallant smile:
"Not badly . . . slow at first . . . There's never knowing . . .
'Twill surely pick up in a little while."

I'd often see them through the winter weather,
Behind the shutters by a light's faint speck,
Poring o'er books, their faces close together,
The lame girl's arm around her mother's neck.
They dressed their windows not one time but twenty,
Each change more pinched, more desperately neat;
Alas! I wondered if behind that plenty
The two who owned it had enough to eat.

Ah, who would dare to sing of tea and coffee?
The sadness of a stock unsold and dead;
The petty tragedy of melting toffee,

The sordid pathos of stale gingerbread.
Ignoble themes! And yet—those haggard faces!
Within that little shop . . . Oh, here I say
One does not need to look in lofty places
For tragic themes, they're round us every day.

And so I saw their agony, their fighting,
Their eyes of fear, their heartbreak, their despair;
And there the little shop is, black and blighting,
And all the world goes by and does not care.
They say she sought her old employer's pity,
Content to take the pittance he would give.
The lame girl? yes, she's working in the city;
She coughs a lot—she hasn't long to live.

Last night MacBean introduced me to Saxon Dane the Poet. Truly, he is more like a blacksmith than a Bard—a big bearded man whose black eyes brood somberly or flash with sudden fire. We talked of Walt Whitman, and then of others.

"The trouble with poetry," he said, "is that it is too exalted. It has a phraseology of its own; it selects themes that are quite outside of ordinary experience. As a medium of expression it fails to reach the great mass of the people."

Then he added: "To hell with the great mass of the people! What have they got to do with it? Write to please yourself, as if not a single reader existed. The moment a man begins to be conscious of an audience he is artistically damned. You're not a Poet, I hope?"

I meekly assured him I was a mere maker of verse.

"Well," said he, "better good verse than middling poetry. And maybe even the humblest of rhymes has its uses. Happiness is happiness, whether it be inspired by a Rossetti sonnet or a ballad by G. R. Sims. Let each one who has something to say, say it in the best way he can, and abide the result . . . After all," he went on, "what does it matter? We are living in a pygmy day. With Tennyson and Browning the line of great poets passed away, perhaps for ever. The world to-day is full of little minstrels, who echo one another and who pipe away tunefully enough. But with one exception they do not matter."

I dared to ask who was his one exception. He answered, "Myself, of course."

Here's a bit of light verse which it amused me to write to-day, as I sat in the sun on the terrace of the Closerie de Lilas:

The Philistine and the Bohemian

She was a Philistine spick and span,
He was a bold Bohemian.
She had the *mode*, and the last at that;
He had a cape and a brigand hat.
She was so *riant* and *chic* and trim;
He was so shaggy, unkempt and grim.
On the rue de la Paix she was wont to shine;
The rue de la Gaî^te/ was more his line.
She doted on Barclay and Dell and Caine;
He quoted Mallarmé/ and Paul Verlaine.
She was a triumph at Tango teas;
At Vorticist's suppers he sought to please.
She thought that Franz Lehar was utterly great;
Of Strauss and Stravinsky he'd piously prate.
She loved elegance, he loved art;
They were as wide as the poles apart:
Yet—Cupid and Caprice are hand and glove—
They met at a dinner, they fell in love.

Home he went to his garret bare,
Thrilling with rapture, hope, despair.
Swift he gazed in his looking-glass,
Made a grimace and murmured: "Ass!"
Seized his scissors and fiercely sheared,
Severed his buccaneering beard;
Grabbed his hair, and clip! clip! clip!
Off came a bunch with every snip.
Ran to a tailor's in startled state,
Suits a dozen commanded straight;
Coats and overcoats, pants in pairs,
Everything that a dandy wears;
Socks and collars, and shoes and ties,

Everything that a dandy buys.
Chums looked at him with wondering stare,
Fancied they'd seen him before somewhere;
A Brummell, a D'Orsay, a *beau* so fine,
A shining, immaculate Philistine.

Home she went in a raptured daze,
Looked in a mirror with startled gaze,
Didn't seem to be pleased at all;
Savagely muttered: "Insipid Doll!"
Clutched her hair and a pair of shears,
Cropped and bobbed it behind the ears;
Aimed at a wan and willowy-necked
Sort of a Holman Hunt effect;
Robed in subtile and sage-green tones,
Like the dames of Rossetti and E. Burne-Jones;
Girdled her garments billowing wide,
Moved with an undulating glide;
All her frivolous friends forsook,
Cultivated a soulful look;
Gushed in a voice with a creamy throb
Over some weirdly Futurist daub—
Did all, in short, that a woman can
To be a consummate Bohemian.

A year went past with its hopes and fears,
A year that seemed like a dozen years.
They met once more . . . Oh, at last! At last!
They rushed together, they stopped aghast.
They looked at each other with blank dismay,
They simply hadn't a word to say.
He thought with a shiver: "Can this be she?"
She thought with a shudder: "This can't be he?"
This simpering dandy, so sleek and spruce;
This languorous lily in garments loose;
They sought to brace from the awful shock:
Taking a seat, they tried to talk.
She spoke of Bergson and Pater's prose,
He prattled of dances and ragtime shows;

She purred of pictures, Matisse, Cezanne,
His tastes to the girls of Kirchner ran;
She raved of Tchaikovsky and Caesar Franck,
He owned that he was a jazz-band crank!
They made no headway. Alas! alas!
He thought her a bore, she thought him an ass.
And so they arose and hurriedly fled;
Perish Illusion, Romance, you're dead.
He loved elegance, she loved art,
Better at once to part, to part.

And what is the moral of all this rot?
Don't try to be what you know you're not.
And if you're made on a muttonish plan,
Don't seek to seem a Bohemian;
And if to the goats your feet incline,
Don't try to pass for a Philistine.

II

A Small Cafe in a Side Street,

June 1914.

The Bohemian Dreams

Because my overcoat's in pawn,
I choose to take my glass
Within a little *bistro* on
The rue du Montparnasse;
The dusty bins with bottles shine,
The counter's lined with zinc,
And there I sit and drink my wine,
And think and think and think.

I think of hoary old Stamboul,
Of Moslem and of Greek,
Of Persian in coat of wool,
Of Kurd and Arab sheikh;
Of all the types of weal and woe,
And as I raise my glass,
Across Galata bridge I know
They pass and pass and pass.

I think of citron-trees aglow,
Of fan-palms shading down,
Of sailors dancing heel and toe
With wenches black and brown;
And though it's all an ocean far

From Yucatan to France,
I'll bet beside the old bazaar
They dance and dance and dance.

I think of Monte Carlo, where
The pallid croupiers call,
And in the gorgeous, guilty air
The gamblers watch the ball;
And as I flick away the foam
With which my beer is crowned,
The wheels beneath the gilded dome
Go round and round and round.

I think of vast Niagara,
Those gulfs of foam a-shine,
Whose mighty roar would stagger a
More prosy bean than mine;
And as the hours I idly spend
Against a greasy wall,
I know that green the waters bend
And fall and fall and fall.

I think of Nijni Novgorod
And Jews who never rest;
And womenfolk with spade and hod
Who slave in Buda-Pest;
Of squat and sturdy Japanese
Who pound the paddy soil,
And as I loaf and smoke at ease
They toil and toil and toil.

I think of shrines in Hindustan,
Of cloistral glooms in Spain,
Of minarets in Ispahan,
Of St. Sophia's fane,
Of convent towers in Palestine,
Of temples in Cathay,
And as I stretch and sip my wine
They pray and pray and pray.

And so my dreams I dwell within,
And visions come and go,
And life is passing like a Cin-
Ematographic Show;
Till just as surely as my pipe
Is underneath my nose,
Amid my visions rich and ripe
I doze and doze and doze.

Alas! it is too true. Once more I am counting the coppers, living on the ragged edge. My manuscripts come back to me like boomerangs, and I have not the postage, far less the heart, to send them out again.

MacBean seems to take an interest in my struggles. I often sit in his room in the rue Saint-Julien-le-Pauvre, smoking and sipping whisky into the small hours. He is an old hand, who knows the market and frankly manufactures for it.

"Give me short pieces," he says; "things of three verses that will fill a blank half-page of a magazine. Let them be sprightly, and, if possible, have a snapper at the end. Give me that sort of article. I think I can place it for you."

Then he looked through a lot of my verse: "This is the kind of stuff I might be able to sell," he said:

A Domestic Tragedy

Clorinda met me on the way
As I came from the train;
Her face was anything but gay,
In fact, suggested pain.
"Oh hubby, hubby dear!" she cried,
"I've awful news to tell . . ."
"What is it, darling?" I replied;
"Your mother—is she well?"

"Oh no! oh no! it is not that,
It's something else," she wailed,
My heart was beating pit-a-pat,
My ruddy visage paled.

Like lightning flash in heaven's dome
The fear within me woke:
"Don't say," I cried, "our little home
Has all gone up in smoke!"

She shook her head. Oh, swift I clasped
And held her to my breast;
"The children! Tell me quick," I gasped,
"Believe me, it is best."
Then, then she spoke; 'mid sobs I caught
These words of woe divine:
"It's coo-coo-cook has gone and bought
A new hat just like mine."

At present I am living on bread and milk. By doing this I can rub along for another ten days. The thought pleases me. As long as I have a crust I am master of my destiny. Some day, when I am rich and famous, I shall look back on all this with regret. Yet I think I shall always remain a Bohemian. I hate regularity. The clock was never made for me. I want to eat when I am hungry, sleep when I am weary, drink—well, any old time.

I prefer to be alone. Company is a constraint on my spirit. I never make an engagement if I can avoid it. To do so is to put a mortgage on my future. I like to be able to rise in the morning with the thought that the hours before me are all mine, to spend in my own way—to work, to dream, to watch the unfolding drama of life.

Here is another of my ballads. It is longer than most, and gave me more trouble, though none the better for that.

The Pencil Seller

A pencil, sir; a penny—won't you buy?
I'm cold and wet and tired, a sorry plight;
Don't turn your back, sir; take one just to try;
I haven't made a single sale to-night.
Oh, thank you, sir; but take the pencil too;
I'm not a beggar, I'm a business man.
Pencils I deal in, red and black and blue;

It's hard, but still I do the best I can.
Most days I make enough to pay for bread,
A cup o' coffee, stretching room at night.
One needs so little—to be warm and fed,
A hole to kennel in—oh, one's all right . . .

Excuse me, you're a painter, are you not?
I saw you looking at that dealer's show,
The *crou^tes* he has for sale, a shabby lot—
What do I know of Art? What do I know . . .
Well, look! That David Strong so well displayed,
"White Sorcery" it's called, all gossamer,
And pale moon-magic and a dancing maid
(You like the little elfin face of her?)—
That's good; but still, the picture as a whole,
The values,—Pah! He never painted worse;
Perhaps because his fire was lacking coal,
His cupboard bare, no money in his purse.
Perhaps . . . they say he labored hard and long,
And see now, in the harvest of his fame,
When round his pictures people gape and throng,
A scurvy dealer sells this on his name.
A wretched rag, wrung out of want and woe;
A soulless daub, not David Strong a bit,
Unworthy of his art . . . How should I know?
How should I know? I'm *Strong*—I painted it.

There now, I didn't mean to let that out.
It came in spite of me—aye, stare and stare.
You think I'm lying, crazy, drunk, no doubt—
Think what you like, it's neither here nor there.
It's hard to tell so terrible a truth,
To gain to glory, yet be such as I.
It's true; that picture's mine, done in my youth,
Up in a garret near the Paris sky.
The child's my daughter; aye, she posed for me.
That's why I come and sit here every night.
The painting's bad, but still—oh, still I see
Her little face all laughing in the light.

So now you understand.—I live in fear
Lest one like you should carry it away;
A poor, pot-boiling thing, but oh, how dear!
"Don't let them buy it, pitying God!" I pray!
And hark ye, sir—sometimes my brain's awhirl.
Some night I'll crash into that window pane
And snatch my picture back, my little girl,
And run and run . . .
I'm talking wild again;
A crab can't run. I'm crippled, withered, lame,
Palsied, as good as dead all down one side.
No warning had I when the evil came:
It struck me down in all my strength and pride.
Triumph was mine, I thrilled with perfect power;
Honor was mine, Fame's laurel touched my brow;
Glory was mine—within a little hour
I was a god and . . . what you find me now.

My child, that little, laughing girl you see,
She was my nurse for all ten weary years;
Her joy, her hope, her youth she gave for me;
Her very smiles were masks to hide her tears.
And I, my precious art, so rich, so rare,
Lost, lost to me—what could my heart but break!
Oh, as I lay and wrestled with despair,
I would have killed myself but for her sake . . .

By luck I had some pictures I could sell,
And so we fought the wolf back from the door;
She painted too, aye, wonderfully well.
We often dreamed of brighter days in store.
And then quite suddenly she seemed to fail;
I saw the shadows darken round her eyes.
So tired she was, so sorrowful, so pale,
And oh, there came a day she could not rise.
The doctor looked at her; he shook his head,
And spoke of wine and grapes and Southern air:
"If you can get her out of this," he said,
"She'll have a fighting chance with proper care."

"With proper care!" When he had gone away,
I sat there, trembling, twitching, dazed with grief.
Under my old and ragged coat she lay,
Our room was bare and cold beyond belief.
"Maybe," I thought, "I still can paint a bit,
Some lilies, landscape, anything at all."
Alas! My brush, I could not steady it.
Down from my fumbling hand I let it fall.
"With proper care"—how could I give her that,
Half of me dead? . . . I crawled down to the street.
Cowering beside the wall, I held my hat
And begged of every one I chanced to meet.
I got some pennies, bought her milk and bread,
And so I fought to keep the Doom away;
And yet I saw with agony of dread
My dear one sinking, sinking day by day.
And then I was awakened in the night:
"Please take my hands, I'm cold," I heard her sigh;
And soft she whispered, as she held me tight:
"Oh daddy, we've been happy, you and I!"
I do not think she suffered any pain,
She breathed so quietly . . . but though I tried,
I could not warm her little hands again:
And so there in the icy dark she died . . .
The dawn came groping in with fingers gray
And touched me, sitting silent as a stone;
I kissed those piteous lips, as cold as clay—
I did not cry, I did not even moan.
At last I rose, groped down the narrow stair;
An evil fog was oozing from the sky;
Half-crazed I stumbled on, I knew not where,
Like phantoms were the folks that passed me by.
How long I wandered thus I do not know,
But suddenly I halted, stood stock-still—
Beside a door that spilled a golden glow
I saw a name, *my name*, upon a bill.
"A Sale of Famous Pictures," so it read,
"A Notable Collection, each a gem,
Distinguished Works of Art by painters dead."

The folks were going in, I followed them.
I stood upon the outskirts of the crowd,
I only hoped that none might notice me.
Soon, soon I heard them call my name aloud:
"A 'David Strong', his *Fete in Brittany*."
(A brave big picture that, the best I've done,
It glowed and kindled half the hall away,
With all its memories of sea and sun,
Of pipe and bowl, of joyous work and play.
I saw the sardine nets blue as the sky,
I saw the nut-brown fisher-boats put out.)
"Five hundred pounds!" rapped out a voice near by;
"Six hundred!" "Seven!" "Eight!" And then a shout:
"A thousand pounds!" Oh, how I thrilled to hear!
Oh, how the bids went up by leaps, by bounds!
And then a silence; then the auctioneer:
"It's going! Going! Gone! *Three thousand pounds!*"
Three thousand pounds! A frenzy leapt in me.
"That picture's mine," I cried; "I'm David Strong.
I painted it, this famished wretch you see;
I did it, I, and sold it for a song.
And in a garret three small hours ago
My daughter died for want of Christian care.
Look, look at me! . . . Is it to mock my woe
You pay three thousand for my picture there?" . . .

O God! I stumbled blindly from the hall;
The city crashed on me, the fiendish sounds
Of cruelty and strife, but over all
"Three thousand pounds!" I heard; "Three thousand pounds!"

There, that's my story, sir; it isn't gay.
Tales of the Poor are never very bright . . .
You'll look for me next time you pass this way . . .
I hope you'll find me, sir; good-night, good-night.

III

The Luxembourg,

June 1914.
On a late afternoon, when the sunlight is mellow on the leaves, I often sit near the Fontaine de Medicis, and watch the children at their play. Sometimes I make bits of verse about them, such as:

Fi-Fi in Bed

Up into the sky I stare;
All the little stars I see;
And I know that God is there
O, how lonely He must be!

> Me, I laugh and leap all day,
> Till my head begins to nod;
> He's so great, He cannot play:
> I am glad I am not God.

>> Poor kind God upon His throne,
>> Up there in the sky so blue,
>> Always, always all alone . . .
>> *"Please, dear God, I pity You."*

Or else, sitting on the terrace of a cafe on the Boul' Mich', I sip slowly a Dubonnet or a Byrrh, and the charm of the Quarter possesses me. I think of men who have lived and loved there, who have groveled and gloried, who have drunk deep and died. And then I scribble things like this:

Gods in the Gutter

I dreamed I saw three demi-gods who in a cafe sat,
And one was small and crapulous, and one was large and fat;
And one was eaten up with vice and verminous at that.

The first he spoke of secret sins, and gems and perfumes rare;
And velvet cats and courtesans voluptuously fair:
"Who is the Sybarite?" I asked. They answered: "Baudelaire."

The second talked in tapestries, by fantasy beguiled;
As frail as bubbles, hard as gems, his pageantries he piled;
"This Lord of Language, who is he?" They whispered "Oscar Wilde."

The third was staring at his glass from out abysmal pain;
With tears his eyes were bitten in beneath his bulbous brain.
"Who is the sodden wretch?" I said. They told me: "Paul Verlaine."

Oh, Wilde, Verlaine and Baudelaire, their lips were wet with wine;
Oh poseur, pimp and libertine! Oh cynic, sot and swine!
Oh votaries of velvet vice! . . . Oh gods of light divine!

Oh Baudelaire, Verlaine and Wilde, they knew the sinks of shame;
Their sun-aspiring wings they scorched at passion's altar flame;
Yet lo! enthroned, enskied they stand, Immortal Sons of Fame.

I dreamed I saw three demi-gods who walked with feet of clay,
With cruel crosses on their backs, along a miry way;
Who climbed and climbed the bitter steep to which men turn and pray.

    And while I am on the subject of the Quarter, let me repeat this, which is included in my Ballads of the Boulevards:

The Death of Marie Toro

We're taking Marie Toro to her home in Pe\re-La-Chaise;
We're taking Marie Toro to her last resting-place.
Behold! her hearse is hung with wreaths till everything is hid
Except the blossoms heaping high upon her coffin lid.
A week ago she roamed the street, a draggle and a slut,
A by-word of the Boulevard and everybody's butt;
A week ago she haunted us, we heard her whining cry,
We brushed aside the broken blooms she pestered us to buy;
A week ago she had not where to rest her weary head . . .
But now, oh, follow, follow on, for Marie Toro's dead.

Oh Marie, she was once a queen—ah yes, a queen of queens.
High-throned above the Carnival she held her splendid sway.
For four-and-twenty crashing hours she knew what glory means,
The cheers of half a million throats, the *de/lire* of a day.
Yet she was only one of us, a little sewing-girl,
Though far the loveliest and best of all our laughing band;
Then Fortune beckoned; off she danced, amid the dizzy whirl,
And we who once might kiss her cheek were proud to kiss her hand.
For swiftly as a star she soared; she had her every wish;
We saw her roped with pearls of price, with princes at her call;
And yet, and yet I think her dreams were of the old Boul' Mich',
And yet I'm sure within her heart she loved us best of all.
For one night in the Purple Pig, upon the rue Saint-Jacques,
We laughed and quaffed . . . a limousine came swishing to the door;
Then Raymond Jolicoeur cried out: "It's Queen Marie come back,
In satin clad to make us glad, and witch our hearts once more."
But no, her face was strangely sad, and at the evening's end:
"Dear lads," she said; "I love you all, and when I'm far away,
Remember, oh, remember, little Marie is your friend,
And though the world may lie between, I'm coming back some day."
And so she went, and many a boy who's fought his way to Fame,
Can look back on the struggle of his garret days and bless
The loyal heart, the tender hand, the Providence that came

To him and all in hour of need, in sickness and distress.
Time passed away. She won their hearts in London, Moscow, Rome;
They worshiped her in Argentine, adored her in Brazil;
We smoked our pipes and wondered when she might be coming home,
And then we learned the luck had turned, the things were going ill.
Her health had failed, her beauty paled, her lovers fled away;
And some one saw her in Peru, a common drab at last.
So years went by, and faces changed; our beards were sadly gray,
And Marie Toro's name became an echo of the past.

You know that old and withered man, that derelict of art,
Who for a paltry franc will make a crayon sketch of you?
In slouching hat and shabby cloak he looks and is the part,
A sodden old Bohemian, without a single *sou*.
A boon companion of the days of Rimbaud and Verlaine,
He broods and broods, and chews the cud of bitter souvenirs;
Beneath his mop of grizzled hair his cheeks are gouged with pain,
The saffron sockets of his eyes are hollowed out with tears.
Well, one night in the D'Harcourt's din I saw him in his place,
When suddenly the door was swung, a woman halted there;
A woman cowering like a dog, with white and haggard face,
A broken creature, bent of spine, a daughter of Despair.
She looked and looked, as to her breast she held some withered bloom;
"Too late! Too late! . . . they all are dead and gone," I heard her say.
And once again her weary eyes went round and round the room;
"Not one of all I used to know . . ." she turned to go away . . .
But quick I saw the old man start: "Ah no!" he cried, "not all.
Oh Marie Toro, queen of queens, don't you remember Paul?"

"Oh Marie, Marie Toro, in my garret next the sky,
Where many a day and night I've crouched with not a crust to eat,
A picture hangs upon the wall a fortune couldn't buy,
A portrait of a girl whose face is pure and angel-sweet."
Sadly the woman looked at him: "Alas! it's true," she said;

441

"That little maid, I knew her once. It's long ago—she's dead."
He went to her; he laid his hand upon her wasted arm:
"Oh, Marie Toro, come with me, though poor and sick am I.
For old times' sake I cannot bear to see you come to harm;
Ah! there are memories, God knows, that never, never die . . ."
"Too late!" she sighed; "I've lived my life of splendor and of shame;
I've been adored by men of power, I've touched the highest height;
I've squandered gold like heaps of dirt—oh, I have played the game;
I've had my place within the sun . . . and now I face the night.
Look! look! you see I'm lost to hope; I live no matter how . . .
To drink and drink and so forget . . . that's all I care for now."

And so she went her heedless way, and all our help was vain.
She trailed along with tattered shawl and mud-corroded skirt;
She gnawed a crust and slept beneath the bridges of the Seine,
A garbage thing, a composite of alcohol and dirt.
The students learned her story and the cafes knew her well,
The Pascal and the Panthe/on, the Sufflot and Vachette;
She shuffled round the tables with the flowers she tried to sell,
A living mask of misery that no one will forget.
And then last week I missed her, and they found her in the street
One morning early, huddled down, for it was freezing cold;
But when they raised her ragged shawl her face was still and sweet;
Some bits of broken bloom were clutched within her icy hold.
That's all . . . Ah yes, they say that saw: her blue, wide-open eyes
Were beautiful with joy again, with radiant surprise . . .

A week ago she begged for bread; we've bought for her a stone,
And a peaceful place in Pe\re-La-Chaise where she'll be well alone.
She cost a king his crown, they say; oh, wouldn't she be proud
If she could see the wreaths to-day, the coaches and the crowd!
So follow, follow, follow on with slow and sober tread,
For Marie Toro, gutter waif and queen of queens, is dead.

IV

The Cafe de Deux Magots,

June 1914.

The Bohemian

Up in my garret bleak and bare
I tilted back on my broken chair,
And my three old pals were with me there,
    Hunger and Thirst and Cold;
Hunger scowled at his scurvy mate:
Cold cowered down by the hollow grate,
And I hated them with a deadly hate
    As old as life is old.

So up in my garret that's near the sky
I smiled a smile that was thin and dry:
"You've roomed with me twenty year," said I,
    "Hunger and Thirst and Cold;
But now, begone down the broken stair!
I've suffered enough of your spite . . . so there!"
Bang! Bang! I slapped on the table bare
    A glittering heap of gold.

"Red flames will jewel my wine to-night;
I'll loose my belt that you've lugged so tight;
Ha! Ha! Dame Fortune is smiling bright;
    The stuff of my brain I've sold;
Canaille of the gutter, up! Away!

You've battened on me for a bitter-long day;
But I'm driving you forth, and forever and aye,
    Hunger and Thirst and Cold."

So I kicked them out with a scornful roar;
Yet, oh, they turned at the garret door;
Quietly there they spoke once more:
    "The tale is not all told.
It's *au revoir*, but it's not good-by;
We're yours, old chap, till the day you die;
Laugh on, you fool! Oh, you'll never defy
    Hunger and Thirst and Cold."

Hurrah! The crisis in my financial career is over. Once more I have weathered the storm, and never did money jingle so sweetly in my pocket. It was MacBean who delivered me. He arrived at the door of my garret this morning, with a broad grin of pleasure on his face.

"Here," said he; "I've sold some of your rubbish. They'll take more too, of the same sort."

With that he handed me three crisp notes. For a moment I thought that he was paying the money out of his own pocket, as he knew I was desperately hard up; but he showed me the letter enclosing the cheque he had cashed for me.

So we sought the Grand Boulevard, and I had a Pernod, which rose to my head in delicious waves of joy. I talked ecstatic nonsense, and seemed to walk like a god in clouds of gold. We dined on frogs' legs and Vouvray, and then went to see the Revue at the Marigny. A very merry evening.

Such is the life of Bohemia, up and down, fast and feast; its very uncertainty its charm.

Here is my latest ballad, another attempt to express the sentiment of actuality:

The Auction Sale

Her little head just topped the window-sill;
She even mounted on a stool, maybe;
She pressed against the pane, as children will,

And watched us playing, oh so wistfully!
And then I missed her for a month or more,
And idly thought: "She's gone away, no doubt,"
Until a hearse drew up beside the door . . .
I saw a tiny coffin carried out.

And after that, towards dusk I'd often see
Behind the blind another face that looked:
Eyes of a young wife watching anxiously,
Then rushing back to where her dinner cooked.
She often gulped it down alone, I fear,
Within her heart the sadness of despair,
For near to midnight I would vaguely hear
A lurching step, a stumbling on the stair.

These little dramas of the common day!
A man weak-willed and fore-ordained to fail . . .
The window's empty now, they've gone away,
And yonder, see, their furniture's for sale.
To all the world their door is open wide,
And round and round the bargain-hunters roam,
And peer and gloat, like vultures avid-eyed,
Above the corpse of what was once a home.

So reverent I go from room to room,
And see the patient care, the tender touch,
The love that sought to brighten up the gloom,
The woman-courage tested overmuch.
Amid those things so intimate and dear,
Where now the mob invades with brutal tread,
I think: "What happiness is buried here,
What dreams are withered and what hopes are dead!"

Oh, woman dear, and were you sweet and glad
Over the lining of your little nest!
What ponderings and proud ideas you had!
What visions of a shrine of peace and rest!
For there's his easy-chair upon the rug,
His reading-lamp, his pipe-rack on the wall,

All that you could devise to make him snug—
And yet you could not hold him with it all.

Ah, patient heart, what homelike joys you planned
To stay him by the dull domestic flame!
Those silken cushions that you worked by hand
When you had time, before the baby came.
Oh, how you wove around him cozy spells,
And schemed so hard to keep him home of nights!
Aye, every touch and turn some story tells
Of sweet conspiracies and dead delights.

And here upon the scratched piano stool,
Tied in a bundle, are the songs you sung;
That cozy that you worked in colored wool,
The Spanish lace you made when you were young,
And lots of modern novels, cheap reprints,
And little dainty knick-knacks everywhere;
And silken bows and curtains of gay chintz . . .
And oh, her tiny crib, her folding chair!

Sweet woman dear, and did your heart not break,
To leave this precious home you made in vain?
Poor shabby things! so prized for old times' sake,
With all their memories of love and pain.
Alas! while shouts the raucous auctioneer,
And rat-faced dames are prying everywhere,
The echo of old joy is all I hear,
All, all I see just heartbreak and despair.

    Imagination is the great gift of the gods. Given it, one does not need to look afar for subjects. There is romance in every face.
    Those who have Imagination live in a land of enchantment which the eyes of others cannot see. Yet if it brings marvelous joy it also brings exquisite pain. Who lives a hundred lives must die a hundred deaths.
    I do not know any of the people who live around me. Sometimes I pass them on the stairs. However, I am going to give my imagination rein, and string some rhymes about them.

Before doing so, having money in my pocket and seeing the prospect of making more, let me blithely chant about

The Joy of Being Poor

I

Let others sing of gold and gear, the joy of being rich;
But oh, the days when I was poor, a vagrant in a ditch!
When every dawn was like a gem, so radiant and rare,
And I had but a single coat, and not a single care;
When I would feast right royally on bacon, bread and beer,
And dig into a stack of hay and doze like any peer;
When I would wash beside a brook my solitary shirt,
And though it dried upon my back I never took a hurt;
When I went romping down the road contemptuous of care,
And slapped Adventure on the back—by Gad! we were a pair;
When, though my pockets lacked a coin, and though my coat was old,
The largess of the stars was mine, and all the sunset gold;
When time was only made for fools, and free as air was I,
And hard I hit and hard I lived beneath the open sky;
When all the roads were one to me, and each had its allure . . .
Ye Gods! these were the happy days, the days when I was poor.

II

Or else, again, old pal of mine, do you recall the times
You struggled with your storyettes, I wrestled with my rhymes;
Oh, we were happy, were we not?—we used to live so "high"
(A little bit of broken roof between us and the sky);
Upon the forge of art we toiled with hammer and with tongs;
You told me all your rippling yarns, I sang to you my songs.
Our hats were frayed, our jackets patched, our boots were down at heel,
But oh, the happy men were we, although we lacked a meal.
And if I sold a bit of rhyme, or if you placed a tale,
What feasts we had of tenderloins and apple-tarts and ale!

And yet how often we would dine as cheerful as you please,
Beside our little friendly fire on coffee, bread and cheese.
We lived upon the ragged edge, and grub was never sure,
But oh, these were the happy days, the days when we were poor.

III

Alas! old man, we're wealthy now, it's sad beyond a doubt;
We cannot dodge prosperity, success has found us out.
Your eye is very dull and drear, my brow is creased with care,
We realize how hard it is to be a millionaire.
The burden's heavy on our backs—you're thinking of your rents,
I'm worrying if I'll invest in five or six per cents.
We've limousines, and marble halls, and flunkeys by the score,
We play the part . . . but say, old chap, oh, isn't it a bore?
We work like slaves, we eat too much, we put on evening dress;
We've everything a man can want, I think . . . but happiness.

Come, let us sneak away, old chum; forget that we are rich,
And earn an honest appetite, and scratch an honest itch.
Let's be two jolly garreteers, up seven flights of stairs,
And wear old clothes and just pretend we aren't millionaires;
And wonder how we'll pay the rent, and scribble ream on ream,
And sup on sausages and tea, and laugh and loaf and dream.

And when we're tired of that, my friend, oh, you will come with me;
And we will seek the sunlit roads that lie beside the sea.
We'll know the joy the gipsy knows, the freedom nothing mars,
The golden treasure-gates of dawn, the mintage of the stars.
We'll smoke our pipes and watch the pot, and feed the crackling fire,
And sing like two old jolly boys, and dance to heart's desire;
We'll climb the hill and ford the brook and camp upon the moor . . .
Old chap, let's haste, I'm mad to taste the Joy of Being Poor.

V

My Garret, Montparnasse,

June 1914.

My Neighbors

To rest my fagged brain now and then,
When wearied of my proper labors,
I lay aside my lagging pen
And get to thinking on my neighbors;
For, oh, around my garret den
There's woe and poverty a-plenty,
And life's so interesting when
A lad is only two-and-twenty.

Now, there's that artist gaunt and wan,
A little card his door adorning;
It reads: "Je ne suis pour personne",
A very frank and fitting warning.
I fear he's in a sorry plight;
He starves, I think, too proud to borrow,
I hear him moaning every night:
Maybe they'll find him dead to-morrow.

Room 4: The Painter Chap

He gives me such a bold and curious look,
That young American across the way,
As if he'd like to put me in a book

(Fancies himself a poet, so they say.)
Ah well! He'll make no "document" of me.
I lock my door. Ha! ha! Now none shall see . . .

Pictures, just pictures piled from roof to floor,
Each one a bit of me, a dream fulfilled,
A vision of the beauty I adore,
My own poor glimpse of glory, passion-thrilled . . .
But now my money's gone, I paint no more.

For three days past I have not tasted food;
The jeweled colors run . . . I reel, I faint;
They tell me that my pictures are no good,
Just crude and childish daubs, a waste of paint.
I burned to throw on canvas all I saw—
Twilight on water, tenderness of trees,
Wet sands at sunset and the smoking seas,
The peace of valleys and the mountain's awe:
Emotion swayed me at the thought of these.
I sought to paint ere I had learned to draw,
And that's the trouble . . .
Ah well! here am I,
Facing my failure after struggle long;
And there they are, my *croutes* that none will buy
(And doubtless they are right and I am wrong);
Well, when one's lost one's faith it's time to die . . .

This knife will do . . . and now to slash and slash;
Rip them to ribands, rend them every one,
My dreams and visions—tear and stab and gash,
So that their crudeness may be known to none;
Poor, miserable daubs! Ah! there, it's done . . .

And now to close my little window tight.
Lo! in the dusking sky, serenely set,
The evening star is like a beacon bright.
And see! to keep her tender tryst with night
How Paris veils herself in violet . . .

Oh, why does God create such men as I?—
All pride and passion and divine desire,
Raw, quivering nerve-stuff and devouring fire,
Foredoomed to failure though they try and try;
Abortive, blindly to destruction hurled;
Unfound, unfit to grapple with the world . . .

And now to light my wheezy jet of gas;
Chink up the window-crannies and the door,
So that no single breath of air may pass;
So that I'm sealed air-tight from roof to floor.
There, there, that's done; and now there's nothing more . . .

Look at the city's myriad lamps a-shine;
See, the calm moon is launching into space . . .
There will be darkness in these eyes of mine
Ere it can climb to shine upon my face.
Oh, it will find such peace upon my face! . . .

City of Beauty, I have loved you well,
A laugh or two I've had, but many a sigh;
I've run with you the scale from Heav'n to Hell.
Paris, I love you still . . . good-by, good-by.
Thus it all ends—unhappily, alas!
It's time to sleep, and now . . . *blow out the gas* . . .

> *Now there's that little midinette*
> *Who goes to work each morning daily;*
> *I choose to call her Blithe Babette,*
> *Because she's always humming gaily;*
> *And though the Goddess "Comme-il-faut"*
> *May look on her with prim expression,*
> *It's Pagan Paris where, you know,*
> *The queen of virtues is Discretion.*

Room 6: The Little Workgirl

Three gentlemen live close beside me—
A painter of pictures bizarre,
A poet whose virtues might guide me,
A singer who plays the guitar;
And there on my lintel is Cupid;
I leave my door open, and yet
These gentlemen, aren't they stupid!
They never make love to Babette.

I go to the shop every morning;
I work with my needle and thread;
Silk, satin and velvet adorning,
Then luncheon on coffee and bread.
Then sewing and sewing till seven;
Or else, if the order I get,
I toil and I toil till eleven—
And such is the day of Babette.

It doesn't seem cheerful, I fancy;
The wage is unthinkably small;
And yet there is one thing I can say:
I keep a bright face through it all.
I chaff though my head may be aching;
I sing a gay song to forget;
I laugh though my heart may be breaking—
It's all in the life of Babette.

That gown, O my lady of leisure,
You begged to be "finished in haste."
It gives you an exquisite pleasure,
Your lovers remark on its taste.
Yet . . . oh, the poor little white faces,
The tense midnight toil and the fret . . .
I fear that the foam of its laces
Is salt with the tears of Babette.

It takes a brave heart to be cheery
With no gleam of hope in the sky;
The future's so utterly dreary,
I'm laughing—in case I should cry.
And if, where the gay lights are glowing,
I dine with a man I have met,
And snatch a bright moment—who's going
To blame a poor little Babette?

And you, Friend beyond all the telling,
Although you're an ocean away,
Your pictures, they tell me, are selling,
You're married and settled, they say.
Such happiness one wouldn't barter;
Yet, oh, do you never regret
The Springtide, the roses, Montmartre,
Youth, poverty, love and—Babette?

> *That blond-haired chap across the way*
> *With sunny smile and voice so mellow,*
> *He sings in some cheap cabaret,*
> *Yet what a gay and charming fellow!*
> *His breath with garlic may be strong,*
> *What matters it? his laugh is jolly;*
> *His day he gives to sleep and song:*
> *His night's made up of song and folly.*

Room 5: The Concert Singer

I'm one of these haphazard chaps
Who sit in cafes drinking;
A most improper taste, perhaps,
Yet pleasant, to my thinking.
For, oh, I hate discord and strife;
I'm sadly, weakly human;
And I do think the best of life
Is wine and song and woman.

Now, there's that youngster on my right
Who thinks himself a poet,
And so he toils from morn to night
And vainly hopes to show it;
And there's that dauber on my left,
Within his chamber shrinking—
He looks like one of hope bereft;
He lives on air, I'm thinking.

But me, I love the things that are,
My heart is always merry;
I laugh and tune my old guitar:
Sing ho! and hey-down-derry.
Oh, let them toil their lives away
To gild a tawdry era,
But I'll be gay while yet I may:
Sing tira-lira-lira.

I'm sure you know that picture well,
A monk, all else unheeding,
Within a bare and gloomy cell
A musty volume reading;
While through the window you can see
In sunny glade entrancing,
With cap and bells beneath a tree
A jester dancing, dancing.

Which is the fool and which the sage?
I cannot quite discover;
But you may look in learning's page
And I'll be laughter's lover.
For this our life is none too long,
And hearts were made for gladness;
Let virtue lie in joy and song,
The only sin be sadness.

So let me troll a jolly air,
Come what come will to-morrow;
I'll be no *cabotin* of care,

No *souteneur* of sorrow.
Let those who will indulge in strife,
To my most merry thinking,
The true philosophy of life
Is laughing, loving, drinking.

> *And there's that weird and ghastly hag*
> *Who walks head bent, with lips a-mutter;*
> *With twitching hands and feet that drag,*
> *And tattered skirts that sweep the gutter.*
> *An outworn harlot, lost to hope,*
> *With staring eyes and hair that's hoary*
> *I hear her gibber, dazed with dope:*
> *I often wonder what's her story.*

Room 7: The Coco-Fiend

I look at no one, me;
I pass them on the stair;
Shadows! I don't see;
Shadows! everywhere.
Haunting, taunting, staring, glaring,
Shadows! I don't care.
Once my room I gain
Then my life begins.
Shut the door on pain;
How the Devil grins!
Grin with might and main;
Grin and grin in vain;
Here's where Heav'n begins:
Cocaine! Cocaine!

A whiff! Ah, that's the thing.
How it makes me gay!
Now I want to sing,
Leap, laugh, play.
Ha! I've had my fling!
Mistress of a king
In my day.

    Just another snuff . . .
    Oh, the blessed stuff!
    How the wretched room
    Rushes from my sight;
    Misery and gloom
    Melt into delight;
    Fear and death and doom
    Vanish in the night.
    No more cold and pain,
    I am young again,
    Beautiful again,
    Cocaine! Cocaine!

Oh, I was made to be good, to be good,
For a true man's love and a life that's sweet;
Fireside blessings and motherhood.
Little ones playing around my feet.
How it all unfolds like a magic screen,
Tender and glowing and clear and glad,
The wonderful mother I might have been,
The beautiful children I might have had;
Romping and laughing and shrill with glee,
Oh, I see them now and I see them plain.
Darlings! Come nestle up close to me,
You comfort me so, and you're just . . . Cocaine.

    It's Life that's all to blame:
    We can't do what we will;
    She robes us with her shame,
    She crowns us with her ill.
    I do not care, because
    I see with bitter calm,
    Life made me what I was,
    Life makes me what I am.
    Could I throw back the years,
    It all would be the same;
    Hunger and cold and tears,
    Misery, fear and shame,

And then the old refrain,
Cocaine! Cocaine!

A love-child I, so here my mother came,
Where she might live in peace with none to blame.
And how she toiled! Harder than any slave,
What courage! patient, hopeful, tender, brave.
We had a little room at Lavilette,
So small, so neat, so clean, I see it yet.
Poor mother! sewing, sewing late at night,
Her wasted face beside the candlelight,
This Paris crushed her. How she used to sigh!
And as I watched her from my bed I knew
She saw red roofs against a primrose sky
And glistening fields and apples dimmed with dew.
Hard times we had. We counted every *sou*,
We sewed sacks for a living. I was quick . . .
Four busy hands to work instead of two.
Oh, we were happy there, till she fell sick . . .

My mother lay, her face turned to the wall,
And I, a girl of sixteen, fair and tall,
Sat by her side, all stricken with despair,
Knelt by her bed and faltered out a prayer.
A doctor's order on the table lay,
Medicine for which, alas! I could not pay;
Medicine to save her life, to soothe her pain.
I sought for something I could sell, in vain . . .
All, all was gone! The room was cold and bare;
Gone blankets and the cloak I used to wear;
Bare floor and wall and cupboard, every shelf—
Nothing that I could sell . . . except myself.

I sought the street, I could not bear
To hear my mother moaning there.
I clutched the paper in my hand.
'Twas hard. You cannot understand . . .
I walked as martyr to the flame,
Almost exalted in my shame.

They turned, who heard my voiceless cry,
"For Sale, a virgin, who will buy?"
And so myself I fiercely sold,
And clutched the price, a piece of gold.
Into a pharmacy I pressed;
I took the paper from my breast.
I gave my money . . . how it gleamed!
How precious to my eyes it seemed!
And then I saw the chemist frown,
Quick on the counter throw it down,
Shake with an angry look his head:
"Your *louis d'or* is bad," he said.

Dazed, crushed, I went into the night,
I clutched my gleaming coin so tight.
No, no, I could not well believe
That any one could so deceive.
I tried again and yet again—
Contempt, suspicion and disdain;
Always the same reply I had:
"Get out of this. Your money's bad."

Heart broken to the room I crept,
To mother's side. All still . . . she slept . . .
I bent, I sought to raise her head . . .
"Oh, God, have pity!" she was dead.

> That's how it all began.
> Said I: Revenge is sweet.
> So in my guilty span
> I've ruined many a man.
> They've groveled at my feet,
> I've pity had for none;
> I've bled them every one.
> Oh, I've had interest for
> That worthless *louis d'or*.

> But now it's over; see,
> I care for no one, me;

Only at night sometimes
In dreams I hear the chimes
Of wedding-bells and see
A woman without stain
With children at her knee.
Ah, how you comfort me,
Cocaine! . . .

BOOK THREE

LATE SUMMER

I

The Omnium Bar, near the Bourse,

Late July 1914.

MacBean, before he settled down to the manufacture of mercantile fiction, had ideas of a nobler sort, which bore their fruit in a slender book of poems. In subject they are either erotic, mythologic, or descriptive of nature. So polished are they that the mind seems to slide over them: so faultless in form that the critics hailed them with highest praise, and as many as a hundred copies were sold.

Saxon Dane, too, has published a book of poems, but he, on the other hand, defies tradition to an eccentric degree. Originality is his sin. He strains after it in every line. I must confess I think much of the free verse he writes is really prose, and a good deal of it blank verse chopped up into odd lengths. He talks of assonance and color, of stress and pause and accent, and bewilders me with his theories.

He and MacBean represent two extremes, and at night, as we sit in the Cafe du Do^me, they have the hottest of arguments. As for me, I listen with awe, content that my medium is verse, and that the fashions of Hood, Thackeray and Bret Harte are the fashions of to-day.

Of late I have been doing light stuff, "fillers" for MacBean. Here are three of my specimens:

The Philanderer

Oh, have you forgotten those afternoons
With riot of roses and amber skies,
When we thrilled to the joy of a million Junes,
And I sought for your soul in the deeps of your eyes?
I would love you, I promised, forever and aye,
And I meant it too; yet, oh, isn't it odd?
When we met in the Underground to-day
I addressed you as Mary instead of as Maude.

Oh, don't you remember that moonlit sea,
With us on a silver trail afloat,
When I gracefully sank on my bended knee
At the risk of upsetting our little boat?
Oh, I vowed that my life was blighted then,
As friendship you proffered with mournful mien;
But now as I think of your children ten,
I'm glad you refused me, Evangeline.

Oh, is that moment eternal still
When I breathed my love in your shell-like ear,
And you plucked at your fan as a maiden will,
And you blushed so charmingly, Guenivere?
Like a worshiper at your feet I sat;
For a year and a day you made me mad;
But now, alas! you are forty, fat,
And I think: What a lucky escape I had!

Oh, maidens I've set in a sacred shrine,
Oh, Rosamond, Molly and Mignonette,
I've deemed you in turn the most divine,
In turn you've broken my heart . . . and yet
It's easily mended. What's past is past.
To-day on Lucy I'm going to call;

For I'm sure that I know true love at last,
And *She* is the fairest girl of all.

The *Petit Vieux*

"Sow your wild oats in your youth," so we're always told;
But I say with deeper sooth: "Sow them when you're old."
I'll be wise till I'm about seventy or so:
Then, by Gad! I'll blossom out as an ancient *beau*.

I'll assume a dashing air, laugh with loud Ha! ha! . . .
How my grandchildren will stare at their grandpapa!
Their perfection aureoled I will scandalize:
Won't I be a hoary old sinner in their eyes!

Watch me, how I'll learn to chaff barmaids in a bar;
Scotches daily, gayly quaff, puff a fierce cigar.
I will haunt the Tango teas, at the stage-door stand;
Wait for Dolly Dimpleknees, bouquet in my hand.

Then at seventy I'll take flutters at roulette;
While at eighty hope I'll make good at poker yet;
And in fashionable togs to the races go,
Gayest of the gay old dogs, ninety years or so.

"Sow your wild oats while you're young," that's what you are told;
Don't believe the foolish tongue—sow 'em when you're old.
Till you're threescore years and ten, take my humble tip,
Sow your nice tame oats and then . . . Hi, boys! Let 'er rip.

My Masterpiece

It's slim and trim and bound in blue;
Its leaves are crisp and edged with gold;
Its words are simple, stalwart too;
Its thoughts are tender, wise and bold.
Its pages scintillate with wit;
Its pathos clutches at my throat:

Oh, how I love each line of it!
That Little Book I Never Wrote.

In dreams I see it praised and prized
By all, from plowman unto peer;
It's pencil-marked and memorized,
It's loaned (and not returned, I fear);
It's worn and torn and travel-tossed,
And even dusky natives quote
That classic that the world has lost,
The Little Book I Never Wrote.

Poor ghost! For homes you've failed to cheer,
For grieving hearts uncomforted,
Don't haunt me now . . . Alas! I fear
The fire of Inspiration's dead.
A humdrum way I go to-night,
From all I hoped and dreamed remote:
Too late . . . a better man must write
That Little Book I Never Wrote.

Talking about writing books, there is a queer character who shuffles up and down the little streets that neighbor the Place Maubert, and who, they say, has been engaged on one for years. Sometimes I see him cowering in some cheap *bouge*, and his wild eyes gleam at me through the tangle of his hair. But I do not think he ever sees me. He mumbles to himself, and moves like a man in a dream. His pockets are full of filthy paper on which he writes from time to time. The students laugh at him and make him tipsy; the street boys pelt him with ordure; the better cafes turn him from their doors. But who knows? At least, this is how I see him:

My Book

Before I drink myself to death,
God, let me finish up my Book!
At night, I fear, I fight for breath,
And wake up whiter than a spook;

And crawl off to a *bistro* near,
And drink until my brain is clear.

Rare Absinthe! Oh, it gives me strength
To write and write; and so I spend
Day after day, until at length
With joy and pain I'll write The End:
Then let this carcase rot; I give
The world my Book—my Book will live.

For every line is tense with truth,
There's hope and joy on every page;
A cheer, a clarion call to Youth,
A hymn, a comforter to Age:
All's there that I was meant to be,
My part divine, the God in me.

It's of my life the golden sum;
Ah! who that reads this Book of mine,
In stormy centuries to come,
Will dream I rooted with the swine?
Behold! I give mankind my best:
What does it matter, all the rest?

It's this that makes sublime my day;
It's this that makes me struggle on.
Oh, let them mock my mortal clay,
My spirit's deathless as the dawn;
Oh, let them shudder as they look . . .
I'll be immortal in my Book.

And so beside the sullen Seine
I fight with dogs for filthy food,
Yet know that from my sin and pain
Will soar serene a Something Good;
Exultantly from shame and wrong
A Right, a Glory and a Song.

How charming it is, this Paris of the summer skies! Each morning I leap up with joy in my heart, all eager to begin the day of work. As I eat my breakfast and smoke my pipe, I ponder over my task. Then in the golden sunshine that floods my little attic I pace up and down, absorbed and forgetful of the world. As I compose I speak the words aloud. There are difficulties to overcome; thoughts that will not fit their mold; rebellious rhymes. Ah! those moments of despair and defeat.

Then suddenly the mind grows lucid, imagination glows, the snarl unravels. In the end is always triumph and success. O delectable *me/tier*! Who would not be a rhymesmith in Paris, in Bohemia, in the heart of youth!

I have now finished my twentieth ballad. Five more and they will be done. In quiet corners of cafes, on benches of the Luxembourg, on the sunny Quays I read them over one by one. Here is my latest:

My Hour

Day after day behold me plying
My pen within an office drear;
The dullest dog, till homeward hieing,
Then lo! I reign a king of cheer.
A throne have I of padded leather,
A little court of kiddies three,
A wife who smiles whate'er the weather,
A feast of muffins, jam and tea.

The table cleared, a romping battle,
A fairy tale, a "Children, bed,"
A kiss, a hug, a hush of prattle
(God save each little drowsy head!)
A cozy chat with wife a-sewing,
A silver lining clouds that low'r,
Then she too goes, and with her going,
I come again into my Hour.

I poke the fire, I snugly settle,
My pipe I prime with proper care;

The water's purring in the kettle,
Rum, lemon, sugar, all are there.
And now the honest grog is steaming,
And now the trusty briar's aglow:
Alas! in smoking, drinking, dreaming,
How sadly swift the moments go!

Oh, golden hour! 'twixt love and duty,
All others I to others give;
But you are mine to yield to Beauty,
To glean Romance, to greatly live.
For in my easy-chair reclining . . .
*I feel the sting of ocean spray;
And yonder wondrously are shining
The Magic Isles of Far Away.*

*Beyond the comber's crashing thunder
Strange beaches flash into my ken;
On jetties heaped head-high with plunder
I dance and dice with sailor-men.
Strange stars swarm down to burn above me,
Strange shadows haunt, strange voices greet;
Strange women lure and laugh and love me,
And fling their bastards at my feet.*

*Oh, I would wish the wide world over,
In ports of passion and unrest,
To drink and drain, a tarry rover
With dragons tattooed on my chest,
With haunted eyes that hold red glories
Of foaming seas and crashing shores,
With lips that tell the strangest stories
Of sunken ships and gold moidores;*

*Till sick of storm and strife and slaughter,
Some ghostly night when hides the moon,
I slip into the milk-warm water
And softly swim the stale lagoon.
Then through some jungle python-haunted,*

Or plumed morass, or woodland wild,
I win my way with heart undaunted,
And all the wonder of a child.

The pathless plains shall swoon around me,
The forests frown, the floods appall;
The mountains tiptoe to confound me,
The rivers roar to speed my fall.
Wild dooms shall daunt, and dawns be gory,
And Death shall sit beside my knee;
Till after terror, torment, glory,
I win again the sea, the sea . . .

Oh, anguish sweet! Oh, triumph splendid!
Oh, dreams adieu! my pipe is dead.
My glass is dry, my Hour is ended,
It's time indeed I stole to bed.
How peacefully the house is sleeping!
Ah! why should I strange fortunes plan?
To guard the dear ones in my keeping—
That's task enough for any man.

So through dim seas I'll ne'er go spoiling;
The red Tortugas never roam;
Please God! I'll keep the pot a-boiling,
And make at least a happy home.
My children's path shall gleam with roses,
Their grace abound, their joy increase.
And so my Hour divinely closes
With tender thoughts of praise and peace.

II

The Garden of the Luxembourg,

Late July 1914.

When on some scintillating summer morning I leap lightly up to the seclusion of my garret, I often think of those lines: "In the brave days when I was twenty-one."

True, I have no loving, kind Lisette to pin her petticoat across the pane, yet I do live in hope. Am I not in Bohemia the Magical, Bohemia of Murger, of de Musset, of Verlaine? Shades of Mimi Pinson, of Trilby, of all that immortal line of laughterful grisettes, do not tell me that the days of love and fun are forever at an end! Yes, youth is golden, but what of age? Shall it too not testify to the rhapsody of existence? Let the years between be those of struggle, of sufferance—of disillusion if you will; but let youth and age affirm the ecstasy of being. Let us look forward all to a serene sunset, and in the still skies "a late lark singing".

This thought comes to me as, sitting on a bench near the band-stand, I see an old savant who talks to all the children. His clean-shaven face is alive with kindliness; under his tall silk hat his white hair falls to his shoulders. He wears a long black cape over a black frock-coat, very neat linen, and a flowing tie of black silk. I call him "Silvester Bonnard". As I look at him I truly think the best of life are the years between sixty and seventy.

A Song of Sixty-Five

Brave Thackeray has trolled of days when he was twenty-one,
And bounded up five flights of stairs, a gallant garreteer;
And yet again in mellow vein when youth was gaily run,

Has dipped his nose in Gascon wine, and told of Forty Year.
But if I worthy were to sing a richer, rarer time,
I'd tune my pipes before the fire and merrily I'd strive
To praise that age when prose again has given way to rhyme,
The Indian Summer days of life when I'll be Sixty-five;

For then my work will all be done, my voyaging be past,
And I'll have earned the right to rest where folding hills are green;
So in some glassy anchorage I'll make my cable fast,—
Oh, let the seas show all their teeth, I'll sit and smile serene.
The storm may bellow round the roof, I'll bide beside the fire,
And many a scene of sail and trail within the flame I'll see;
For I'll have worn away the spur of passion and desire . . .
Oh yes, when I am Sixty-five, what peace will come to me.

I'll take my breakfast in my bed, I'll rise at half-past ten,
When all the world is nicely groomed and full of golden song;
I'll smoke a bit and joke a bit, and read the news, and then
I'll potter round my peach-trees till I hear the luncheon gong.
And after that I think I'll doze an hour, well, maybe two,
And then I'll show some kindred soul how well my roses thrive;
I'll do the things I never yet have found the time to do . . .
Oh, won't I be the busy man when I am Sixty-five.

I'll revel in my library; I'll read De Morgan's books;
I'll grow so garrulous I fear you'll write me down a bore;
I'll watch the ways of ants and bees in quiet sunny nooks,
I'll understand Creation as I never did before.
When gossips round the tea-cups talk I'll listen to it all;
On smiling days some kindly friend will take me for a drive:
I'll own a shaggy collie dog that dashes to my call:
I'll celebrate my second youth when I am Sixty-five.

Ah, though I've twenty years to go, I see myself quite plain,
A wrinkling, twinkling, rosy-cheeked, benevolent old chap;
I think I'll wear a tartan shawl and lean upon a cane.
I hope that I'll have silver hair beneath a velvet cap.
I see my little grandchildren a-romping round my knee;

So gay the scene, I almost wish 'twould hasten to arrive.
Let others sing of Youth and Spring, still will it seem to me
The golden time's the olden time, some time round Sixty-five.

From old men to children is but a step, and there too, in the shadow of the Fontaine de Medicis, I spend much of my time watching the little ones. Childhood, so innocent, so helpless, so trusting, is somehow pathetic to me.

There was one jolly little chap who used to play with a large white Teddy Bear. He was always with his mother, a sweet-faced woman, who followed his every movement with delight. I used to watch them both, and often spoke a few words.

Then one day I missed them, and it struck me I had not seen them for a week, even a month, maybe. After that I looked for them a time or two
 and soon forgot.

Then this morning I saw the mother in the rue D'Assas. She was alone and in deep black. I wanted to ask after the boy, but there was a look in her face that stopped me.

I do not think she will ever enter the garden of the Luxembourg again.

Teddy Bear

O Teddy Bear! with your head awry
And your comical twisted smile,
You rub your eyes—do you wonder why
You've slept such a long, long while?
As you lay so still in the cupboard dim,
And you heard on the roof the rain,
Were you thinking . . . what has become of *him*?
And when will he play again?

Do you sometimes long for a chubby hand,
And a voice so sweetly shrill?
O Teddy Bear! don't you understand
Why the house is awf'ly still?
You sit with your muzzle propped on your paws,
And your whimsical face askew.

Don't wait, don't wait for your friend . . . because
He's sleeping and dreaming too.

Aye, sleeping long . . . You remember how
He stabbed our hearts with his cries?
And oh, the dew of pain on his brow,
And the deeps of pain in his eyes!
And, Teddy Bear! you remember, too,
As he sighed and sank to his rest,
How all of a sudden he smiled to you,
And he clutched you close to his breast.

I'll put you away, little Teddy Bear,
In the cupboard far from my sight;
Maybe he'll come and he'll kiss you there,
A wee white ghost in the night.
But me, I'll live with my love and pain
A weariful lifetime through;
And my Hope: will I see him again, again?
Ah, God! If I only knew!

After old men and children I am greatly interested in dogs. I will go out of my way to caress one who shows any desire to be friendly. There is a very filthy fellow who collects cigarette stubs on the Boul' Mich', and who is always followed by a starved yellow cur. The other day I came across them in a little side street. The man was stretched on the pavement brutishly drunk and dead to the world. The dog, lying by his side, seemed to look at me with sad, imploring eyes. Though all the world despise that man, I thought, this poor brute loves him and will be faithful unto death.

From this incident I wrote the verses that follow:

The Outlaw

A wild and woeful race he ran
Of lust and sin by land and sea;
Until, abhorred of God and man,
They swung him from the gallows-tree.
And then he climbed the Starry Stair,

And dumb and naked and alone,
With head unbowed and brazen glare,
He stood before the Judgment Throne.

The Keeper of the Records spoke:
"This man, O Lord, has mocked Thy Name.
The weak have wept beneath his yoke,
The strong have fled before his flame.
The blood of babes is on his sword;
His life is evil to the brim:
Look down, decree his doom, O Lord!
Lo! there is none will speak for him."

The golden trumpets blew a blast
That echoed in the crypts of Hell,
For there was Judgment to be passed,
And lips were hushed and silence fell.
The man was mute; he made no stir,
Erect before the Judgment Seat . . .
When all at once a mongrel cur
Crept out and cowered and licked his feet.

It licked his feet with whining cry.
Come Heav'n, come Hell, what did it care?
It leapt, it tried to catch his eye;
Its master, yea, its God was there.
Then, as a thrill of wonder sped
Through throngs of shining seraphim,
The Judge of All looked down and said:
"Lo! here is ONE who pleads for him.

"And who shall love of these the least,
And who by word or look or deed
Shall pity show to bird or beast,
By Me shall have a friend in need.
Aye, though his sin be black as night,
And though he stand 'mid men alone,
He shall be softened in My sight,
And find a pleader by My Throne.

"So let this man to glory win;
From life to life salvation glean;
By pain and sacrifice and sin,
Until he stand before Me—*clean*.
For he who loves the least of these
(And here I say and here repeat)
Shall win himself an angel's pleas
For Mercy at My Judgment Seat."

I take my exercise in the form of walking. It keeps me fit and leaves me free to think. In this way I have come to know Paris like my pocket. I have explored its large and little streets, its stateliness and its slums.

But most of all I love the Quays, between the leafage and the sunlit Seine. Like shuttles the little steamers dart up and down, weaving the water into patterns of foam. Cigar-shaped barges stream under the lacework of the many bridges and make me think of tranquil days and willow-fringed horizons.

But what I love most is the stealing in of night, when the sky takes on that strange elusive purple; when eyes turn to the evening star and marvel at its brightness; when the Eiffel Tower becomes a strange, shadowy stairway yearning in impotent effort to the careless moon.

Here is my latest ballad, short if not very sweet:

The Walkers

(He speaks.)

Walking, walking, oh, the joy of walking!
Swinging down the tawny lanes with head held high;
Striding up the green hills, through the heather stalking,
Swishing through the woodlands where the brown leaves lie;
Marveling at all things—windmills gaily turning,
Apples for the cider-press, ruby-hued and gold;
Tails of rabbits twinkling, scarlet berries burning,
Wedge of geese high-flying in the sky's clear cold,
Light in little windows, field and furrow darkling;
Home again returning, hungry as a hawk;

Whistling up the garden, ruddy-cheeked and sparkling,
Oh, but I am happy as I walk, walk, walk!

(She speaks.)

Walking, walking, oh, the curse of walking!
Slouching round the grim square, shuffling up the street,
Slinking down the by-way, all my graces hawking,
Offering my body to each man I meet.
Peering in the gin-shop where the lads are drinking,
Trying to look gay-like, crazy with the blues;
Halting in a doorway, shuddering and shrinking
(Oh, my draggled feather and my thin, wet shoes).
Here's a drunken drover: "Hullo, there, old dearie!"
No, he only curses, can't be got to talk . . .
On and on till daylight, famished, wet and weary,
God in Heaven help me as I walk, walk, walk!

III

The Cafe de la Source,

Late in July 1914.

The other evening MacBean was in a pessimistic mood.

"Why do you write?" he asked me gloomily.

"Obviously," I said, "to avoid starving. To produce something that will buy me food, shelter, raiment."

"If you were a millionaire, would you still write?"

"Yes," I said, after a moment's thought. "You get an idea. It haunts you. It seems to clamor for expression. It begins to obsess you. At last in desperation you embody it in a poem, an essay, a story. There! it is disposed of. You are at rest. It troubles you no more. Yes; if I were a millionaire I should write, if it were only to escape from my ideas."

"You have given two reasons why men write," said MacBean: "for gain, for self-expression. Then, again, some men write to amuse themselves, some because they conceive they have a mission in the world; some because they have real genius, and are conscious they can enrich the literature of all time. I must say I don't know of any belonging to the latter class. We are living in an age of mediocrity. There is no writer of to-day who will be read twenty years after he is dead. That's a truth that must come home to the best of them."

"I guess they're not losing much sleep over it," I said.

"Take novelists," continued MacBean. "The line of first-class novelists ended with Dickens and Thackeray. Then followed some of the second class, Stevenson, Meredith, Hardy. And to-day we have three novelists of the third class, good, capable craftsmen. We can trust ourselves comfortably in their hands. We read and enjoy them, but do you think our children will?"

"Yours won't, anyway," I said.

"Don't be too sure. I may surprise you yet. I may get married and turn *bourgeois*."

The best thing that could happen to MacBean would be that. It might change his point of view. He is so painfully discouraging. I have never mentioned my ballads to him. He would be sure to throw cold water on them. And as it draws near to its end the thought of my book grows more and more dear to me. How I will get it published I know not; but I will. Then even if it doesn't sell, even if nobody reads it, I will be content. Out of this brief, perishable Me I will have made something concrete, something that will preserve my thought within its dusty covers long after I am dead and dust.

Here is one of my latest:

Poor Peter

Blind Peter Piper used to play
All up and down the city;
I'd often meet him on my way,
And throw a coin for pity.
But all amid his sparkling tones
His ear was quick as any
To catch upon the cobble-stones
The jingle of my penny.

And as upon a day that shone
He piped a merry measure:
"How well you play!" I chanced to say;
Poor Peter glowed with pleasure.
You'd think the words of praise I spoke
Were all the pay he needed;
The artist in the player woke,
The penny lay unheeded.

Now Winter's here; the wind is shrill,
His coat is thin and tattered;
Yet hark! he's playing trill on trill
As if his music mattered.

And somehow though the city looks
Soaked through and through with shadows,
He makes you think of singing brooks
And larks and sunny meadows.

Poor chap! he often starves, they say;
Well, well, I can believe it;
For when you chuck a coin his way
He'll let some street-boy thieve it.
I fear he freezes in the night;
My praise I've long repented,
Yet look! his face is all alight . . .
Blind Peter seems contented.

A day later.

On the terrace of the Closerie de Lilas I came on Saxon Dane. He was smoking his big briar and drinking a huge glass of brown beer. The tree gave a pleasant shade, and he had thrown his sombrero on a chair. I noted how his high brow was bronzed by the sun and there were golden lights in his broad beard. There was something massive and imposing in the man as he sat there in brooding thought.

MacBean, he told me, was sick and unable to leave his room. Rheumatism. So I bought a cooked chicken and a bottle of Barsac, and mounting to the apartment of the invalid, I made him eat and drink. MacBean was very despondent, but cheered up greatly.

I think he rather dreads the future. He cannot save money, and all he makes he spends. He has always been a rover, often tried to settle down but could not. Now I think he wishes for security. I fear, however, it is too late.

The Wistful One

I sought the trails of South and North,
I wandered East and West;
But pride and passion drove me forth
And would not let me rest.

> And still I seek, as still I roam,
> A snug roof overhead;
> Four walls, my own; a quiet home . . .
> "You'll have it—*when you're dead.*"

MacBean is one of Bohemia's victims. It is a country of the young. The old have no place in it. He will gradually lose his grip, go down and down. I am sorry. He is my nearest approach to a friend. I do not make them easily. I have deep reserves. I like solitude. I am never so surrounded by boon companions as when I am all alone.

But though I am a solitary I realize the beauty of friendship, and on looking through my note-book I find the following:

If You Had a Friend

If you had a friend strong, simple, true,
Who knew your faults and who understood;
Who believed in the very best of you,
And who cared for you as a father would;
Who would stick by you to the very end,
Who would smile however the world might frown:
I'm sure you would try to please your friend,
You never would think to throw him down.

And supposing your friend was high and great,
And he lived in a palace rich and tall,
And sat like a King in shining state,
And his praise was loud on the lips of all;
Well then, when he turned to you alone,
And he singled you out from all the crowd,
And he called you up to his golden throne,
Oh, wouldn't you just be jolly proud?

If you had a friend like this, I say,
So sweet and tender, so strong and true,
You'd try to please him in every way,
You'd live at your bravest—now, wouldn't you?
His worth would shine in the words you penned;
You'd shout his praises . . . yet now it's odd!

You tell me you haven't got such a friend;
You haven't? I wonder . . . *What of God?*

To how few is granted the privilege of doing the work which lies closest to the heart, the work for which one is best fitted. The happy man is he who knows his limitations, yet bows to no false gods.

MacBean is not happy. He is overridden by his appetites, and to satisfy them he writes stuff that in his heart he despises.

Saxon Dane is not happy. His dream exceeds his grasp. His twisted, tortured phrases mock the vague grandiosity of his visions.

I am happy. My talent is proportioned to my ambition. The things I like to write are the things I like to read. I prefer the lesser poets to the greater, the cackle of the barnyard fowl to the scream of the eagle. I lack the divinity of discontent.

True Contentment comes from within. It dominates circumstance. It is resignation wedded to philosophy, a Christian quality seldom attained except by the old.

There is such an one I sometimes see being wheeled about in the Luxembourg. His face is beautiful in its thankfulness.

The Contented Man

"How good God is to me," he said;
"For have I not a mansion tall,
With trees and lawns of velvet tread,
And happy helpers at my call?
With beauty is my life abrim,
With tranquil hours and dreams apart;
You wonder that I yield to Him
That best of prayers, a grateful heart?"

"How good God is to me," he said;
"For look! though gone is all my wealth,
How sweet it is to earn one's bread
With brawny arms and brimming health.
Oh, now I know the joy of strife!
To sleep so sound, to wake so fit.

Ah yes, how glorious is life!
I thank Him for each day of it."

"How good God is to me," he said;
"Though health and wealth are gone, it's true;
Things might be worse, I might be dead,
And here I'm living, laughing too.
Serene beneath the evening sky
I wait, and every man's my friend;
God's most contented man am I . . .
He keeps me smiling to the End."

To-day the basin of the Luxembourg is bright with little boats. Hundreds of happy children romp around it. Little ones everywhere; yet there is no other city with so many childless homes.

The Spirit of the Unborn Babe

The Spirit of the Unborn Babe peered through the window-pane,
Peered through the window-pane that glowed like beacon in the night;
For, oh, the sky was desolate and wild with wind and rain;
And how the little room was crammed with coziness and light!
Except the flirting of the fire there was no sound at all;
The Woman sat beside the hearth, her knitting on her knee;
The shadow of her husband's head was dancing on the wall;
She looked with staring eyes at it, she looked yet did not see.
She only saw a childish face that topped the table rim,
A little wistful ghost that smiled and vanished quick away;
And then because her tender eyes were flooding to the brim,
She lowered her head . . . "Don't sorrow, dear," she heard him softly say;
"It's over now. We'll try to be as happy as before
(Ah! they who little children have, grant hostages to pain).
We gave Life chance to wound us once, but never, never more . . ."
The Spirit of the Unborn Babe fled through the night again.

The Spirit of the Unborn Babe went wildered in the dark;
Like termagants the winds tore down and whirled it with the snow.
And then amid the writhing storm it saw a tiny spark,
A window broad, a spacious room all goldenly aglow,
A woman slim and Paris-gowned and exquisitely fair,
Who smiled with rapture as she watched her jewels catch the blaze;
A man in faultless evening dress, young, handsome, debonnaire,
Who smoked his cigarette and looked with frank admiring gaze.
"Oh, we are happy, sweet," said he; "youth, health, and wealth are ours.
What if a thousand toil and sweat that we may live at ease!
What if the hands are worn and torn that strew our path with flowers!
Ah, well! we did not make the world; let us not think of these.
Let's seek the beauty-spots of earth, Dear Heart, just you and I;
Let other women bring forth life with sorrow and with pain.
Above our door we'll hang the sign: *'No children need apply* . . . '"
The Spirit of the Unborn Babe sped through the night again.

The Spirit of the Unborn Babe went whirling on and on;
It soared above a city vast, it swept down to a slum;
It saw within a grimy house a light that dimly shone;
It peered in through a window-pane and lo! a voice said: "Come!"
And so a little girl was born amid the dirt and din,
And lived in spite of everything, for life is ordered so;
A child whose eyes first opened wide to swinishness and sin,
A child whose love and innocence met only curse and blow.
And so in due and proper course she took the path of shame,
And gladly died in hospital, quite old at twenty years;
And when God comes to weigh it all, ah! whose shall be the blame
For all her maimed and poisoned life, her torture and her tears?
For oh, it is not what we do, but what we have not done!
And on that day of reckoning, when all is plain and clear,
What if we stand before the Throne, blood-guilty every one? . . .
Maybe the blackest sins of all are Selfishness and Fear.

IV

The Cafe de la Paix,

August 1, 1914.
Paris and I are out of tune. As I sit at this famous corner the faint breeze is stale and weary; stale and weary too the faces that swirl around me; while overhead the electric sign of Somebody's Chocolate appears and vanishes with irritating insistency. The very trees seem artificial, gleaming under the arc-lights with a raw virility that rasps my nerves.

"Poor little trees," I mutter, "growing in all this grime and glare, your only dryads the loitering ladies with the complexions of such brilliant certainty, your only Pipes of Pan orchestral echoes from the clamorous cafes. Exiles of the forest! what know you of full-blossomed winds, of red-embered sunsets, of the gentle admonition of spring rain! Life, that would fain be a melody, seems here almost a malady. I crave for the balm of Nature, the anodyne of solitude, the breath of Mother Earth. Tell me, O wistful trees, what shall I do?"

Then that stale and weary wind rustles the leaves of the nearest sycamore, and I am sure it whispers: "Brittany."

So to-morrow I am off, off to the Land of Little Fields.

Finistere

Hurrah! I'm off to Finistere, to Finistere, to Finistere;
My satchel's swinging on my back, my staff is in my hand;
I've twenty *louis* in my purse, I know the sun and sea are there,
And so I'm starting out to-day to tramp the golden land.
I'll go alone and glorying, with on my lips a song of joy;

I'll leave behind the city with its canker and its care;
I'll swing along so sturdily—oh, won't I be the happy boy!
A-singing on the rocky roads, the roads of Finistere.

Oh, have you been to Finistere, and do you know a whin-gray town
That echoes to the clatter of a thousand wooden shoes?
And have you seen the fisher-girls go gallivantin' up and down,
And watched the tawny boats go out, and heard the roaring crews?
Oh, would you sit with pipe and bowl, and dream upon some sunny quay,
Or would you walk the windy heath and drink the cooler air;
Oh, would you seek a cradled cove and tussle with the topaz sea!—
Pack up your kit to-morrow, lad, and haste to Finistere.

Oh, I will go to Finistere, there's nothing that can hold me back.
I'll laugh with Yves and Le/on, and I'll chaff with Rose and Jeanne;
I'll seek the little, quaint *buvette* that's kept by Mother Merdrinac,
Who wears a cap of many frills, and swears just like a man.
I'll yarn with hearty, hairy chaps who dance and leap and crack their heels;
Who swallow cupfuls of cognac and never turn a hair;
I'll watch the nut-brown boats come in with mullet, plaice and conger eels,
The jeweled harvest of the sea they reap in Finistere.

Yes, I'll come back from Finistere with memories of shining days,
Of scaly nets and salty men in overalls of brown;
Of ancient women knitting as they watch the tethered cattle graze
By little nestling beaches where the gorse goes blazing down;
Of headlands silvering the sea, of Calvarys against the sky,
Of scorn of angry sunsets, and of Carnac grim and bare;
Oh, won't I have the leaping veins, and tawny cheek and sparkling eye,
When I come back to Montparnasse and dream of Finistere.

Two days later.

Behold me with staff and scrip, footing it merrily in the Land of Pardons. I have no goal. When I am weary I stop at some *auberge*; when I am rested I go on again. Neither do I put any constraint on my spirit. No subduing of the mind to the task of the moment. I dream to heart's content.

My dreams stretch into the future. I see myself a singer of simple songs, a laureate of the under-dog. I will write books, a score of them. I will voyage far and wide. I will . . .

But there! Dreams are dangerous. They waste the time one should spend in making them come true. Yet when we do make them come true, we find the vision sweeter than the reality. How much of our happiness do we owe to dreams? I have in mind one old chap who used to herd the sheep on my uncle's farm.

Old David Smail

He dreamed away his hours in school;
He sat with such an absent air,
The master reckoned him a fool,
And gave him up in dull despair.

When other lads were making hay
You'd find him loafing by the stream;
He'd take a book and slip away,
And just pretend to fish . . . and dream.

His brothers passed him in the race;
They climbed the hill and clutched the prize.
He did not seem to heed, his face
Was tranquil as the evening skies.

He lived apart, he spoke with few;
Abstractedly through life he went;
Oh, what he dreamed of no one knew,
And yet he seemed to be content.

I see him now, so old and gray,
His eyes with inward vision dim;

And though he faltered on the way,
Somehow I almost envied him.

At last beside his bed I stood:
"And is Life done so soon?" he sighed;
"It's been so rich, so full, so good,
I've loved it all . . ."—and so he died.

Another day.

Framed in hedgerows of emerald, the wheat glows with a caloric fervor, as if gorged with summer heat. In the vivid green of pastures old women are herding cows. Calm and patient are their faces as with gentle industry they bend over their knitting. One feels that they are necessary to the landscape.

To gaze at me the field-workers suspend the magnificent lethargy of their labors. The men with the reaping hooks improve the occasion by another pull at the cider bottle under the stook; the women raise apathetic brown faces from the sheaf they are tying; every one is a study in deliberation, though the crop is russet ripe and crying to be cut.

Then on I go again amid high banks overgrown with fern and honeysuckle. Sometimes I come on an old mill that seems to have been constructed by Constable, so charmingly does Nature imitate Art. By the deserted house, half drowned in greenery, the velvety wheel, dipping in the crystal water, seems to protest against this prolongation of its toil.

Then again I come on its brother, the Mill of the Wind, whirling its arms so cheerily, as it turns its great white stones for its master, the floury miller by the door.

These things delight me. I am in a land where Time has lagged, where simple people timorously hug the Past. How far away now seems the welter and swelter of the city, the hectic sophistication of the streets. The sense of wonder is strong in me again, the joy of looking at familiar things as if one were seeing them for the first time.

The Wonderer

I wish that I could understand
The moving marvel of my Hand;
I watch my fingers turn and twist,
The supple bending of my wrist,
The dainty touch of finger-tip,
The steel intensity of grip;
A tool of exquisite design,
With pride I think: "It's mine! It's mine!"

Then there's the wonder of my Eyes,
Where hills and houses, seas and skies,
In waves of light converge and pass,
And print themselves as on a glass.
Line, form and color live in me;
I am the Beauty that I see;
Ah! I could write a book of size
About the wonder of my Eyes.

What of the wonder of my Heart,
That plays so faithfully its part?
I hear it running sound and sweet;
It does not seem to miss a beat;
Between the cradle and the grave
It never falters, stanch and brave.
Alas! I wish I had the art
To tell the wonder of my Heart.

Then oh! but how can I explain
The wondrous wonder of my Brain?
That marvelous machine that brings
All consciousness of wonderings;
That lets me from myself leap out
And watch my body walk about;
It's hopeless—all my words are vain
To tell the wonder of my Brain.

But do not think, O patient friend,
Who reads these stanzas to the end,
That I myself would glorify . . .
You're just as wonderful as I,
And all Creation in our view
Is quite as marvelous as you.
Come, let us on the sea-shore stand
And wonder at a grain of sand;
And then into the meadow pass
And marvel at a blade of grass;
Or cast our vision high and far
And thrill with wonder at a star;
A host of stars—night's holy tent
Huge-glittering with wonderment.

If wonder is in great and small,
Then what of Him who made it all?
In eyes and brain and heart and limb
Let's see the wondrous work of Him.
In house and hill and sward and sea,
In bird and beast and flower and tree,
In everything from sun to sod,
The wonder and the awe of God.

August 9, 1914.

  For some time the way has been growing wilder. Thickset hedges have yielded to dykes of stone, and there is every sign that I am approaching the rugged region of the coast. At each point of vantage I can see a Cross, often a relic of the early Christians, stumpy and corroded. Then I come on a slab of gray stone upstanding about fifteen feet. Like a sentinel on that solitary plain it overwhelms me with a sense of mystery.

  But as I go on through this desolate land these stones become more and more familiar. Like soldiers they stand in rank, extending over the moor. The sky is cowled with cloud, save where a sullen sunset shoots blood-red rays across the plain. Bathed in that sinister light stands my army of stone, and a wind swooping down seems to wail amid its ranks. As in a glass darkly I can see the skin-clad men, the women with their tangled hair, the beast-like feast, the cowering terror of the night. Then the sunset is cut off suddenly, and a clammy mist shrouds that silent army. So it is almost with a shudder I take my last look at the Stones of Carnac.

But now my pilgrimage is drawing to an end. A painter friend who lives by the sea has asked me to stay with him awhile. Well, I have walked a hundred miles, singing on the way. I have dreamed and dawdled, planned, exulted. I have drunk buckets of cider, and eaten many an omelette that seemed like a golden glorification of its egg. It has all been very sweet, but it will also be sweet to loaf awhile.

Oh, It Is Good

Oh, it is good to drink and sup,
And then beside the kindly fire
To smoke and heap the faggots up,
And rest and dream to heart's desire.

Oh, it is good to ride and run,
To roam the greenwood wild and free;
To hunt, to idle in the sun,
To leap into the laughing sea.

Oh, it is good with hand and brain
To gladly till the chosen soil,
And after honest sweat and strain
To see the harvest of one's toil.

Oh, it is good afar to roam,
And seek adventure in strange lands;
Yet oh, so good the coming home,
The velvet love of little hands.

So much is good . . . We thank Thee, God,
For all the tokens Thou hast given,
That here on earth our feet have trod
Thy little shining trails of Heaven.

V

August 10, 1914.

I am living in a little house so near the sea that at high tide I can see on my bedroom wall the reflected ripple of the water. At night I waken to the melodious welter of waves; or maybe there is a great stillness, and then I know that the sand and sea-grass are lying naked to the moon. But soon the tide returns, and once more I hear the roistering of the waves.

Calvert, my friend, is a lover as well as a painter of nature. He rises with the dawn to see the morning mist kindle to coral and the sun's edge clear the hill-crest. As he munches his coarse bread and sips his white wine, what dreams are his beneath the magic changes of the sky! He will paint the same scene under a dozen conditions of light. He has looked so long for Beauty that he has come to see it everywhere.

I love this friendly home of his. A peace steals over my spirit, and I feel as if I could stay here always. Some day I hope that I too may have such an one, and that I may write like this:

I Have Some Friends

I have some friends, some worthy friends,
And worthy friends are rare:
These carpet slippers on my feet,
That padded leather chair;
This old and shabby dressing-gown,
So well the worse of wear.

I have some friends, some honest friends,
And honest friends are few;

My pipe of briar, my open fire,
A book that's not too new;
My bed so warm, the nights of storm
I love to listen to.

I have some friends, some good, good friends,
Who faithful are to me:
My wrestling partner when I rise,
The big and burly sea;
My little boat that's riding there
So saucy and so free.

I have some friends, some golden friends,
Whose worth will not decline:
A tawny Irish terrier, a purple shading pine,
A little red-roofed cottage that
So proudly I call mine.

All other friends may come and go,
All other friendships fail;
But these, the friends I've worked to win,
Oh, they will never stale;
And comfort me till Time shall write
The finish to my tale.

Calvert tries to paint more than the thing he sees; he tries to paint behind it, to express its spirit. He believes that Beauty is God made manifest, and that when we discover Him in Nature we discover Him in ourselves.

But Calvert did not always see thus. At one time he was a Pagan, content to paint the outward aspect of things. It was after his little child died he gained in vision. Maybe the thought that the dead are lost to us was too unbearable. He had to believe in a coming together again.

The Quest

I sought Him on the purple seas,
I sought Him on the peaks aflame;
Amid the gloom of giant trees
And canyons lone I called His name;
The wasted ways of earth I trod:
In vain! In vain! I found not God.

I sought Him in the hives of men,
The cities grand, the hamlets gray,
The temples old beyond my ken,
The tabernacles of to-day;
All life that is, from cloud to clod
I sought . . . Alas! I found not God.

Then after roamings far and wide,
In streets and seas and deserts wild,
I came to stand at last beside
The death-bed of my little child.
Lo! as I bent beneath the rod
I raised my eyes . . . and there was God.

A golden mile of sand swings hammock-like between two tusks of rock. The sea is sleeping sapphire that wakes to cream and crash upon the beach. There is a majesty in the detachment of its lazy waves, and it is good in the night to hear its friendly roar. Good, too, to leap forth with the first sunshine and fall into its arms, to let it pummel the body to living ecstasy and send one to breakfast glad-eyed and glowing.

Behind the house the greensward slopes to a wheat-field that is like a wall of gold. Here I lie and laze away the time, or dip into a favorite book, Stevenson's *Letters* or Belloc's *Path to Rome*. Bees drone in the wild thyme; a cuckoo keeps calling, a lark spills jeweled melody. Then there is a seeming silence, but it is the silence of a deeper sound.

After all, Silence is only man's confession of his deafness. Like Death, like Eternity, it is a word that means nothing. So lying there I hear the breathing of the trees, the crepitation of the growing grass, the seething of the sap and the movements of innumerable insects. Strange how I think with distaste of the spurious glitter of Paris, of my garret, even of my poor little book.

I watch the wife of my friend gathering poppies in the wheat. There is a sadness in her face, for it is only a year ago they lost their little one. Often I see her steal away to the village graveyard, sitting silent for long and long.

The Comforter

As I sat by my baby's bed
That's open to the sky,
There fluttered round and round my head
A radiant butterfly.

And as I wept—of hearts that ache
The saddest in the land—
It left a lily for my sake,
And lighted on my hand.

I watched it, oh, so quietly,
And though it rose and flew,
As if it fain would comfort me
It came and came anew.

Now, where my darling lies at rest,
I do not dare to sigh,
For look! there gleams upon my breast
A snow-white butterfly.

My friends will have other children, and if some day they should read this piece of verse, perhaps they will think of the city lad who used to sit under the old fig-tree in the garden and watch the lizards sun themselves on the time-worn wall.

The Other One

"Gather around me, children dear;
The wind is high and the night is cold;
Closer, little ones, snuggle near;
Let's seek a story of ages old;
A magic tale of a bygone day,
Of lovely ladies and dragons dread;
Come, for you're all so tired of play,
We'll read till it's time to go to bed."

So they all are glad, and they nestle in,
And squat on the rough old nursery rug,
And they nudge and hush as I begin,
And the fire leaps up and all's so snug;
And there I sit in the big arm-chair,
And how they are eager and sweet and wise,
And they cup their chins in their hands and stare
At the heart of the flame with thoughtful eyes.

And then, as I read by the ruddy glow
And the little ones sit entranced and still . . .
He's drawing near, ah! I know, I know
He's listening too, as he always will.
He's there—he's standing beside my knee;
I see him so well, my wee, wee son . . .
Oh, children dear, don't look at me—
I'm reading now for—the Other One.

For the firelight glints in his golden hair,
And his wondering eyes are fixed on my face,
And he rests on the arm of my easy-chair,
And the book's a blur and I lose my place:
And I touch my lips to his shining head,
And my voice breaks down and—the story's done . . .
Oh, children, kiss me and go to bed:
Leave me to think of the Other One.

Of the One who will never grow up at all,
Who will always be just a child at play,
Tender and trusting and sweet and small,
Who will never leave me and go away;
Who will never hurt me and give me pain;
Who will comfort me when I'm all alone;
A heart of love that's without a stain,
Always and always my own, my own.

Yet a thought shines out from the dark of pain,
And it gives me hope to be reconciled:
That each of us must be born again,
And live and die as a little child;
So that with souls all shining white,
White as snow and without one sin,
We may come to the Gates of Eternal Light,
Where only children may enter in.

So, gentle mothers, don't ever grieve
Because you have lost, but kiss the rod;
From the depths of your woe be glad, believe
You've given an angel unto God.
Rejoice! You've a child whose youth endures,
Who comes to you when the day is done,
Wistful for love, oh, yours, just yours,
Dearest of all, the Other One.

Catastrophe

Brittany,

August 14, 1914.

And now I fear I must write in another strain. Up to this time I have been too happy. I have existed in a magic Bohemia, largely of my own making. Hope, faith, enthusiasm have been mine. Each day has had its struggle, its failure, its triumph. However, that is all ended. During the past week we have lived breathlessly. For in spite of the exultant sunshine our spirits have been under a cloud, a deepening shadow of horror and calamity . . . WAR.

Even as I write, in our little village steeple the bells are ringing madly, and in every little village steeple all over the land. As he hears it the harvester checks his scythe on the swing; the clerk throws down his pen; the shopkeeper puts up his shutters. Only in the cafes there is a clamor of voices and a drowning of care.

For here every man must fight, every home give tribute. There is no question, no appeal. By heredity and discipline all minds are shaped to this great hour. So to-morrow each man will seek his barracks and become a soldier as completely as if he had never been anything else. With the same docility as he dons his baggy red trousers will he let some muddle-headed General hurl him to destruction for some dubious gain. To-day a father, a home-maker; to-morrow fodder for cannon. So they all go without hesitation, without bitterness; and the great military machine that knows not humanity swings them to their fate. I marvel at the sense of duty, the resignation, the sacrifice. It is magnificent, it is FRANCE.

And the Women. Those who wait and weep. Ah! to-day I have not seen one who did not weep. Yes, one. She was very old, and she stood by her garden gate with her hand on the uplifted latch. As I passed she looked at me with eyes that did not see. She had no doubt sons and grandsons who must fight, and she had good reason, perhaps, to remember the war of *soixante-dix*. When I passed an hour later she was still there, her hand on the uplifted latch.

August 30th.

The men have gone. Only remain graybeards, women and children. Calvert and I have been helping our neighbors to get in the harvest. No doubt we aid; but there with the old men and children a sense of uneasiness and even shame comes over me. I would like to return to Paris, but the railway is mobilized. Each day I grow more discontented. Up there in the red North great things are doing and I am out of it. I am thoroughly unhappy.

Then Calvert comes to me with a plan. He has a Ford car. We will all three go to Paris. He intends to offer himself and his car to the Red Cross. His wife will nurse. So we are very happy at the solution, and to-morrow we are off.

Paris.

Back again. Closed shutters, deserted streets. How glum everything is! Those who are not mobilized seem uncertain how to turn. Every one buys the papers and reads grimly of disaster. No news is bad news.

I go to my garret as to a beloved friend. Everything is just as I left it, so that it seems I have never been away. I sigh with relief and joy. I will take up my work again. Serene above the storm I will watch and wait. Although I have been brought up in England I am American born. My country is not concerned.

So, going to the Do^me Cafe, I seek some of my comrades. Strange! They have gone. MacBean, I am told, is in England. By dyeing his hair and lying about his age he has managed to enlist in the Seaforth Highlanders. Saxon Dane too. He has joined the Foreign Legion, and even now may be fighting.

Well, let them go. I will keep out of the mess. But why did they go? I wish I knew. War is murder. Criminal folly. Against Humanity. Imperialism is at the root of it. We are fools and dupes. Yes, I will think and write of other things . . .

MacBean has enlisted.

I hate violence. I would not willingly cause pain to anything breathing. I would rather be killed than kill. I will stand above the Battle and watch it from afar.

Dane is in the Foreign Legion.

How disturbing it all is! One cannot settle down to anything. Every day I meet men who tell the most wonderful stories in the most casual way. I envy them. I too want to have experiences, to live where life's beat is most intense. But that's a poor reason for going to war.

And yet, though I shrink from the idea of fighting, I might in some way help those who are. MacBean and Dane, for example. Sitting lonely in the Do^me, I seem to see their ghosts in the corner. MacBean listening with his keen, sarcastic smile, Saxon Dane banging his great hairy fist on the table till the glasses jump. Where are they now? Living a life that I will never know. When they come back, if they ever do, shall I not feel shamed in their presence? Oh, this filthy war! Things were going on so beautifully. We were all so happy, so full of ambition, of hope; laughing and talking over pipe and bowl, and in our garrets seeking to realize our dreams. Ah, these days will never come again!

Then, as I sit there, Calvert seeks me out. He has joined an ambulance corps that is going to the Front. Will I come in?

"Yes," I say; "I'll do anything."

So it is all settled. To-morrow I give up my freedom.

BOOK FOUR

WINTER

I

The Somme Front,

January 1915.

There is an avenue of noble beeches leading to the Chateau, and in the shadow of each glimmers the pale oblong of an ambulance. We have to keep them thus concealed, for only yesterday morning a Taube flew over. The beggars are rather partial to Red Cross cars. One of our chaps, taking in a load of wounded, was chased and pelted the other day.

The Chateau seems all spires and towers, the glorified dream of a Parisian pastrycook. On its terrace figures in khaki are lounging. They are the volunteers, the owner-drivers of the Corps, many of them men of wealth and title. Curious to see one who owns all the coal in two counties proudly signing for his *sou* a day; or another, who lives in a Fifth Avenue palace, contentedly sleeping on the straw-strewn floor of a hovel.

Here is a rhyme I have made of such an one:

Priscilla

Jerry MacMullen, the millionaire,
Driving a red-meat bus out there—
How did he win his *Croix de Guerre*?

Bless you, that's all old stuff:
Beast of a night on the Verdun road,
Jerry stuck with a woeful load,
Stalled in the mud where the red lights glowed,
Prospect devilish tough.

"Little Priscilla" he called his car,
Best of our battered bunch by far,
Branded with many a bullet scar,
Yet running so sweet and true.
Jerry he loved her, knew her tricks;
Swore: "She's the beat of the best big six,
And if ever I get in a deuce of a fix
Priscilla will pull me through."

"Looks pretty rotten right now," says he;
"Hanged if the devil himself could see.
Priscilla, it's up to you and me
To show 'em what we can do."
Seemed that Priscilla just took the word;
Up with a leap like a horse that's spurred,
On with the joy of a homing bird,
Swift as the wind she flew.

Shell-holes shoot at them out of the night;
A lurch to the left, a wrench to the right,
Hands grim-gripping and teeth clenched tight,
Eyes that glare through the dark.
"Priscilla, you're doing me proud this day;
Hospital's only a league away,
And, honey, I'm longing to hit the hay,
So hurry, old girl . . . But hark!"

Howl of a shell, harsh, sudden, dread;
Another . . . another . . . "Strike me dead
If the Huns ain't strafing the road ahead
So the convoy can't get through!
A barrage of shrap, and us alone;
Four rush-cases—you hear 'em moan?

Fierce old messes of blood and bone . . .
Priscilla, what shall we do?"

Again it seems that Priscilla hears.
With a rush and a roar her way she clears,
Straight at the hell of flame she steers,
Full at its heart of wrath.
Fury of death and dust and din!
Havoc and horror! She's in, she's in;
She's almost over, she'll win, she'll win!
Woof! Crump! right in the path.

Little Priscilla skids and stops,
Jerry MacMullen sways and flops;
Bang in his map the crash he cops;
Shriek from the car: "Mon Dieu!"
One of the *blessé/s* hears him say,
Just at the moment he faints away:
"Reckon this isn't my lucky day,
Priscilla, it's up to you."

Sergeant raps on the doctor's door;
"Car in the court with *couché/s* four;
Driver dead on the dashboard floor;
Strange how the bunch got here."
"No," says the Doc, "this chap's alive;
But tell me, how could a man contrive
With both arms broken, a car to drive?
Thunder of God! it's queer."

Same little *blessé/* makes a spiel;
Says he: "When I saw our driver reel,
A Strange Shape leapt to the driving wheel
And sped us safe through the night."
But Jerry, he says in his drawling tone:
"Rats! Why, Priscilla came in on her own.
Bless her, she did it alone, alone . . ."
Hanged if I know who's right.

As I am sitting down to my midday meal an orderly gives me a telegram:

Hill 71. Two couche/s. Send car at once.

The uptilted country-side is a checker-board of green and gray, and, except where groves of trees rise like islands, cultivated to the last acre. But as we near the firing-line all efforts to till the land cease, and the ungathered beets of last year have grown to seed. Amid rank unkempt fields I race over a road that is pitted with obus-holes; I pass a line of guns painted like snakes, and drawn by horses dyed khaki-color; then soldiers coming from the trenches, mud-caked and ineffably weary; then a race over a bit of road that is exposed; then, buried in the hill-side, the dressing station.

The two wounded are put into my car. From hip to heel one is swathed in bandages; the other has a great white turban on his head, with a red patch on it that spreads and spreads. They stare dully, but make no sound. As I crank the car there is a shrill screaming noise . . . About thirty yards away I hear an explosion like a mine-blast, followed by a sudden belch of coal-black smoke. I stare at it in a dazed way. Then the doctor says: "Don't trouble to analyze your sensations. Better get off. You're only drawing their fire."

Here is one of my experiences:

A Casualty

That boy I took in the car last night,
With the body that awfully sagged away,
And the lips blood-crisped, and the eyes flame-bright,
And the poor hands folded and cold as clay—
Oh, I've thought and I've thought of him all the day.

For the weary old doctor says to me:
"He'll only last for an hour or so.
Both of his legs below the knee
Blown off by a bomb . . . So, lad, go slow,
And please remember, he doesn't know."

So I tried to drive with never a jar;
And there was I cursing the road like mad,
When I hears a ghost of a voice from the car:
"Tell me, old chap, have I 'copped it' bad?"
So I answers "No," and he says, "I'm glad."

"Glad," says he, "for at twenty-two
Life's so splendid, I hate to go.
There's so much good that a chap might do,
And I've fought from the start and I've suffered so.
'Twould be hard to get knocked out now, you know."

"Forget it," says I; then I drove awhile,
And I passed him a cheery word or two;
But he didn't answer for many a mile,
So just as the hospital hove in view,
Says I: "Is there nothing that I can do?"

Then he opens his eyes and he smiles at me;
And he takes my hand in his trembling hold;
"Thank you—you're far too kind," says he:
"I'm awfully comfy—stay . . . let's see:
I fancy my blanket's come unrolled—
My *feet*, please wrap 'em—they're cold . . . they're cold."

There is a city that glitters on the plain. Afar off we can see its tall cathedral spire, and there we often take our wounded from the little village hospitals to the rail-head. Tragic little buildings, these emergency hospitals—town-halls, churches, schools; their cots are never empty, their surgeons never still.

So every day we get our list of cases and off we go, a long line of cars swishing through the mud. Then one by one we branch off to our village hospital, puzzling out the road on our maps. Arrived there, we load up quickly.

The wounded make no moan. They lie, limp, heavily bandaged, with bare legs and arms protruding from their blankets. They do not know where they are going; they do not care. Like live stock, they are labeled and numbered. An orderly brings along their battle-scarred equipment, throwing open their rifles to see that no charge remains. Sometimes they shake our hands and thank us for the drive.

In the streets of the city I see French soldiers wearing the *fourragere*. It is a cord of green, yellow or red, and corresponds to the *Croix de Guerre*, the *Me/daille militaire* and the Legion of Honor. The red is the highest of all, and has been granted only to one or two regiments. This incident was told to me by a man who saw it:

The Blood-Red *Fourragere*

What was the blackest sight to me
Of all that campaign?
A naked woman tied to a tree
With jagged holes where her breasts should be,
Rotting there in the rain.

On we pressed to the battle fray,
Dogged and dour and spent.
Sudden I heard my Captain say:
"Voila\! Kultur has passed this way,
And left us a monument."

So I looked and I saw our Colonel there,
And his grand head, snowed with the years,
Unto the beat of the rain was bare;
And, oh, there was grief in his frozen stare,
And his cheeks were stung with tears!

Then at last he turned from the woeful tree,
And his face like stone was set;
"Go, march the Regiment past," said he,
"That every father and son may see,
And none may ever forget."

Oh, the crimson strands of her hair downpoured
Over her breasts of woe;
And our grim old Colonel leaned on his sword,
And the men filed past with their rifles lowered,
Solemn and sad and slow.

But I'll never forget till the day I die,
As I stood in the driving rain,
And the jaded columns of men slouched by,
How amazement leapt into every eye,
Then fury and grief and pain.

And some would like madmen stand aghast,
With their hands upclenched to the sky;
And some would cross themselves as they passed,
And some would curse in a scalding blast,
And some like children cry.

Yea, some would be sobbing, and some would pray,
And some hurl hateful names;
But the best had never a word to say;
They turned their twitching faces away,
And their eyes were like hot flames.

They passed; then down on his bended knee
The Colonel dropped to the Dead:
"Poor martyred daughter of France!" said he,
"O dearly, dearly avenged you'll be
Or ever a day be sped!"

Now they hold that we are the best of the best,
And each of our men may wear,
Like a gash of crimson across his chest,
As one fierce-proved in the battle-test,
The blood-red *Fourragere*.

For each as he leaps to the top can see,
Like an etching of blood on his brain,
A wife or a mother lashed to a tree,
With two black holes where her breasts should be,
Left to rot in the rain.

So we fight like fiends, and of us they say
That we neither yield nor spare.
Oh, we have the bitterest debt to pay . . .

Have we paid it?—Look—how we wear to-day
Like a trophy, gallant and proud and gay,
Our blood-red *Fourragere*.

It is often weary waiting at the little *poste de secours*. Some of us play solitaire, some read a "sixpenny", some doze or try to talk in bad French to the *poilus*. Around us is discomfort, dirt and drama.

For my part, I pass the time only too quickly, trying to put into verse the incidents and ideas that come my way. In this way I hope to collect quite a lot of stuff which may some day see itself in print.

Here is one of my efforts:

Jim

Never knew Jim, did you? Our boy Jim?
Bless you, there was the likely lad;
Supple and straight and long of limb,
Clean as a whistle, and just as glad.
Always laughing, wasn't he, dad?
Joy, pure joy to the heart of him,
And, oh, but the soothering ways he had,
Jim, our Jim!

But I see him best as a tiny tot,
A bonny babe, though it's me that speaks;
Laughing there in his little cot,
With his sunny hair and his apple cheeks.
And my! but the blue, blue eyes he'd got,
And just where his wee mouth dimpled dim
Such a fairy mark like a beauty spot—
That was Jim.

Oh, the war, the war! How my eyes were wet!
But he says: "Don't be sorrowing, mother dear;
You never knew me to fail you yet,
And I'll be back in a year, a year."
'Twas at Mons he fell, in the first attack;
For so they said, and their eyes were dim;

But I laughed in their faces: "He'll come back,
Will my Jim."

Now, we'd been wedded for twenty year,
And Jim was the only one we'd had;
So when I whispered in father's ear,
He wouldn't believe me—would you, dad?
There! I must hurry . . . hear him cry?
My new little baby . . . See! that's him.
What are we going to call him? Why,
Jim, just Jim.

Jim! For look at him laughing there
In the same old way in his tiny cot,
With his rosy cheeks and his sunny hair,
And look, just look . . . his beauty spot
In the selfsame place . . . Oh, I can't explain,
And of course you think it's a mother's whim,
But I know, I know it's my boy again,
Same wee Jim.

Just come back as he said he would;
Come with his love and his heart of glee.
Oh, I cried and I cried, but the Lord was good;
From the shadow of Death he set Jim free.
So I'll have him all over again, you see.
Can you wonder my mother-heart's a-brim?
Oh, how happy we're going to be!
Aren't we, Jim?

II

In Picardy,

January 1915.

The road lies amid a malevolent heath. It seems to lead us right into the clutch of the enemy; for the star-shells, that at first were bursting overhead, gradually encircle us. The fields are strangely sinister; the splintered trees are like giant toothpicks. There is a lisping and a twanging overhead.

As we wait at the door of the dugout that serves as a first-aid dressing station, I gaze up into that mysterious dark, so alive with musical vibrations. Then a small shadow detaches itself from the greater shadow, and a gray-bearded sentry says to me: "You'd better come in out of the bullets."

So I keep under cover, and presently they bring my load. Two men drip with sweat as they carry their comrade. I can see that they all three belong to the Foreign Legion. I think for a moment of Saxon Dane. How strange if some day I should carry him! Half fearfully I look at my passenger, but he is a black man. Such things only happen in fiction.

This is what I have written of the finest troops in the Army of France:

Kelly of the Legion

Now Kelly was no fighter;
He loved his pipe and glass;
An easygoing blighter,
Who lived in Montparnasse.
But 'mid the tavern tattle

He heard some guinney say:
"When France goes forth to battle,
The Legion leads the way.

> *"The scourings of creation,*
> *Of every sin and station,*
> *The men who've known damnation,*
> *Are picked to lead the way."*

Well, Kelly joined the Legion;
They marched him day and night;
They rushed him to the region
Where largest loomed the fight.
"Behold your mighty mission,
Your destiny," said they;
"By glorious tradition
The Legion leads the way.

> *"With tattered banners flying*
> *With trail of dead and dying,*
> *On! On! All hell defying,*
> *The Legion sweeps the way."*

With grim, hard-bitten faces,
With jests of savage mirth,
They swept into their places,
The men of iron worth;
Their blooded steel was flashing;
They swung to face the fray;
Then rushing, roaring, crashing,
The Legion cleared the way.

> *The trail they blazed was gory;*
> *Few lived to tell the story;*
> *Through death they plunged to glory;*
> *But, oh, they cleared the way!*

Now Kelly lay a-dying,
And dimly saw advance,

With split new banners flying,
The *fantassins* of France.
Then up amid the *melee*
He rose from where he lay;
"Come on, me boys," says Kelly,
"The Layjun lades the way!"

> *Aye, while they faltered, doubting*
> *(Such flames of doom were spouting),*
> *He caught them, thrilled them, shouting:*
> *"The Layjun lades the way!"*

They saw him slip and stumble,
Then stagger on once more;
They marked him trip and tumble,
A mass of grime and gore;
They watched him blindly crawling
Amid hell's own affray,
And calling, calling, calling:
"The Layjun lades the way!"

> *And even while they wondered,*
> *The battle-wrack was sundered;*
> *To Victory they thundered,*
> *But . . . Kelly led the way.*

Still Kelly kept agoing;
Berserker-like he ran;
His eyes with fury glowing,
A lion of a man;
His rifle madly swinging,
His soul athirst to slay,
His slogan ringing, ringing,
"The Layjun lades the way!"

> *Till in a pit death-baited,*
> *Where Huns with Maxims waited,*
> *He plunged . . . and there, blood-sated,*
> *To death he stabbed his way.*

Now Kelly was a fellow
Who simply loathed a fight:
He loved a tavern mellow,
Grog hot and pipe alight;
I'm sure the Show appalled him,
And yet without dismay,
When Death and Duty called him,
He up and led the way.

So in Valhalla drinking
(If heroes meek and shrinking
Are suffered there), I'm thinking
'Tis Kelly leads the way.

We have just had one of our men killed, a young sculptor of immense promise.

When one thinks of all the fine work he might have accomplished, it seems a shame. But, after all, to-morrow it may be the turn of any of us. If it should be mine, my chief regret will be for work undone.

Ah! I often think of how I will go back to the Quarter and take up the old life again. How sweet it will all seem. But first I must earn the right. And if ever I do go back, how I will find Bohemia changed! Missing how many a face!

It was in thinking of our lost comrade I wrote the following:

The Three Tommies

That Barret, the painter of pictures, what feeling for color he had!
And Fanning, the maker of music, such melodies mirthful and
 mad!
And Harley, the writer of stories, so whimsical, tender and glad!

To hark to their talk in the trenches, high heart unfolding to heart,
Of the day when the war would be over, and each would be true
 to his part,
Upbuilding a Palace of Beauty to the wonder and glory of Art . . .

Yon's Barret, the painter of pictures, yon carcass that rots on the wire;
His hand with its sensitive cunning is crisped to a cinder with fire;
His eyes with their magical vision are bubbles of glutinous mire.

Poor Fanning! He sought to discover the symphonic note of a shell;
There are bits of him broken and bloody, to show you the place where he fell;
I've reason to fear on his exquisite ear the rats have been banqueting well.

And speaking of Harley, the writer, I fancy I looked on him last,
Sprawling and staring and writhing in the roar of the battle blast;
Then a mad gun-team crashed over, and scattered his brains as it passed.

Oh, Harley and Fanning and Barret, they were bloody good mates o' mine;
Their bodies are empty bottles; Death has guzzled the wine;
What's left of them's filth and corruption . . . Where is the Fire Divine?

I'll tell you . . . At night in the trenches, as I watch and I do my part,
Three radiant spirits I'm seeing, high heart revealing to heart,
And they're building a peerless palace to the splendor and triumph of Art.

Yet, alas! for the fame of Barret, the glory he might have trailed!
And alas! for the name of Fanning, a star that beaconed and paled,
Poor Harley, obscure and forgotten . . .
Well, who shall say that they failed!

No, each did a Something Grander than ever he dreamed to do;
And as for the work unfinished, all will be paid their due;
The broken ends will be fitted, the balance struck will be true.

So painters, and players, and penmen, I tell you: Do as you please;
Let your fame outleap on the trumpets, you'll never rise up to these—
To three grim and gory Tommies, down, down on your bended knees!

Daventry, the sculptor, is buried in a little graveyard near one of our posts. Just now our section of the line is quiet, so I often go and sit there. Stretching myself on a flat stone, I dream for hours.

Silence and solitude! How good the peace of it all seems! Around me the grasses weave a pattern, and half hide the hundreds of little wooden crosses. Here is one with a single name:

AUBREY.

Who was Aubrey I wonder? Then another:

To Our Beloved Comrade.

Then one which has attached to it, in the cheapest of little frames, the crude water-color daub of a child, three purple flowers standing in a yellow vase. Below it, painfully printed, I read:

To My Darling Papa—Thy Little Odette.

And beyond the crosses many fresh graves have been dug. With hungry open mouths they wait. Even now I can hear the guns that are going to feed them. Soon there will be more crosses, and more and more. Then they will cease, and wives and mothers will come here to weep.

Ah! Peace so precious must be bought with blood and tears. Let us honor and bless the men who pay, and envy them the manner of their dying; for not all the jeweled orders on the breasts of the living can vie in glory with the little wooden cross the humblest of these has won . . .

The Twa Jocks

Says Bauldy MacGreegor frae Gleska tae Hecky MacCrimmon frae Skye:
"That's whit I hate maist aboot fechtin'—it makes ye sae deevilish dry;
Noo jist hae a keek at yon ferm-hoose them Gairmans are poundin' sae fine,
Weel, think o' it, doon in the dunnie there's bottles and bottles o' wine.

A' hell's fairly belchin' oot yonner, but oh, lad, I'm ettlin' tae try . . ."

"If it's poose she'll be with ye whateffer,"
says Hecky MacCrimmon frae Skye.

Says Bauldy MacGreegor frae Gleska: "Whit price fur a funeral wreath?
We're dodgin' a' kinds o' destruction, an' jist by the skin o' oor teeth.
Here, spread yersel oot on yer belly, and slither along in the glaur;
Confoond ye, ye big Hielan' deevil! Ye don't realize there's a war.
Ye think that ye're back in Dunvegan, and herdin' the wee bits o' kye."
"She'll neffer trink wine in Dunfegan," says Hecky MacCrimmon frae Skye.

Says Bauldy MacGreegor frae Gleska: "Thank goodness! the ferm-hoose at last;
There's no muckle left but the cellar, an' even that's vanishin' fast.
Look oot, there's the corpse o' a wumman, sair mangelt and deid by her lane.

Quick! Strike a match . . . Whit did I tell ye!
A hale bonny box o' shampane;
Jist knock the heid aff o' a bottle . . .
Haud on, mon, I'm hearing a cry . . ."
"She'll think it's a wean that wass greetin',"
says Hecky MacCrimmon frae Skye.

    Says Bauldy MacGreegor frae Gleska:
    "Ma conscience! I'm hanged but yer richt.

It's yin o' thae waifs of the war-field, a' sobbin' and shakin' wi' fricht.
Wheesht noo, dear, we're no gaun tae hurt ye.

    We're takin' ye hame, my wee doo!

We've got tae get back wi' her, Hecky. Whit mercy we didna get fou!

    We'll no touch a drap o' that likker—
        that's hard, man, ye canna deny . . ."
    "It's the last thing she'll think o' denyin',"
    says Hecky MacCrimmon frae Skye.

Says Bauldy MacGreegor frae Gleska: "If I should get struck frae the rear,
Ye'll tak' and ye'll shield the wee lassie, and rin for the lines like a deer.
God! Wis that the breenge o' a bullet? I'm thinkin' it's cracket ma spine.
I'm doon on ma knees in the glabber; I'm fearin', auld man, I've got mine.

    Here, quick! Pit yer erms roon the lassie.
        Noo, rin, lad! good luck and good-by . . .
    "Hoots, mon! it's ye baith she'll be takin',"
    says Hecky MacCrimmon frae Skye.

Says Corporal Muckle frae Rannoch: "Is that no' a picture tae frame?
Twa sair woundit Jocks wi' a lassie jist like ma wee Jeannie at hame.
We're prood o' ye baith, ma brave heroes. We'll gie ye a medal, I think."
Says Bauldy MacGreegor frae Gleska: "I'd raither ye gied me a drink.

I'll no speak for Private MacCrimmon, but oh, mon, I'm perishin' dry . . ."

"She'll wush that Loch Lefen wass whuskey," says Hecky MacCrimmon frae Skye.

III

Near Albert,

February 1915.

Over the spine of the ridge a horned moon of reddish hue peers through the splintered, hag-like trees. Where the trenches are, rockets are rising, green and red. I hear the coughing of the Maxims, the peevish nagging of the rifles, the boom of a "heavy" and the hollow sound of its exploding shell.

Running the car into the shadow of a ruined house, I try to sleep. But a battery starts to blaze away close by, and the flame lights up my shelter. Near me some soldiers are in deep slumber; one stirs in his sleep as a big rat runs over him, and I know by experience that when one is sleeping a rat feels as heavy as a sheep.

But how *can* one possibly sleep? Out there in the dark there is the wild tattoo of a thousand rifles; and hark! that dull roar is the explosion of a mine. There! the purring of the rapid firers. Desperate things are doing. There will be lots of work for me before this night is over. What a cursed place!

As I cannot sleep, I think of a story I heard to-day. It is of a Canadian Colonel, and in my mind I shape it like this:

His Boys

"I'm going, Billy, old fellow. Hist, lad! Don't make any noise.
There's Boches to beat all creation, the pitch of a bomb away.
I've fixed the note to your collar, you've got to get back to my
    Boys,
You've got to get back to warn 'em before it's the break of day."

The order came to go forward to a trench-line traced on the map;
I knew the brass-hats had blundered, I knew and I told 'em so;
I knew if I did as they ordered I would tumble into a trap,
And I tried to explain, but the answer came like a pistol: "Go."

Then I thought of the Boys I commanded—I always called them
    "my Boys"—
The men of my own recruiting, the lads of my countryside;
Tested in many a battle, I knew their sorrows and joys,
And I loved them all like a father, with more than a father's pride.

To march my Boys to a shambles as soon as the dawn of day;
To see them helplessly slaughtered, if all that I guessed was true;
My Boys that trusted me blindly, I thought and I tried to pray,
And then I arose and I muttered: "It's either them or it's you."

I rose and I donned my rain-coat; I buckled my helmet tight.
I remember you watched me, Billy, as I took my cane in my hand;
I vaulted over the sandbags into the pitchy night,
Into the pitted valley that served us as No Man's Land.

I strode out over the hollow of hate and havoc and death,
From the heights the guns were angry, with a vengeful snarling of
    steel;
And once in a moment of stillness I heard hard panting breath,
And I turned . . . it was you, old rascal, following hard on my heel.

I fancy I cursed you, Billy; but not so much as I ought!
And so we went forward together, till we came to the valley rim,
And then a star-shell sputtered . . . it was even worse than I
    thought,
For the trench they told me to move in was packed with Boche to
    the brim.

They saw me too, and they got me; they peppered me till I fell;
And there I scribbled my message with my life-blood ebbing away;
"Now, Billy, you fat old duffer, you've got to get back like hell;
And get them to cancel that order before it's the dawn of day.

"Billy, old boy, I love you, I kiss your shiny black nose;

> Now, home there . . . Hurry, you devil,
> or I'll cut you to ribands . . . See . . ."

Poor brute! he's off! and I'm dying . . . I go as a soldier goes.
I'm happy. My Boys, God bless 'em! . . . It had to be them or me.

    Ah! I never was intended for a job like this. I realize it more and more every day, but I will stick it out till I break down. To be nervous, over-imaginative, terribly sensitive to suffering, is a poor equipment for the man who starts out to drive wounded on the battlefield. I am haunted by the thought that my car may break down when I have a load of wounded. Once indeed it did, and a man died while I waited for help. Now I never look at what is given me. It might unnerve me.

    I have been at it for over six months without a rest. When an attack has been going on I have worked day and night, until as I drove I wanted to fall asleep at the wheel.

    The winter has been trying; there is rain one day, frost the next. Mud up to the axles. One sleeps in lousy barns or dripping dugouts. Cold, hunger, dirt, I know them all singly and together. My only consolation is that the war must soon be over, and that I will have helped. When I have time and am not too tired, I comfort myself with scribbling.

The Booby-Trap

I'm crawlin' out in the mangolds to bury wot's left o' Joe—
Joe, my pal, and a good un (God! 'ow it rains and rains).
I'm sick o' seein' him lyin' like a 'eap o' offal, and so
I'm crawlin' out in the beet-field to bury 'is last remains.

'E might 'a bin makin' munitions—'e 'adn't no need to go;
An' I tells 'im strite, but 'e arnsers, "'Tain't no use chewin' the fat;
I've got to be doin' me dooty wiv the rest o' the boys" . . . an' so
Yon's 'im, yon blob on the beet-field wot I'm tryin' so 'ard to git
    at.

There was five of us lads from the brickyard; 'Enry was gassed at
  Bapome,
Sydney was drowned in a crater, 'Erbert was 'alved by a shell;
Joe was the pick o' the posy, might 'a bin sifely at 'ome,
Only son of 'is mother, 'er a widder as well.

She used to sell bobbins and buttons—'ad a plice near the Waterloo
  Road;
A little, old, bent-over lydy, wiv glasses an' silvery 'air;
Must tell 'er I planted 'im nicely,
cheer 'er up like . . . (Well, I'm blowed,
That bullet near catched me a biffer)—I'll see the old gel if I'm
  spared.

She'll tike it to 'eart, pore ol' lydy, fer 'e was 'er 'ope and 'er joy;
'Is dad used to drink like a knot-'ole, she kept the 'ome goin', she
  did:
She pinched and she scriped fer 'is scoolin', 'e was sich a fine
  'andsome boy
('Alf Flanders seems packed on me panties)—
'e's 'andsome no longer, pore kid!

This bit o' a board that I'm packin' and draggin' around in the
  mire,
I was tickled to death when I found it. Says I, "'Ere's a nice little
  glow."
I was chilled and wet through to the marrer, so I started to make
  me a fire;
And then I says: "No; 'ere, Goblimy, it'll do for a cross for Joe."

Well, 'ere 'e is. Gawd! 'Ow one chinges a-lyin' six weeks in the
  rain.
Joe, me old pal, 'ow I'm sorry; so 'elp me, I wish I could pray.
An' now I 'ad best get a-diggin' 'is grave (it seems more like a
  drain)—
And I 'opes that the Boches won't git me till I gits 'im safe planted
  away.

*(As he touches the body there is a tremendous explosion.
He falls back shattered.)*

A booby-trap! Ought to 'a known it! If that's not a bastardly trick!
Well, one thing, I won't be long goin'. Gawd! I'm a 'ell of a sight.
Wish I'd died fightin' and killin'; that's wot it is makes me sick . . .

>Ah, Joe! we'll be pushin' up dysies . . .
>   together, old Chummie . . . good-night!

To-day I heard that MacBean had been killed in Belgium.
I believe he turned out a wonderful soldier. Saxon Dane, too,
has been missing for two months. We know what that means.

It is odd how one gets callous to death, a mediaeval callousness.
When we hear that the best of our friends have gone West, we have
a moment of the keenest regret; but how soon again we find the
heart to laugh! The saddest part of loss, I think, is that one so soon
gets over it.

Is it that we fail to realize it all? Is it that it seems a strange and
hideous dream, from which we will awake and rub our eyes?

Oh, how bitter I feel as the days go by! It is creeping more and
more into my verse. Read this:

Bonehead Bill

I wonder 'oo and wot 'e was,
That 'Un I got so slick.
I couldn't see 'is face because
The night was 'ideous thick.
I just made out among the black
A blinkin' wedge o' white;
Then *biff!* I guess I got 'im *crack*—
The man I killed last night.

I wonder if account o' me
Some wench will go unwed,
And 'eaps o' lives will never be,
Because 'e's stark and dead?

Or if 'is missis damns the war,
And by some candle light,
Tow-headed kids are prayin' for
The Fritz I copped last night.

I wonder, 'struth, I wonder why
I 'ad that 'orful dream?
I saw up in the giddy sky
The gates o' God agleam;
I saw the gates o' 'eaven shine
Wiv everlastin' light:
And then . . . I knew that I'd got mine,
As 'e got 'is last night.

Aye, bang beyond the broodin' mists
Where spawn the mother stars,
I 'ammered wiv me bloody fists
Upon them golden bars;
I 'ammered till a devil's doubt
Fair froze me wiv affright:
To fink wot God would say about
The bloke I corpsed last night.

I 'ushed; I wilted wiv despair,
When, like a rosy flame,
I sees a angel standin' there
'Oo calls me by me name.
'E 'ad such soft, such shiny eyes;
'E 'eld 'is 'and and smiled;
And through the gates o' Paradise
'E led me like a child.

'E led me by them golden palms
Wot 'ems that jeweled street;
And seraphs was a-singin' psalms,
You've no ideer 'ow sweet;
Wiv cheroobs crowdin' closer round
Than peas is in a pod,

'E led me to a shiny mound
Where beams the throne o' God.

And then I 'ears God's werry voice:
"Bill 'agan, 'ave no fear.
Stand up and glory and rejoice
For 'im 'oo led you 'ere."
And in a nip I seemed to see:
Aye, like a flash o' light,
*My angel pal I knew to be
The chap I plugged last night.*

Now, I don't claim to understand—
They calls me Bonehead Bill;
They shoves a rifle in me 'and,
And show me 'ow to kill.
Me job's to risk me life and limb,
But . . . be it wrong or right,
This cross I'm makin', it's for 'im,
The cove I croaked last night.

IV

A Lapse of Time and a Word of Explanation

The American Hospital, Neuilly,
January 1919.

Four years have passed and it is winter again. Much has happened. When I last wrote, on the Somme in 1915, I was sickening with typhoid fever. All that spring I was in hospital.

Nevertheless, I was sufficiently recovered to take part in the Champagne battle in the fall of that year, and to "carry on" during the following winter. It was at Verdun I got my first wound.

In the spring of 1917 I again served with my Corps; but on the entry of the United States into the War I joined the army of my country. In the Argonne I had my left arm shot away.

As far as time and health permitted, I kept a record of these years, and also wrote much verse. All this, however, has disappeared under circumstances into which there is no need to enter here. The loss was a cruel one, almost more so than that of my arm; for I have neither the heart nor the power to rewrite this material.

And now, in default of something better, I have bundled together this manuscript, and have added to it a few more verses, written in hospitals. Let it represent me. If I can find a publisher for it, *tant mieux*. If not, I will print it at my own cost, and any one who cares for a copy can write to me—

Stephen Poore,
12 *bis*, Rue des Petits Moineaux,
Paris.

Michael

"There's something in your face, Michael, I've seen it all the day;
There's something quare that wasn't there when first ye wint away . . ."

"It's just the Army life, mother, the drill, the left and right,
That puts the stiffinin' in yer spine and locks yer jaw up tight . . ."

"There's something in your eyes, Michael, an' how they stare and stare—
You're lookin' at me now, me boy, as if I wasn't there . . ."

"It's just the things I've seen, mother, the sights that come and come,
A bit o' broken, bloody pulp that used to be a chum . . ."

"There's something on your heart, Michael, that makes ye wake at night,
And often when I hear ye moan, I trimble in me fright . . ."

"It's just a man I killed, mother, a mother's son like me;
It seems he's always hauntin' me, he'll never let me be . . ."

"But maybe he was bad, Michael, maybe it was right
To kill the inimy you hate in fair and honest fight . . ."

"I did not hate at all, mother; he never did me harm;
I think he was a lad like me, who worked upon a farm . . ."

"And what's it all about, Michael; why did you have to go,
A quiet, peaceful lad like you, and we were happy so? . . ."

"It's thim that's up above, mother, it's thim that sits an' rules;
We've got to fight the wars they make, it's us as are the fools . . ."

"And what will be the end, Michael, and what's the use, I say,
Of fightin' if whoever wins it's us that's got to pay? . . ."

"Oh, it will be the end, mother, when lads like him and me,
That sweat to feed the ones above, decide that we'll be free . . ."

"And when will that day come, Michael, and when will fightin'
  cease,
And simple folks may till their soil and live and love in peace? . . ."

"It's coming soon and soon, mother, it's nearer every day,
When only men who work and sweat will have a word to say;
When all who earn their honest bread in every land and soil
Will claim the Brotherhood of Man, the Comradeship of Toil;
When we, the Workers, all demand: 'What are we fighting for?' . . .
Then, then we'll end that stupid crime, that devil's madness—
  War."

The Wife

"Tell Annie I'll be home in time
To help her with her Christmas-tree."
That's what he wrote, and hark! the chime
Of Christmas bells, and where is he?
And how the house is dark and sad,
And Annie's sobbing on my knee!

The page beside the candle-flame
With cruel type was overfilled;
I read and read until a name
Leapt at me and my heart was stilled:
My eye crept up the column—up
Unto its hateful heading: *Killed*.

And there was Annie on the stair:
"And will he not be long?" she said.
Her eyes were bright and in her hair
She'd twined a bit of riband red;
And every step was daddy's sure,
Till tired out she went to bed.

And there alone I sat so still,
With staring eyes that did not see;
The room was desolate and chill,
And desolate the heart of me;
Outside I heard the news-boys shrill:
"Another Glorious Victory!"

A victory . . . Ah! what care I?
A thousand victories are vain.
Here in my ruined home I cry
From out my black despair and pain,
I'd rather, rather damned defeat,
And have my man with me again.

They talk to us of pride and power,
Of Empire vast beyond the sea;
As here beside my hearth I cower,
What mean such words as these to me?
Oh, will they lift the clouds that low'r,
Or light my load in years to be?

What matters it to us poor folk?
Who win or lose, it's we who pay.
Oh, I would laugh beneath the yoke
If I had *him* at home to-day;
One's home before one's country comes:
Aye, so a million women say.

"Hush, Annie dear, don't sorrow so."
(How can I tell her?) "See, we'll light
With tiny star of purest glow
Each little candle pink and white."
(They make mistakes. I'll tell myself
I did not read that name aright.)
Come, dearest one; come, let us pray
Beside our gleaming Christmas-tree;
Just fold your little hands and say
These words so softly after me:

"God pity mothers in distress,
And little children fatherless."

*"God pity mothers in distress,
And little children fatherless."*

* * * * *

What's that?—a step upon the stair;
A shout!—the door thrown open wide!
My hero and my man is there,
And Annie's leaping by his side . . .
The room reels round, I faint, I fall . . .
"O God! Thy world is glorified."

Victory Stuff

What d'ye think, lad; what d'ye think,
As the roaring crowds go by?
As the banners flare and the brasses blare
And the great guns rend the sky?
As the women laugh like they'd all gone mad,
And the champagne glasses clink:
Oh, you're grippin' me hand so tightly, lad,
I'm a-wonderin': what d'ye think?

D'ye think o' the boys we used to know,
And how they'd have topped the fun?
Tom and Charlie, and Jack and Joe—
Gone now, every one.
How they'd have cheered as the joy-bells chime,
And they grabbed each girl for a kiss!
And now—they're rottin' in Flanders slime,
And they gave their lives—for *this*.

Or else d'ye think of the many a time
We wished we too was dead,
Up to our knees in the freezin' grime,
With the fires of hell overhead;

When the youth and the strength of us sapped away,
And we cursed in our rage and pain?
And yet—we haven't a word to say . . .
We're glad. We'd do it again.

I'm scared that they pity us. Come, old boy,
Let's leave them their flags and their fuss.
We'd surely be hatin' to spoil their joy
With the sight of such wrecks as us.
Let's slip away quietly, you and me,
And we'll talk of our chums out there:
You with your eyes that'll never see,
Me that's wheeled in a chair.

Was It You?

"Hullo, young Jones! with your tie so gay
And your pen behind your ear;
Will you mark my cheque in the usual way?
For I'm overdrawn, I fear."
Then you look at me in a manner bland,
As you turn your ledger's leaves,
And you hand it back with a soft white hand,
And the air of a man who grieves . . .

"Was it you, young Jones, was it you I saw
(And I think I see you yet)
With a live bomb gripped in your grimy paw
And your face to the parapet?
With your lips asnarl and your eyes gone mad
With a fury that thrilled you through . . .
Oh, I look at you now and I think, my lad,
Was it you, young Jones, was it you?

"Hullo, young Smith, with your well-fed look
And your coat of dapper fit,
Will you recommend me a decent book
With nothing of War in it?"
Then you smile as you polish a finger-nail,

And your eyes serenely roam,
And you suavely hand me a thrilling tale
By a man who stayed at home.

*"Was it you, young Smith, was it you I saw
In the battle's storm and stench,
With a roar of rage and a wound red-raw
Leap into the reeking trench?
As you stood like a fiend on the firing-shelf
And you stabbed and hacked and slew . . .
Oh, I look at you and I ask myself,
Was it you, young Smith, was it you?*

"Hullo, old Brown, with your ruddy cheek
And your tummy's rounded swell,
Your garden's looking jolly *chic*
And your kiddies awf'ly well.
Then you beam at me in your cheery way
As you swing your water-can;
And you mop your brow and you blithely say:
'What about golf, old man?'

*"Was it you, old Brown, was it you I saw
Like a bull-dog stick to your gun,
A cursing devil of fang and claw
When the rest were on the run?
Your eyes aflame with the battle-hate . . .
As you sit in the family pew,
And I see you rising to pass the plate,
I ask: Old Brown, was it you?*

"Was it me and you? Was it you and me?
(Is that grammar, or is it not?)
Who groveled in filth and misery,
Who gloried and groused and fought?
Which is the wrong and which is the right?
Which is the false and the true?
The man of peace or the man of fight?
Which is the ME and the YOU?"

V

Les Grands Mutilés

I saw three wounded of the war:
And the first had lost his eyes;
And the second went on wheels and had
No legs below the thighs;
And the face of the third was featureless,
And his mouth ran cornerwise.
So I made a rhyme about each one,
And this is how my fancies run.

The Sightless Man

Out of the night a crash,
A roar, a rampart of light;
A flame that leaped like a lash,
Searing forever my sight;
Out of the night a flash,
Then, oh, forever the Night!

Here in the dark I sit,
I who so loved the sun;
Supple and strong and fit,
In the dark till my days be done;
Aye, that's the hell of it,
Stalwart and twenty-one.

Marie is stanch and true,
Willing to be my wife;

Swears she has eyes for two . . .
Aye, but it's long, is Life.
What is a lad to do
With his heart and his brain at strife?

There now, my pipe is out;
No one to give me a light;
I grope and I grope about.
Well, it is nearly night;
Sleep may resolve my doubt,
Help me to reason right . . .

(He sleeps and dreams.)

I heard them whispering there by the bed . . .
Oh, but the ears of the blind are quick!
Every treacherous word they said
Was a stab of pain and my heart turned sick.
Then lip met lip and they looked at me,
Sitting bent by the fallen fire,
And they laughed to think that I couldn't see;
But I felt the flame of their hot desire.
He's helping Marie to work the farm,
A dashing, upstanding chap, they say;
And look at me with my flabby arm,
And the fat of sloth, and my face of clay—
Look at me as I sit and sit,
By the side of a fire that's seldom lit,
Sagging and weary the livelong day,
When every one else is out on the field,
Sowing the seed for a golden yield,
Or tossing around the new-mown hay . . .

Oh, the shimmering wheat that frets the sky,
Gold of plenty and blue of hope,
I'm seeing it all with an inner eye
As out of the door I grope and grope.
And I hear my wife and her lover there,
Whispering, whispering, round the rick,

Mocking me and my sightless stare,
As I fumble and stumble everywhere,
Slapping and tapping with my stick;
Old and weary at thirty-one,
Heartsick, wishing it all was done.
Oh, I'll tap my way around to the byre,
And I'll hear the cows as they chew their hay;
There at least there is none to tire,
There at least I am not in the way.
And they'll look at me with their velvet eyes
And I'll stroke their flanks with my woman's hand,
And they'll answer to me with soft replies,
And somehow I fancy they'll understand.
And the horses too, they know me well;
I'm sure that they pity my wretched lot,
And the big fat ram with the jingling bell . . .
Oh, the beasts are the only friends I've got.
And my old dog, too, he loves me more,
I think, than ever he did before.
Thank God for the beasts that are all so kind,
That know and pity the helpless blind!

Ha! they're coming, the loving pair.
My hand's a-shake as my pipe I fill.
What if I steal on them unaware
With a reaping-hook, to kill, to kill? . . .
I'll do it . . . they're there in the mow of hay,
I hear them saying: "He's out of the way!"
Hark! how they're kissing and whispering . . .
Closer I creep . . . I crouch . . . I spring . . .

(He wakes.)

Ugh! What a horrible dream I've had!
And it isn't real . . . I'm glad, I'm glad!
Marie is good and Marie is true . . .
But now I know what it's best to do.
I'll sell the farm and I'll seek my kind,
I'll live apart with my fellow-blind,

And we'll eat and drink, and we'll laugh and joke,
And we'll talk of our battles, and smoke and smoke;
And brushes of bristle we'll make for sale,
While one of us reads a book of Braille.
And there will be music and dancing too,
And we'll seek to fashion our life anew;
And we'll walk the highways hand in hand,
The Brotherhood of the Sightless Band;
Till the years at last shall bring respite
And our night is lost in the Greater Night.

The Legless Man

(The Dark Side)

My mind goes back to Fumin Wood, and how we stuck it out,
Eight days of hunger, thirst and cold, mowed down by steel and flame;
Waist-deep in mud and mad with woe, with dead men all about,
We fought like fiends and waited for relief that never came.
Eight days and nights they rolled on us in battle-frenzied mass!
"Debout les morts!" We hurled them back. By God! they did not pass.

They pinned two medals on my chest, a yellow and a brown,
And lovely ladies made me blush, such pretty words they said.
I felt a cheerful man, almost, until my eyes went down,
And there I saw the blankets—how they sagged upon my bed.
And then again I drank the cup of sorrow to the dregs:
Oh, they can keep their medals if they give me back my legs.

I think of how I used to run and leap and kick the ball,
And ride and dance and climb the hills and frolic in the sea;
And all the thousand things that now I'll never do at all . . .
Mon Dieu! there's nothing left in life, it often seems to me.
And as the nurses lift me up and strap me in my chair,
If they would chloroform me off I feel I wouldn't care.

Ah yes! we're "heroes all" to-day—they point to us with pride;
To-day their hearts go out to us, the tears are in their eyes!
But wait a bit; to-morrow they will blindly look aside;
No more they'll talk of what they owe, the dues of sacrifice
(One hates to be reminded of an everlasting debt).
It's all in human nature. Ah! the world will soon forget.

My mind goes back to where I lay wound-rotted on the plain,
And ate the muddy mangold roots, and drank the drops of dew,
And dragged myself for miles and miles when every move was pain,
And over me the carrion-crows were retching as they flew.
Oh, ere I closed my eyes and stuck my rifle in the air
I wish that those who picked me up had passed and left me there.

(The Bright Side)

Oh, one gets used to everything!
I hum a merry song,
And up the street and round the square
I wheel my chair along;
For look you, how my chest is sound
And how my arms are strong!

Oh, one gets used to anything!
It's awkward at the first,
And jolting o'er the cobbles gives
A man a grievous thirst;
But of all ills that one must bear
That's surely not the worst.

For there's the cafe open wide,
And there they set me up;
And there I smoke my *caporal*
Above my cider cup;
And play *manille* a while before
I hurry home to sup.

At home the wife is waiting me
With smiles and pigeon-pie;
And little Zi-Zi claps her hands
With laughter loud and high;
And if there's cause to growl, I fail
To see the reason why.

And all the evening by the lamp
I read some tale of crime,
Or play my old accordion
With Marie keeping time,
Until we hear the hour of ten
From out the steeple chime.

Then in the morning bright and soon,
No moment do I lose;
Within my little cobbler's shop
To gain the silver *sous*
(Good luck one has no need of legs
To make a pair of shoes).

And every Sunday—oh, it's then
I am the happy man;
They wheel me to the river-side,
And there with rod and can
I sit and fish and catch a dish
Of *goujons* for the pan.

Aye, one gets used to everything,
And doesn't seem to mind;
Maybe I'm happier than most
Of my two-legged kind;
For look you at the darkest cloud,
Lo! how it's silver-lined.

The Faceless Man

I'm dead.
Officially I'm dead. Their hope is past.
How long I stood as missing! Now, at last
                I'm dead.
Look in my face—no likeness can you see,
No tiny trace of him they knew as "me".
How terrible the change!
Even my eyes are strange.
So keyed are they to pain,
That if I chanced to meet
My mother in the street
She'd look at me in vain.

When she got home I think she'd say:
"I saw the saddest sight to-day—
A *poilu* with no face at all.
Far better in the fight to fall
Than go through life like that, I think.
Poor fellow! how he made me shrink.
No face. Just eyes that seemed to stare
At me with anguish and despair.
This ghastly war! I'm almost cheered
To think my son who disappeared,
My boy so handsome and so gay,
Might have come home like him to-day."

I'm dead. I think it's better to be dead
When little children look at you with dread;
And when you know your coming home again
Will only give the ones who love you pain.
Ah! who can help but shrink? One cannot blame.
They see the hideous husk, not, not the flame
Of sacrifice and love that burns within;
While souls of satyrs, riddled through with sin,
Have bodies fair and excellent to see.
Mon Dieu! how different we all would be

If this our flesh was ordained to express
Our spirit's beauty or its ugliness.

(Oh, you who look at me with fear to-day,
And shrink despite yourselves, and turn away—
It was for you I suffered woe accurst;
For you I braved red battle at its worst;
For you I fought and bled and maimed and slew;
For you, for you!
For you I faced hell-fury and despair;
The reeking horror of it all I knew:
I flung myself into the furnace there;
I faced the flame that scorched me with its glare;
I drank unto the dregs the devil's brew—
Look at me now—for *you* and *you* and *you* . . .)

* * * * *

I'm thinking of the time we said good-by:
We took our dinner in Duval's that night,
Just little Jacqueline, Lucette and I;
We tried our very utmost to be bright.
We laughed. And yet our eyes, they weren't gay.
I sought all kinds of cheering things to say.
"Don't grieve," I told them. "Soon the time will pass;
My next permission will come quickly round;
We'll all meet at the Gare du Montparnasse;
Three times I've come already, safe and sound."
(But oh, I thought, it's harder every time,
After a home that seems like Paradise,
To go back to the vermin and the slime,
The weariness, the want, the sacrifice.
"Pray God," I said, "the war may soon be done,
But no, oh never, never till we've won!")

Then to the station quietly we walked;
I had my rifle and my haversack,
My heavy boots, my blankets on my back;
And though it hurt us, cheerfully we talked.

We chatted bravely at the platform gate.
I watched the clock. My train must go at eight.
One minute to the hour . . . we kissed good-by,
Then, oh, they both broke down, with piteous cry.
I went . . . Their way was barred; they could not pass.
I looked back as the train began to start;
Once more I ran with anguish at my heart
And through the bars I kissed my little lass . . .

Three years have gone; they've waited day by day.
I never came. I did not even write.
For when I saw my face was such a sight
I thought that I had better . . . stay away.
And so I took the name of one who died,
A friendless friend who perished by my side.
In Prussian prison camps three years of hell
I kept my secret; oh, I kept it well!
And now I'm free, but none shall ever know;
They think I died out there . . . it's better so.

To-day I passed my wife in widow's weeds.
I brushed her arm. She did not even look.
So white, so pinched her face, my heart still bleeds,
And at the touch of her, oh, how I shook!
And then last night I passed the window where
They sat together; I could see them clear,
The lamplight softly gleaming on their hair,
And all the room so full of cozy cheer.
My wife was sewing, while my daughter read;
I even saw my portrait on the wall.
I wanted to rush in, to tell them all;
And then I cursed myself: "You're dead, you're dead!"
God! how I watched them from the darkness there,
Clutching the dripping branches of a tree,
Peering as close as ever I might dare,
And sobbing, sobbing, oh, so bitterly!

But no, it's folly; and I mustn't stay.
To-morrow I am going far away.

I'll find a ship and sail before the mast;
In some wild land I'll bury all the past.
I'll live on lonely shores and there forget,
Or tell myself that there has never been
The gay and tender courage of Lucette,
The little loving arms of Jacqueline.

A man lonely upon a lonely isle,
Sometimes I'll look towards the North and smile
To think they're happy, and they both believe
I died for France, and that I lie at rest;
And for my glory's sake they've ceased to grieve,
And hold my memory sacred. Ah! that's best.
And in that thought I'll find my joy and peace
As there alone I wait the Last Release.

L'ENVOI

We've finished up the filthy war;
We've won what we were fighting for . . .
(Or have we? I don't know).
But anyway I have my wish:
I'm back upon the old Boul' Mich',
And how my heart's aglow!
Though in my coat's an empty sleeve,
Ah! do not think I ever grieve
(The pension for it, I believe,
Will keep me on the go).

So I'll be free to write and write,
And give my soul to sheer delight,
Till joy is almost pain;
To stand aloof and watch the throng,
And worship youth and sing my song
Of faith and hope again;
To seek for beauty everywhere,
To make each day a living prayer
That life may not be vain.

To sing of things that comfort me,
The joy in mother-eyes, the glee
Of little ones at play;
The blessed gentleness of trees,
Of old men dreaming at their ease
Soft afternoons away;
Of violets and swallows' wings,
Of wondrous, ordinary things
In words of every day.

To rhyme of rich and rainy nights,
When like a legion leap the lights
And take the town with gold;
Of taverns quaint where poets dream,
Of cafes gaudily agleam,
And vice that's overbold;
Of crystal shimmer, silver sheen,
Of soft and soothing nicotine,
Of wine that's rich and old,

Of gutters, chimney-tops and stars,
Of apple-carts and motor-cars,
The sordid and sublime;
Of wealth and misery that meet
In every great and little street,
Of glory and of grime;
Of all the living tide that flows—
From princes down to puppet shows—
I'll make my humble rhyme.

So if you like the sort of thing
Of which I also like to sing,
Just give my stuff a look;
And if you don't, no harm is done—

In writing it I've had my fun;
Good luck to you and every one—
And so
                    Here ends my book.

BIBLIOBAZAAR

The essential book market!

Did you know that you can get any of our titles in large print?

Did you know that we have an ever-growing collection of books in many languages?

Order online:
www.bibliobazaar.com

Find all of your favorite classic books!

Stay up to date with the latest government reports!

At BiblioBazaar, we aim to make knowledge more accessible by making thousands of titles available to you- *quickly and affordably*.

Contact us:
BiblioBazaar
PO Box 21206
Charleston, SC 29413

Printed in Great Britain by
Amazon.co.uk, Ltd.,
Marston Gate.